THE LEEWARD ISLANDS SQUADRON

The Second Carlisle & Holbrooke
Naval Adventure

Chris Durbin

Chris Durbin

To
Philip Missen MBE
Operations Manager, Porthcawl Lifeboat
Royal National Lifeboat Institution
Saving Lives at Sea

The Leeward Islands Squadron

The Leeward Islands Squadron Copyright © 2018 by Chris Durbin. All Rights Reserved.

Chris Durbin has asserted his rights under the Copyright, Design and Patents act, 1988, to be identified as the author of this work.

No part of this book may be reproduced in any form or by any electronic or mechanical means including information storage and retrieval systems, without permission in writing from the author. The only exception is by a reviewer, who may quote short excerpts in a review.

Cover designed by Book Beaver.

This book is a work of fiction. Names, characters, places, and incidents either are products of the author's imagination or are used fictitiously. Any resemblance to actual persons, living or dead, events, or locales is entirely coincidental.

ISBN: 9781980919568

Chris Durbin
Visit my website at www.chris-durbin.com

First Edition: 2018

CONTENTS

	The Seven Years War	1
	The Captain	3
	Principal Characters	4
Prologue	Privateers	9
Chapter 1	The Commodore	19
Chapter 2	Sealed Orders	27
Chapter 3	Chiara's Letter	40
Chapter 4	Medina Prepares	51
Chapter 5	Jackson	58
Chapter 6	Attack on Port Louis	63
Chapter 7	Change of Command	77
Chapter 8	Redemption	91
Chapter 9	Fire Ship	98
Chapter 10	Fort Royal	103
Chapter 11	Take, Sink or Burn	112
Chapter 12	Mission Accomplished	122
Chapter 13	Death at Sea	137
Chapter 14	Carlisle Bay	149
Chapter 15	Passage to Antigua	152
Chapter 16	English Harbour	160
Chapter 17	A Cruise	175
Chapter 18	Fort Louis	182

Chapter 19	Prizes	190
Chapter 20	Ambuscade	198
Chapter 21	Escape	214
Chapter 22	Passage North	228
Chapter 23	A Commercial Venture	236
Chapter 24	Consequences	245
Chapter 25	News from Nice	250
Chapter 26	Barbuda	256
Chapter 27	Theories	265
Chapter 28	St. Bartholomew	271
Chapter 29	Mutiny	278
Chapter 30	The Hunt	285
Chapter 31	Scorpion	295
Chapter 32	L'Arques	301
Chapter 33	Reunion	307
Epilogue	Pitt's Strategy	313
	Nautical Terms	318
	Bibliography	319
	The Author	321
	Feedback	323

LIST OF CHARTS

The North Atlantic	5
The Lesser Antilles	6
Port Louis, Grenada	7
Fort Royal, Martinique	8

THE SEVEN YEARS WAR

1756: Disaster on Land and Sea

The Seven Years War (known in America as The French and Indian War) can justly be described as the first global conflict. It was fought in Europe, North America, the West and East Indies, Africa and all the oceans of the world. By its end, Britain was the undisputed master of North America and India and, most importantly, of the trade routes between the home islands and her colonies. The war marked the start of Britannia's one-hundred and sixty-three years of ruling the waves, from the Annus Mirabilis of 1759 to the Washington Naval Treaty of 1922.

However, the first year of the war – 1756 – didn't end well for Britain. Minorca had been lost to the French through naval mismanagement, Calcutta had been besieged and taken by the Nawab of Bengal and Montcalm had captured Fort Oswego on Lake Ontario for the French. The first Newcastle administration had fallen, and the government was rocked by the trial of Admiral Byng. But through this gloom, Lord Anson, the First Lord of the Admiralty, before he was temporarily cast into the wilderness along with the Duke of Newcastle, had started to deploy his ships to counter-attack.

This is the fictitious story of Captain Edward Carlisle and his first lieutenant, George Holbrooke, as they form the tip of the spear that Anson thrust into the French West Indian possessions.

If any of Carlisle or Holbrooke's exploits – either ashore or afloat – seem a little unlikely, then I recommend that you read Augustus Hervey's Journal which was published in 2002 by Chatham Publishing. Hervey spent much of the Seven Years War at sea in command and was present at several battles and other operations, including the disastrous battle of Minorca. When you read his startlingly frank account of those times, you will agree that a novelist has no need of overstatement when writing of the Royal Navy of the mid-eighteenth century.

THE CAPTAIN

Regulations and Instructions, 1734

Lastly, Whereas the Charge and Command of the Ship, and of the Officers and Men serving therein, are entirely entrusted to the Captain, and the Welfare and good Management of the Whole does in especial Manner depend upon his Economy and Prudence, he is to understand… he is himself responsible for the whole Conduct and good Government of the Ship, and for the due Execution of all Regulations here set down, which concern the several Duties of the Officers and Company of the Ship, who are to obey him in all Things, which he shall direct them for His Majesty's Service.

PRINCIPAL CHARACTERS

Fictional Characters

Captain Robert Jermy: Commanding Officer, *Wessex* and Commodore of the squadron.

Captain Edward Carlisle: Commanding Officer, *Medina*.

Lieutenant Miles Godwin: First Lieutenant, *Wessex*.

Lieutenant George Holbrooke: First Lieutenant, *Medina*.

James Thompson: Sailing Master, *Wessex*.

John Hosking: Sailing Master, *Medina*.

John Chalmers: Chaplain, *Wessex*.

Able Seaman Jackson: Captain's Coxswain, *Medina*.

Able Seaman Whittle: A follower of Captain Carlisle's from his home in Virginia.

Lady Chiara Angelini: Captain Carlisle's friend.

Historical Characters

The Duke of Newcastle: Prime Minister of Great Britain from 1754-1756 and 1757-1762.

The Duke of Devonshire: Prime Minister of Great Britain 1756-1757.

William Pitt: Leader of the House of Commons 1756-1761.

Lord George Anson: First Lord of the Admiralty 1751-1756 and 1757-1762.

Rear Admiral Thomas Frankland: Commander-in-Chief, Leeward Islands Station.

The Leeward Islands Squadron

THE NORTH ATLANTIC 1756-1757

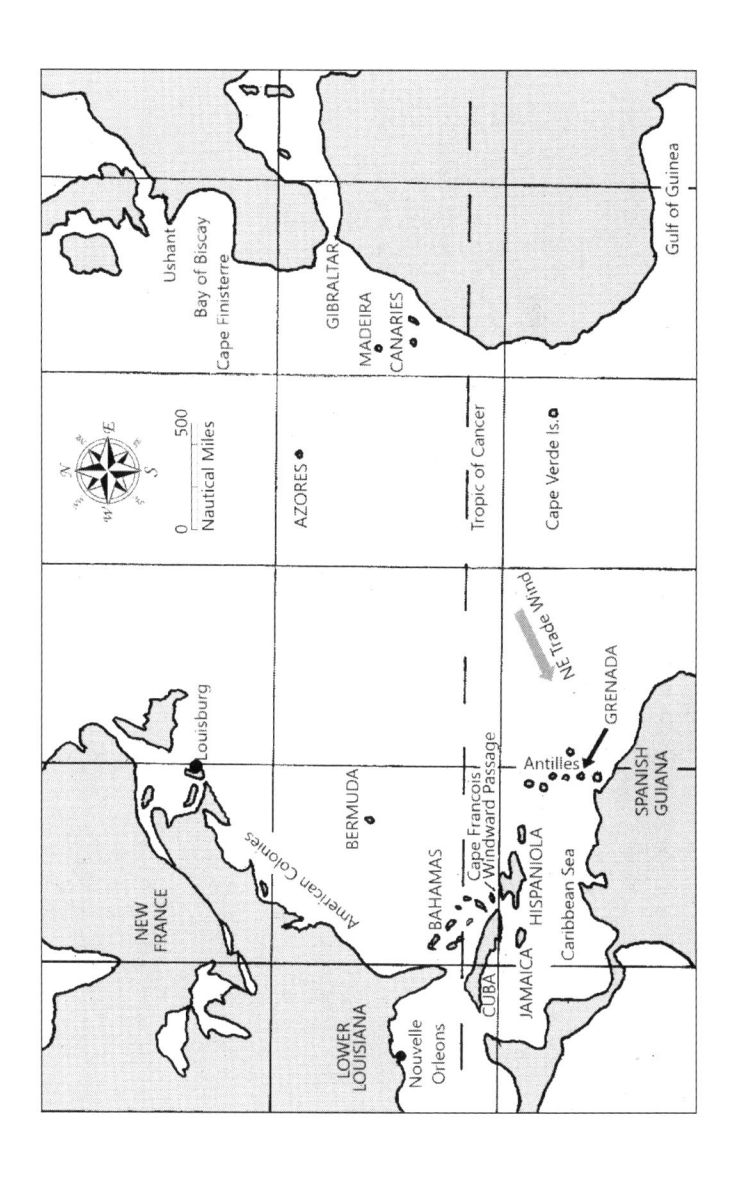

Chris Durbin

THE LESSER ANTILLES 1756-1757

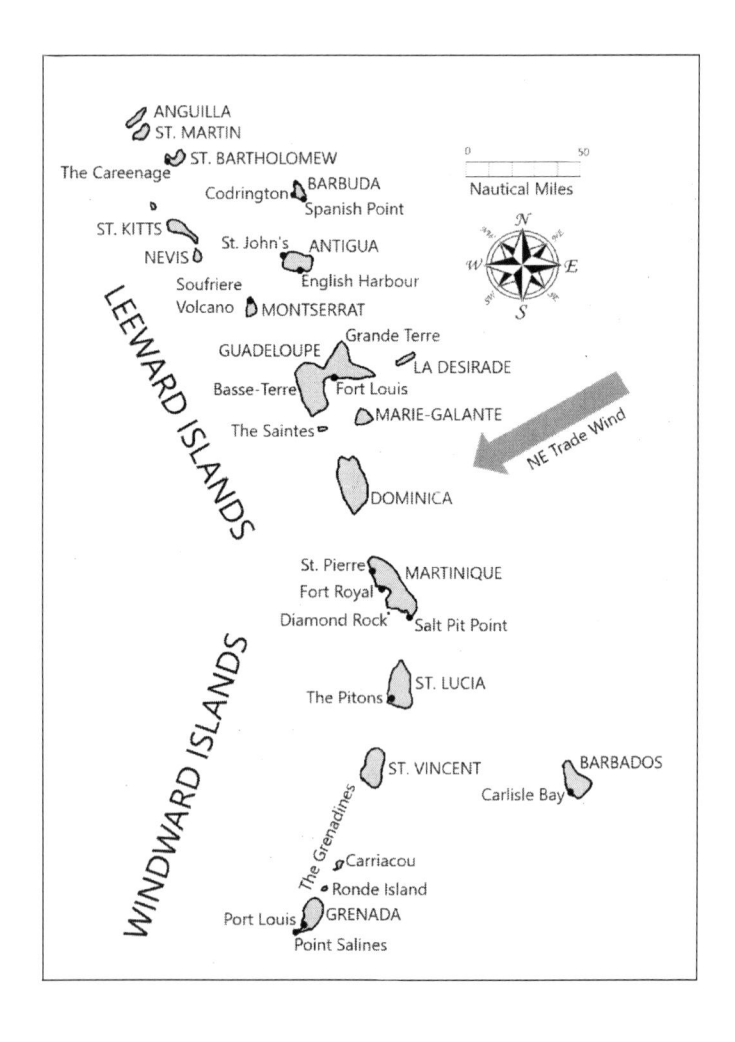

The Leeward Islands Squadron

PORT LOUIS, GRENADA 1756-1757

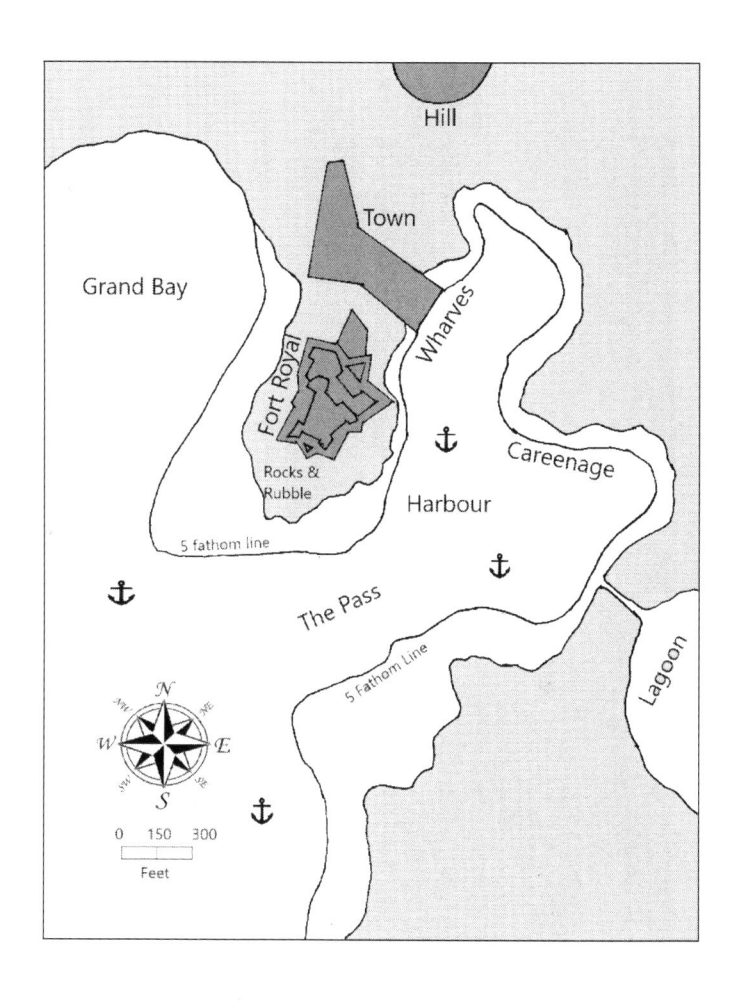

Chris Durbin

FORT ROYAL, MARTINIQUE 1757

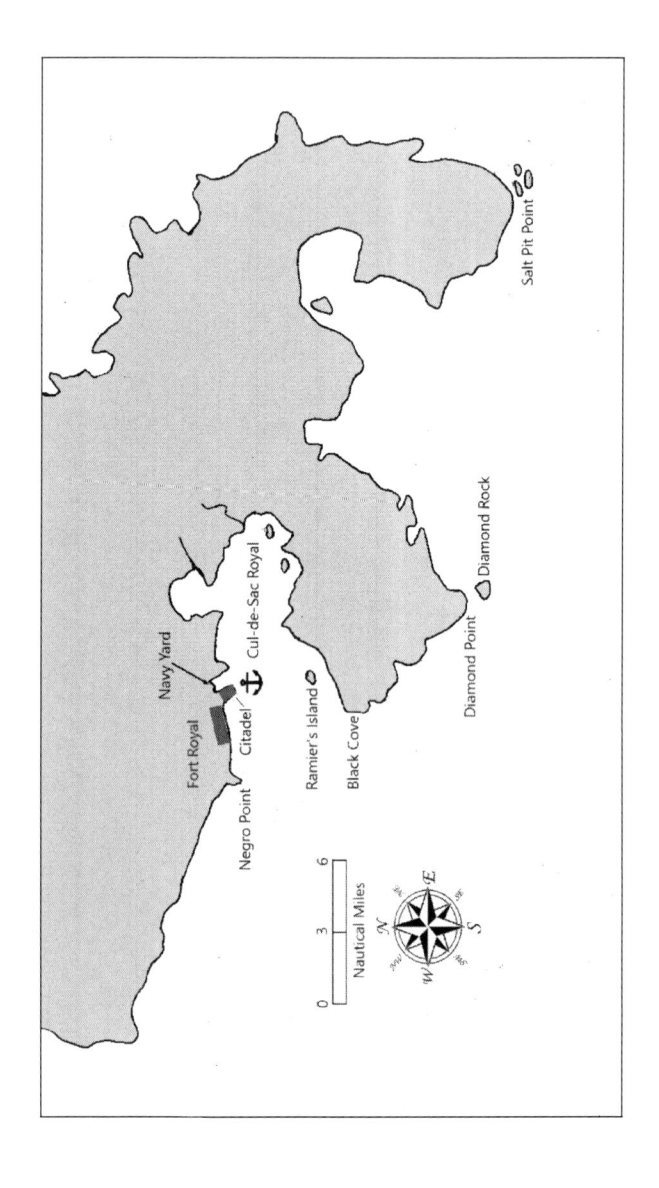

The Leeward Islands Squadron

PROLOGUE

Privateers

Monday, fifteenth of November 1756
Medina, at Sea, Ushant east-southeast 17 leagues

There were no lights showing in *Medina*. Even the tiny binnacle lantern had been extinguished, and the slow match at the guns had been covered with tarpaulins to prevent the privateers detecting her presence. The frigate ghosted along under her lower sails alone, the light north-westerly breeze providing enough steerage way to keep her head to the southwest as she kept pace with the convoy a mile to windward. The swell building from the west suggested that these light airs would not last the night, but it was the next few hours that concerned Captain Carlisle.

'Deck ho! I see 'em, sir, broad on the larboard beam.' Even the lookout was speaking softly – as much as a man can do when calling to the quarterdeck from the masthead.

'Both of them? Where are they heading?'

'Same course as us sir, two brigs under full sail about two miles away.'

'Very well, Whittle. Let me know if they alter course but keep a sharp lookout all round.'

Carlisle breathed a sigh of relief. He had staked his reputation on the two French brig-corvettes using their superior speed to cross the convoy's wake as soon as the light faded. His conference with the convoy commander had been unsatisfactory, shouted across fifty yards of heaving sea. Carlisle had pressed his opinion as hard as he could – his conviction that the attack would come from leeward, not from windward where the enemy was first sighted. Captain Jermy was a sick man, which may have accounted for his lack of tactical thought. It was evident to Carlisle that the French privateers would want a clear run back to France if they should be fortunate enough to cut out one of the Levanters – the Turkey Merchants as they were sometimes called – or even an East Indiaman. Backing her captain's hunch and in defiance of orders, Medina had reduced sail and slipped quietly through the convoy as soon as Carlisle was confident that the brigs could no longer distinguish him from the ships of the convoy.

'Mister Holbrooke,' he said to his first lieutenant, 'let the men know the situation, it's probably best if you walk down to the guns and tell them individually. We can expect no immediate help from Wessex, not until we start firing.' The commodore's ship had remained resolutely to windward of the convoy, where the privateers were last seen.

'Aye-aye sir,' replied Holbrooke. He lowered his voice, 'it looks like we are in the right position after all.' This was the closest that Holbrooke could come to open criticism of the captain of Wessex, four years senior to Carlisle on the captain's list and commodore of this small squadron by courtesy of those few years.

Carlisle took a few turns up and down the quarterdeck. In his last commission, he would have been staring eagerly to leeward, hoping for a glimpse of the brigs. Since then he had learned to trust his lookouts who surely had better eyes than he had and could be relied upon to report any change. He needed this time to decide on his next move, and he knew that he had two options. The obvious and safe course of action was to disrupt the attack immediately by opening fire – long range though it was – and bringing Wessex hurrying through the convoy to help. That would at least hold off the brigs while they decided on their next move and may even cause the privateer masters to give up. After all, the wind was set to increase, and the convoy would consequently move much faster on its way across the Bay of Biscay, making attacks more difficult. However, Carlisle had an embryonic reputation as a fighting captain, a reputation won in the desperate fight to take Vulcain earlier that year in the Mediterranean, and if it were to persist, that reputation had to be fed and nurtured. Apparently, his frigate had not yet been identified by the two brigs, Medina having reduced sail specifically to blend in with the three East Indiamen who habitually shortened sail overnight. The four Levanters were forced to copy the Indiamen or lose the protection of the convoy, and their insurance. The bold option was to wait until the brigs were committed to the attack and then spring the trap. He could damage them, perhaps even take one, but a determined French attacker had at least a chance of carrying off a prize in a confused night-time melee. Carlisle turned over the alternatives in his mind, but the deciding factor was the cohesion of his crew. When he commissioned Medina only last month, he had been permitted to turn over most of his people from his previous command, Fury. His complement had been made up with a draft from the press tender – competent seamen for the most part, but there was still a clear split between the old Furies and the new men. Carlisle hoped that the first taste of action would bring them together, and it was that thought that tipped the balance.

'Mister Hosking,' he said to the sailing master. 'Bring her onto the wind; we will move closer to the convoy.'

He was committed. Now, when he opened fire, the brigs would be too close for Wessex to intervene in time. He was consciously cutting his superior officer out of the action, or that is how it would look in a court martial.

Carlisle had sent the crew to quarters at dusk, but the frigate had been cleared for action long before then. They were all at their stations now, not stripped to the waist as they had generally been in the Mediterranean, but still wearing shirts, waistcoats and jackets against the North Atlantic in November. It could be a long wait before the Frenchmen made their move.

Holbrooke returned silently to the quarterdeck. 'The men are in good heart sir, looking forward to a little action.' He looked over the larboard quarter to where the lookout had reported the privateers, 'I fancy I can just see them now, a pale patch against the darkness.'

It was a dark night. The moon and stars were hidden by a blanket of low cloud that almost met the sea, and the light wind was doing nothing to disperse it. The dew had already started to fall, dampening the miles of hemp cordage and causing the bosun and his mates to scurry from fore to aft, feeling the tension on the shrouds.

Carlisle gave a sideways glance to leeward. He didn't know why, but it was much easier to detect objects in the dark that way. Holbrooke was correct. The two brigs were just visible from the deck, they had all sail set and were beating up towards the convoy in a most determined manner.

'At least you won't have to worry about Fury's old demi-battery this time Mister Holbrooke,' said Carlisle. 'Your twenty-eight guns are all under your own eye now.'

Holbrooke smiled. Medina was of a newer generation than Fury; in fact, she had only completed fitting out last month. Medina had four more nine-pounders than the older frigate, but the critical point was that they were all on the upper deck in two long batteries and only the four three-pounders were on the quarterdeck. There were no guns at all on the fo'c'sle and none on the lower deck. It gave the first lieutenant a far greater degree of control over the ship's main armament.

'They are moving up fast now sir,' observed Holbrooke. 'They certainly have a good turn of speed; about a point free of the wind I would say.'

'Wonderfully fast, those brig-corvettes. But then they don't have to carry three months stores and water, and their scantlings don't have to stand the rigours of years on blockade duty. Out and back in less than a week is their normal routine. I'll let them come closer before we spring the trap,' replied Carlisle.

Medina was close astern of the last Levanter, with the Indiamen clustered at the head of the convoy. The brigs were now a mile to the east of the frigate. In this meagre visibility, it was unlikely that the masters of the convoyed ships would have seen the threat approaching from leeward. Carlisle watched intently, waiting for the moment when he judged that the brigs would perceive the trap that had been set for them.

'There they go,' said the master as the two brigs put up their helms and started to come off the wind. They had spotted the frigate lying in wait for them.

'Stand by larboard battery,' roared Holbrooke.

'Put up your helm Mister Hosking,' shouted Carlisle. 'Mister Holbrooke, fire when your guns bear.'

Medina turned smoothly to larboard. When the lead privateer was squarely on her beam, Holbrooke gave the order and the battery opened with a roar, all guns erupting nearly simultaneously to send a hundred and fourteen pounds of cast iron across the eight cables of water that now separated them. It was difficult to see any damage; the telescope was useless in this light, and the new night-glasses that Carlisle had heard about had not yet made its way to sea. However, it looked like the lead privateer was struggling with her fore-topsail, so perhaps they had scored some hits.

Carlisle recognised this as the moment of greatest danger. He could see that after a few minutes hesitation the stern-most Indiaman had hardened onto the wind in an instinctive desire to put the greatest possible distance between them and their attackers, and the others were in the act of following suit. Wessex would have heard the thunder of Medina's guns and would have seen the flash on this dark night; she would surely come down to assist. But in the meantime, the brigs could split up and attack the head and tail of the convoy. If they did that there was at least an even chance that they could snap up a valuable prize in the confusion and darkness. Carlisle knew that he had to keep the French privateers on the back foot.

'Mister Hosking, lay a course to intercept the second brig. I expect her to attack the rear of the convoy. Mister Holbrooke, have you reloaded?'

'Yes sir, loaded with ball.'

'Deck there! I can see the commodore coming down now, it looks like he will pass ahead of the convoy.'

Good, at least Jermy was thinking. If Medina was engaged astern, as the flashes from her broadside would suggest, then Wessex should be at the head of the convoy. As if on cue, the lead brig altered course to larboard and headed southwest.

'Mister Holbrooke, one broadside for our friend as we pass. Aim for her masts.'

A staggered broadside this time, carefully aimed by each gun captain. Now that the brig was nearer, holes could be seen in her sails, and there were a few parted lines, hanging slack in the light breeze, but no critical damage. She sped on southwest unaware that Wessex was heading for the same point.

Carlisle carefully observed the two brigs. Their intention was clear: one would attack the head of the convoy while the other would attack the rear. Medina couldn't deal with both attacks, and one of them would surely make off with a prize. A large, well-practised and ruthless prize crew could board and be underway to France in ten minutes. That would leave one of the brigs to continue to harry the convoy, preventing the escort from chasing the retreating prize. The whole plan relied on Wessex being unable to interfere in time to shift the balance. They didn't yet know how close Wessex was to the head of the convoy. Carlisle felt confident that between them, the fifty-gun fourth rate and the twenty-eight-gun frigate, they could hold off the two privateers.

'Deck ho! Wessex has veered; she's bows on to us.'

Carlisle couldn't believe his ears, but a glance to

windward showed him the truth of the lookout's hail.

'Put the ship about Mister Hosking.' Carlisle pounded the quarterdeck rail with his fist. How could Jermy be so foolish? His action meant that the first brig would be free to take his pick of the convoy while the second – the decoy – led them further astern.

'Mister Holbrook, a broadside from the larboard guns as they bear.'

In an instant, the situation had changed. The first brig, the one that displayed Medina's shot holes in her sails, was far ahead and evidently preparing to lay alongside the leading Indiaman. A sudden flash and eruption of smoke, followed quickly by the sharp report of the brig's broadside, showed that she was close enough to her prey for even her light guns to come into play, six-pounders at best but more likely three or four-pounders. The Indiaman – she looked like the Beaufort, an old and small ship for the John Company – seemed too panicked to realise that her best defence was to veer and run down to Medina. She appeared overly concerned with boarding nets and bringing her own battery into action. By sheer weight of broadside, she should be able to hold her own. After all, she had thirty-two guns, which in the navy would put her in the fifth rate, one above Medina. But her crew was pitifully small, and she would barely have a hundred men to serve them and to manage the sails; far too few and utterly insufficient to repel a French privateer's boarding party. The drama unfolded in front of the group gathered on Medina's quarterdeck. To their horror, they saw the brig crash alongside the Indiaman. A horde of Frenchmen, hardly slowed by the boarding nets, poured onto her decks. They watched helplessly as her halyard was slashed and her ensign fell over the stern to trail behind, a splash of red in her grey and white wake, easily visible in the light from the lanterns that had just sprung to life in her stern windows.

'Did the Frenchman know that Medina had changed

course? Probably not,' thought Carlisle. She was well-enough handled, but she was no King's ship and would lack the discipline that kept Whittle at Medina's masthead looking all around the horizon. With his countryman at the masthead, Carlisle could concentrate on the battle, leaving the wider surveillance in good hands. 'Mister Holbrooke, Mister Hosking. I would rather not be fighting three hundred French privateers on the deck of the Indiaman, it's not worth the casualties that we would take. So, we'll advertise our presence and threaten to trap her between Medina and her prize. A broadside now Mister Holbrooke, to leeward. I don't want to harm the Beaufort. Mister Hosking, steer a course to bring me alongside the brig, but I trust that she will see sense and sheer off before we arrive.' Carlisle knew very well that his actions could easily be misconstrued as cowardice, and he saw that same understanding in the master's face as he turned away to give his orders. The master didn't yet know him.

Medina's larboard battery fired, the shot landing harmlessly a mile or so towards Ushant.

'That got their attention,' said Carlisle to the quarterdeck in general. 'Now, let's see what they do. Mister Holbrooke, stand by to board her over our starboard side, in case they're a bloody-minded crew and don't care to withdraw.'

'Jackson, muster your boarders on the fo'c'sle,' shouted Holbrooke to the captain's coxswain, the leader of the boarders for the larboard watch.

'Aye-aye sir,' replied Jackson. There was a close understanding between these two men, forged in combat in the Mediterranean. It was Jackson who steered the boat into St. Stephen's cove in Minorca under the guns of de Richelieu's siege batteries. It was Jackson who had crowded alongside Holbrooke when he boarded Vulcain from their little barca-longa and turned the tide of the battle, slashing wildly with his cutlass to protect the lieutenant's unguarded left side. And it was Jackson again who dragged the three-pounder into position on St. Honorat Island and stood, exposed, in the bright sunshine waiting for the supposed corsair to negotiate a truce. Yes, Holbrooke would be pleased to have Jackson seconding him if they had to settle this business on the deck of the French privateer.

The privateer did indeed see sense. The scene was almost comical as the French boarders hurriedly – very hurriedly – retraced their movements, the final dozen having to jump for their lives and liberty across the widening chasm as the brig sheered away and put her stern to the wind. The very last man paused indecisively on the gunwale, terrified of the widening gap and the grey sea rushing below him. He glanced behind and gathered himself to make the leap but too late; a Lascar, a native seaman of the East Indies, swung at him with a boarding axe that bit deep into his shoulder and he tumbled forward to be lost in the tumbling wake.

'Mister Hosking. Put up your helm, and bring us across her stern,' he said pointing to the fleeing privateer. 'We'll give her a raking broadside to remember us by. Is your larboard battery ready Mister Holbrooke?'

'Ready, aye, ready,' replied Holbrooke wiping the powder stains from his face. Slowly Medina drew across the brig's stern, and slowly – too slowly – the brig moved away to the southeast. The range was only two cables, point-blank for nine-pounders, when Holbrooke gave the command, 'Fire!' There were experienced men among the gun crews, men from the old Fury who had three times engaged the heavy frigate Vulcain and three times raked her from stern to stem. It was hardly credible, but to Carlisle, it looked as though every shot had found its mark. The windows and planking of her stern just ceased to exist, and the whole run of her upper deck was revealed, a tangle of overturned guns and mangled flesh. Yet somehow her two masts were still standing, and her sails were still drawing as she slowly and painfully sailed out of range and was swallowed in the blackness.

'There's no more fight left in her, gentlemen, we can leave her to make her way home.' Carlisle glanced over to the Beaufort. She looked intact, and a reassuring wave from her master left little doubt as to his next action. 'Mister Hosking, haul your wind and place us astern of the convoy. We'll leave Wessex to deal with her privateer. I don't expect we'll see any more of ours today.'

The sailing master gave him a curious look. It was a look of surprise and recognition, a sideways glance and slight tilt of the head in acknowledgement of a job well done. Carlisle realised that he had been under suspicion by this older man. He had been suspected of cowardice when he declined to lay himself alongside the privateer and fight it out toe to toe. But Hosking was an old campaigner and could see that Carlisle had been correct; a dangerous attack had been repulsed without any casualties. It may not make the broadsheets in London, but it was a thoroughly professional piece of work.

CHAPTER ONE

The Commodore

Tuesday, sixteenth of November 1756
Medina, at Sea, Ushant northeast 50 leagues

The foretold wind arrived in the morning watch, a moderate westerly with a little south in it that swept away the gloom and the low clouds and wafted the convoy on its voyage south-by-west at a respectable six knots, close hauled on the starboard tack. However, the rising sun revealed a convoy visibly shaken by the night's activity. The three Indiamen and the four Levanters clung tightly to each other and showed no tendency to stray far from the protection of their escorts. *Beaufort* still had stray lines and ripped sails, but she was holding her place in the convoy, her decks and rigging crawling with men engaged in the skilled work of repairing timber, canvas and cordage.

'Will the commodore call for you, sir?' asked the master. Carlisle had been considering just that question when his thoughts had been interrupted. There was no doubt that his actions could be regarded as insubordinate on the one hand and lacking conduct, even cowardly, on the other. *He* knew that his tactics had been correct. He was right to persuade the commodore to split his forces. It had been hard, waiting until the privateers were committed before revealing his presence, but again it was the best thing to do. His greatest professional gamble was probably warning-off the first brig rather than engaging in hand-to-hand fighting on the deck of an Indiaman, but without a doubt he had prevented unnecessary casualties among his crew while still achieving his objective. He also knew that Jermy was wrong to ignore the first brig and steer for the tail of the convoy. If *Medina* hadn't reversed course at the critical moment it was quite likely that *Beaufort* would now be a prize under a French battery somewhere on the

Brittany coast. But these were difficult concepts to articulate because they were founded on the proposition that his lawfully appointed superior was incompetent. Any of his actions, correct though they were, could be turned against him in an inquiry or – God forbid – a court martial. Carlisle crossed his fingers behind his back, a personal superstition that age and responsibility had failed to eradicate.

So, taken all-in-all, he would rather not have to justify himself to Jermy. If the commodore felt any irritation after the actions of the night, then Carlisle would just have to hope that he would have forgotten it before the Indiamen parted company north of Madeira. And in any case, *Beaufort* didn't look very severely damaged, and the privateers appeared to have fared worse than the convoy in that short battle. But as with any dealings of this sort, it had been a risky business.

Here was Chalmers, another but a more welcome interruption. A sixth-rate's establishment included a chaplain, but in practice they were rarely seen on such small ships. David Chalmers, however, was a follower of Carlisle's, had served as his chaplain in *Fury* and was pleased to find a berth in his new command.

'May I congratulate you on a successful defence of the convoy sir?'

'You may, Mister Chalmers.' Carlisle smiled and paused his pacing, the two men stood side-by-side between the three-pounders looking to leeward at the convoy. 'However, I wonder whether the commodore will see it that way. He may feel that I have been a little too independent for his taste. To tell you the truth, I'd rather not have to explain myself to him just now; I'm hoping he is indisposed.'

'Ah, I was also pondering that possibility. I wonder whether it would be advisable to take the initiative? To grasp fate by the forelock?' Carlisle looked quizzically at Chalmers.

'There's a Greek god, he's not very well known nowadays; *Caerus*, the representation of fortune. He has a lock of hair on his forehead, but he's bald behind. It's said that a man can grasp his own fate when *Caerus* is approaching, but after he has passed there is nothing to hold on to.' A happy inspiration allowed Chalmers to add a naval perspective, for clarity. 'He has missed his tide.'

Carlisle looked even more puzzled and with a laugh, replied. 'And how should I grasp this mythical forelock, Mister Chalmers? With what vessel should I catch my tide? What is the practical application of this advice?'

Chalmers turned to face Carlisle and in a lower tone, in the hope that the sailing master, the quartermaster and the helmsman, all of whom were within four paces, should be unable to hear. 'Well, perhaps you could write to the commodore and congratulate him on his victory? And if that letter could reach him before his breakfast …'

But Carlisle missed the last few words as he caught the significance of this advice. He turned to the mate of the watch, his manner transformed into one of immediate and determined action. 'Pass the word for my clerk. He is to be in my day cabin in two minutes with his pen and his inkhorn. Mister Hosking, close the commodore and indicate that I wish to send a boat.' He turned back to the chaplain, 'Mister Chalmers, would you do me the pleasure of assisting in drafting this note?'

In ten minutes the letter was written and sealed. *Medina* lay-to under the lee of *Wessex*, the two ships gently rising and falling on the swell. Carlisle could see Jermy on his quarterdeck; he had the disapproving look of a man who was preparing to very much dislike this communication from his subordinate. The letter was delivered, and Jermy limped below, grasping the hammock netting as he descended to the main deck and thence to his cabin. He looked like an old man, which he wasn't, or like a sick man which, undoubtedly, he was. The boat returned. Carlisle let *Medina* linger a while, keeping pace with *Wessex* as she slowly gathered way to catch up with the convoy, which had itself spilt its wind to avoid straying too far from its escort. Just when Carlisle felt that he could not, with decency, delay any longer his return to his station, he saw Jermy heaving himself back up to the quarterdeck. Gone was the disapproving look and with what could almost be described as a cheery wave, the commodore indicated his pleasure and beckoned for Carlisle to regain his station.

Dealing with superiors, Carlisle found, needed a great deal of subtlety. Those four years of additional seniority that Jermy enjoyed would make Carlisle subordinate to him for the rest of his naval career. No force on earth could advance Carlisle faster than Jermy, and only a temporary and unlikely appointment as commodore could exchange their positions – and then for just as long as the appointment lasted.

Chalmers watched this exchange from the lee side of the quarterdeck. 'The problem with Captain Carlisle,' Chalmers mused, 'is that he underestimates the strength of his own position.' It was quite likely that Jermy had been nervously anticipating what Carlisle may write to his friends in England, regarding his commodore's conduct. And letters could be trusted to the Indiamen to be sent home from Madeira, which was only a week away. After all, it was well known that Jermy, probably through no fault of his own, had never been in action with the enemy, while Carlisle was becoming well known as a successful frigate captain with an important victory to his credit. What Jermy could not know is that Carlisle had no friends in England, or more correctly, none in anything remotely resembling high places. For Edward Carlisle was a colonial American whose only home was in Virginia; he was the sole colonial on the post-captain's list, and he was struggling to find his niche in English society.

Holbrooke had the afternoon watch. There was little to do. The weather was fair, and their present course would give them a landfall off Cape Finisterre in three or four days, even allowing for the pace of the lumbering John Company ships and the Turkey Merchants. He had a very cordial relationship with his captain; it had survived the younger man's earlier disillusionment with the service and his captain's clearly stated disappointment in his performance. This bond had been greatly strengthened by Holbrooke's determined and aggressive action that had secured for Carlisle his great victory only five months ago. There had been a lot of change in Holbrooke's life since then. He had passed for lieutenant, received his commission with none of the usual delays and had been appointed second-in-command of Carlisle's small frigate *Fury*. When *Fury* had been decommissioned in Portsmouth, he had been asked by Carlisle to be his first lieutenant in this larger frigate. An indulgent Admiralty, conscious that the capture of *Vulcain*, a far, more powerful frigate than *Fury*, had not been adequately acknowledged, was keen to offer what scraps it could to Carlisle. Holbrooke was duly appointed. His commission lay in his cabin, a tangible and treasured reminder of the distance he had travelled in such a short space of time.

He remembered his reunion with his father in Portsmouth and the pride of a parent who had, until then, despaired of his son fulfilling his potential. His father had been a sailing master; he had never been in a position to regard a commission as an achievable ambition for himself, but he was brimming with pride now that his son had achieved that goal.

Neither Carlisle nor Holbrooke had lingered long in Portsmouth. *Fury* needed a refit and Carlisle was owed a reward for his successful single-ship action, the first of this war. Their Lordships had judged to a nicety the absolute minimum that they could offer Carlisle. They had balanced the natural justice of a substantial reward against their need to play down the recent disastrous events in the Mediterranean that had led to the loss of Minorca and the ongoing and highly political court martial of Admiral Byng. If Carlisle had been well connected, he could have expected a small ship-of-the-line or even a knighthood, but the combined effects of his own obscurity and the political situation had resulted in a commission to command *Medina*. In one respect, Carlisle should be extremely pleased with this new ship – just off the stocks from John Randall's yard at Cuckold's Point in Rotherhithe. She was a modern thirty-two-gun frigate built to the draught of the *Lyme*, but with more headroom below decks – an excellent ship for cruising against the enemy and with boundless potential as a prize taker. But Holbrooke was only too aware that Carlisle needed greater recognition for very personal reasons. He had an understanding with a young woman in Nice; or had her family yet fled to Leghorn in anticipation of a French invasion? Chiara Angelini was no common prize; she was the niece of a Sardinian viscountess and a lady in her own right. Holbrooke knew that Carlisle needed some visible display of eligibility before he would be allowed to claim this remarkable woman as his own – and command of a frigate, however new, was an insufficient mark of the Admiralty's favour to impress the Angelini family.

Holbrooke, however, was content with his own reward. He had received his lieutenant's commission a year earlier than was theoretically allowed – with the connivance of his village parson who he had falsified his date of birth – and he had been appointed as second-in-command of the newest frigate in King George's navy. And that meant that he stayed with Carlisle, a matter of no small importance to Holbrooke.

Carlisle and Holbrooke had posted up the London Road and on to Sheerness, where *Medina* had been fitting out. They were joined by a large proportion of the people from *Fury*, augmented by a draft from the press tender in the Pool of London. After a short shakedown cruise, they had joined *Wessex* at The Downs and sailed with this convoy of merchantmen for the East Indies and the eastern Mediterranean. Holbrooke knew that *Medina* would not take either of these convoys to its destination. The Turkey Merchants would leave the convoy at thirty-seven degrees north for their own passage through the Gut and into the Mediterranean, while the East Indiamen would be escorted as far as Madeira. No, *Medina's* destination lay elsewhere. Carlisle had told his officers when they left The Downs that they were sailing under sealed orders – those intriguing, almost romantic, articles that all *Medina's* officers had heard of, but none had sailed under until this time. Not that the orders were on board *Medina*; they were held by the commodore in *Wessex*, and it was entirely possible that he would be unwilling to share them, or he may be prohibited from disclosing their contents to Carlisle even when they had been opened.

The Admiralty would be unlikely to send two of its much-needed ships all the way to Madeira only for them to turn around and head for the North Sea, the Baltic or the French Atlantic Coast, but the Mediterranean was still a possibility, or anywhere in the South Atlantic or the Americas. Holbrooke knew that he could rule out the East Indies as they had only been ordered to store for three months. It was difficult to guess what was in their Lordship's minds and Anson was known to be unusually secretive about his dispositions. 'However, that's a normal consequence of a naval career – laying in clothes and cabin stores for warm seas and ending up in the high latitudes of the Barents Sea,' thought Holbrook, but he was still betting on the other side of the Atlantic. It made sense that a confidential mission to the Americas would need to fulfil a dual purpose and convoying as far as Madeira was not even out of their way. This was the usual route to pick up the northeast trade winds at about thirty degrees north, which could take them to the Caribbean or further north to the American Colonies or the St. Lawrence River. But only two ships? What could they achieve? And if they were destined to join a more significant force then why the secrecy?

CHAPTER TWO

Sealed Orders

Tuesday, thirtieth of November 1756
Medina, at Sea, Madeira east-northeast 35 leagues

The two ships rode comfortably to the westerly swell, their heads pointing southwest, and their fore-topsails backed, lying to in response to the signal for *Medina's* captain to wait upon the commodore. They had parted company with the Turkey Merchants at the latitude of Lisbon and were not sorry to see those wretchedly slow ships disappear over the south-eastern horizon, bound through the Gut for the Eastern Mediterranean. The Indiamen had left them at thirty-five north and would be anchored in the fair Bay of Funchal by now, taking on wood, water and fresh provisions. No doubt they would also be taking on some good Madeira wine for the long passage to India.

Only a generation ago it would have been unthinkable for a naval squadron to have passed so close to Madeira without stopping to replenish its supplies. However, the technological innovations of the last twenty years had transformed the ability of British men-of-war to keep the sea. The output from the victualling yards, those wonders of the modern age, ensured that every King's ship that sailed from England was provided with the best of supplies. They had salted meat, prepared and preserved to the highest standard, fresh water in clean barrels, small beer brewed only yards from the dockyard gates and fresh vegetables to be consumed before they rotted. By the mid-eighteenth century it was disease – scurvy principally – that limited the time a ship could spend at sea. These innovations meant that a squadron such as Jermy commanded could sail to the West Indies or the Cape without having to touch land. It was a significant advantage if secrecy was necessary, but it deprived the ships' companies of one of the best runs ashore in the world, and it was potentially ruinous for the Madeiran economy.

Perhaps less than a dozen people in *Medina* knew that the commodore had sealed orders, but each of that dozen understood that Carlisle had likely been summoned to hear the content of those orders – instructions that could take them anywhere in the world. It was a hard pull for the longboat's crew into the weather. They were on the edge of the trade wind and although the sea had not yet built up to that regular series of waves, so characteristic of the area either side of the Tropic of Cancer, every third or fourth was large enough to send a spray of salt water onto the rowers and break their rhythm. But a few capfuls of salt water couldn't take the edge off their anticipation, for they knew their captain was invited for dinner and they expected to lie alongside for an hour or two and looked forward to the traditional hospitality of their *Wessex* opposite numbers – their *Oppos* in the language of the sea.

Carlisle was relieved to see that Jermy appeared in better health than a week ago; perhaps this beautiful weather and sea air was good for him. He walked, if not like a young man, at least less like a man with one foot in the grave. Jermy met Carlisle at the entry port, that convenient aperture in the hull of two-decked ships that allowed personages of great dignity – admirals or captains – to come onboard without having to either scramble over the gunwale or squeeze through a gun port. It was Carlisle's first visit to *Wessex,* and although protocol didn't insist that Jermy's officers should be introduced to him, it would have been more usual than otherwise. Post-captains were the most immediate sources of patronage, and lieutenants, master's mates and midshipmen needed to meet those who could, perhaps, benefit their careers. Post-captains also required the opportunity to meet a wide range of potential followers, so the custom of introductions had real benefits beyond a mere social nicety. But Jermy led him straight past the line of side boys, under the curious gaze of the officers on the quarterdeck and down to the great cabin. These fifty-gun ships had been built to take an admiral on foreign stations, even if the fitting out had not always been completed to quite the necessary standard, and *Wessex* boasted a dining table capable of seating ten people in comfort, fourteen with a push. However, there were only four at dinner today, as this was understood to be a working meal.

As a commodore by courtesy only, Jermy didn't have a flag captain, but his first lieutenant was a man of seniority and experience. Miles Godwin was older than Carlisle, and he responded politely when introduced. And yet there was just something in his attitude that Carlisle didn't quite like, a slight reserve and a drawing back of his body as they shook hands. Carlisle knew that he was too ready to see an insult to his colonial heritage, but he had become skilled at noticing the little signs, and he was almost sure that he saw them now in Godwin. It wouldn't be unlikely; a mixture of envy at Carlisle's rank and recent fame, and English-bred notions of superiority over colonists were almost to be expected. Carlisle let it pass.

The fourth at the table was James Thompson, Jermy's sailing master. Carlisle found it difficult to form an impression of Thompson. In a way, he was typical of his breed, a professional seaman who was secure in his warranted status and not troubled by the need for his captain's approval in the way that every other man on board was. But again, there was something a little odd in the sailing master's demeanour, a reserve that Carlisle had not expected. It seemed to Carlisle that he was there under sufferance – that the presence of *Medina's* captain was an awkward necessity – more resented than welcomed.

The great cabin was laid up for dinner with an

imposing display of polished walnut, gleaming silver and sparkling glassware. The stern windows – vast in comparison to *Medina's* – had been cleaned both inside and out. Some unknown hand must have dangled precariously on a bosun's chair over the taffrail with a line hauling him in against the inward slope of the stern to achieve that perfection. The only jarring detail was a broad stretch of unpainted canvas hung against the larboard bulkhead, which puzzled Carlisle until he realised that it was large enough to cover three or four charts. He looked more closely, and he could see that a corner of thick paper was just showing below the lower edge of the canvas.

With sherries in hand and the introductions complete, Jermy motioned toward the canvas-covered side of the cabin in what was evidently a rehearsed move. Carlisle hadn't credited his superior with a sense of the dramatic, but then he hardly knew him. In fact, on reflection, it seemed more likely that Jermy was economising on his movement because every step appeared to cause him pain and his sprightliness at the entry port apparently came at a price. The canvas cover was removed to show three charts. A quick glance ended Carlisle's speculation about their destination. The largest covered the whole of the North Atlantic, from Iceland to Brazil and from the Channel to the Gulf of Mexico. The next showed the chain of seemingly insignificant dots that made up the Windward and Leeward Islands at the eastern extremity of the Caribbean Sea, from Puerto Rico to Trinidad. But the last was the most interesting; it was a large-scale chart of the most southerly of the Windward Islands – Grenada and that treacherous series of islets stretching away to the north, the Grenadines.

Carlisle's mind was running ahead, and his first thought was for those highly polished windows. They were already in the realm of the northeast trade winds, as his damp coat testified, and it would be a dead run from Madeira to Grenada. The windows would be salt stained within minutes of their bearing away for the Antilles; so much for the labours of that unknown seaman. His second thought was to wonder whether Godwin and Thomson had already been told their destination. He glanced to his left at the sailing master; he certainly knew, and the look on his face told Carlisle that his initial reserve was caused by embarrassment at having been informed before Carlisle, an unfortunate deviation from the usual protocol, but perhaps justified. A more extended look to his right confirmed that the first lieutenant also was aware of their destination. But in Godwin's case, the slight smirk and the confident return of the inspection told Carlisle all he needed to know; he was glad that he had Holbrooke as his second-in-command rather than this jealous and probably scheming subordinate.

Jermy appeared to have missed this interchange or at least chose to ignore it. While Carlisle had been assessing the commodore's officers, Jermy had lowered himself carefully into his chair at the head of the table. After closing his eyes for a few seconds, his pain apparent in the lines on his face, he gestured the three officers to take their own seats.

'Gentlemen,' said Jermy. He seemed to gain strength when seated, reinforcing Carlisle's view that he probably suffered from gout and its attendant debilitating pain. He remembered Augustus Hervey in the Mediterranean, a very active officer, but suffering from that common eighteenth-century wealthy man's illness and frequently confined to his cabin for days or weeks on end. It was supposed to be associated with over-indulgence in rich foods, spirits and fortified wines; by his great bulk and the easy way that Jermy tossed off his sherry and beckoned the servant to refill it, Carlisle could easily believe that to be the case. 'Our destination, as you see, is revealed.' There was no acknowledgement that he had chosen to disclose this vital information to a lieutenant and a sailing master before a post-captain, the *de facto* and *de jure* second-in-command of the expedition.

'Our orders – *my* orders,' he corrected himself, 'having sent the convoy on its various ways, are to proceed to Grenada where I am to destroy the nest of privateers lying at Port Louis. I am then to look for Admiral Frankland at Carlisle Bay in Barbados or English Harbour in Antigua and join the Leeward Islands Squadron.'

'Why that curious insistence that the orders were for Jermy himself?' thought Carlisle. Insecurity, lack of self-confidence? Or was he merely keeping his first lieutenant in his place? Either way, it was an unfortunate rhetorical device to deploy at the start of a relationship where each party would be dependent upon the goodwill and support of the other, where success or failure rested in no small extent upon co-operation. Those who had no experience of the navy assumed that it was ruled by a strict hierarchy, reinforced by an iron disciple, that kept subordinates faithful to the wishes of their superiors. Carlisle and anyone who had spent even a short time at sea knew that this was far from the truth. Each squadron and each ship was a little fiefdom to itself and admirals, commodores and captains were bred to independence of thought and action to an extent that would startle anyone with no experience of life in a man-of-war. Jermy must surely know that Carlisle had it in his power to make or break this expedition.

Carlisle knew Grenada from a visit during the peace between the wars so he could contribute to planning for the first part of the mission. However, he was not acquainted with Thomas Frankland; he knew him only by his reputation. The admiral had been in the West Indies and Bahamas on-and-off since the last war and had commanded the Leeward Island station for over a year. He was known as an able commander, but he was stubborn and had a short temper. He had succeeded in quarrelling both with his predecessor and with the local authorities in Antigua. Nevertheless, Frankland had a vast knowledge of his station, having been an investor and active participant in several commercial undertakings, including, of course, the import of African slaves for the plantations. He was a man with extensive personal business interests that stretched far beyond his naval duties.

'You know, I am sure, that Grenada is ideally situated to intercept our Guinea trade on its way to any of our islands in the Lesser Antilles, or Jamaica, or our American Colonies.' Jermy gave Carlisle a significant look meant to indicate that he knew where Carlisle came from. 'So, this doesn't directly concern our West Indies convoys which can gather at Barbados or Antigua without interference from these privateers, but it does concern the import of the raw material for the plantations – the West African slaves.'

Carlisle was pleased to see that Jermy at least had a good grasp of the strategic imperatives on this side of the Atlantic. Having grown up in Virginia, he well understood that the economy of the southern colonies was reliant upon a constant supply of imported manpower. Some of this was satisfied by indentured servants and petty criminals from Britain, but the most significant source of labour was provided by slaves who were forcibly removed from their homes in the lands clustered around the Gulf of Guinea. The prevailing trade winds and sea currents dictated that the route from West Africa to Georgia, the Carolinas, Virginia and Maryland must cross the mid-Atlantic to the coast of Spanish Guiana. From there it passed to windward of the Lesser Antilles and the Bahamas and followed the North American coast past Florida. Spain owned Florida and had no present quarrel with Britain, but the French navy contested much of the remainder of the route. There was a kind of operational balance from Barbados northwards along the Windward and Leeward Islands, the principal French base at Martinique being countered by British cruisers from their primary home at English Harbour in Antigua and their seasonal deployed base at Carlisle Bay in Barbados.

Admiral Frankland had no useful anchorages south of Barbados, and even if he had, there were no additional ships to station there. Consequently, the passage between Tobago to the south and Barbados to the north was unprotected and led directly past Grenada with its excellent sheltered harbour of Port Louis, secure under the French guns of Fort Royal. This passage was the most dangerous part of the route for the slaver, from the barracoons of West Africa to the slave markets of the Jamaica, Antigua and the American Colonies. Their Lordships, presumably under pressure from Lord Halifax, president of the Board of Trade and Plantations, had deployed Jermy's small force to disrupt the French privateers until Frankland could be reinforced with sufficient cruisers to protect the whole of his extensive area of command.

Carlisle knew all about slavery. He understood its role in the economy of the Colonies, and he knew about the human suffering that it caused. On the rare occasions that he thought about slavery, it led him to be glad that he had been born the *second* son of his tobacco plantation-owning and, therefore, slave-owning father. He had no moral choice to make, unlike his elder brother who would inherit the plantation along with its slaves and indentured servants. He guessed that his brother, a blunt, unimaginative man like his father, would not expend a moment on the moral question of slavery, but would put all his effort into getting the most economic benefit from the system. 'Good luck to him,' thought Carlisle. 'I am well out of it.' But in the back of his mind, Carlisle knew that he was being disingenuous; his moralising didn't extend to an analysis of the part that he would be playing in securing the slaving supply chain at this its most vulnerable point.

Jermy continued. 'With this trade wind, we can expect to be off Grenada in little more than two weeks, about the eighteenth of December if we are fortunate.'

The Leeward Islands Squadron

Thompson nodded his agreement. Of course, the master would have been consulted unless Jermy's orders expressly prohibited it. It was Thompson's responsibility to navigate the squadron successfully across more than four thousand miles of trackless ocean; he had to be consulted. Carlisle cursed his own prickly temperament that took offence so quickly. And if Thompson had been told, it would have been hard for Jermy to keep the secret from his first lieutenant, but that didn't excuse the damned smug expression on Godwin's face.

'You will see,' Jermy pointed to the large-scale chart of the island of Grenada, 'that the French capital is located here on the leeward side of the island, Port Louis they call it. The harbour and anchorage are protected by a fortress in the Vauban style – it's fifty years old, and I know little else about it.'

Carlisle, however, was quite well acquainted with Port Louis and Fort Royal. He couldn't say quite why he didn't immediately offer his knowledge, something about the atmosphere in the cabin – it was all wrong – it made him suspect that his help might not be welcomed, and he didn't want to risk a rebuff. The fort, as he remembered it, watched over the anchorage from its well-chosen position on a high promontory that poked like a swollen thumb into the Grand Bay, as the French called it, and enclosed the shallow harbour of Port Louis. It commanded the seaward approach from all points of the compass from the south through east to north and gave protection to larger vessels anchored in the bay. There was a higher peak to the north of the fort that offered a view right down to the southerly tip of the island. The French had set up a simple signalling system between the height and the fort so that in good visibility nothing could approach Port Louis without betraying its presence for at least an hour before arrival. The well-remembered scene came to Carlisle's mind; the bright Caribbean sunshine, the sea breeze nullifying the trade wind and wafting them into the small harbour, the exchange of salutes as befitted friendly nations. Fort Royal had looked like a child's toy castle with comical puffs of smoke marking the position of the batteries, a peaceful scene but he could easily see it turning nasty. He imagined his frigate caught in that plunging fire – heated shot almost certainly – and no escape once committed to that lethal bottle-neck. He remembered four bastions and a kind of hornwork toward the interior of the island, the curtain of which was covered by a ravelin. How many guns? He thought about thirty to forty in all, perhaps two dozen commanding the anchorage and the remainder covering the bay to the north and the landward approaches – twenty-four pounders and nine-pounders. A moderately strong squadron could probably reduce the fort, but the French were undoubtedly capable of holding off a small two-decker and a frigate. He hoped, without any real conviction, that Jermy had a well-considered plan.

Jermy continued. 'I know little of the fort that is not revealed in that plan of the anchorage, but like all of these fortifications it's vulnerable to a surprise attack.' He paused and passed his hand across his eyes as a look of intense pain creased his features. Carlisle noticed that these fits appeared more frequently the longer they talked; it looked past time for the commodore to lie down. 'Mister Thompson here assures me that the sea breeze won't set in until the forenoon watch, too late for a surprise attack at dawn, but we can be certain that the French will not be keeping a good lookout to the south. If they anticipate an attack at all, they will believe it will come from the north, from Mister Frankland's squadron.'

'Surely he wasn't planning to come into the anchorage with the sea breeze? The sea breeze that would probably last all through the long day making it difficult, if not impossible, to beat out of the harbour again,' thought Carlisle, astonished at the naivety of it.

But Jermy continued remorselessly. He had the look of a man set upon a path when he didn't really relish its destination. 'I plan to round this southerly point of the island – Point Salines – at the end of the morning watch and then attack the anchorage with the first of the sea breeze.'

'Good God,' thought Carlisle. 'We'll be helpless under the guns of the fort. Even if there is no lookout on the peak behind the fort, we will be seen at dawn from the watchtowers on the southeast side of the island, and it's only four or five miles from there to Port Louis, a gentle stroll for a soldier. Fort Royal will have two hours to prepare, and there will be no escape with a steady wind from the sea.'

Jermy continued. '*Wessex* will engage the fort. *Medina*, assisted by *Wessex's* boats, will take, sink, burn and destroy everything in the anchorage and harbour as expeditiously as possible. I don't need to tell you that I will spend as little time as possible under the guns of the fort, but if need be, I will anchor until the sea breeze fades and allows us to leave.'

Carlisle tried to maintain a poker face, but his shock must have shown. How could it not when presented with such a suicidal plan? Jermy turned to him with a contorted expression, part pain, but largely disapproval. 'You have a comment, Captain Carlisle?' Jermy looked as though the last thing that he wanted was a critique of his plan.

'If I may be permitted an observation, sir?'

Jermy merely nodded. It was difficult to read his facial expressions when they were so dominated by his physical agony.

'I know this harbour and fort sir.' Carlisle outlined the defences of Port Louis as he remembered them. 'There is no room to manoeuvre once we are abreast the fort and the sea breeze will prevent us leaving when we are in. Certainly, we will be able to do great execution in the anchorage and harbour, but we run a considerable risk from the guns of the fort. They command the whole of the anchorage and the inner harbour.'

'And what would you suggest as an alternative, captain?' asked Jermy, grimacing in pain. 'Perhaps we should sail away to Barbados and report our failure without even trying? We must be prepared to take our knocks, nothing can be achieved otherwise.'

Carlisle was taken aback. Jermy had as good as accused him of cowardice in front of junior officers. Thompson looked appalled; Godwin was barely able to conceal his delight. 'You command sir,' he replied stiffly, 'and I am ready to play my part.' Carlisle could think of nothing better to say in the face of such blind stupidity.

'I am pleased that you understand that Captain Carlisle, I do indeed command. Now here are my orders.'

Carlisle tried not to show his discomfort and anger as the commodore outlined the details of his plan. Against a smaller, less well-armed fortification – perhaps a few batteries protected by earthworks – the strategy may well have worked, but it would still be dangerous under any circumstances. Against two dozen twenty-four pounders with heated shot firing from behind solid masonry and with no surprise, no room to manoeuvre and no chance of a sailing retreat, the plan was suicidal. Carlisle ruefully reflected that a man with higher moral courage would have continued to argue another course of action, but he just couldn't do it, not after having had his physical courage almost openly questioned. Was this another manifestation of his prickliness about his colonial heritage? Probably, he thought; but still, there it was, the cross he had to bear through his career.

As Carlisle was pulled back to *Medina*, he reflected ruefully upon the factors that influence a man's decision-making. Not the obvious physical, tangible factors, such as wind, tide, enemy strength, the size of one's own forces, powder, water and stores – these had an objective reality that the naval mind could easily encompass. No, he was thinking of the influences that lay below the surface. Jermy, for example, was in such pain that any prolonged period of thought was probably impossible. When he had once developed a plan, he was in no mental state to revise it and certainly not in a state to take criticism, however constructive. It was also likely also that Jermy felt the shadow of Carlisle's reputation. In his case, it nurtured a dogged refusal to accept advice from his junior and a steadfast determination to risk anything for a fast and famous victory. Carlisle himself – and he readily conceded this weakness – was too conscious by far of his colonial heritage, and that made him over-sensitive to insults and slights. Another man would have handled his commodore better, would have dissuaded him from this disastrous plan. But the dice had been cast and the objective reality – the objective naval fact – was that *Medina* would be taken under the guns of Fort Royal in obedience to the commodore's orders, regardless of the consequences.

'And God help us all,' thought Carlisle.

CHAPTER THREE

Chiara's Letter

Thursday, ninth of December 1756
Medina, at Sea, Madeira east-northeast 500 leagues

Mid-Atlantic, and the steady northeast trade wind was hastening the two men-of-war to their rendezvous with the enemy. Two lonely ships, for although this was the main highway for the westbound trade from Europe to the whole of North and Central America, all the vessels were heading in the same direction, and at broadly similar speeds. If two ships met, then they generally stayed in sight for days. If they didn't meet, then even this well-travelled path was apparently deserted. There were no sea-birds this far from land, just the occasional whale spouting in the distance or a group of dolphins sporting under the bows and, occasionally, a shoal of flying fish taking to the air to escape their predators – there was nothing else. Jermy's small squadron was alone under the blue sky and the high, white clouds.

The two hundred men in *Medina* had little to do. The frigate was new, and her standing and running rigging were still in good order, her sails had not yet been thinned by the sun and wind, nor chafed by contact with the myriad of hempen ropes. Her hull was sound, an hour at the chain pump was all that was required to keep the bilge clear, and there were always a few men who had incurred the displeasure of the first lieutenant or the bosun to be set to that task. And with the wind blowing steadily from astern and the commodore strangely reluctant to spread his stuns'ls, there was little need to touch the sheets from one watch to the next. The forenoons were spent in training the crew. Gun drills, musketry, cutlasses, boarding pikes and axes, rigging and unrigging the boats on their cradles in the waist and introducing the landsmen to the complexities of the equipment. What was left of the afternoon, after dinner and the issue of beer, wine or rum, was taken up with routine maintenance. The dogs, those anomalous two-hour watches designed to break up the sequence of duties so that each day every man had a different duty cycle, were set aside for recreation. It was true that, except for a few specialists, every man of the crew had to stand watch; four hours on, four hours off throughout the day and night. But in practice, it required only a handful of seamen to steer the ship, keep a lookout and monitor the sails and rigging. During the night watches, half of each watch could find a quiet spot in the lee scuppers and doze away much of their four hours on deck. If life on board a man-of-war could ever be described in idyllic terms, a westbound transatlantic passage in fine weather answered that description.

Carlisle was taking his ease in the great cabin on this glorious afternoon. He had spent much of the past nine days planning for his part on the attack on Port Louis, and now he felt that his preparations were well underway. This was the first occasion since taking command of *Medina* that Carlisle found himself with time on his hands and the leisure to indulge in his guilty pastime – an innocent enough pleasure, in all truth. He removed the small key to his writing desk that he kept on the fob of his watch-chain and opened one of the small drawers on the side. The name *Davenport* had not yet been applied to this design of campaign desk; that would have to wait for the captain of that name later in the century. But the style was becoming popular with sea officers who had enough space for such luxuries and Carlisle had used some of the advance of prize money that his agent had provided from the capture of *Vulcain*, to make this indulgent purchase.

He removed a small bundle of letters, tied together by a powder-blue ribbon with a lock of auburn hair twisted into the bow. Carlisle pressed them briefly to his face to catch the fading remains of the scent of the writer and was transported in his imagination back to the garden behind the villa overlooking the harbour at Nice. The faint trace of perfume evoked memories of the soft Mediterranean breezes and the harsh Mediterranean sun, the cold tramontanas and mistrals that made his watch over Toulon so miserable and the desperate fights with the French frigates. He remembered John Keltie, his first lieutenant in those days, shot down in his moment of triumph as he struck the French ensign from the stern of the captured *Vulcain*. But it was the memory of the rose garden and the beautiful Italian lady that held Carlisle's attention.

He selected the latest letter. It was dated from Nice in the final week of October and had been hurried by overland courier to Calais and thence to England by the good offices of the governor of that Sardinian province – General Paterson, an expatriate Scot in the service of King Charles Emmanuel. The writer could be relied upon for the practical side of correspondence. Each letter was clearly marked with the date and the place where it was written, and each letter was sequentially numbered. Chiara was no scatter-brained miss. She knew that the journeys of a letter sent to a ship at sea were too indefinite to trust to vague headings such as '*The fourteenth, at home,*' which may be sufficient when writing from London to a friend in Bath. However, when letters could take months or perhaps years to reach their destination and cause grievous disorientation in the reader when eventually they arrive out of sequence, something more definite is required. He returned the remainder of the package of letters to the drawer. The sun was past its zenith and scurrying away to the west, so the cabin was in relative darkness. The best light was to be found by sitting on the cushioned benches at the rear of the cabin, where the sunlight came streaming through the skylight overhead. The voices on the quarterdeck hardly disturbed him at all, and he had long ago learned to filter out the sound of the wind in the rigging, whether it was a whisper or a roar. The creaking of the steering tackles and the groaning of the rudder as it swung on its gudgeons just below him were merely the background hum of life at sea.

'Saturday the thirtieth of October, Casa Angelini, Nice ... My dearest Edward,' it began. It was *almost* a wholly correct letter from a young woman to the man with whom she had an understanding, approved of by her family. Almost, but not entirely; for the mores of Nice where not the same as those that would be recognised in Georgian England or indeed in colonial Virginia. Chiara was not always discreet and had an unnervingly matter-of-fact way of referring to their relationship and shared experiences. Carlisle was relieved that as well as correctly dating a letter, the writer understood the need for firmly sealing it; but then, having been brought up in Sardinian court society, that hotbed of intrigue and illicit affairs, how could she not? Chiara Angelini was the niece of a person of consequence in Sardinia, she was of marriageable age and could have expected to be the titled lady of a grand estate, given the likelihood of a good match. But Chiara had her own ideas and appeared to have set her heart upon this unknown and penniless post-captain from the Colonies. Obscure, friendless and with neither interest nor patronage to assure his promotion and employment.

This letter and its predecessors reassured Carlisle that his affections were still reciprocated – there seemed to be a real mutual attraction, and Chiara was not reticent about expressing that attraction in the letter. But Carlisle was ever the critical analyst of his own affairs, and although not exactly a pessimist, he took a realistic view of his prospects both in the navy and in this affair of the heart. How could this perfect woman, who would be fought over – literally duelled for – in England, how could she possibly choose a future with Edward Carlisle, second son of a Virginia plantation owner and by great good fortune a post-captain in George II's navy? Carlisle had seen enough of Sardinian society to know that in his absence Chiara would have been bombarded with offers, some honourable but many not so, regardless – or perhaps because of – her known attachment to him. How long could she withstand that? And if her aunt, Viscountess Angelini should decide that after all this sea-captain was not a suitable match for her niece, for how long would she defy that formidable woman's wishes? He was well on the way to snatching a miserable few hours from this beautiful day when there was a knock at the cabin door. He hastily stuffed the letter under the seat cushion and composing himself as best he could, called loudly, 'Come!'

The door opened, and the friendly face of the Reverend John Chalmers appeared, an unearthly orange glow from the bright afternoon sun framing his silhouette and giving him an uncanny resemblance to the religious icons that Carlisle had seen so often in Italy.

'Good afternoon sir,' he said as he stepped into the cabin having determined that the captain could be disturbed, 'do you have a few moments?'

Carlisle briefly toyed with the idea of sending the chaplain packing so that he could return to his self-inflicted punishment with Chiara's letter. The captain of a man-of-war always had the credible excuse that he was too busy with more important matters. However, the two men had a close relationship, and Carlisle had a nagging feeling that the chaplain saw straight through him, that he knew his captain's innermost thoughts. He probably would not be taken in by a plea of overwork when there was no paperwork on the desk, and none of his officers was present to make his life difficult by requiring decisions that they were quite capable of making without his intervention. He stood up and as he did so the letter, so evidently a feminine letter, fell out from under the cushion.

Carlisle was put to a stumbling, undignified effort to retrieve it and place it, as nonchalantly as he could, back into the desk.

'I've as many moments as you wish Mister Chalmers. As you see, I was hardly engaged in the King's business,' he said, an involuntary sheepish grin lifting the corners of his mouth. The chaplain merely nodded in acknowledgement, a grave half-smile advertising his ever willingness to talk. If Carlisle had wished to discuss his relationship with Chiara Angelini, there would be no better person than Chalmers to hear him. In many ways, the chaplain was the perfect counsellor. He never looked surprised at anything he was told, rarely gave advice unless asked and had an unfailingly alternative perspective – he was able to see things from a wholly different viewpoint to that which had been bred into the naval mind. Carlisle sometimes felt like a child – a not very bright child – when he was talking to Chalmers, although they were of similar age and social background.

'I've come to offer a report on lessons that I have been giving to the young gentlemen,' he said. This didn't fool Carlisle at all; he guessed that the chaplain had decided that it was time for him to check on his captain and offer any advice that may be required. God knew, he sometimes needed it. Chalmers' help in his dealings with the commodore after the fight with the privateers had been worth more than an extra deck of guns to Carlisle. Without that wise counsel, his relationship with Jermy would be fragile, to say the least, and the effectiveness of the squadron would be diminished accordingly. For form's sake, Carlisle listened to the chaplain's report, detailing which midshipmen were progressing in mathematics, in grammar, which showed promise, which would need significant further instruction before they could be considered for a lieutenant's board. Chalmers showed more enthusiasm for teaching than anyone he had yet encountered in a man-of-war, far more than any sailing master or schoolmaster and certainly more than any other chaplain. Chalmers had even started to teach the ship's boys their letters, many of whom had no previous experience of education and had come to the navy from the Foundling Hospital or the new Marine Society, established earlier that year specifically to provide boys for the navy. He had been pleased to be able to award Chalmers the extra pay that came with the duty of instructing the young gentlemen. He knew that without his naval pay, Chalmers was not provided for at all, had no benefice and no prospect of one. The few extra shillings a week were of the greatest importance to him. Chalmers had, in fact, become a follower of Carlisle's, each dependent upon the other for loyalty and patronage.

'Will you take a glass of Madeira, Chalmers?' He raised his voice and called for his servant who hurried off to retrieve a bottle from the stygian depths where it was kept as cool as anything could be in that latitude. 'Let's close the skylight for a while,' he said more softly. 'I fear that the helmsmen make too much capital from trading on my conversations.'

Chalmers accepted the wine and admired its colour for a moment while he sat quietly, waiting for Carlisle to start the conversation. The subject was obvious, and he knew enough of Carlisle's affairs to be sure that only one woman would be writing to him on such delicate paper. Unless, of course, this was a letter from the viscountess, but the viscountess would only write to forbid the relationship, and Carlisle was not such a good actor as to be able to hide such a reversal of his fortunes for a month. He knew the subject of the conversation, but not how it would be addressed.

'Are you familiar with Madeira, Chalmers?' asked Carlisle. 'I mean the wine, not the island, although of course, the one comes from the other.'

'I've taken it occasionally,' the chaplain admitted, 'but my knowledge is at best indifferent. This, however, seems a particularly good example. The flavour of toasted sugar – molasses even – comes through wonderfully.'

'The commodore of the Indiamen gave me half a dozen cases in appreciation of our action against the privateers. It's the *vinho da rhoda*, literally the *wine of the round trip*.'

Chalmers looked politely blank.

'Madeira has been the favoured wine in Virginia since before I was born. The best of the best is the wine that has been to India and back, enduring periods of intense heat for a year a more. You would think that it would kill the wine, but it's the fortification with cane spirit – rum of a kind – that preserves it while the heat gives it this flavour. The result is this beautifully rounded offering. You know, an opened bottle can be kept for years so long as its re-corked; no other wine can equal it.' Carlisle swirled the reddish-amber liquid around his glass and studied it against the light from the stern windows. 'For this bottle, we can thank the wine exporting house of Newton and Spence and the Honourable East India Company. It's perhaps the best gift I've ever received. I'll treasure it as a reminder of home and serve it to only my particular friends.'

Chalmers bowed and took an appreciative sip. 'Why is it,' he said, 'that a knowledge of the antecedents of wine heightens the pleasure of drinking it? Before you told me its history, I took it as a variety of sherry or possible port; but now I can appreciate it fully.' He cradled the Madeira and gloated over it like a miser over his hoard of gold.

The two men sat in silence, lost in their own thoughts.

'Chiara sends her best wishes to you.'

Chalmers nodded, 'so that is how he wishes to start,' he thought.

'I hope you'll return my very best to Chiara and respects to the viscountess in your next letter sir,' he said.

'I will, I will,' Carlisle looked thoughtful. 'But I wish I could be certain that this friendship – our understanding – can survive these long months and many miles.'

'So, here's the heart of the matter,' thought Chalmers.

'When we left The Downs, like you I had no idea where we were bound. I even dared to hope that we may take the Turkey merchants up the Mediterranean and have time to visit Nice or Leghorn on the way back. Although I dare say, the French army may have had something to say about that.' Carlisle took a few turns across the cabin under the stern windows; a sure sign of his mental agitation. 'But now it seems that we are to join the Leeward Islands Squadron, and it could be years before we return home.' He paused, his face ill-lit by the sunshine coming through the glass skylight. He looked old and disheartened. 'I fear that I may be behaving dishonourably in encouraging this understanding between us. Certainly, she could do better than me and must be under great pressure from half the nobility of Sardinia and the Italian states.'

In his agitation, Carlisle stared at Chalmers, apparently expecting a response. But Chalmers was too good a listener to be rushed into replying. He deliberately took a sip of his Madeira. 'Such a shame to let this grow warm,' he said, risking the loss of the moment, but he knew that Carlisle would not value a snap response. 'If I may comment?' he asked, after another pause. Carlisle nodded.

'Lady Chiara has a great fondness for you Carlisle, not founded on any delusions of your social standing or of your professional prospects, although as an aside I believe you don't do yourself justice in that regard. No, she values you for your own personal qualities, and that's a far more stable foundation for a partnership.' Carlisle opened his mouth to respond, then closed it, feeling like a schoolboy unable to form the right words to contribute to a debate. 'Remember, we have seen that she values her aunt's advice and takes it very seriously, but she is her own woman and, in the end, will take advice but not orders.'

'You think, then, that the viscountess may be against our understanding?'

The Leeward Islands Squadron

Again, Chalmers paused. 'This excellent wine really is the best stage prop imaginable,' he thought as he took another leisurely sip.

'No, I don't. The viscountess knows you well and more importantly, and to the point, she knows her niece. She must have witnessed her rejecting a dozen suitors over the years and by now must be aware that no amount of persuasion will make her choose a man whom she doesn't want. Chiara appears unaffected by dukedoms or noble titles, and that can't have been missed by her aunt. I believe that the Viscountess is your greatest ally in this business.'

Carlisle turned his back and gazed thoughtfully at the blue-grey Atlantic slipping gently astern. There was a good swell running, and he had the fascinating sensation of seeing a far horizon for a few seconds, followed by a few fathoms of smooth swell rising above his eye-line. A good metaphor for the changeable mood that he was in. Oh, for some certainty!

'Then you don't believe I am acting dishonourably?' he asked, turning to look directly at his friend, 'because I couldn't abide that.'

'Certainly not. If you detect any cooling in Chiara's letters, I hope we can talk about it, as friends, before you take any irreversible steps. Imagine what effect it will have on her if the tone of your letters becomes cool. You may feel powerless and isolated here at sea; imagine how much worse it must be for Chiara, surrounded all day by predatory men and even now, perhaps, flying from a French advance into the Savoy.'

'Ah, can King Charles Emmanuel stay neutral in this war? Does he even wish to do so? I expect Newcastle and Anson would dearly love to know that,' said Carlisle. Neither he nor Chalmers could possibly know that the Duke of Newcastle's administration had collapsed a bare few weeks after they left England, casting Anson into unemployment, a victim of the widespread fury at the loss of Minorca. Only four days ago, the Duke of Devonshire had formed a new government.

'But let's not confuse high politics with personal relationships, my dear Carlisle. You may have to suffer separation for a while, but the prize is worth the wait. However, I think you know that.'

Carlisle gazed for a long minute at the swell rising and falling in the ship's wake, lost in thought and apparently oblivious to Chalmers presence. Eventually, when he turned around, he seemed surprised to see the chaplain, calmly sitting at the table, drinking his Madeira.

'Your advice, as always, is well taken, my best of advisers. I see you have a little of your Madeira left, perhaps we could make a toast?' Chalmers stood facing his captain – his friend. 'To Lady Chiara!'

CHAPTER FOUR

Medina Prepares

Saturday, eighteenth of December 1756
Medina, at Sea, Grenada west-by-north 10 leagues

The northeast trade winds had blown steadily for the past eighteen days and had carried the two ships across the Atlantic in elegant style, eating up a steady hundred and fifty miles from noon to noon each day. Medina could easily have made two hundred miles each day, but the old fifties were notoriously poor sailors, and a steady six knots was all that could rightly be expected of them. Wherever Wessex's best point of sailing lay, it undoubtedly wasn't with the wind right astern. She had a most unfortunate motion before the wind, tucking her backside sideways into each approaching wave and waddling downwind like an old matron heading for market, a piglet under each arm.

Carlisle had spent those days preparing his ship and boats for the coming attack on Grenada. He had not confided all his misgivings to his officers, not even to Holbrooke, whom he trusted more than any other man – not yet. In the absence of any further instructions from Jermy, Carlisle had assumed that his first objective would be to destroy the privateers in the harbour and the anchorage before turning his attention to any other vessels that may be there; taking prizes would be a tertiary objective. While he could be reasonably confident that his great guns could sink any large but lightly-built privateers in the anchorage, for the smaller vessels that lay deep in the harbour where Medina's cannon could not reach, the surest method of destruction was fire. The boat gun in the longboat may blaze away at its fastest rate of one round every four minutes, but wooden ships could withstand a lot of that kind of punishment without sinking. Whereas fire, if not quickly brought under control, was a much more certain means of annihilation. He had ordered the gunner to prepare packages of combustible materials for each of the boats and to train selected reliable hands in their use. The great guns had not been neglected; they had been run in and out every day during the dog watches, and each weapon had fired ten practice rounds. It was noticeable that Wessex's guns had fired only a bare minimum of shot, perhaps two or three per gun. Either Jermy was supremely confident in his gunnery, or he was sadly underestimating the task of taking on the twenty-four pounders of Fort Royal – twenty-four pounders firing from behind solid masonry and with the furnaces for heated shot close at hand.

A knock at the door of the great cabin heralded the entrance of George Holbrooke.

'Take a seat, Mister Holbrooke.'

Carlisle had always believed that men responded well to the trust of their superiors. There was an old saying that hovered on the edge of his conscious thought, something along the lines of; Give a man your trust, and he will invariably exceed your expectations. In the case of Holbrooke, his confidence had been rewarded tenfold. Only a year ago, this young man who stood before him was a master's mate on the verge of being turned out of Carlisle's previous command, judged by his captain to be lacking in the qualities required of a sea officer and a bad influence on the men. It was only Carlisle's debt of gratitude to Holbrooke's father, who had saved him in similar circumstances in the last war, that had given Carlisle pause. Whether the critical factor was Carlisle's trust or the excitement of battle and action against the enemy, or a mixture of the two, Holbrooke had proved his worth. As a consequence, he had gained a commission and was now the first lieutenant of a frigate, at least two or three years before he could reasonably have expected such a weighty responsibility.

'How goes the training for the cutting-out parties?' asked Carlisle.

'Very well sir. The men have responded with all the enthusiasm that we expected, you could almost say that they are looking forward to it. Of course, they don't really believe in the combustibles,' he laughed. 'Even as they are taught how to set fire to a merchantman, they are imagining carrying them out to sea as lawful prizes, unburned and with their value intact.'

'Well, I hope we may be able to indulge them – and ourselves – but don't count on being able to carry away prizes under the guns of Fort Royal.'

Carlisle stood and made his habitual half-dozen paces in front of the stern windows.

'In fact, in a way you've hit upon the very issue that I want to discuss with you. Would you close the skylight Holbrooke? I'd rather we were not overheard.'

Three or four people – the mate of the watch, the quartermaster and the helmsmen – were legitimately stationed on the quarterdeck within earshot of the skylight. But Carlisle was sure that the number had been doubled when the first lieutenant was called for, only a day away from expected contact with the enemy. Medina's people were no less inquisitive than any others. Closing the skylight was a public acknowledgement that a private conversation was taking place. The disadvantage was that nature abhorring a vacuum, conjecture would take the place of fact. The desire for information would be fed one way or another.

'I won't hide from you, Holbrooke, that I have deep misgivings about this operation.'

Holbrooke considered interrupting with an assurance that his captain's confidences were safe with him, but he rejected it as being unnecessary. In any case, he had his own concerns. He had conducted boats under the guns of shore batteries in the Mediterranean; he had felt the nakedness of being in an open boat when the enemy was firing their cannon from behind solid walls, and it wasn't a happy memory.

'Any hope of success rests upon surprise, and I am convinced that we'll have none.' Carlisle described to Holbrooke how the French could have hours of notice before their arrival. 'That's my first objection. My second is that Wessex, even with our support, can achieve nothing against Fort Royal. The weight of metal is similar, but our enemies have the advantage of height, protection and heated shot. I don't doubt the commodore's courage, but it would take a miracle for him to prevail against those odds.'

Carlisle was pacing continually now, a transparent betrayal of his state of mind.

'And finally, the winds are all wrong. The sea breeze will pin us in the bay, under the French guns, until well into the dogs. We may well destroy whatever shipping is in the harbour, but if we suffer any damage to sails or rigging, then nothing short of a miracle will allow us to retire without loss. Two of King George's ships may go into the bay, but I won't be surprised if less than that number come out again.'

Holbrooke looked shocked. Of course, he knew there would be risks, but to have them so nakedly exposed by his captain forced home the grave danger that they would face.

'I've therefore decided upon an – ah – modification to my orders. You'll understand now why I insisted that we are not overheard,' the captain said, casting a look at the closed skylight.

Holbrooke's furtive glance at the pantry door was interpreted correctly by Carlisle. 'Smart has been sent to the galley to question the cook about French West Indian cuisine, he'll be gone a long time.' Holbrooke nodded and smiled. The ship's cook was the only black man holding a warrant that Holbrooke had ever met. He had been a slave in the French West Indies, a cook who had won his freedom by swimming out to a British sloop during the last war. He had been pressed, of course, British men-of-war were always hungry for able-bodied men, and a year later the seaman had earned his cook's warrant under Admiral Knowles at Havana by the simple expedient of interposing his foot between a Spanish round shot and its final resting place at the base of the mizzen mast. Knowles was so impressed that the ball had failed to cause major damage to his ship that he swore it was due to being impeded by the able seaman's foot – which incidentally had been amputated in the cockpit not fifteen minutes later. The admiral had immediately written an application for a cook's warrant which he dispatched with his official report after the battle.

'The commodore has ordered that all boats should be employed in destroying the shipping in the harbour with Medina covering them and using her own batteries to assist in the destruction. That I will do, but with this alteration – and this is where I need your support.'

Holbrooke nodded. This was a dangerous business, discussing modifications to the commodore's orders. If anyone should ever hear of this, then two careers would be in grave jeopardy.

'You will command the longboat …'

That surprised Holbrooke. He had assumed that he would be needed on board Medina to manage the batteries and be ready to second Captain Carlisle.

'… because I need the longboat to be preserved and ready to tow Medina or Wessex – or both – out of the bay if the action takes the turn that I fear.'

What Carlisle needed, as he explained to his first lieutenant, was to have his largest ship's boat – the longboat – appear to take part in the business of commerce destruction, while remaining close enough to Medina to tow her out of range of the fort when the destruction was complete. Or when the frail frigate's timbers could take no more punishment. He explained that the longboat would be double-banked (if the commodore should question that, it could be explained away as prize crews) and all preparations for towing should be complete in the boat and in Medina. Holbrooke was to concentrate on the nearest merchant ships and direct the other boats to those deeper in the harbour. Carlisle confidently expected that the fort would focus its firepower upon the two ships, probably mainly upon Wessex, at least initially, and leave the boats unmolested.

Carlisle and Holbrooke were close friends, they owed each other a debt of honour for their successes. Carlisle because Holbrooke had led a near-suicidal flanking attack on the French frigate Vulcain six months ago, saving the captain from ignominious defeat when he had over-reached himself in boarding his larger adversary. Holbrooke because without Carlisle's forbearance he would have been cast aside in Mahon before ever he had the chance to reach for glory in that desperate battle – a battle that led directly to his early commission as a lieutenant. But even this close friendship was constrained by naval protocol, and each knew that they had already pushed to its limit the conventional relationship between a captain and his second-in-command. Nevertheless, Holbrooke felt impelled to speak.

'Wouldn't the commodore be amenable to incorporating this into his plan, sir? Perhaps it's worth asking for a meeting before the action …'

But Carlisle was already shaking his head, sadly but emphatically.

'No, he would not. How can I put this? The fact is that for whatever reason, I don't enjoy the commodore's confidence. I have already gone as far as I can in offering my advice – too far perhaps. I will not go further. No, Holbrooke, we must obey the commodore's orders, exert ourselves to the utmost in carrying out our part in his plan while retaining a reserve for our own safety. That is your role. The other boats can be left to cause mayhem among the privateers and merchantmen in the harbour, but you must defy your own instincts and preserve the longboat as our means of escape. I hope – I hope, that it won't be necessary, but I fear otherwise.'

CHAPTER FIVE

Jackson

Saturday, eighteenth of December 1756
Medina, at Sea, Grenada west-by-north 10 leagues

Jackson laughed softly to himself. He remembered the day when he was turned over from *Fury* into *Medina*, following his captain and lieutenant into this newer frigate.

'Jackson, just Jackson?' The purser had asked. 'That's not good enough, what's your Christian name,' he demanded. Jackson had looked from the pen poised over the muster list and up to the moist eyes sunk into the round, bespectacled face and had almost laughed. The purser was recording his entry into *Medina*, making him legally a part of the ship's company until she was decommissioned, sunk or captured. There was a long line of men behind him, mostly volunteers but a few taken up by the press to fill out the complement.

'I've got no Christian name, sir. It's just Jackson.' He shifted his gaze to look steadfastly over the purser's shoulder. He heard some muted laughter behind him. He had a Christian name, of course. He was regularly baptised – or so his mother had led him to understand – in the half-derelict garrison church at the back of Portsmouth Point, behind the Square Tower. His mother told him proudly that he had been baptised in the same church that Charles II had married his foreign princess. It seemed unlikely to Jackson, the building really was in a poor state and looked nothing like a royal palace, although he had heard that there were plans to refurbish it. He had visited the church when *Fury* had been paid off, it was his only point of anchorage with the shore – he had no home, no parents, no brothers or sisters, no relatives and no friends who weren't seamen like himself. He had never known his father, who had sailed in an East Indiaman before the young Jackson was born and had been drowned off the Cape. His mother had died of smallpox when Jackson was eleven. But he was lucky; Britain was at war again, and he was taken on board the ninety-gun *Namur* as a servant to the bosun. He had not had a home ashore since that day. Jackson had always assumed that there was some record of his baptism in the garrison church and he was determined to hunt it down when he had a decent spell ashore. Because he really couldn't believe that his mother would weigh him down with *that* Christian name, even with its supposed royal connections. And he certainly wasn't going to tell the purser – or anyone else – what it was.

The purser looked sceptically at Jackson. He felt that he was being *strung a line*, as these sailors said, but it was unlikely that he would get any more out of this man in front of him. However, he was diligent in his own way, and a single name would stand out like a white topsail in a squall on the new muster list.

'Well, I'm going to have to put an 'X' where your Christian name should be, I can't leave it blank. Are you sure you don't have one?'

'No Christian name, sir, and I don't want an 'X' beside my name. That's the mark of an unlettered man, and I can read – aye and write pretty well.' His gaze didn't shift from a point over the purser's left shoulder.

'Then I must have something, Jackson,' replied the purser. If this man in front of him could dig in his heels over this issue, then so could he. And the purser was sure that Jackson was lying to him. 'If it's not an 'X,' what's it to be?'

This was the first time that Jackson had been challenged on this issue. It was the fault of the new muster forms, of course. The old pages could accommodate a single name without looking incomplete, but not the new ones. Jackson thought for a moment as the purser impatiently tapped his fingernails on the wooden desk.

'Jack, sir. Jack Jackson. But it's not my name,' he continued, doggedly, 'it's just a pusser's name.'

The purser looked at him sharply. Was this insolence? 'Probably not,' he thought. It was just like the lower deck to have a cryptic phrase for an assumed name and *pusser's name* at least sounded plausible.

With a resigned sigh and a few strokes of the pen, Jackson, first name unknown, was entered onto *Medina*'s books as Jack Jackson.

'Next!' called the purser as Jackson stepped aside.

'Eli.' Stated the old quartermaster, looking the purser straight in the eye.

'Surname?' demanded the unsuspecting purser.

'Ain't got one … sir.'

The line of men erupted into laughter while the unfortunate purser stared resignedly at his muster sheet. It was going to be a long day.

Jackson had some serious thinking to do and needed some solitude to do it. If he were the captain, he could step into his cabin or clear the windward side of the quarterdeck. If he were a warrant officer, he could retire to his tiny partitioned sleeping compartment. But an able seaman, even if he was also the captain's coxswain, shared his sleeping quarters with a hundred and fifty other men, and he had none of these options. But Jackson knew where to go, and in these tropical regions, it was a pleasant enough place. He ran hand-over-hand up the foremast shrouds and popped up through the lubber's hole, surprising three men who were engaged in a game of knucklebones in the foretop – a form of gambling of dubious legality in a King's ship.

'Sling your hooks, mates,' he said, not unpleasantly, with a jerk of his thumb towards the lubber's hole. Two of the men were in their first commission and looked inclined to disagree, but the third had served with Jackson in *Fury*. He led the way out of the top with a respectful nod to his old shipmate. The authority of the captain's coxswain was too great for argument.

This was a critical commission for Jackson; he could feel the tide behind him and was determined to catch it. Ever since he had been ordered to take the young Holbrooke into Toulon inner harbour under cover of darkness to count the French fleet, he had felt that Captain Carlisle trusted him. In fact, he was sure that his selection for that expedition in Toulon, and the later service in various hired tenders and prizes, had been no coincidence. He wasn't chosen at random from among the other senior able seamen, he was specifically selected. With that knowledge, Jackson was just biding his time before he formally requested to be nominated for a bosun's warrant. He knew that there was tremendous competition back in England where people waited years for a spare berth. But here in the West Indies, it was quite common for the commander-in-chief to award provisional warrants in the confident expectation that they would be endorsed by the Navy Board. So, this was his opportunity. If he waited until they returned to Britain, he would be the last in a long line of hopefuls.

He had seen how Carlisle worked and he had watched with interest as Holbrooke had matured into his first lieutenant's berth. He knew enough about sea officers to recognise that these two were quite exceptional in their courage and enterprise. He could feel it in his bones; these two would achieve great things. The question was, how should he – Jackson – position himself to benefit from his officers' good fortunes?

'Let's just suppose,' he thought, 'that Holbrooke gets his step to commander on this station. Should I stay with Carlisle, and wait for the bosun to be transferred or retire? Or should I jump ship with Holbrooke and ask to be his bosun?' It was all highly theoretical, but Jackson knew that these things happened very suddenly. The capture of another man-of-war and Holbrooke could – probably would – be whisked away, perhaps back to England, before Jackson would have a chance to fetch his wake. And that is why he needed to make his decision now. He knew that the attack on the fort and anchorage tomorrow was a dicey affair – he could sense the unease among the officers. It could be that in the confusion a French frigate was cut out, and Holbrooke could be lost to him in a matter of weeks.

It wasn't that he didn't want to stay with his captain, but Carlisle was established in this command with a competent and not-very-aged bosun. It could be years before Jackson's opportunity arose if he stayed in *Medina*.

Jackson was a gambling man – there was no moral angle to him dislodging the knucklebones players from the foretop – and he was prepared to gamble now. Holbrooke, it must be. He would talk to the lieutenant at the next opportunity and sow the seeds for them shifting berth together when – if – Holbrooke should be promoted.

Happy with his decision, Jackson settled back against the stowed stuns'ls and whistled to himself as he watched the sunset and counted the first planets and stars making their appearance, one-by-one as day gave way to night. He wasn't troubled by the regular comings-and-goings as the watch on deck checked the set of the sails, sweated down the halyards and adjusted the sheets. He was at peace with the world. He had a plan.

The Leeward Islands Squadron

CHAPTER SIX

Attack on Port Louis

Sunday, nineteenth of December 1756
Medina, at Sea, Port Louis east-northeast 6 nautical miles

The small squadron had rounded Point Salines at the southwest tip of Grenada with the sun already well on her way to the zenith. Each ship was trailing a string of boats manned and ready to be slipped as soon as they were within a reasonable range of their objectives. As predicted, the sea breeze had set in with the forenoon watch, and it was wafting them gently towards the land. So far all had gone according to the commodore's plan and the southwest shore of Grenada, its green forests, plantations, sandy beaches and rocky outcrops, passed peacefully to starboard. There was no hint of warlike preparation, but as Carlisle well knew, that perception was deceptive. They had undoubtedly been observed as much as three hours ago, and whatever else the French were, they were not stupid, nor incompetent. There were adequate roads in this southern part of the island, and Fort Royal would have been alerted by now. But none of this was yet evident to Commodore Jermy's squadron, and the peaceful scene lulled even the most hardened sailor's fears.

Carlisle and Holbrooke stood side by side on the quarterdeck. *Medina* had been cleared for action for the past hour, and the men had eaten their breakfast of oatmeal porridge and small beer. The guns were run out, splinter nets were rigged, the yards had been chained, the decks sanded, and water buckets refilled; all possible preparations had been made. Both men regarded this operation with the utmost concern, and the gravity of the situation showed on their faces as they watched the shore slip by.

They could just discern the outline of the Fort Royal now. 'God, it looks huge,' thought Holbrooke. Not nearly as imposing as St. Philip's fort in Minorca, which he was intimately familiar with, having run messages into the beleaguered garrison under de Richelieu's guns only six months ago. But Fort Royal was imposing enough for a small Caribbean island. 'Could this tiny squadron really prevail in an open assault under those battlements?' he asked himself. The scale of this undertaking was just becoming apparent.

Even with his telescope, it was too far to see any details. But there was undoubtedly a thin plume of smoke rising from the fort; cookhouse fires or heated shot? They would soon know. Shifting his view slightly to the right, he could see the anchorage and behind that, the warehouses and jetties of Port Louis guarded by the fort. He could see three vessels in the outer anchorage, a ship and two brigs. There was a third brig alongside the jetties and two smaller schooners behind her. The inner anchorage was empty. At this distance, they could all be privateers, or they could be more-or-less innocent merchantmen. Perhaps those at anchor were more likely to be the former and those alongside the latter, as merchantmen could more easily load and unload their cargoes at a jetty than at anchor.

Carlisle had the same opinion. 'Mister Holbrooke, I don't like the look of the anchored ships. They're too much for the boats to take on; I'll engage those with our broadsides. The boats are to give them a wide berth and proceed to burn the vessels on the jetty. Remember your station in the longboat; keep close to *Medina* and annoy the privateers, if that is what they are.'

'Aye-aye sir. Perhaps I should leave you now and join the longboat.'

The three boats were towing close alongside the frigate, so it was a matter of moments for Holbrooke to step from the mizzen chains into the bows of the longboat. It took longer to make his way to the stern as the boat was packed with men, far above its usual pulling complement, so that the oars could be double-banked if necessary. They would need all the muscle that they could safely stow in the boat if they were to pull *Medina* or *Wessex* out of action against the sea breeze. He was comforted to see Jackson sat with his arm across the tiller – a solid nucleus of seamanlike competence.

Carlisle watched the commodore's ship intently, looking for a signal, but Jermy apparently thought that the plan was clear enough, because *Wessex's* halyards remained bare. He could see Jermy on his quarterdeck in earnest conversation with Thompson, the master. Godwin stood some distance apart right at the quarterdeck rail where presumably he could best control the guns.

Carlisle watched as Jermy walked across to the leeward side; he was moving more stiffly than before, holding onto railings and halyards to steady himself. Even from this distance, it was apparent that the pain was intense, and it was a significant effort of will to remain upright. Thompson stood beside the wheel. He looked neither at his commodore nor at the first lieutenant but stared intently at the sails. The wind was almost dead astern, just a trifle on the starboard quarter and the vast lateen mizzen and the fore and main coarses had been furled to improve visibility from the quarterdeck. The gun ports were open on both sides, and the guns were run out, which must have been a relief to the crews as the day was becoming hot already and the breeze through the open ports would be welcome.

'Mister Hosking, we are a little too close to *Wessex*, clew up the main topsail and take some of the way off her.' The sailing master had noticed the edge in Carlisle's voice. He was as sensitive as a cat to the subtle variations in his captain's voice, and he could tell that Carlisle was nervous. For his part, Hosking was not at all happy with this enterprise. This was perhaps the most exposed position in the ship, and he had a wealth of experience at sea to tell him that this was a desperate gamble, bringing two ships into a defended anchorage against a prepared enemy.

Less than a mile to go now and the details of the fort were becoming visible. Carlisle was puzzled to see that the guns had not been run out. Could it be that the defenders were unprepared? Had Jermy achieved the surprise that he had hoped for? With a jolt, Carlisle remembered why the cannon certainly could not be run out. The heated shot was only loaded at the last moment. Otherwise, it would burn through the damp wadding and ignite the powder charge prematurely. He could imagine the crews beside the furnaces; bellows working briskly, the armourer turning the shot on its grid over the coals. The loaders waiting with their double-handed cradles to take the shot directly from the furnace to the waiting guns. When would they open fire? There was no point in waiting too long, in Carlisle's opinion. They should be firing at half a mile, so any moment now.

'Sir, the commodore's first lieutenant is waving,' said Hosking. 'It looks like he is attracting your attention.' He was indeed, and his meaning was obvious, *Wessex's* boats were being dispatched now, and he wanted *Medina* to do the same. Jermy looked in no fit state to wave at anyone, he was barely managing to stay upright.

'Bosun, away pinnace and yawl,' called Carlisle. 'Hold the longboat alongside for now.' He watched as the two boats slipped their painters and moved away toward the anchorage. A little too early in Carlisle's opinion; he would have waited a while to conserve the strength of the crews. His two master's mates were in those boats, bright young men he could ill-afford to lose. He hoped they would obey his orders and keep clear of the privateers, saving their efforts for the merchantmen at the jetties.

Looking up at the fort, Carlisle was just in time to see the opening shots of the battle. He saw the empty embrasures suddenly change shape as the ugly, black mouths of the guns thrust through them, almost simultaneously. That was good drill by the French gunners, they must have been well trained for an action of this kind. He just had time to count eight guns when the whole curtain of the battlements erupted in smoke and flame, not less than six of the guns firing in unison, the remaining a few seconds later. There was nothing to show that they were using heated shot except the smoke from the furnace and the very short time between running out and firing. There was always a loss of accuracy with heated shot because the gunners were naturally reluctant to stand behind the gun, right in the line of the deadly recoil, and to point it correctly once the balls had rolled, sizzling down the barrel.

Medina was astern of *Wessex,* and the French were aiming for the commodore's ship. There were no hits from this first salvo, and the grouping of the fall of shot was all over the place, as you would expect when the commander of the battery had but seconds to point the guns between loading and firing. In Carlisle's opinion it would be better if the guns fired individually, then their gun captains could make better use of the brief few seconds available to them.

The other disadvantage with heated shot was that the rate of fire was significantly reduced, perhaps to half of the natural pace. Ideally, a fort would use a mixture of heated and cold shot to maintain the tempo while still exploiting the battery's potential destructive power. As if in agreement, smaller puffs of smoke were appearing below and between the big guns; nine-pounders, Carlisle estimated. These were firing cold shot and achieving much better practice, faster and more accurate, and small waterspouts were already straddling the commodore's ship.

The shot was falling thick and fast around *Wessex* and Carlisle could see that it was only a matter of time before she started to be damaged. Jermy was holding his fire, but surely not for much longer. Almost immediately he saw then heard the flagship's larboard battery open fire.

Quickly raising the telescope to his eye, he observed the results of the broadside; clouds of dust and eruptions of earth and loose masonry all along the base of the fort. Too short, not enough elevation, but it would give the French gunners pause for thought. The fort had the advantage of height, something approaching a hundred feet above the fragile wooden ships. And now that advantage started to tell. *Wessex* was taking hits, only from the nine-pounders so far, but the enormous waterspouts left by the hot shot were creeping closer.

'Mister Hosking, down helm and bring the larboard battery to bear on that first ship,' said Carlisle, indicating the nearest ship-rigged vessel, certainly a privateer now that she could be clearly seen. The privateer lay with her bows to the wind pointing directly at *Medina*. Part of her crew was frantically trying to get a spring from the furthest aft larboard gun port to the anchor cable to bring their own guns to bear, while the other half was piling into boats to make their escape. The fort may have been prepared for the attack, but the ships at anchor had either been forgotten, or the message had taken too long to reach them. Either way, *Medina's* first target was a sitting duck, ready to be raked from forward to aft.

Carlisle was handicapped by having sent his first lieutenant and both master's mates away in the boats, but this was the moment for his midshipmen to rise to the occasion. Nevertheless, he would control the firing of the battery himself.

'Mister Wishart, larboard battery stand by,' he called down into the waist.

'Aye-aye sir,' replied the midshipman. David Wishart had been a midshipman in *Fury* with Carlisle. He had fought several engagements, the last of which saw his uncle, *Fury's* first lieutenant, killed by a French musket. Wishart had avenged that death by hurling the French marksman from the mizzen top to the deck – he had proved his steadiness and his courage; he would soon be ready for promotion to master's mate.

'Aim at the base of her foremast, Mister Wishart.'

Medina turned deliberately to starboard. The Frenchmen working on the spring scattered, abandoning their task, as the frigate's full battery became visible. It must have been a fearful sight indeed; twelve nine-pound cannon on the deck, two three pounders on the quarterdeck and the swivel guns in the tops and along the hammock rails, all pointing directly at the small, frail privateer.

'Fire!' shouted Carlisle, and the whole broadside discharged its load of nine-pound balls almost simultaneously. Caribbean privateers were not made to take that kind of punishment; they were the smallest and flimsiest ship-rigged vessels afloat and were never intended to withstand the broadside of a rated man-of-war. The foremast went by the board, taking the main topmast with it. The bowsprit and jib boom hung drunkenly under the stem, and the beakhead was utterly destroyed.

Down on *Medina's* main deck, the gun captains were raising their hands as their guns were reloaded.

'Mister Wishart, fire as soon as each gun is ready.'

The midshipman raised his hat in response, swelling with pride at the responsibility of handling the whole battery in action. Carlisle could see that he needed only to point out the targets; the management of the guns was in good hands.

The battery was firing now in ones and twos, and at this close range almost every shot told. Carlisle could see large holes in the privateer's larboard bow, but so far, no hits on the waterline, nothing fatal.

'Mister Thompson, you can see our next target; lay me across her bows,' said Carlisle pointing to the second privateer, a brig. The crew of the brig had no illusions about their impending fate and were taking to the boats as fast as they could.

Carlisle had to admit that, for all his scepticism, the

attack was proceeding as well as he could have hoped. The six boats, four from *Wessex* and *Medina's* pinnace and yawl, were approaching the vessels moored along the jetty. Holbrooke in the longboat was busy throwing combustibles into the crippled first privateer, while his crew harassed the retreating privateer boats with brisk musketry. He was obeying his orders, staying close to *Medina*.

Then, in a moment the tide of the battle turned. A wisp of heat haze that started in *Wessex's* stern turned into an angry swirl of black smoke.

'The flagship's fire is slackening sir,' said the master. 'Looks like she has a right problem on her poop deck.'

A problem indeed and clearly the guns crews were being stripped to provide firefighters. With the wind at her stern, the fire was moving steadily forward, consuming the poop deck as it did so. The quarterdeck would soon be in danger.

'They must put the wind on their bow soon, or they will lose control.' The master was almost shouting at Carlisle in his anguish.

Carlisle waved to Holbrooke in the longboat, but the lieutenant had already seen the problem and was turning his boat toward the flagship, the rowers bending their oars in response to his urgings. Carlisle wondered how long their enthusiasm would last; nobody relished being near a burning man-of-war. If the fire really took hold it would be only a matter of time before the danger to their rescuers overcame their sense of duty. After the initial risk of the fire transferring to the rescuing boats, the loaded guns would start to explode, sending their shot who-knew-where. Then the flames would creep downwards, and when they reached the magazine, the whole ship would blow, taking with it any boats that had stayed too close. Holbrooke had the men under control for the moment, but for how long?

Wessex was lying southwest of the fort. 'If she veers now,' thought Carlisle, 'and passes between the four-fathom bank and the fort, she could just about weather the point of land to the north and escape from the bay. But she will take a lot more punishment before she is clear.'

And that was just what Jermy was attempting, he had brought his helm to weather, and his stern had just passed through the wind, his mizzen swinging over to starboard. Carlisle breathed a sigh of relief; perhaps they could escape after all, but at that moment the fates intervened again. Before his horrified eyes, Carlisle saw a lick of flame rise from the poop and catch the mizzen. In a second it was gone, consumed by the fire. With no leverage aft, *Wessex* immediately put before the wind again, driving directly for the pass and closer to the guns of Fort Royal.

Godwin, in *Wessex*, saw the danger and was gesticulating urgently at the longboat, waving Holbrooke in to drag *Wessex's* bows around to the west. Little did he know that this was the duty that Holbrooke was prepared for. There was a stout cable faked down in the longboat and a heaving line bent on to its end. All Holbrooke had to do was bring *Wessex's* bows around; he didn't need to tow the two-decker any great distance. As soon as the wind was on the larboard bow, the square mizzen topsail would provide the balance for the headsails, and she would be able to lie on the wind.

'Jackson, stand by the heaving line,' yelled Holbrooke to the coxswain. 'I'll take the tiller.' Jackson vaulted over the rowers, now double-banked in their need for speed. By the time he had taken up the heaving line, the longboat was under *Wessex's* bows. Holbrooke could see the flagship's frantic efforts to prepare a hawser for towing and could see that it would be too late. By the time the hawser had been cleared they would be too far through the pass to be able to make their escape, and even closer to the deadly gunnery of Fort Royal.

'I have a tow ready.' He called up to Godwin, who he could see directing efforts on the fo'c'sle. The flagship's first lieutenant raised his arm, but it was evident that he couldn't understand Holbrooke,

'Jackson, hold up the hawser, let them see we are ready.'

The inboard bow oar and Jackson between them held a few fathoms of the hawser at head height. Yet still *Wessex* didn't see, they were all bending to their work of preparing their own towing cable.

'Oh, you blind sods, look below!' bellowed Jackson in exasperation. That brought Godwin's head up. He looked annoyed at being addressed so, but at last, he grasped the situation.

The longboat was now directly under *Wessex's* larboard bow. 'Heave when you are ready Jackson,' called Holbrooke. But Jackson had already drawn back his arm. He flung the tightly coiled line from his right hand, the monkey's fist at the end dragging out the small coils and, as the weight of line in the air started to have its effect, drawing out the larger coils in his left hand. The line snaked out straight and true to be caught by a seaman's outstretched arm from the rail of the head. The heaving line was passed to another seaman leaning through the hawse hole and thence to the eager team, ready to heave in the hawser. Holbrooke had to concede that Godwin had his men well organised. The heaving line ran rapidly inboard. Next came the hawser stoppered to the heaving line and that moved almost as fast. A great shout came from *Wessex,* and there was Godwin at the fo'c'sle rail making the universal sign with his crossed wrists over his head – the hawser had been secured to the bits.

'Haul down the slack Jackson. Stroke oar, secure to the holdfast.' The larboard rowers flattened themselves against the thwarts as the hawser swung over their heads and the weight was taken on the stern of the boat. 'Now, give way together,' ordered Holbrooke. He blessed Carlisle's foresight in doubling his boat's crew. The wooden shafts bent as the brawny oarsmen strained every sinew. There was a rush through the water as the longboat took up the slack, then a sharp rebound as the whole ponderous weight of the two-decker brought the boat to a standstill, then dragged it backwards.

'Steady,' shouted Holbrooke. 'Watch the stroke oar.' He looked over his shoulder. *Wessex* looked enormous from this angle; how could he ever hope to move that great bulk? The longboat steered crazily with this great weight dragging her stern around. Holbrooke knew what he must do. 'Jackson, back here and take the tiller.' Jackson was the expert; he had at least ten more years at sea and had spent much of that handling boats under every conceivable condition. Holbrooke could not match that experience.

Jackson again hurdled the rowers and took the tiller. 'Row short Nobby,' was his first order to the stroke oar. Short, sharp tugs would be better to get the flagship's bows swinging; the long, deep strokes could wait until the vast mass of the flagship was in motion.

Holbrooke looked again at *Wessex*. Was she starting to turn? Yes, there was a definite movement. But now the next problem presented itself. The gunners in the fort, seeing their prey being manoeuvred away from them, had turned the nine-pounders – their secondary armament – onto the longboat. At first, this wasn't evident to Holbrooke, but when he was regularly soaked by the spray from near-misses, it became an inescapable fact. Luckily the oarsmen were now fully occupied in their task; putting them in danger from a burning two-decker was terrible enough, but then exposing them, almost stationary until *Wessex* began to move, under the guns of a fortress was asking too much.

Jackson understood. His body tense, his muscles taut, he pushed back and fore in time with the stroke oar, an irresistible example to the oarsmen who were left with no leisure to contemplate their danger.

Holbrooke could see with satisfaction the dead-straight line from the bows of the longboat, through the towing bridle at the stern, to the point where the hawser disappeared through the hawse hole of the two-decker. It was bar-taught with only a slight catenary. The longboat's bows were to the west, and the whole of the effort was being transmitted efficiently to turn the ship onto the wind. Holbrooke could see nothing of *Medina*; she was hidden by *Wessex's* bulk. But he could see that Jermy was swinging his yards around, close-hauled on the larboard tack. Nobody could approach the poop which was still on fire, and any efforts to bend on a new lateen mizzen would be futile. *Wessex* would need to claw off this lee shore with the canvas she had available. Holbrooke could see that the flagship's rate of fire had slackened as the guns crews had been re-deployed to fire fighting and to sail trimming. But that was of no consequence, and the violence of Fort Royal was starting to look like a minor irritation in the face of a lee shore with a damaged rig and the fire on the poop still raging.

In five minutes Holbrooke's task was completed. At a wave from Godwin, the tow was slipped, and *Wessex* started moving sedately away to the northwest. Looking up, Holbrooke could see that the fire on the poop was being brought under control, although the stern above the quarterdeck was a charred parody of its former glory. He could see *Medina* now. Carlisle had also tacked and was engaging the fort with his starboard battery as he stood out for the safety of the open sea in *Wessex's* wake. Seeing the two ships in retreat, the remainder of the boats had turned back toward them and were stretching out with all their might to get out of range of the fort's guns as quickly as possible. Only Lynton's boat appeared to have achieved anything, and it was towing a small flush-decked schooner barely larger than itself.

'Back your topsails Mister Hosking,' ordered Carlisle. 'We'll hold our position until we can cover the boats' withdrawal.'

The starboard battery was in fine form, firing as fast as they could reload. *Medina* had not yet taken any significant damage, but Carlisle was acutely aware that this couldn't last. The fort's nine-pounders were almost at point-blank range, and it was only the smoke from the two ships' cannons blowing into the French gunners' eyes that had preserved them so far. He had no intention of delaying his departure to hoist in the boats, he just wanted them all to shelter behind *Medina* as they were escorted out of danger. The fort was still concentrating its fire on *Wessex*, but the guns on the southeast side of the fort could no longer point at the flagship and so were now targeting the frigate.

'Hot work Mister Hosking.'

'Aye sir, and it'll get hotter before it ends. Look at those boats stretching out now, they don't want to be left behind to face that cannonade alone.'

'I do believe our French friends have not helped themselves though. I wouldn't be using hot shot now, a faster and more accurate fire with cold shot from those twenty-four pounders would make life very uncomfortable for us.'

'I dare say you are right sir. But those nine-pounders are not improving our looks,' said the master as the cradle for the longboat was destroyed where it stood, mercifully with no human casualties.

'Oh, for a fireship now. We could burn those privateers where they lie.'

But Hosking was not a man for wishful thinking. With a barely audible humph he said, 'we can get underway now sir, the boats are almost here.'

And so ended Jermy's action at Fort Royal. The tally was one privateer damaged and a small trading schooner taken as a prize to set against what looked like severe damage to a fourth-rate. There was a palpable sense of failure in the squadron as it withdrew to the northwest. There would be celebrations at Fort Royal today, but none in the great cabin of *Wessex*.

CHAPTER SEVEN

Change of Command

Sunday, nineteenth of December 1756
Medina, at Sea, Ronde Island southeast 9 nautical miles

Medina followed *Wessex* out of the Grand Bay and northward. *Medina's* three boats were strung out astern of her and the captured schooner, now manned by Charles Lynton and a small prize crew, sailed obediently in her wake. Carlisle conceded that perhaps the safest and most convenient route to Barbados was to beat up to leeward of the islands and then round either St. Vincent or St. Lucia and then beat back to the east. Undoubtedly that was Jermy's plan, although Carlisle was beginning to despair of his commodore's planning. The squadron's orders clearly stated that following their attack on Grenada, they should look for the Leeward Islands Squadron in Barbados. What the orders didn't state, and Carlisle knew nothing of any additional verbal directions that Jermy may have received, was what level of success was required at Grenada. Probably it wasn't specified, but it was inconceivable that their Lordships would be content with the little that had been achieved. The damage to *Wessex* didn't look too bad now that the fire had been extinguished, nothing that the dockyard at English Harbour couldn't put right in a few weeks. However, set against the modest gains, the squadron's account was squarely in deficit.

'Come!' called Carlisle in response to a knock on the cabin door. He was pleased to see Holbrooke enter, looking a little cleaner than when he had last seen him fresh from his exertions in the longboat. 'Take a seat Mister Holbrooke, you have a report?'

'Yes sir,' Holbrooke withdrew a sheet of paper from his

waistcoat pocket. 'First, the casualties sir.' He didn't need the paper for that, the company of *Medina* was small enough for its first lieutenant to know everyone by name, and the casualties were seared into his mind. 'One dead sir. Able Seaman Claverty died in the yawl, bow oar, he was struck by a musket ball and expired almost immediately. It appears that the yawl came nearest to the jetties and was surprised by a squad of soldiers running down from the fort. They were lucky to get away so lightly, perhaps the soldiers had run too hard for accurate musketry.' Holbrooke paused to allow his captain to comment.

'A good man, he will be missed. A volunteer, I believe, with a number of ships behind him.'

'Yes sir, he has no family in the muster book, but I'll inquire among the hands.' Holbrooke continued.

'There are four wounded, sir, but only one seriously. Jenkins of the afterguard, also yawl crew, his elbow was shattered by a musket ball from the same volley that killed Claverty. Mister Carlton is removing the arm now as far below the shoulder as he dares. He says that Jenkins has as much chance of recovery as anyone in that condition.'

Carlisle knew nothing of his surgeon's capabilities even after a long transatlantic passage; there had been little sickness and no requirement for surgery since leaving The Downs. At least the man was getting on with his gruesome job without any kind of fuss. Carlisle remembered surgeons in other ships who would not proceed with any type of operation without having the captain view the patient, perhaps to share the guilt if the surgery proved ineffective.

'Let Mister Carlton know that I would like his report as soon as he is at leisure. What of the physical damage Mister Holbrooke?'

'Well, it's not serious sir. I will ask the carpenter to give you a detailed report as soon as he has made everything safe in case of heavy weather. There are two shot holes in the gundeck on the starboard side and one lodged against

The Leeward Islands Squadron

the gammoning, but the turns are not cut through, and the bowsprit isn't in any danger at present. The bosun is preparing to replace the whole gammoning before dark.'

Carlisle nodded. The gammoning – the turns of strong cordage that held the base of the bowsprit fast to the head – was one of the weakest points in any ship.

'The worst damage is to the longboat's cradle. Chips reckons that he has a day's work there.'

'Does he have the timber for a repair?'

'Yes sir, at least to make safe until we can get to the yard at English Harbour.'

'Very well. And our prize? How did young Charles manage to cut out that schooner in all the confusion? He must have kept a cool head.'

'It appears that when the alarm was given, those of the privateers' crew that were ashore commandeered the schooner to take them out to the ships and brig anchored in the bay. There was a deal of confusion when they met the weaker-hearted of their friends coming the other way in the privateers' boats, and most of them jumped out of the schooner and into the boats and headed back for the shore. In the confusion, Lynton and the pinnace crew snapped her up.'

'Does she have a cargo?'

'She does sir, but of no great worth; she is stuffed with hay. I guess that she had recently arrived at Port Louis from elsewhere in the island, or perhaps from one of the smaller islands to the north and hadn't yet unloaded.'

'Aye, there is no value in hay unless we need a bonfire,' replied Carlisle smiling, 'but the hull may be worth something. I'll discuss it with the commodore, but meanwhile, we can spare Mister Lynton and four men to keep her in company.'

One of the advantages of the skylight was that, often, Carlisle heard a message intended for him before the messenger could make his way to the cabin door.

'Mister Smith,' he heard the master call. 'My

compliments to Captain Carlisle and the flagship is requesting that we close her.'

Carlisle, therefore, had the time to compose his reply so that the astonished Smith, one of the new young gentlemen that he had embarked in Sheerness, received his return message almost before he had completed his own delivery.

'My compliments to Mister Hosking. Close *Wessex* but keep to her leeward, we will need to be at about fifty yards if we are to have a conversation.'

Carlisle and Holbrooke looked at each other. What orders did Jermy have for them? Was he planning to tamely continue to Barbados, which seemed most likely? Or was he planning some further action against Port Louis?

It had been an easy matter to close within hailing distance of the flagship. *Medina* was inherently the faster ship, and in any case, *Wessex* had been under very easy sail as she headed northward away from Port Louis. Hosking had merely sheeted home the topsails, which had been spilling wind for the past two hours, and the frigate moved quickly up to the two-decker's quarterdeck. Carlisle was surprised to see Lieutenant Godwin and Thompson, the sailing master, standing side-by-side at the lee rail of the quarterdeck.

Godwin put the speaking trumpet to his mouth. 'Captain Carlisle. I regret to inform you that the commodore is not well, he's unable to leave his cabin. Will you come aboard and wait upon him?'

'What a curious way to put it,' thought Carlisle. This was not phrased as an order from the commodore, and it almost sounded that Jermy was not the instigator of this meeting. He considered asking for details of the commodore's condition but bit his tongue. It was not a fit subject for a bellowed conversation across fifty yards of sea, a conversation that could be heard by anyone in either ship who cared to listen. And Carlisle had another reason. He didn't want to be beholden to this Miles Godwin for information. He still smarted from their previous meeting.

The flagship put down her helm and backed her topsail to take her way off. *Medina* followed her actions, and within a few minutes, the two ships were lying-to, quite comfortable in this gentle tail-end of the trade wind. The yawl was pulled up to the waist – a poor choice of boat in Carlisle's opinion as the unfortunate Claverty's blood had barely been swabbed away from the bow thwart that he had been occupying. Carlisle descended the short distance into the boat to the wail of the side boys' calls. It was a slightly greater effort to make his way onto the waist of *Wessex*, encumbered by carpenters and bosun's crew, busily setting to right the punishment that she had taken at the hands of the French gunners. There were many shot-holes from the smaller cannon but mercifully few from the twenty-four-pound heated shot. Carlisle was now convinced that the fort could have done more damage with cold shot – a faster rate of fire and greater accuracy could have resulted in the complete wrecking of the squadron. Hot-shot was considerably over-rated, in his opinion. As he walked towards the commodore's quarters, he looked up at the poop deck. It was devastated, burned down almost to the level of the quarterdeck at its after end. Of the taffrail and its gilded ornaments, there was no sign. No evidence either of the stern lanterns, those visible marks of distinction that separated a ship-of-the-line from the workaday frigates and smaller vessels. The great cabin was exposed to the elements and only by the grace of God had the fire been extinguished before it had spread as far forward as the commodore's dining and sleeping cabins.

The scene that awaited him in the commodore's sleeping cabin was not reassuring. The surgeon was an older man with white hair and a strangely prominent pot belly, looking for all the world like a Hogarth cartoon of a ship's surgeon. He would not have looked out of place as a character in Gin Lane or Beer Street. He stood beside the suspended cot, wringing his hands, with the demeanour of a man who had the cares of the world on his shoulders. Godwin not even troubling to introduce him to Carlisle, just strode straight over to the cot and started speaking.

'He tripped and fell as we were disengaging and he hasn't …'

'One moment Mister Godwin, perhaps I could hear from the medical man.' This earned a hard stare from the lieutenant, but he gave way as the surgeon braced himself to make a coherent report.

'There must be a reckoning between us before long,' thought Carlisle and he kept his gaze on Godwin until the lieutenant turned away with a show of business.

'Now sir,' he said to the surgeon. 'Would you give me a summary of the commodore's medical condition?'

'Well, sir …' started the surgeon, his hands twitching nervously as he self-consciously fought to avoid wringing them together again. 'Well sir, I was called to the quarterdeck by a messenger saying that the commodore had fallen. I expected the worst, but straightaway I could easily see that he was not hurt – I mean there was no blood or broken bones.' He glanced warily at Godwin, for support perhaps, but the lieutenant chose not to face him.

'Go on in your own words Mister – ah …'

'Oh. Green, Surgeon Daniel Green, sir.'

Never, never had Carlisle met such an obsequious surgeon, not even on the smallest rated ship and not in any naval hospital. How he had ever been appointed to a fourth-rate was a mystery. But the man must be encouraged: he was the proper person to care for Jermy, in fact, the only person who could care for him.

'Very well, Mister Green, proceed.'

'Well sir, I had the men bring the commodore below on one of the cabin partitions and place him in this cot, but he hasn't opened his eyes or stirred at all. I am at a

The Leeward Islands Squadron

loss, sir.'

The man was utterly pathetic. Carlisle was close to losing his temper. 'Then you don't know what ails him?'

'No sir, I don't.' The surgeon's distress at this inquisition was evident. He had stopped trying to keep his body language under control and was now clutching his palms together over his round belly so tightly that the veins in the back of his hands were standing proud from the thin skin, purple and pulsating.

'Then tell me, what was the commodore's condition before the engagement? I know from my own observation that he was in pain and had difficulty walking.'

Again, the surgeon glanced uncertainly at Godwin who now returned a steady stare. Something had passed between these two before Carlisle had arrived. He was determined to understand the condition of the commodore and the prognosis for his recovery because until he did recover, or until Carlisle took a decisive step, the question of command of the squadron and command of *Wessex* was open. Was that the basis of the exchanged glances between the surgeon and the first lieutenant?

'The commodore suffered from an ailment that I took to be gout. That, in any case, is what his physician told me before we sailed. But I have never seen gout like this. His pulse has been low for the past week, and he has been unable to spend more than an hour on deck, and then only in a chair set up for him on the quarterdeck. I've been bleeding him twice a week since Sheerness.'

'Bah!' said Godwin. 'This is nothing to do with his gout. He fell when a nine-pounder came inboard and took a breadth of wood out of the mizzen mast. I've seen men killed outright by the wind of a passing shot, the commodore is lucky to be alive.'

Godwin looked furious, it appeared that he had rehearsed a story with the surgeon who, under Carlisle's interrogation, was now deviating from the agreed line.

'The commodore's gout was no worse than many

others that I have seen. He would have recovered in a few weeks,' the first lieutenant continued, his jaw jutting and his face a study in arrogant defiance.

Ignoring Godwin, Carlisle leaned into the cot and put his ear to the commodore's mouth. At first, he could detect no breath, no stirring at all. He held up his hand for silence, and as he waited and became accustomed to the ambient movement of air in the cabin, he found that he could feel the very faintest breath; slow and weak, but nevertheless the man was still breathing.

'Well Mister Green, I take it you have nothing more to add.'

Carlisle was aware of the delicate situation that was likely to develop if the question of command was raised. As the next senior officer in the squadron, leadership of the two ships would fall to him, but the command of *Wessex*? That was more difficult. Lawfully, it should probably devolve on Miles Godwin as the ship's second-in-command, and this temporary captain would then be able to make life very difficult for the new temporary commodore. Godwin would know where Jermy's orders were kept and may choose not to give away that information readily. He could even destroy important documentation. And by the frightened look of the commodore's secretary, whom Carlisle had just spotted in the shadows beside the quarter gallery, he would have little opposition within the flagship. It seemed that Godwin, not Jermy, had been the natural leader, or autocrat, of this floating community.

That look on the secretary's face – he remembered his name now, Clarkson – and the exchange of glances between the secretary and the first lieutenant spurred Carlisle to immediate action. There was a budding conspiracy developing before his eyes, and it must be stopped – now. It was clear that Jermy was not in a fit state to direct the squadron and in Carlisle's opinion would

The Leeward Islands Squadron

not be for some time, if ever.

'Mister Godwin, Mister Clarkson, we should leave Mister Green with the commodore, but I would like to speak with you in the dining cabin.' He needed the secretary as a witness to the conversation that he planned. He would have preferred the master join them, but that would be unwise with the squadron still in pilotage waters.

Godwin showed signs of resisting; he clearly resented Carlisle giving orders in his ship, but the ingrained habits of discipline and the captain's decisive move toward the cabin broke his resistance. Carlisle left no time for Godwin to settle or to take the initiative.

'Mister Godwin, what were the last orders that the commodore gave for the movement of the squadron?'

The first lieutenant was taken off-balance. He had expected a conversation about the succession of command. But Carlisle was not prepared to walk into that trap. Legally, Jermy commanded the squadron until he was unequivocally incapacitated, and insufficient time had elapsed since his collapse to make that determination. These were tricky legal grounds, and Carlisle had no doubt that Godwin would exploit any irregularities.

Godwin just stared stupidly at Carlisle.

'Perhaps I am not clear. The last direct orders that I received from the commodore regarded the attack on Port Louis. By his turning away and signalling a recall for the boats, I understood that he had ordered a withdrawal. I now understand that soon after ordering the recall, the commodore fell to the deck and has not been able to issue any orders since that time. My question is this; before he collapsed, did he give any orders for the deployment of the squadron?'

'No sir, he did not.' Godwin could now see the where this was leading, and he could see the trap that Carlisle had opened for him. But there was no way back without overt insubordination.

'I see. Then in the four hours that have elapsed since

the commodore's incapacitation, his temporary incapacitation, I am sure, can you tell me to what purpose *Wessex* has been leading the squadron to the north? Away from Port Louis?'

Godwin was in an awkward situation now. Like Carlisle, he had assumed that the order to turn away from Fort Royal was a precursor to withdrawing to Barbados. He had been happy to continue that course rather than to consult this colonial upstart, as he should have done as soon as the commodore fell. His prejudices had led him down a dangerous path.

Carlisle could see that he would get no immediate answer from the first lieutenant.

'I see,' he said with heavy significance, still looking at Godwin. 'Mister Clarkson, can you add anything? Did the commodore give you any orders that Mister Godwin may have missed?'

'N-no, sir.' The wretched man was stammering in his nervousness. He cast an anxious sideways glance at Godwin.

'What on earth had this Godwin persuaded him to say, or not say?' thought Carlisle. He knew that he must maintain the momentum, he mustn't surrender the initiative. He decided that he could take a few minutes of the master's time without any detriment to the navigation.

'Mister Godwin, please ask the sentry to pass the word for Mister Thompson.'

Godwin half turned but then swung back towards Carlisle, a truculent, aggressive expression on his face.

'I cannot see the point of this discussion …,' he started. But Carlisle was prepared for just such a reaction, and he sharply retorted.

'Mister Godwin, I didn't ask your opinion, you will do as I ask. Immediately if you please.'

In the face of a direct order and with the secretary as a witness, he could only comply. The secretary was looking more and more scared by the moment.

'Had these two colluded to keep him out of the chain of command?' wondered Carlisle. It wasn't impossible. Certainly, Godwin had a personal grudge against him, and he may have thought to keep the frigate captain at arm's length until they should meet the Leeward Islands Squadron. A dangerous gamble, in Carlisle's opinion.

Carlisle had to think fast to retain control of this situation. Godwin had every right to excuse himself to deal with ship's affairs; after all the flagship had taken significant damage in the battle, and it was the first lieutenant's first duty to see that repairs were being carried out. But Carlisle didn't want Godwin out of his sight until this business was concluded, and he didn't want him talking alone to the sailing master.

'Mister Godwin,' he called to the first lieutenant's retreating back. 'Just call to the sentry, I need your advice in the cabin if you please.'

One look at Godwin told Carlisle that he had been correct. He had prevented the first lieutenant from going in search of the master.

The sailing master only had a matter of a few yards to cover from his position beside the wheel. He hurried into the cabin looking worried and flustered, but the polite greeting he gave to Carlisle was in marked contrast to the dark, glowering looks of the first lieutenant.

'Good afternoon Mister Thompson, I hope not to keep you long. I believe you are aware of the commodore's condition? That he is unconscious?'

'Aye sir, I am aware. I saw him fall.' The master's initial friendly greeting had been partly replaced by wariness. He was unsure of the tone of the meeting or where it was leading.

'I had asked you here to determine what the commodore's intention was before he became incapacitated. I have already ascertained that neither Lieutenant Godwin nor Mister Clarkson had any orders other than to turn away from the fort and to recall the boats. I now need to know whether he gave you any further orders.'

The master paused. He could sense that this was an important question – he didn't really know why – but the atmosphere in the small dining cabin told him that he should consider carefully before replying.

'The commodore's last orders to me were to set a course to weather the northerly arm of the bay, Point Bois Maurice on the chart.' He thought again for a moment. 'I then heard him order the midshipman to make the boat recall signal. He was becoming very weak, and I was just about to suggest that he sit in the chair that we kept lashed under the break of the poop when he fell.'

'He gave you no orders for a course to be set after you had weathered the point?'

'No sir, that would have been my next question in a few minutes after we had settled on our course to windward. However, that is when we lost the mizzen, and we'd have been weathering no point at all if it had not been for the prompt help of your lieutenant.'

Godwin looked even more furious at this acknowledgement that they owed their immediate salvation to *Medina*.

Carlisle could see from the faces of the three men around him that they were starting to recognise the errors that had been made since the commodore's fall. He was almost sure that Godwin was the instigator and he thought he knew why.

The first lieutenant opened his mouth to speak, but Carlisle rode straight over this interruption. 'I will give you an opportunity to speak again in a moment Mister Godwin.'

Turning back to the master, Carlisle held his gaze and asked very deliberately, 'Why, therefore Mister Thompson, did you continue for nearly four hours on a northerly heading after weathering the point? On whose orders?'

The Leeward Islands Squadron

The master's emotional turmoil was written on his face. Carlisle had once been told that in these circumstances, one should never ask a question unless one already knew the answer. In this case, Carlisle was confident that he did know the answer. The master was too straightforward a person to have taken it on his own initiative to set a course away from the enemy. But Thompson was saved the difficulty of answering.

'Sir, I ordered the master to steer north,' said Godwin, interrupting, with death on his face. 'It was clearly the commodore's intention to proceed to Barbados in accordance with his written orders.'

'Mister Godwin, I will pass over your interruption of the master when he is preparing to answer my question. However, I have this observation to make.' He fixed the first lieutenant with a steady gaze. 'The commodore's orders stated that he was to proceed to Barbados after having reduced Port Louis as a base for privateers. That has not been accomplished. And yet, I find that the squadron has been withdrawn from action against the enemy without consulting the most senior officer who was in a fit condition to make that decision.'

Godwin blanched. This was a serious accusation against him. A very senior admiral was awaiting court martial in England for actions not very different to these, albeit on a much larger scale; the shadow of Byng's decision at Minorca was already starting to have its effect on the navy. The master and the secretary both involuntarily leaned away from Godwin, concerned now at being guilty by association.

Carlisle let his statement hang for a few moments, for emphasis, before continuing.

'Mister Thompson, is the squadron in a safe position to lie-to?'

'It is, sir. The wind is steady from east-northeast, and we have two hundred miles sea-room before we would fetch up on Blanco Island. If it veers at all, we will have the whole Caribbean Sea under our lee.'

'Very well, then signal the squadron to lie-to.' He turned to face Miles Godwin. 'Until the commodore is conscious, I will determine what actions the squadron should take, based upon their Lordships orders to the commodore.'

'Keep moving forward,' Carlisle said to himself. 'Don't allow a power void.'

'Mister Clarkson, be so kind as to bring me the commodore's orders.'

He turned again to the first lieutenant, 'Mister Godwin, you will command *Wessex*, obedient to my directions, until the commodore regains his health. For now, you are to concentrate on repairing the damage and restoring the fighting capability of the ship.' That placed the command of *Wessex* firmly under Carlisle's gift – Godwin was commanding at Carlisle's behest. The critical principle of who commanded the squadron had been established by *fiat*.

Godwin appeared to hesitate, perhaps to disagree. But there really was nothing in Carlisle's orders that he could take exception to, except maybe the assumption that Jermy was unable to command. And he had just missed his opportunity to argue that point.

CHAPTER EIGHT

Redemption

Monday, twentieth of December 1756
Wessex, at sea, Ronde Island southeast 5 leagues

Carlisle had spent the night on board *Wessex*. He would have been far more comfortable in *Medina*, but he didn't trust Godwin out of his sight and was determined to be on hand when – if – the commodore should regain his wits. He had sent for his own servant and for Whittle, ostensibly to allow Jermy's personal staff to concentrate on the wellbeing of the commodore but his real reason was to have some friendly faces around him. He was comfortable with Thompson, but Godwin had a grudge and had altogether too much influence over the other officers. Ideally, he would have called Holbrooke over to second him, but that would have left *Medina* without a commission officer.

Jermy had not stirred overnight. He had again quizzed Green, but it had become evident to Carlisle that his own judgement was just as valuable as that of the timid surgeon. If this state persisted, he would have to extract some kind of a written report from the man, by outright bullying if necessary. However, for the moment the surgeon was best left to tend to the commodore in his own way.

Privately, Carlisle was preparing to take the squadron back into action without the support of the commodore and in the teeth of Godwin's objections. He would concede this to Godwin: the first lieutenant had driven the hands overnight to make good the damage to the great cabin and poop deck, to repair the shot holes in the hull and to set a new lateen mizzen sail. The cabin would not be habitable until they had the services of the yard at

English Harbour, but at least it was made watertight with a spare topsail hauled taught over the gap, and the mounting points for the backstay snatch blocks had been reinforced. For all practical purposes, *Wessex* was ready to go back into action. She looked ugly, but she could fight.

Carlisle could hear the poop deck being flogged dry over his head – a gentle sound that would not disturb the unconscious commodore. He had nowhere to go in the ship other than this tiny dining cabin, which was fast becoming claustrophobic. His position was anomalous, to say the least; Godwin was in temporary command of the ship while Carlisle was in temporary command of the squadron. Any other officer that he knew would have offered this almost-commodore the use of the quarterdeck, but not Godwin, and Carlisle wasn't going to squander his store of moral advantage in a silly squabble over a place to walk. Nevertheless, he felt physically constrained, and there was something – a relevant thought – hovering on the edge of his consciousness. Something that was said to him yesterday, a piece of the jigsaw that fitted into a vital space – perhaps.

Carlisle thought over the numberless reports that he had received after they broke off the action with Fort Royal, mentally ticked them off in chronological order until he came to Holbrooke's description of the prize. That was it! The cargo of the schooner was hay and that fitted with two other fragments of the puzzle. He had made an offhand comment about fire ships in relation to the anchored privateers, but a load of hay wouldn't make the best fire ship – too much smoke and not enough persistent flame. But he had noticed how the smoke from the squadron's guns had blown down upon the fort and affected their aim. The guns didn't create enough smoke to change the balance, but a schooner load of hay? Maybe, just maybe.

'Sentry, my compliments to the officer of the watch,

and would he please signal *Medina* into hailing range?'

The ideas were tumbling through his mind now, thick and fast. He needed his own people here, but first, he needed the latest information on Jermy. He walked across the passageway to Jermy's sleeping cabin. Green was there, fussing with the bedclothes for want of any decisive medical intervention; he apparently had no idea how to treat the commodore.

'Mister Green, how fortuitous that I should meet you here.' The surgeon jumped in surprise; Carlisle hadn't realised that he had entered so quietly, but there was a natural tendency to move and to speak softly in the presence of sickness.

'What is the commodore's condition this morning?' He held the unfortunate surgeon in his gaze, offering him no option but to reply. But the surgeon just opened and closed his mouth, nothing came out.

'Come, sir, it's a simple question, what is the commodore's condition?'

'Well sir …' Carlisle realised with a resigned sigh that this was how Green started all replies when asked his opinion. He seemed to believe that if he began in a temporising tone, he would not be held responsible for any inaccuracies.

'Well sir, the commodore is much the same as yesterday. His breath and his pulse are both very faint. Normally I would want to let blood at this stage, but I am not sure that his constitution will stand it.'

'I should think not Mister Green.' Carlisle shuddered at the thought of letting blood from this already weakened man. 'Do you have any prognosis regarding his return to health? When do you believe he may regain consciousness?'

'Well sir …, I cannot really say. He may wake up at any time, but he is showing no signs of doing so.'

'Thank you, Mister Green, is that all you can tell me?'

The wretched man merely nodded.

'In that case, I need a written statement to that effect. Call for the secretary, he can help with the wording, but I expect the statement to say exactly what you have just told me, and I want it within thirty minutes. Do you understand, sir?'

Without waiting for a reply, Carlisle left the cabin and walked up to what was left of the poop deck. *Medina* was already bearing up to close the flagship. He could see Holbrooke and Hosking standing side-by-side behind the hammock nets. Looking down to *Wessex's* quarterdeck, he caught Godwin staring up at him, pure malevolence writ large upon his face. They locked eyes for a few moments before Godwin turned away to his business. Thompson was supervising the helm, making sure that a straight course was being steered because *Medina* clearly intended to come very close. Carlisle liked Thompson; he just had to find a way of gaining his trust.

'Mister Holbrooke,' called Carlisle across the rapidly closing gap. Please come over to the flagship at two bells for orders.' Carlisle chose his words carefully with Godwin listening. The intended meeting was more like a conference, but he wanted to leave no doubt about who would be making the decisions. He remembered the conference – the council of war – that Admiral Byng had called after his battle off Minorca and its disastrous consequences. There would be no divided decision-making while Carlisle was commanding.

'Gentlemen,' began Carlisle, looking over the assembled officers, 'I have called you together to let you know how I intend to complete the accomplishment of the orders which their Lordships were pleased to entrust to Commodore Jermy.'

Carlisle was cautious in his selection of words; they could quickly come back to haunt him. In fact, if the action he was about to set in train resulted in a court martial or even an inquiry, his words would undoubtedly be repeated, embellished or redacted according to the memory or inclination of the witness. There must be no assumption that Jermy was anything other than temporarily unable to take command of the squadron and the ship. He cast his eyes around the room. They were meeting in the forward end of the ruined great cabin. It was strangely gloomy; the windows that only hours before had stretched the breadth of the stern had been destroyed by the fire, and the spare topsail that covered the empty space and the last few feet of the overhead poop deck let in only a fraction of the usual light. The smell of smoke, everyday wood smoke overlain by the smell of burned shipboard substances – tar, paint and cordage – hung in the air. But it was surprising how mild the scent was; the salt sea air sweeping through the gaps in the makeshift covering carried away the odours as fast as they emerged. Holbrooke was there, but Carlisle had not felt justified in calling for the master from *Medina*, not in hostile waters. It was difficult to remember that they were still only a few miles from French-held Grenada, the whole scene being so peaceful. Godwin was in attendance by right, as the temporary commander of *Wessex*. Thompson was also there as Carlisle needed his navigational skills. It would look odd in a subsequent inquiry if he had not sought the master's advice on this plan and in any case, Carlisle had admired Thompson's bearing since the commodore's incapacity. He had also called Charles Lynton over from the prize; the master's mate would have an essential contribution to the gathering.

Carlisle toted up the opposing forces. He was supported by two reliable officers from his own ship, and he believed he had the better part of Thompson's loyalty. In contrast, Godwin looked exposed – shoulders hunched, arms crossed, glaring around him under dark eyebrows – the very image of frustrated antagonism.

'Before I begin I will read Mister Green's assessment of the commodore's physical condition.' Carlisle read the few words, the surgeon's nervousness was evident in the way that he refused to commit himself. The patient's symptoms were described most elastically, leaving room for a miraculous recovery enabled by the extraordinary medical care he was receiving, or a swift demise from an untreatable ailment that pre-dated his coming under Green's care. Patients may come, and patients may go, on their feet or feet-first, but this surgeon would bumble along to a new set of unwary victims, untouched by the consequences of his ineptitude. Nevertheless, unsatisfactory though it was from a medical perspective, the statement met Carlisle's needs. It acknowledged that Jermy was unconscious and didn't attempt to estimate when he may recover sufficiently to command the squadron. That left Carlisle free to act.

'I intend a second attempt on the privateers at Port Louis.' Carlisle paused to let his audience take in that statement. It wasn't quite intended as a challenge, but by the dogged, glowering look on Godwin's face, the first lieutenant took it as such. He didn't, however, feel in a strong enough position to question the orders of this upstart temporary commodore, this usurper. He knew that his actions in taking the squadron away from the scene of action without any plan to further annoy the enemy left him open to the most serious charges in the whole articles of war: cowardice or failing to do his utmost in the face of the enemy. Charges that carried only one penalty – death.

'We must make another attempt on Port Louis, but we must have a means of minimising Fort Royal's capacity to prevent us doing so.' That much was evident and uncontroversial.

'I intend to use our prize, the schooner, as a fireship, although perhaps not in the way that you imagine.' He had their interest now. A fireship! But how would a single fireship alter the situation?

'Mister Lynton, the schooner has a full load of hay, is

that correct?'

'Yes, sir. She's fairly stuffed with hay, right up to the hatch coamings. It's baled tight and bound with some sort of vine. It'll burn well.' The wistful look on the young man's face belied his show of enthusiasm. He had no desire to see this pleasant command of his go up in smoke.

'So, gentlemen. This is my plan …'

CHAPTER NINE

Fire Ship

Tuesday, twenty-first of December 1756
Medina, at Sea, off Port Louis, Grenada

The sun had not yet shown itself over the bulk of Grenada to larboard as *Wessex* and *Medina* hurried down the western side of the island with the prize schooner tucked in beside the flagship. At this inflexion point in the heating and cooling of the land, there was neither a sea breeze nor a land breeze to disturb the northeast trade wind, and the three vessels were making eight knots with the wind on their quarter and all plain sail set. The surprise was one aspect of the plan, and Carlisle knew that this side of the island was less well served with roads than the southeast, from where they had been observed on their earlier approach. *Wessex* had left a trail of smoke on the previous day as she rounded the point and was lost to sight from the fort. Even if the commander of Fort Royal had sent a galloper to follow them up the coast, the last view of the squadron would have shown them limping away over the northwest horizon. Carlisle had more respect for the French military mind than to assume that they would become complacent. Probably they would have decided that they had seen the last of the British squadron, but they would nevertheless be prepared.

Carlisle was pleased with the way the meeting had concluded. He had successfully isolated Godwin and, he believed, had won over Thompson. Best of all, he had found an enthusiastic commander for the fire ship in *Wessex's* third lieutenant, John Curtis, who had been recommended by Thompson. Curtis was very young, barely older than Holbrooke, and felt confined by his lowly position in a ship that manifestly was lacking in enterprise. Carlisle would have liked to ask Holbrooke to take the fire ship command, dangerous though it was. He had complete faith in Holbrooke, but if the first lieutenant was absent when the frigate was carried into action, then he, as the captain, must undoubtedly have returned to take command and his reasons for wanting to stay in *Wessex* hadn't changed. Young Lynton was naturally devastated to be passed over, but he was just too inexperienced, and his leadership skills had not yet matured. That is why he had been given the schooner in the first place, to hone his management of the men, but a desperate venture like this was another thing entirely and required the authority of the King's commission to improve the chances of success.

They had spent the remainder of Monday preparing the schooner for its new and presumably short-lived existence as a fire ship. If this were to have been a traditional use of a fire ship – against enemy vessels, usually while they were at anchor – she would have been prepared differently. Fire ship construction was a well-understood art in the navy and involved considerable structural modification to the selected vessel. Many, in fact, were purpose-built for the role. But in this case, Carlisle didn't have the time, the materials or the need for such elaborate modifications. The iron chambers, the fire barrels, the composition of pitch, tallow, corn powder, mealed powder, sulphur, rosin and saltpetre could all be dispensed with because all that Carlisle needed was smoke and plenty of it. The schooner had no gun ports, so her hull was crudely scuttled in four places on each side to allow a free draft of air. Some of the hay bales had been lifted out of the hold and arranged on the upper deck as protection from small arms and light cannon. A four-foot-thick, solidly packed hay bale would retard a nine-pound shot sufficiently to blunt much of its destructive power, and no musket bullets would penetrate even halfway through. But that wasn't the principal purpose for re-arranging the cargo. There needed to space deep in the hold where the fires could be started, and the cavity must communicate with the scuttles to generate enough draft to nurture the blaze. It was one of those curious contradictions of life at sea. Fire was the ever-present terror of seamen and once well alight, a fire in a wooden ship was almost impossible to extinguish until it had burnt its way down to the waterline. On the other hand, it was notoriously tricky to start and to maintain a fire deliberately.

Carlisle never ceased to be amazed at the range of skills found among the people of a man-of-war. When it became known in *Wessex* that the fire ship needed to make vast quantities of smoke from hay, the bosun came to the quarterdeck, leading a landsman – a huge, lumbering hulk of a man. He was one of the unskilled hands brought aboard before the ship sailed from Sheerness, embarrassed and awkward in the presence of a captain.

'Davis here claims to know something of hay fires sir, don't you Davis?'

The landsman nodded dumbly. The bosun, not in the least constrained by the presence of his subject standing right beside him continued, 'he won't say where his knowledge comes from sir, but he was a volunteer from somewhere on the London road, Rochester way I believe, and I guess that he was running from the law. Rick-burning no doubt. It may be worth listening to him.'

It required a lot of patience to get the information out of Davis, who was used to becoming conveniently dumb in the presence of authority. But he did have real knowledge, and it was from his advice, carefully extracted, that the final disposition of the hay bales was decided.

'If you want flames sir, like you would at night, then the hay needs to be bone dry, if possible. But if you want smoke, like you want to annoy folk in the day, then you need a lower tier of dry hay, plenty of space around it for air and a top tier of wet hay. That will burn all day and smoke out two fields downwind of it.'

Pity the poor farmers who had Davis for a neighbour; the man was obsessed with fire, a real arsonist. Carlisle turned him over the carpenter who was responsible for the preparation of the fire-ship – or smoke-ship as she was being called.

There had been little change in the commodore's state. He hadn't moved, but his breathing and pulse had not deteriorated any further. It appeared to Carlisle that he was unlikely to recover soon. Perhaps his best chance was to be landed at a hospital as quickly as possible. There was no naval hospital at English Harbour. The nearest was at Port Royal in Jamaica, and that was a thousand miles to leeward – out of the question even for a sick post-captain. Barbados had no naval facility at all, but there must be some sort of army hospital, Carlisle imagined, but would Jermy would do better there than in his own ship at sea?

Carlisle pushed this line of thought away. Whatever the consequences to Jermy, it was quite clear that the squadron's duty lay in a second attempt at the privateers in Port Louis. After that, he would follow the sealed orders and beat up to Barbados. If the Leeward Island Squadron was not there, then he would reach along the windward side of the island chain to English Harbour in Antigua. But for now, he should concentrate on the task at hand. There was one last consideration for the commodore, Carlisle called for the surgeon.

'Mister Green, it's time to take the Mister Jermy below into safety. You have prepared a space in the Orlop?'

'Yes, sir. I'll take him there immediately. May I ask Mister Godwin for some hands?'

'Yes, you may. I expect to go into action in thirty minutes. You will need to send one of your mates to tend the commodore, you may be needed in the cockpit.'

The surgeon bowed in acknowledgement. He appeared positively frightened of Carlisle, but then Carlisle reflected, he was probably terrified of anyone in power. There was little real difference between Surgeon Green and Landsman Davis; both were wary of authority and functionally useless. They were only separated by an accident of birth and a smattering of education.

CHAPTER TEN

Fort Royal

Tuesday, twenty-first of December 1756
Wessex, at sea, The Grand Bay

With a steady breeze on their beam, the squadron stood boldly in towards the fort under fighting sail: topsails, headsails and mizzen. The sun shone brightly on the scene, and all looked peaceful, but nobody watching from the deck of *Wessex* had any illusions. Carlisle hoped that the squadron may have achieved some surprise this time, but that would only mean that the garrison would be working more frantically to prepare for the battle. He imagined that the furnaces had been kept alight since their last attack and that the bellows would by now be plying heartily to bring them up to the required intense heat. It made little difference whether the French had been informed by a horseman taking the long road from the north, or whether the first they knew of a new attack was the appearance of the squadron around Point Bois Maurice – the garrison's guns would be ready by the time *Wessex* came within range.

In a way, this was the sort of work that the poor, derided two-decked fifties were retained for. Since Minorca, it had become clear that sixty guns were the minimum qualification for the line of battle, and even they were rapidly being replaced by the newer seventy-fours. If the fifties had a role in the modern navy, it was in this kind of colonial operation where a frigate was not powerful enough and lacked the protection of heavy timbers, but the deployment of a valuable third-rate was not justifiable. Every man-of-war was a design compromise: trading firepower, protection, speed, manoeuvrability, manpower and cost against each other to come up with the right formula for the task. In this case and for this role the Navy Board may just have got the balance right. Nevertheless, Carlisle could still have wished for the extra weight of broadside and thickness of oak that a genuine line-of-battle ship would have provided.

The two-decker again led the way into the Grand Bay with the frigate a cable-length astern, but this time they approached from the northwest, rather than the southwest. The schooner was tucked under *Wessex's* starboard quarter, concealed from watchers in the fort. A keen eye would be able to make out her masts through the much more extensive ship's rigging, but in their haste to prepare, Carlisle thought it unlikely that the soldiers would guess its purpose.

'What speed are we making Mister Thompson?' asked Carlisle, more to ease the tension than for any need to know. This kind of theatre worked well on the quarterdeck hands, but Carlisle had the distinct impression that the sailing master, old in the ways of the navy and accustomed to dealing with young post-captains, wasn't deceived.

'Stream the log,' he called to the mate of the watch.

Command of a two-decker, thought Carlisle, was entirely different from commanding a frigate. Although the fundamentals were the same, everything was on a larger scale. He looked down, there were more people on the quarterdeck, not only to work the four guns located there – six-pounders, rather than *Medina's* tiny three-pounders – but there were more people for everything. There were midshipmen underfoot, four steersmen stood at the wheel and there were hands standing by the signal halyards. However, perhaps the most significant difference was the view of the gun-decks. In *Medina*, he could look down from the quarterdeck rail onto a good half of his great guns, with the rest of the battery just below his feet. He could observe at first hand the organisation of the gun crews, he could feel the temper of the men. From *Wessex's* poop deck he could, by leaning over the rail, see just four guns on each side of the upper deck, and that from a relatively long distance. Those four were almost as many guns as he could have seen in *Medina,* but on a two-decked man-of-war that was merely a quarter of their number and with the larger twenty-four pounders on the lower deck and the twelve-pounders on the upper deck, it was just an eighth of the ship's broadside weight. He didn't enjoy that remoteness. When he went into action against *Vulcain* in the Mediterranean, he had felt that he could communicate instantly with his main armament. In *Wessex* he would have to rely upon Godwin to transmit his orders and for master's mates and midshipmen to accurately pass them on to the crews. Nevertheless, he appreciated this greater weight of broadside, eight hundred and twenty-eight pounds in total against *Medina's* two hundred and twenty-eight. That, and the superior thickness of the timbers and planking was why it was implausible that a frigate could stand toe-to-toe against a ship-of-the-line, even one of the smallest such as *Wessex*, and that was why he was going to use her to soak up the fort's fire.

'A point to larboard Mister Thompson.' He wanted the fort to believe that he was in earnest about engaging them. He wanted them to forget the frigate and concentrate their fire on *Wessex*. That would make sense to the commander of the fort. The privateers were close enough to be under his most immediate protection, and an intruder must brave the fire of the heated shot to achieve anything against the vessels in the inner harbour.

Carlisle carefully watched the fort. Yes, there was the heat haze from the furnaces, making the French royal standard shimmer grotesquely.

'I still believe they would be better advised to concentrate on cold shot,' said Carlisle, the fact that nobody was in ear-shot betrayed his mounting nervousness. Cold shot, a faster rate of fire and higher accuracy would ensure that the fort would make short work of any wooden ships that dared to trespass within its range. This heated shot seemed like a distraction to Carlisle – a fatal distraction, he hoped.

'They're running out,' shouted the signal midshipman, his eye glued to his telescope. Carlisle raised his own telescope just in time to see their first shots. There was little to fear at this long range, but of course, the French had no reason to hold their fire. It was probably to their advantage that the guns were warmed through and the range tried.

'Hold your fire, Mister Godwin,' he called down to the upper deck. *Wessex* moved closer and closer to the fort. 'God, those spouts look enormous,' he thought as the fort's second salvo dropped short and on their bow.

They were closer still. 'Stand by the broadside,' Carlisle called. The ship was in dead silence as the fort, their tormentor of two days ago, drew nearer. Soon *Wessex* would start taking punishment. 'Too bad,' thought Carlisle. That was the purpose of a ship-of-the-line, to stand and take the enemy's shots. If his plan worked, then he would clear out this coven of privateers and be on his way to Barbados in a few hours. Of course, if *Wessex* was hit, then he, Edward Carlisle, was in the most exposed position possible. He was directing operations from the poop deck, rather than the better-protected quarterdeck so that he could more easily see the fort and privateers ahead of him, and he could look over his shoulder to see *Medina* astern and the schooner to starboard. The poop deck felt even more exposed than usual with the last fifteen feet covered in a makeshift tarpaulin, the hammock nets missing, and the stern lanterns lost, their mounting brackets burned away from the stern timbers. But it couldn't be helped; this was the best place for visibility.

Looking ahead he could see the privateersmen leaving their vessels, tumbling into their already overcrowded boats and pulling fast for the inner harbour. They must have felt confident that the squadron had been beaten and would not return otherwise they would surely have moved their vessels into the inner harbour – would have run them aground if necessary – rather than leave them in this exposed anchorage. They had no desire to fight men-of-war and were even more lightly built than a frigate. One broadside from either of the attacking ships would sink them where they lay. They could see the danger to themselves and, true to their essentially commercial nature, were preserving their bodies for another day when they could prey on fat merchantmen rather than withstand the gunnery of King's ships.

A ripping sound overhead told where a nine-pounder, elevated more than its fellows, had found its target. The bosun sensibly ignored it. Nothing vital had parted, and the small loss of sailing efficiency from a hole in the main topsail was irrelevant.

'Mister Godwin, you may open fire on the fort,' shouted Carlisle. He had to think before each order that he gave, had to remember that he commanded the squadron, but not *Wessex*, that was Godwin's prerogative. Before Jermy was incapacitated, the commodore had commanded both the squadron and the ship, which made the chain of authority much shorter and simpler, but Carlisle didn't have the power to usurp the second-in-command's right to command in his captain's absence. Not without some real and verifiable cause. Thankfully, Godwin appeared wary of antagonising Carlisle; he was probably concerned at what would be said about his having withdrawn the squadron yesterday, without orders.

Carlisle's order was relayed by the master's mate on the quarterdeck, but the first lieutenant had heard Carlisle, and before the repeated command had reached him, twenty-five linstocks had been pressed to their touch-holes, and four hundred and fourteen pounds of cast iron shot was hurtling towards the grey masonry of Fort Royal. *Wessex* recoiled with the shock; it seemed to Carlisle that she actually moved a few yards sideways in the water. This was Carlisle's first experience of firing a full broadside from a ship-of-the-line. The only other occasions that he had been on such a large ship had been in times of peace when whole broadsides were discouraged as too expensive in powder and shot and too ruinous to the ship's fabric. He was impressed. He was even more impressed when he saw the results on the fort. The shot had been well pitched-up, and the embrasures had been swept most thoroughly. It was difficult to tell for sure, but it looked like at least one shot had gone clean through an embrasure, passing between the merlons without touching them. The gun's muzzle was partly withdrawn, and at an odd angle. It must have been hit in the act of running out. That heated shot still in its barrel would be causing all sorts of anxiety and would undoubtedly disturb the rhythm of the adjacent guns. And rhythm was all-important for the management of heated shot. He may have a real dislike for Godwin, and he indeed mistrusted him, but he could only admire the way that the first lieutenant had drilled his gun crews. That must have been accomplished on the Atlantic crossing without any help or even encouragement from a desperately sick commodore, and with a high number of landsmen in the crew.

But *Wessex* was also taking punishment. A midshipman came running up the poop-deck ladder to report a gun overturned on the lower deck. The fire started by the heated shot had been quickly extinguished, and the weapons on either side were being brought back into action. He had no information on casualties.

'Now,' thought Carlisle. 'Now is the time.' He leaned over what was left of the starboard hammock rails and waved to Curtis in the schooner. 'Proceed Mister Curtis,' he shouted. 'And good luck to you.'

Curtis waved in acknowledgement and sheeted home his fore and main sails. The schooner was released from her pedestrian pace alongside the flagship and moved fast up towards her bow.

'Back your topsails Mister Thompson, this is where we stand and fight.'

He looked over his shoulder to *Medina*. Holbrooke had already started hauling in his sheets and was moving up on *Wessex's* leeward quarter. The frigate didn't have the acceleration of the much lighter schooner, but she was no sluggard. He felt a burst of pride for his ship – pride and a fervent hope that she would emerge intact from this desperate gamble.

Wessex's larboard battery was firing now as fast as each gun could reload. There must be some steady officers on that lower gun deck, keeping the crews focussed on their drills. The rate of fire was reasonable also, a continuous thunder and hail of iron interrupting the fort's gunners, preventing them achieving the deliberate rhythm that was so essential if the hot shot was to be used efficiently. The process of supplying the ball at the correct temperature to each gun at just the right point in its reloading cycle was much more critical than when using cold shot. Just another factor that convinced Carlisle that the French commander was unwise to put his faith in this cumbersome ammunition.

Wessex was almost stationary now; this was her most vulnerable moment when she presented the easiest of targets for the fort. She couldn't lie in this position for long. Eventually, the French guns would hit something vital, a critical spar, the rudder or – God forbid – a lucky shot may start a fire near the magazine. But Carlisle had no intention of letting the fort have a clear target. He looked forward, and there was the schooner cutting across the two-decker's bow. Curtis had timed it to perfection. He was close-hauled on the port tack; the steady trade wind being diminished by the rising sea breeze and he was just shaving ahead of *Wessex's* jib-boom. It was vital that he should reach his objective without needing to waste time in tacking, but it looked like the wind would solve that problem.

Carlisle considered demanding a higher rate of fire from Godwin to cover the schooner, but immediately rejected it – he could see that *Wessex's* guns were being worked as fast as they could be. Any superfluous orders now would only exasperate the first lieutenant. In any case, *Medina* would soon start to add her modest weight to the bombardment as she moved ahead of *Wessex* and her cannon were unmasked.

It was astonishing how fast the schooner was moving. In the time that Carlisle had been considering the situation, she had covered most of the distance to the fort. As he watched, she slackened her sheets, the way came off her, and she grounded gently on the rocky shallows below the fort and directly in line with *Wessex*. Carlisle had to control himself, the tension of these next few moments was so intense. Would Curtis manage to put up the smoke screen before the fort realised his intention? He watched in dread as he saw an artillery officer pointing to the small vessel and two of the nine-pounders shifted to this new target.

That was when the subtlety of Carlisle's plan was unveiled. What would the fort think of the schooner? They would immediately conclude that she must be stuffed full of fighting men with the intention of making a frontal assault on the battlements. She would be looking to defend her walls rather than nullify a fire-ship. Another distraction for the harassed French gunners and a few vital minutes gained before the fort's commander realised his mistake.

Within two minutes the smoke was starting to pour up from the hatches, the draught of air surging in through her scuttled sides became almost visible in its intensity. Carlisle saw Curtis and his three volunteers scramble down the side of the schooner into the jolly boat as the fort's guns started to raise clouds of splinters from the wrecked craft, bringing down her mainmast, with her sails still set. But it was too late for the fort. Billows of grey smoke were now pouring from the grounded schooner; the rising sea breeze, not yet determined in its direction, diffusing the smoke and carried it in a broad swathe towards the fort only a hundred yards away. In three more minutes, Carlisle could barely see the fort at all; the French artillerymen must have only occasional glimpses of their target as they were hampered by the thick billows of hay-smoke rolling into their gun platforms. They continued to fire, but the shots were wild and the rate of fire even slower than before. The schooner was perfectly visible from the great two-decker, and Carlisle watched as the jolly boat raised a lug sail and after hesitating on the best course to reach safety chose an easy reach over to *Medina*, rather than a beat into the eye of the wind to meet *Wessex*. That was clear thinking from Curtis.

CHAPTER ELEVEN

Take, Sink or Burn

Tuesday, twenty-first of December 1756
Medina, at Sea, The Grand Bay

Why, man, he doth bestride the narrow world like a Colossus, and we petty men walk under his huge legs and peep about. The lines that Shakespeare put into Cassius' mouth – in envy of great Caesar – came unbidden to Holbrooke's conscious mind as he stood on the quarterdeck of *Medina*, surveying his command. They must have been lurking there, deep below his waking thoughts, ready for this occasion. He had commanded a frigate before, taking the captured *Vulcain* from the Tyrrhenian Sea back to Gibraltar; a long and anxious passage with contrary winds, a small crew and a damaged ship. But today it was different, today he was taking one of His Majesty's frigates into action against the French. He had a full crew and an experienced sailing master, who was carefully leaving enough space for the temporary captain – himself, George Holbrooke, as he had to remember – to pace the weather side of the quarterdeck. He had a few moments leisure to think, and the ever-introspective Holbrooke analysed his situation yet again. There was a curious mindset that went with command of a man-of-war, quite distinct from other types of authority. By a single word, he could bring instant ruin to his ship and its two hundred men. He could put her aground by a misguided helm order, he could carry too much sail and lose a mast, he could apply poor tactical choices and be raked by a broadside. Quite likely none of these highly skilled and experienced people on the quarterdeck would dare to correct him until it was too late. It was like living in a kind of bubble, protected from the usual give-and-take of social intercourse.

If, for example, he ordered a turn of two points to larboard now and the sheets to be hauled in, the master and the quartermaster would instantly respond, and in a very few minutes he would be between *Wessex* and the enemy, taking the kind of punishment that no frigate was constructed to withstand. Hosking may remonstrate, but probably not. It was a tactical decision and strictly none of his business. People would die, and quite likely, through want of an intact frigate, the whole venture would fail.

If he made a joke, everyone would laugh. If he made a facetious comment, everyone would nod sagely. And he was only the temporary commander of *Medina*. How must it affect Carlisle, subjected to that kind of deference all day, every day? A Colossus indeed.

Medina was following close astern of *Wessex* as they approached the fort, and both Holbrooke and Hosking were carefully watching the flagship. There would be no formal signal; but as soon as her topsails started to swing around, Holbrooke knew that he must haul aft his own sheets and overtake her to starboard, following close behind Curtis in the schooner, who was waiting for the same cue to start his perilous enterprise. The wind was tricky; Hosking and the quartermaster were anxiously watching the quarterdeck dog-vane and the luffs of the topsails as the sea-breeze began to assert itself. This was vital to Carlisle's plan. The wind from the sea would blow the smoke from the burning hay down onto the fort.

If the sea-breeze failed, then Carlisle would have to turn away and wait for the change. It all hinged on the rate at which the land heated up as the sun rose. The solid earth reacted more rapidly than the sea to the sun's heat. Unlike the sea, a fluid element that could move the heat from the surface through vertical currents, the warmed land could not quickly dissipate its heat which instead was trapped in the very top layer. Consequently, the surface of the earth heated up much faster than the surface of the sea, causing a temperature gradient between the two during the day. The air above the land was heated by the earth, rising and creating a temporary low pressure. Wind from the sea rushed in to compensate – that was what mariners meant when they spoke of the sea breeze. On this leeward side of the island, at some point in the morning or forenoon, the sea-breeze would defeat the northeast trade wind, and the conditions would be right to smoke out the fort. The change had started half an hour ago, but it was still fitful. Even at this stage the trade wind could re-assert itself and destroy the squadron's plan of attack. As Holbrooke watched, the feathers and corks of the dog-vane on the starboard side of the quarterdeck were streaming weakly across the deck. Good enough in Holbrooke's opinion. The breeze would only grow stronger from now as the full force of the sun hit Grenada's high land. Hosking thought so too, and he nodded encouragingly in Holbrooke's direction. What a fickle natural phenomenon on which to hang a strategy that was taking the squadron's five hundred men into imminent peril. What a testament to the organisation and discipline of the navy that the five hundred men carried out their orders without question.

Medina's boats were being towed alongside, manned and ready to play their part. The longboat was again ordered to stay close to the frigate in case it became embayed by this rising sea-breeze, while the pinnace and yawl were to pull deep into the bay to sink or burn the small vessels in the inner harbour. The privateers at anchor would be dealt with by *Medina's* broadsides.

'Flagship's backing her topsails sir,' reported the master. 'The way is coming off her ... quickly.' This was as close as Hosking would come to nudging his captain into action and Holbrooke came back to the present with a start. It was too easy as a captain to assume that everything would continue functioning without his intervention.

Hosking would be extremely reluctant to alter course without orders while Holbrooke was on the quarterdeck. If Holbrooke was not paying attention, the chain of command was fractured.

'Very well Mister Hosking. Come to starboard, haul aft the sheets and let's get at those privateers.'

'Aye-aye sir.' He turned to relay the orders, but the bosun and quartermaster had already heard, and the whole intricate structure was in motion. The fo'c'sle, waist and quarterdeck seethed with purposeful energy as the waisters heaved on the sheets to tighten the sails and catch every ounce of the gathering breeze. The steersmen turned the wheel, the quartermaster carefully watching the distance to *Wessex's* quarter gallery as the frigate gathered pace and the gap between the two ships narrowed.

'Away boats,' called Holbrooke. The painters were slipped, and the pinnace and yawl dropped quickly astern, to turn under *Wessex's* quarter and shoot through the gap that was opening between the frigate and the flagship as *Medina* gathered pace towards her prey.

Holbrooke looked over his shoulder; the fort was shrouded in grey smoke. Not a very thick smoke but sufficient to frustrate the aim of the French artillerymen. They were still firing; he could see the flashes as each gun discharged and a brief thickening of the smoke as the guns added their blacker clouds to the overall gloom. *Wessex* was firing well, apparently without any significant damage to herself. The flagship's aim was not affected by the smoke as the outline of the fort was clearly visible, and the orange glare of each French discharge provided excellent aiming points. *Wessex* was more stable now, lying-to in this friendly breeze and providing a firm platform for accurate gunnery. The flagship's boats were pulling strongly for the harbour. Her longboat, like *Medina's*, lying on her oars to windward, was ready to haul the ship out of the bay if that became necessary. But Holbrooke knew that Carlisle's dispositions had taken the sea-breeze into account, and the great ship had given itself sufficient sea room to beat out of the bay when their work was done, unless her rigging or sails became damaged, or her rudder was hit.

'Mister Hosking. Lay us alongside the first privateer at a quarter-cable and hold us there until we have finished with her.' He took in the whole panorama with a single sweep of his gaze before the work of pounding the frail anchored ships into sinking wrecks took over the main part of his attention. The battle of the fort appeared to be going well, and the boats were pulling fast into the harbour, a few stray shots from the eastern walls of the fort speeding them on their way. But they would soon be too deep into the harbour to be worried by the fort. The jolly-boat was pulling towards *Medina*, he noticed, but he could ignore that. Curtis would have the sense to come to *Medina's* disengaged side, and the bosun would take the boat in tow and bring Curtis and his band of heroes on board. The boats from the privateers had long-since reached the harbour. The three privateers, Holbrooke's personal objective, lay peacefully at anchor, abandoned by their crews – not a soul could be seen on board.

'Mister Lynton, hold your fire until we have the first privateer abeam, depress your guns and aim for the waterline, I believe you will receive no fire in return.'

Lynton waved his hat in acknowledgement and turned to his eager gun crews. The cannon of the upper deck had been double-shotted for this first broadside. A nine-pound ball was not large by naval standards and would be of little account in a fleet action, but against the thin planking of a French privateer, and at this range, it would be deadly.

Lynton posed dramatically atop the grating over the main hatch, his sword drawn and his hat in his left hand. The privateer was so close that he could clearly see its masts over *Medina's* gunwales and he watched both his guns and his target with hawk-like intensity. The gun crews were poised at their weapons, levering the mountings around with the hand spikes to keep them trained on the enemy as they approached the critical position. The gun captains were alternately watching their target through the gun port, motioning to the crew to train forward or aft and casting glances at Lynton, all the while blowing on their linstocks to keep the match alive. Holbrooke watched as the master's mate coolly ordered more depression on the number eight gun. Lynton appeared to have it all under control, and Holbrooke turned back to the task of positioning his command for the maximum destructive effect.

It occurred to Holbrooke – even at this critical point as he was about to bring a frigate into action for the first time, his mind still churned away, examining itself – that if he did nothing, gave no more orders, the ship would go into action perfectly well without his further guidance. He had set up the approach to the target, given orders for manoeuvring and engaging, and those things would all happen now without any further intervention from him.

Medina was nearly abeam the first privateer, a small, narrow, black-hulled ship-rigged vessel. Holbrooke could see its name picked out in white against the black counter, '*La Mouette*,' a good name for such a sleek, fast ship, *The Seagull*. He saw Lynton cast a sideways glance at him. The younger man knew very well that he was to engage without further orders, but Holbrooke was commanding for the first time in an engagement, and this was Lynton's first time in control of the whole battery. Holbrooke was pleased to see that the glance was intended to confirm that Holbrooke had no new orders, and Lynton turned back to his study of the target and his guns.

La Mouette looked the picture of peace and tranquillity. She was lying almost beam-on to the wind; there must be a current here running from the south to the north across the harbour entrance, the gathering sea-breeze not yet having enough force to swing her to face the sea. *Medina's* bows were alongside the privateer's mainmast, and the way was coming off her as Hosking backed the topsails with his scratch team of waisters, all that was available after the guns and the boats had taken the cream of the crew. Holbrooke hoped that Lynton wouldn't leave it too late. They would have a limited time in this position as they would be blown gradually down onto the privateer, with little forward movement to give them steerage way. But as Holbrooke considered whether to order Lynton to open fire, the whole broadside discharged simultaneously. A hundred and fourteen pounds of cast iron smashed into *La Mouette*, every round hitting the unfortunate vessel – they could hardly miss at that range – and at least half of the shot tore large holes in the planking along the waterline. Lynton must have timed that to perfection. *Medina* was not rolling much, but the little motion that she had would have been enough to cause the shots to strike too high, or worse still to tear up the water between the two ships if they had not fired at the correct moment. The devastation was impressive and immediate. The privateer staggered and started listing to starboard. To starboard! Holbrooke glanced at the height of her masts – yes, there was sufficient distance between the two ships so that even if the privateer capsized, her poles would fall clear of *Medina*. Clearly, Hosking had the same thought, and he was carefully watching the distance, his fingers drumming nervously against his thigh, as the two ships drifted slowly towards each other.

The second broadside completed the destruction, opening the fragile craft along the waterline for two-thirds of her length. The inrush of water was now distributing itself more evenly in the hold, and she was starting to right herself, but there was no stopping her descent and the water quickly moved up to her gunwales. Holbrooke would not have believed that a ship, even one as small as this frail vessel, could be destroyed so rapidly. He had always assumed that a wooden vessel would float for a long time, even when thoroughly waterlogged. But *La*

Mouette must have had a substantial cargo, perhaps molasses or sugar taken out of a British West Indiaman. In any case, she was doomed. Holbrooke blew a single blast on his whistle before the third broadside could be fired.

'Mister Hosking, you may move on to the brig now.'

This would be trickier. The privateer brig had swung with the wind and *Medina* would be approaching across her bow. That slight current must be localised in the main channel where the first privateer had anchored. Holbrooke didn't want to run down her beam into the harbour mouth, where there was too much chance of being embayed. Although the longboat was waiting to tow them out if necessary, it was far safer to avoid getting the frigate into that dangerous position.

'Mister Lynton, double-shot the guns again. We will be crossing her bow, so don't fire a broadside, each gun is to engage independently as it bears. Aim for the cutwater and let's see if we can open this one up like the last.'

The brig appeared as deserted as the ship had been, but she sank in a much more dramatic fashion after two rounds from each gun had entirely destroyed the massive timbers where her keel rose to become the prow. The butts of the planks were released from their rebates and opened like a peeled banana on either side of the cutwater. The water rushed in, and as the bows settled, the stern rose theatrically. In the end, it was the combined weight of her foremast and the cable suspended below her bows that dragged her down, probably her cargo had shifted also. She pitch-poled and sank rapidly, bows-first, the rush of air blowing out the windows of her modest stern-gallery.

Holbrooke had time to look astern and see that the tops of the masts of the first ship were still visible where she had rested upright on the bottom. The brig, however, disappeared entirely leaving a widening circle of debris – broken planks, hatch gratings, hen-coops, barrels, cordage. It was possible that the French could salvage the ship-rigged privateer – with a lot of effort and expense – but the brig was lost. In both cases, the wrecks must be removed before Port Louis could safely be used again.

'Cease firing,' shouted Holbrooke, and then he remembered to blow the single blast on his whistle. But Lynton had already given the order to his crews, the utter destruction of the brig apparent for all to see and there was no point in wasting ammunition.

'I would like to give her a little sea-room before we start on the next ship, may I bring her to the wind?' asked Hosking.

'Yes, master. Please do so,' replied Holbrooke. He looked back at *Wessex*. She appeared in good order, and her guns were firing with a steady rhythm, although she had apparently been hit more than once.

The fort was not aiming at *Medina* at all. Those guns that could not train on *Wessex* were firing at the boats, without success so far. In the harbour, he could see three or four plumes of smoke, presumably where the boats were following their orders to sink or destroy, but not to take prizes. Holbrooke, however, was under no such orders and he had been permitted explicitly by Carlisle to take a prize if there was sufficient time, but under no circumstances was he to cause a delay in the squadron's withdrawal. He could see that the boats were not yet returning from the harbour, so perhaps he had time.

'We will tack and withdraw a little Mister Hosking so that we can release the longboat to cut out that last privateer. Will that give us enough sea-room without the longboat's help?'

'Aye sir, this sea breeze looks settled now, and I can weather either headland from here.'

Holbrooke picked up a speaking-trumpet and hailed the longboat. 'Mister Smith, we will take that last ship as a prize. Seize your towing hawser to her cable and cut away the anchor. Make as much offing as you can under oars. I will give you a prize crew once you are out of the bay.

'Aye-aye sir,' came the faint, but enthusiastic reply.

That was a beautiful ship and would sell quickly in Antigua, probably to resume her old profession of privateering, but under the British flag rather than the French. It wouldn't make the crews of *Wessex* and *Medina* wealthy, but it would undoubtedly be a useful supplement to their pay. The cutting-out of the last ship could be left to Smith and his longboat crew. Holbrooke turned his attention back to the harbour.

CHAPTER TWELVE

Mission Accomplished

Tuesday, twenty-first of December 1756
Wessex, at Sea, The Grand Bay

Thompson glanced over his shoulder at Carlisle. 'Warm work sir,' he said, 'I don't doubt that one of those hot-shot will reach us soon.' Carlisle exchanged a glance with the petty officer in charge of the fire party, a steady man, a bosun's mate in his day-job. The normal watchbill allocated a man from each gun as fire party, to be released from the gun crew when a fire had been detected. However, this was not a normal situation, and *Wessex* was brazenly facing a fort that had already proved its competence with hot shot. Today, ten men were free from all duties except this one, to watch for fire and respond quickly. Two of them were constantly keeping the pair of elm-tree pumps in motion, a steady trickle of cool water running through canvas hoses over each deck and losing itself back into the ocean through the scuppers. The remainder were stationed beside their buckets on the gun-decks, the fo'c'sle, the quarterdeck and the poop deck. The petty officer knuckled his forehead in acknowledgement and returned to his vigil, conscious now of his captain's attention, ostentatiously turning his head this way and that to search for tell-tale wisps of smoke of a lighter grey than the guns were producing. Carlisle almost laughed, the man would know soon enough if they were hit by a twenty-four-pound hot shot.

Crash! Carlisle spun on his heels and looked up for the source of the noise. A shot had struck the quarters of the main yard, severing it about ten feet in from the starboard yardarm. But there was something different about that shot. Carlisle searched back through his memory of the last few seconds. Yes, that was it, the weird ululation just before the crash. The French gunners were using chain shot to disable their tormentor, and that was a twenty-four pounder. Had they abandoned the heated shot? Quite probably, the rigging of *Wessex* was a much easier target than her hull, and with the smoke from the burning cargo of hay in their eyes, they needed a mark that gave them a higher probability of achieving hits. It was a sensible switch of ammunition. In this gathering sea breeze, a disabled ship must drift inshore, eventually to take the ground under the guns of the fort, to be burned by her crew and abandoned to the French.

'Mister Godwin,' the first lieutenant turned to face him. 'The towing hawser is laid along?'

'Aye sir, it is. Two hawsers in case of an accident. They're faked down on the fo'c'sle; there's more space there, and they're led back through the hawse-hole. The heaving line is bent on ready to go.'

'Very well. You see that the French are trying to disable us now?'

'Yes sir, bosun is securing the main yard now.'

'Curious,' thought Carlisle. Under the stress of action, the man forgot to be surly. His attitude was almost agreeable. It was curious also that both Thompson and Godwin had accepted his position; not just as the temporary commander of the squadron, which was his by right, but they also appeared to accept his interference in the management of the ship. He knew that he was on dangerous ground here and could not, without real necessity, formally usurp Godwin's right to command during the lawful captain's indisposition. But Godwin was either avoiding confrontation or was just more comfortable in the role of second-in-command. In truth, it was difficult to separate the functions of squadron command and flagship command when the squadron consisted of merely a fifty-gun ship and a frigate, but Godwin could reasonably have forced the issue.

The sailing master joined the conversation. 'That old mainsail is neither here-nor-there in beating out of the bay in this wind sir, but I would rather have the topsail if I can. I've told the bosun to lash the yardarm back onto the quarter and secure it until the carpenter can fish one of the reserve spars into place. It'll be good enough for the tacks of the topsail.'

Chain and bar shot was regularly howling overhead, and there was a steady stream of knotting and splicing to keep the bosun's crew busy. The French appeared to have entirely ceased firing at the ship's hull, and they probably had abandoned their heated shot.

'Mister Godwin!' The first lieutenant raised his head from the guns. 'The bosun will need more men soon.'

Godwin nodded in understanding and turned away to start re-distributing his resources.

Carlisle wondered about casualties among *Wessex's* gun crews – there must be some at least. The danger to the bosun's men was evident, and as they moved about the tops and the rigging they had the hunched look of men trying to minimise the size of the target that they presented to the French guns.

The howl of a chain shot was followed by a crash of breaking timber. Carlisle looked up to see large chunks of the fabric of the foretop and its hammock cranes fall to the deck, followed by a rain of splinters, severed ropes, solid wooden blocks and wrecked hammocks. The splinter nets performed their duty and caught the worst of the debris before it fell onto the heads and shoulders of the men on the deck. But, as he watched, a lone seaman, with a despairing wail, lost his grip on the damaged woodwork of the foretop and fell backwards, his arms flailing and a look of horror on his face. He hit the fo'c'sle rail, his body bending back on itself in at an angle that no living backbone could endure. The impact was not audible above the din of battle, nor the second fall as the now-lifeless

The Leeward Islands Squadron

figure dropped from the rail down to the upper deck, landing between two of the guns. One of the gunners gave him a cursory look, shook his head and at a motioned command from the gun captain, dragged him clear to lie in a crumpled heap against the coaming of the main hatch. It hardly interrupted the tempo of the gun crew, as they heaved on the tackles and ran their twelve-pounder out to send another iron ball screaming over the water to the fort. A human life had been extinguished, leaving no trace at the scene of the tragedy, no blood at all.

Carlisle dragged his eyes away from the scene. He could see that Holbrooke had completed the destruction of the larger privateers, two had been sunk, and the third was under tow. He could also see the boats returning from the inner harbour, he counted all six of them.

'Mister Thompson, there is nothing to keep us here now. How do you propose to leave the bay?'

Thompson had been anticipating the question. 'The wind has backed into the west-southwest now and looks set in that direction. I'll gather way on the starboard tack then bring her about and take her out to the northwest. We have just enough sea-room, but it will be tight.'

'We could tow her head around with the longboat, that would give us more space.'

'That it would, sir.' He looked over the starboard side of the ship. The longboat was close in under the hawse-hole, just where she should be.

The bosun was shamelessly eavesdropping, and the master's order was lost as the bosun, disregarding his advanced years, vaulted the quarterdeck rail and ran forward along the gang boards to the fo'c'sle. Taking up the heaving line he ran out on the cathead. The longboat was so close that he could just drop the line into the stern where the coxswain quickly pulled in the towing hawser – there was no need for a lighter messenger with the boat so handy under the ship's bows. A bridle had been rigged in the stern of the longboat. It was a matter of seconds for the hawser to be secured to the bridle, then a minute or so for the longboat to pull far enough ahead so that the angle of the tow was not too steep to dissipate the rower's efforts and for the fo'c'sle crew to haul down the slack and make fast. Within five minutes of the master's order, the longboat had taken the strain and started the arduous task of shifting the bows of the great two-decker through the wind. *Wessex* had a thirty-foot longboat, a great brute of a vessel, used for all the heavy work of the ship. The longboat carried eight oars on each side and every oar – except for the bow oars where the narrowing of the boat made the thwarts too cramped – had been double-banked. A total of thirty brawny men were putting their hearts into the work. Nothing that floated could long resist that sheer force, and within a minute *Wessex* started to turn, her sails were sheeted home, and her bow moved slowly into the wind. Shot continued to howl overhead, and one nine-pounder raised a water fountain close alongside the longboat, drenching the coxswain and the stroke oar. There was a brief loss of pulling power, and the steady rhythm was momentarily destroyed as the stroke oar waved uselessly in the air, breaking the beat of the remaining oarsmen, who took their timing from him. The coxswain quickly regained order with a few commands, punctuated by passionate curses which, if they lacked originality, at least had the force of conviction.

    The critical point was fast approaching. The bows must be rapidly dragged through the eye of the wind to reduce the time that *Wessex* was a mere mass of uncontrollable windage, blowing slowly down upon the waiting fort. The boat's coxswain, recognising the danger, urged his rowers to their greatest effort, his whole body setting the timing for the strokes, moving backwards and forwards, his muscles tensed and his left hand holding the tiller. The foresails shivered, the ship was dead in the water, but still, the longboat exerted its sideways pressure. Now the jib, the outer jib and the forestaysail played their part as the wind caught them aback and added their leverage to the pulling power of the oarsmen. The bows were swinging fast now.

'Let go and haul,' shouted Thompson to the fo'c'sle.

Crash! The deck shook under Carlisle's feet. This impact was much larger and seemed to be from a hit on the stern. Fearing the worst, he looked over the poop rail onto the quarterdeck. The wheel was still manned, and Thompson was still standing, steady as a rock, bringing the ship onto her new course to escape the bay. His worst fears had not been realised. He had imagined the ship's vulnerable stern being subjected to raking fire from the fort as she turned through the wind.

'Don't you worry sir,' shouted the quartermaster presuming upon the intimacy of action and his great age. 'That was just a pair of them old chain shot hitting us. They can't make it through solid oak, but they do cause quite a judder, ha, ha.' He looked up at the luffs of the fore-topsail that could easily be seen in the absence of the sails on the mainmast. 'I've known it worse than this sir. Aye, far worse.' His Devon accent, still soft and round after all these years at sea, turned all his esses into zeds and elongated each word; it took a moment for Carlisle to tune into his speech.

'Old George was with Benbow at his last fight,' observed the nearest helmsman, a middle-aged man himself, pigtailed and scarred. 'Powder monkey he was,' and then in a lower tone, to be deniable, 'or so he claims.'

'Aye, I was,' replied the quartermaster, glaring at his challenger. 'And Brave Benbow wouldn't have been worried by some chain shot, so nor shall we youngster. You just mind your course, you goddamned lubber.'

'Good God,' thought Carlisle, 'was it possible?' He calculated rapidly, a ten-year-old ship's boy in 1702, when Benbow was killed, would be sixty-four now, or thereabouts. This grey-whiskered old sea-dog below him could easily be that age. If so he was already at sea when Carlisle's father was born – he probably still mourned Queen Anne and thought these Hanoverians just a passing phase. A few lines of the old ale-house song, a favourite in his youth in Virginia and still sung in gunrooms and messes throughout the fleet, came unbidden to his mind.

Come all you seamen bold
and draw near, and draw near,
Come all you seamen bold and draw near.
It's of an Admiral's fame,
O brave Benbow was his name,
How he fought all on the main,
you shall hear, you shall hear.

Just remembering the first line transported him back to his childhood home in Williamsburg, catching snatches of the song as he passed Shields Tavern on some errand or other, pursued by the smells of rum and tobacco, of horse dung and old leather.

Wessex gathered pace on the larboard tack. The master was correct; the loss of the main course and main topsail mattered hardly at all in this wind.

'How's the helm, quartermaster?' he called down to the quarterdeck.

'She steers fine, sir. Perhaps takes a little more weather helm, but don't you worry about her.'

'Perhaps this man goes through life telling people not to worry,' he thought. 'A comfortable friend to have, perhaps it's a result of hailing from a rural county like Devon.' Carlisle remembered what he had read about Benbow's last fight, a desperate affair off Cape Santa Marta some 900 miles west of here. Benbow lost a leg early in the action, and some of his captains failed to support the flag, two of whom were later shot for cowardice. Benbow died some two months later. If this quartermaster had been at Benbow's last fight then, by comparison, everything else in life might well be nothing to worry about.

With the wind on her larboard bow and the fort now abeam, *Wessex* could concentrate her starboard battery on covering the retreat of *Medina* and her prize. Through his telescope, Carlisle could see that Holbrooke was speaking to the frigate's returning pinnace. As he watched, the pinnace spun around and headed at speed towards the longboat. A figure made a flying leap from the longboat into the pinnace – Carlisle thought it looked like Smith, the bright young midshipman who would very soon make a good master's mate. Smith, if it were he, landed without dignity in the stern-sheets, and the pinnace continued almost without missing a stroke towards the captured privateer. Good. It looked like Holbrooke had that situation well under control. In a couple of minutes, the privateer should have at least a few headsails and a mizzen to relieve the strain on the longboat's rowers. In fifteen minutes he would expect to see topsails and then she could proceed on her own out of the bay. But for now, Carlisle's duty was to engage the fort with an intense fire to cover the retreat of *Medina* and the privateer. If the frigate was not suited to absorb twenty-four-pound shot, then the privateer was doubly unsuited. He had seen what *Medina's* nine-pounders could do to these lightly-built craft; a single unlucky shot from the fort could sink her outright.

'Mister Thompson. Now that we are through the wind bring her to on this tack. I want the whole starboard battery to bear on the fort until *Medina* and the prize are out of range. I estimate thirty minutes will be sufficient. Mister Godwin, we will give you a steady platform. I want those French gunners to fear for their lives every time they run out. Don't give them the leisure to aim properly.'

'Aye-aye, sir.' Replied Godwin with a confident wave. He had lost one of his larboard guns to an unfortunate shot that had damaged the oak carriage, but his starboard battery was undamaged, and Carlisle could see that the crews were willing enough. The guns ran in and out with a fine rhythm, spitting iron, flame and smoke at a speed which did credit to Godwin's drills.

The burning schooner was still doing its job. Perhaps the smoke was just starting to thin a little, and from time-to-time, a flaw in the wind gave the fort a clear view of *Wessex*, but it was never long enough to allow the gunners to take careful aim.

'Look over there, to the right of the fort sir.' The master pointed at the base of the promontory on which the fort was built. A party of about thirty soldiers were scrambling over the rocks and discarded masonry, clearly heading for the schooner. They carried two long poles – they looked like flag-staffs – and each man had a bucket. 'What an absurd attempt!' thought Carlisle. That schooner was firmly aground, probably bilged on the rocks, her lower planking stove in by the force of the grounding. They would need hours to move her, and those pathetic buckets would hardly make any impact on the burning hay. But of course, the commander of the fort did not know the squadron's intention. *Wessex* could be settling down to a long slogging match in an attempt to subdue and then assault the fort. Carlisle knew the truth. Barring accidents they would be away in half an hour, but it would do no harm to hide that from the French.

'Mister Godwin, direct the six-pounders to load with grape-shot and annoy those soldiers. It doesn't matter if they hit the schooner, the grape will do no harm to her that hasn't been done already, but it will stop the soldiers putting out the fire.'

Wessex carried four six-pounders on the quarterdeck and another two on the fo'c'sle. Carlisle couldn't see the four under his feet – he was still on the poop deck where he had the best overview of the action – but he could easily see the fo'c'sle. There was a midshipman there in charge of the guns. He looked somewhat older than the typical run of young gentlemen, in his mid-twenties at least. Carlisle saw him take the order from Godwin, saw him direct the captain of the gun to continue loading the ball which was on its way to the muzzle of the gun. He watched as the midshipman pointed out the target and then stepped clear to allow the crew to run the gun out. The gun captain squinted down the length of the barrel, motioned for a little more left traverse, then he stepped to the side. One of the crew had his hand over the touch-hole to prevent the priming powder being blown away, or a stray spark igniting it prematurely. The gun captain swiftly lowered the linstock, and the gun jumped and ran backwards, pulling taught the tackles that were designed to restrict its backward movement. Carlisle looked for the fall of shot. Not bad, it had landed a little low and between the soldiers and the schooner towards which they were scrambling as fast as they could. The whole mass of soldiers paused, dropped to the ground, seeking cover behind the rocks, momentarily unwilling to go forward into the ground which they now knew was being swept by the ship's guns. An officer drew his sword and ran to the front, his gestures unmistakable, *follow me!* A few of the soldiers started to move, then they were all on their feet again, running hard for the cover that the schooner would offer. Carlisle hadn't doubted the *esprit de corps* of the French army, and now he had a compelling demonstration. The officer had done well to get them moving again, but there had been no real unwillingness, just a few seconds of doubt.

Carlisle almost found himself hoping that the brave soldiers would reach the relative safety of the schooner's hull, but it was not to be. The two six-pounders below him on the quarterdeck fired almost simultaneously when the soldiers still had another fifty yards of rough ground to cover. The order for grapeshot had reached the quarterdeck six-pounders just after they had fired their round-shot at the fort, so this second salvo was the true anti-personnel ammunition. Carlisle was impressed that the grapeshot had been stored ready for use beside each gun; it would have been easy to forget that detail in the preparations for action. This was a reasonable distance for this heavier anti-personnel ammunition. It was beyond the effective range of the case-shot which in a six-pounder would fire forty musket balls in quite a wide cone, too widely dispersed at that range. But it was just right for the eleven half-pound balls tightly wrapped in a canvas bag that made up the six-pounders' grapeshot. The range was great enough to allow the pattern of balls to open into a cone that would cover about fifteen yards of width but close enough for accuracy and to keep the pattern sufficiently concentrated for lethal effect.

One of the guns – the first to fire – was not so well laid and the balls merely churned up a portion of the sea and scattered stone chips from the rocks at the water's edge. But the second was elevated just right. If it had been traversed a little further left it would have utterly destroyed that valiant group of men, but as it was it just caught the stragglers. Five fell, struck down like wooden pins on a bowling alley. Carlisle trained his telescope on the tragic group. There was little that could be done for a man hit by half a pound of cast iron travelling at around eleven-hundred feet per second. Two of them didn't move at all, but three of them were apparently still living. Perhaps they had merely been hit by stone chips flung up by the boulders that they had been scrambling over. He watched the officer. He was a middle-aged man, and he had lost his hat and his wig, exposing the short, grey hair beneath. Calling to four of his men he ran back to help the wounded soldiers. Carlisle had seen enough.

'Mister Godwin, tell the guns to concentrate their fire upon the schooner, do not fire upon the wounded men.'

Godwin waved in acknowledgement, and at that moment, before the order could be relayed to the midshipman on the fo'c'sle, his six-pounder fired its round of grape. Carlisle had an immediate premonition of tragedy. By the time he turned back towards the little group of wounded and their rescuers, they were no more. They had been caught in the centre of the pattern of grapeshot, and whether by direct impact or by flying stone chips, they had been annihilated, barely a movement was seen from the ten men. He heard the howl of anger from their friends who nevertheless and quite sensibly continued running for the schooner.

Carlisle turned towards the fo'c'sle, rage contorting his face, but he quickly took control of himself. It wasn't the fault of the midshipman or his gun crew. They had no leisure to pick and choose their target, being wholly occupied in loading and firing with barely enough time for aiming. They would probably have merely seen a group of men, the same enemy that they had been ordered to engage only a few moments before. They didn't even now understand what they had done but were rapidly loading again with grape-shot, levering the gun to the left to point at the schooner now that their previous target had been dealt with. In all fairness, they were more to be commended than criticised. Not for the first time, Carlisle had been forcibly reminded of the need for the ship's officers to be free from involvement in the mechanics of fighting the ship so that they could retain a measure of clarity for making the right decisions promptly. If he had shouted his order to Godwin only a few seconds earlier – as soon as he saw the effect of the quarterdeck gun – that pointless and inhuman slaughter could have been averted. A display of mercy would not even have helped the French officer on his mission as he would have been severely hampered by the three wounded men, and Carlisle could see that the second-in-command was already rallying the survivors.

'Mister Godwin, keep those soldiers off the deck of the schooner, space out the fire of the six-pounders so that they are continuously engaged.'

While this drama was being enacted, the pinnace crew had left their boat towing on a painter behind the captured privateer, and the first of the headsails had been set and was just starting to draw. Carlisle would have set the mizzen first to avoid too much sideways pressure being put on the tow, but he could see that the mizzen was being released from its brails and would soon be balancing the rig. The task of the longboat was visibly eased, and he could see both vessels starting to move faster. They now had to choose the right time to drop the tow, though not until the prize had steerage way and was on a course which would allow her to clear the northern headland. How frustrating, to be watching this critical operation without being able to influence it in any way!

Meanwhile, *Wessex* had her own battle to fight. The soldiers sent to extinguish the fire in the schooner were thoroughly pinned down. One or two brave souls had scaled the hull, fighting their way through the choking smoke, but there was little that they could do. If left to themselves, without *Wessex's* lethal grape-shot, they may have been able to quench the fire and in a short while to reduce the amount of smoke, but that was not to be, and the officer left in charge must be rapidly realising what a fool's errand he had been sent on.

'Captain Carlisle!' That was the master calling from the quarterdeck. 'I strongly recommend that we get underway immediately. We are being blown down towards the shallows, and very soon we won't be able to weather the point.' Thompson was not entirely his imperturbable self. What sailing master could be, lying-to with the shore five cables under his lee and a captain apparently determined to remain in that position indefinitely?

However, Carlisle wasn't going to be rushed. He was sure that Thompson had given himself some room for error. He looked carefully over at the frigate and its prize. They were still within range of the fort's guns but would only have to withstand one or two more firing and reloading cycles before they were beyond effective range. The fort was still wreathed in smoke, and there was nothing that the group of soldiers could do in under an hour that would change the situation. Carlisle could see for himself that the flagship would soon be perilously close to the land. A leadsman had been calling the depth since they entered the bay, stolidly carrying out his task from the fo'c'sle head with the six-pounders firing at his elbow. 'By the deep sixteen,' he called. Sixteen fathoms, that was plenty of water for a ship that drew less than twenty feet, but Carlisle knew that it shoaled fast here. Thompson was becoming agitated. The ordinarily rock-solid sailing master was almost dancing with frustration.

'Very well Mister Thompson. Get us underway but keep us in range of the fort as long as possible.'

The fore-topsail was swung around, the sheets hardened in, and *Wessex* slowly moved off. North-northwest was the course to comfortably clear Point Bois Maurice and escape this wind-bound bay. Her battery could still point at the fort, and she kept up a regular fire as she withdrew. Both *Medina* and the prize could sail a little higher, and although they were still in the danger zone, the range was rapidly becoming too high for accurate shooting from the fort. The French gunnery really was poor. *Wessex* had received only a few hits, and none had caused severe damage. Carlisle tried to imagine himself in the position of the French artillery commander. His gunners were blinded by the thick smoke rolling in through the embrasures, and there was apparently nothing he could do about it. His attempt to move the schooner or put out the fire had failed with a tragic loss of life. Most of the time, the Frenchmen could see their target through the smoke, but it was in fleeting images only and not for long enough to allow the careful aiming of the guns which would have proved lethal to Carlisle's plans. Also, his gunners had sustained casualties. Carlisle had seen several of *Wessex's* twenty-four and eighteen-pound shot bring up showers of rock chippings around the embrasures and he was confident that some had gone clean through. At least one of the fort's guns had been silent for some time. The Frenchman was rapidly being educated about the limits of the effectiveness of heated shot and the advantages of seaborne mobility. There would be some harsh words between him and the fort's commander, no doubt.

The final shots from the fort raised waterspouts a cable short of *Wessex's* stern and well clear of the higher-pointing and faster-sailing *Medina* and her prize. The two-decker had been faithful to the purpose for which she had been built. She had absorbed the wrath of the fort to allow her nimbler consort to destroy first the enemy's commerce raiders and second the enemy's trade itself. The last that Fort Royal saw of the squadron was its topsails disappearing around the northern headland as it left the Grand Bay and sailed away to the north. Carlisle noted with satisfaction that the schooner was still emitting billows of thick smoke, the party sent to extinguish it probably having insufficient buckets for the job. He guessed that the unfortunate vessel would continue to burn all day if they didn't get a portable pump down onto the foreshore.

CHAPTER THIRTEEN

Death at Sea

Thursday, twenty-third of December 1756
Medina, at Sea, St. Vincent southeast 18 leagues

Two days had passed since the second attack on Port Louis. In that time the squadron had beat north-northwest, or as close as they could lie, against a steady northeast trade wind, but progress was painfully slow with *Wessex* favouring her wounded main yard. Barbados was almost dead to windward of Grenada, an inescapable fact of geography and the general circulation of air in the North Atlantic. Sailors have known this for hundreds of years and have planned their voyages accordingly. So, in an ideal world, one ruled by geography and meteorology and not by Admiralty orders, the squadron would have called at Barbados before Granada. But Edward Carlisle had no such luxury. He was under orders to call at Carlisle Bay – there was an almost childish delight in heading for a place with which he shared a name – to look for the Leeward Islands Squadron, and if they weren't there to stretch right across the Windward and Leeward islands to English Harbour in Antigua. Privately, Carlisle considered it unlikely that he would find the squadron at Barbados. There was no reason for Admiral Frankland to be there when the French were at Martinique, and the trade of Britain predominantly passed through the passages between the islands in the north of the chain. Frankland was short of ships at this early stage of the war. He would welcome the additional strength of even this small squadron, but he wouldn't feel the need to meet them on their journey. Unless he had word of a threat to Barbados, it was unlikely that Carlisle Bay would be disturbed by the presence of the Leeward Islands

Squadron.

It was just a part of life at sea, this continual battle to sail against the wind. They had fought for every inch to windward – to the *west* – to clear the Grand Bay. Then, when the sea-breeze faded as they left the influence of the island, and the trade wind regained its ascendancy, they had continued to fight for every inch to windward, but now trying to make ground to the *east*. The plan was to beat up to the latitude of St. Lucia and then put the wind on their larboard bow and – hopefully – be able to sail through the passage between St. Vincent and St. Lucia and so in a single tack to Carlisle Bay. Any change in the constancy of the northeast trade wind would alter the plan. If the wind veered, they would be tacking through the passage; if it backed, they would have a pleasant reach to their destination and knock a day or two off the voyage.

Wessex was nearly whole again. A spare t'gallant yard had been fished to the end of the main yard. It wouldn't withstand a Caribbean hurricane, but it would get them to English Harbour, given average luck. The poop deck, however, was not repairable at sea. Carlisle had quizzed the carpenter, a young and very active man who appeared to know his trade. The best he could do was to create a framework over the great cabin and fit the spare topsail more snuggly, well frapped down with strong ropes, so that the weather was kept out. The bulkhead at the forward end of the great cabin had also been reinforced and made weather-tight. The only real detriment to the accommodation of the ship was the loss of the great cabin and the after end of the poop deck. Otherwise, *Wessex* was whole and fit for sea if a little ungainly with her drooping stern. But she was slow, she always had been, particularly with the wind on her bow, and she was a sore trial to the fast-sailing *Medina*.

Jermy had been returned to his dining cabin, still unconscious, barely alive in fact. The surgeon had nothing new to say, and after a conference with *Medina's* surgeon, they concluded that all they could do was keep him comfortable until he could be landed at Bridgetown – to whatever facilities that place offered. Carlisle had considered heading directly for Antigua, but they could hardly have reached there any earlier, and the health of the commodore did not – in his judgement – justify disobeying the Admiralty's written orders.

'Well, Holbrooke, this is fine weather,' said Carlisle, 'it's good to be back in my own ship.' He stretched his head over the weather hammock netting and savoured the salt air, blowing clean across thousands of miles of ocean to speed the squadron on its way. The people were in excellent spirits, and their losses in Port Louis had been forgotten. They had their prize in company; she could be seen just to leeward of them, a nice little ship-rigged ex-privateer that would fetch a decent price when they presented her to the Vice-Admiralty court in English Harbour. And this weather and the constant care needed to get the most out of the ship was good for the men. If they could just make their own way to Barbados and not have to drag that slug of a two-decker with them, this passage would be perfect. Ever since the command of the squadron had devolved onto their captain, they had resented having to trim their pace for *Wessex*. When she carried a functioning commodore, it was only natural that *Medina* should conform to her speed, but now she was to all intents and purposes the junior ship, her continued holding back of her betters was barely endurable.

'What do you think of this weather Mister Hosking? will it last?'

'It looks well enough to me sir, the true and honest trade wind.'

The master, feeling a slight change in the strength of the wind, cast a glance at the luff of the mainsail and then at the steersmen. He nodded in satisfaction as the quartermaster ordered the helm put down a fraction to take advantage of the gust.

'We're clear of the hurricane season, and the glass is steady, so I see no reason why we shouldn't hold this wind for the next few days.' He swept the horizon, using his hand to shield his eyes from the glare of the sun. 'But we must watch for squalls nevertheless sir. You see those great towering clouds to windward?' Carlisle had indeed seen them. He remembered them well from his previous service in these parts. 'They can bring strong squalls, perhaps sixty knots in the gusts and torrential rain, and sometimes the wind backs very quickly. Nothing like the genuine hurricane, but if you are caught with your t'gallants set, it can be right awkward.'

'Thank you, Mister Hosking. Perhaps you would write a note on the slate for the officers and speak to each of them explaining the danger. Now, when do you believe we will be able to fetch Carlisle Bay? When should we tack?' That called for a detailed discussion, and the two men went below to the great cabin to study the charts.

'Perhaps by the end of the afternoon watch sir? Unless this wind backs, in which case we can tack as soon as we like. There's plenty of water between the islands.'

They were disturbed by a knock on the door, heralding the entrance of Midshipman Smith.

'Beg pardon sir, Mister Holbrooke's compliments and *Wessex* has put up her helm and is closing on us; it looks like she wants to speak.'

'Very good, I'll be on deck in two minutes.'

He pointed to Martinique on the chart. 'I don't want to be seen from Martinique, just in case the French have a strong squadron lurking to the south of the island. It's no part of our orders to interfere in the balance of forces without Admiral Frankland. As you say unless the wind changes we can come about at seven bells in the afternoon watch to allow the hands to make all secure before the dogs.'

Carlisle bounded lightly up the ladder and onto the

quarterdeck. Whatever Godwin had to say would probably ruin his day, but at least he could make the most of this carefree feeling while it lasted. The great two-decker was still a cable away when Carlisle reached the quarterdeck. He could see Godwin standing beside the larboard mizzen shrouds, evidently preparing to hail as soon as the distance closed.

'Watch your course quartermaster and pay attention to the dog-vane.' He heard Holbrooke say. There was always a danger when two large ships came this close, particularly when they were sailing on a bowline. This was not the time for *Medina* to be caught aback by a fluke of the wind.

Closer and closer came *Wessex*. She looked enormous at half a cable, but she needed to be at a quarter of a cable for a shouted conversation, or preferably less. From this perspective, it was easy to see the attraction of these fifty-gun ships to a cash-starved Admiralty. They cost a fraction of the money needed to build a modern seventy-four and yet for a colonial presence they fulfilled the need splendidly. They looked imposing, could accommodate a flag officer and a small retinue and could fight anything below the third rate. The danger was in believing the fantasy that they could stand in the line of battle. Those days were gone and unlikely to return.

'Captain Carlisle, will you come on board, sir?' Godwin was leaning forward over the hammock netting to get his message across as soon as possible. He looked tense, unsmiling, vulnerable. Carlisle had not, until now, seen the dour first lieutenant in anything but an incipient rage, and this was a new aspect of this strange man. Carlisle paused for a moment. His immediate instinct was to ask why. But surely this concerned Jermy and therefore was not a fit subject for a public discussion. No, he would have to go, with the loss of at least a few hours on their passage and a probable soaking in this brisk breeze.

'Very well. Follow my movements, we will lie-to.'

He turned to his own first lieutenant. 'Mister

Holbrooke, let's keep this simple. Bring the longboat alongside to leeward; I'll have no ceremony, and the regular boat's crew will do.'

It was an easy thing to say, but there was a heavy swell and getting the boat safely alongside, and fendered was no simple task. There was a deliberate and barely concealed tardiness in getting the boat ready for the captain. He may have wanted no ceremony and may well have been happy with a boat's crew from the watch on deck, but his own coxswain and his own boat's crew were having none of it. When eventually the longboat was ready for his embarkation, it was manned by the captain's boat's crew, led by Jackson, correctly dressed, if not shaved, and prepared to make a proper impression on *Wessex*.

Carlisle's first impression on entering the makeshift cabin was the smell. It was a noxious odour, a little akin to gangrene, which like any sailor who had entered a sick bay a week after a hard-fought battle, was quite familiar to him. But gangrene wasn't quite right – there was a musty smell overlaying it, the smell of sick older people. The surgeon looked even more worried than usual. He made no attempt to control his actions as he wrung his hands together in anguish and uncertainty. He started to speak, but Carlisle waved impatiently for silence and, overcoming his nausea, approached the cot which was swinging gently as the ship moved to the long Atlantic swell. He was shocked at what he saw. Jermy had been critically unwell when he last saw him the day before, but his decline since then had been rapid. The flesh had fallen away from his face leaving a grotesquely prominent nose and sunken eye sockets. The skin on his forehead was stretched tight, and his cheeks had developed discoloured spots; dark spots, almost black. He was barely recognisable as the pink, well-fed man that he first met in Sheerness a scant few weeks ago.

'He looks dead!' thought Carlisle, 'have they been concealing it, waiting for me to make the discovery?' He leaned into the cot and once again put his ear close to Jermy's mouth. Nothing. He waited. The cabin was in complete silence, the normal workings of the ship were hushed in respect and shock – the ship's company well knew the significance of Carlisle's visit. After twenty seconds or so of patient stillness, he could just detect the very faintest sound of the man's slowly beating heart and the sluggish expansion and contraction of his lungs. It was so slight that he could not feel any hint of the breath leaving his mouth or nostrils, nor see any rise and fall of his chest. Yet, the commodore still lived.

'Make your report Mister Green,' said Carlisle, without taking his eyes from the dying man, for he needed no medical opinion to tell him that Jermy was close to the end. At times of great drama or pathos, in the intervals between any decisions he had to make, Carlisle's mind was apt to wander. His early education had largely been wasted, but sometimes a few choice examples of poetry and prose rose to the surface, more-or-less as daydreams. The presence of imminent and unpreventable death was both pitiful and frightening, and Carlisle thought Hamlet's analogy for death most apt and suitably sombre, perfectly composed for occasions such as this, *the undiscovered country from whose bourn no traveller returns.*

The wretched surgeon stammered out his report. It was of little value, but the death of a post-captain was a solemn occasion and required to be recorded. He detailed the commodore's decline, accelerating over the last twenty-four hours, his opinion that death was very close. But he refused to speculate on how much more time remained for the decaying semi-corpse before them. There was nothing he could do.

'Very well, Mister Green. Then I will stay here with the commodore. You should continue to attend him, and if any appropriate treatment comes to mind, then you must apply it.' There was a seat beside the cot, lashed to the ring bolts in the deck that were ordinarily used for the tackles of the six-pounder, but the gun had been shifted aft into the remains of the great cabin.

'Mister Godwin!' The first lieutenant was startled out of his reverie. Whether he was contemplating that *undiscovered country* or whether he was fretting about his fate under the command of a man to whom he had been so openly insolent, was not clear. But Godwin was a worried man, that much was certain. 'Mister Godwin,' he repeated. 'Send my boat back to *Medina*. Tell the coxswain that I will remain in *Wessex* for the time being and then signal the squadron to get underway.'

The first lieutenant nodded wordlessly. 'And Mister Godwin,' Carlisle called softly to him, 'let there be silence abaft the mainmast. No carpenters, no holystoning. Orders are to be given in a whisper. Is that clear?'

'Aye-aye, sir.' Carlisle noted that Godwin's reply was the first that he had addressed to Carlisle without an ugly sneer.

'And send the commodore's clerk to me.'

Carlisle settled to his lonely vigil. Inevitably – and very soon, he judged – he would have to formally take command of the squadron until they should meet Admiral Frankland, and that could be anything from a few days to a few weeks. In that time, they could be chasing enemy merchantmen, grappling with privateers or fighting for their lives against the French West Indies squadron. Carlisle knew all about *Medina,* and he had a good idea of the capabilities of *Wessex*, but he still had the feeling that there was something disjointed about the larger ship, something odd about the way the officers spoke to each other. It wasn't that there was any open hostility, just a lack of that human contact that made for a cohesive leadership team. He suspected that Godwin was in some way either actively responsible or the unwitting propagator of this sad situation. Either way, he intended to get to the heart of the problem, and he would start with the written records. Jermy's clerk had brought the fair log for him to inspect, a certain delicacy preventing him asking for the captain's own journal, not while he still lived and breathed.

To a landsman, the log looked like a soulless record of the ship's activities. Here were compiled the daily doings of this floating family; courses steered, winds and weather, beef and water casks opened, sails sighted, punishments administered. There was nothing about the *feeling* in the ship and even fewer personal reflections on its officers. But even in this factual catalogue, this wasteland of the finer senses, some inferences could be drawn. There had been several complaints about the food, that first and sure sign of dissatisfaction. Cross-referring to the record of casks opened, Carlisle was satisfied that there was nothing unusual about them. The beef and pork casks had all been salted and packed very recently at the victualling yard at Deptford and presumably shipped down to Sheerness in the weeks before *Wessex* sailed. The other provisions were likewise fresh – at least by naval standards. The record of punishments was less encouraging. The impression that Carlisle gleaned from the logs was that *Wessex* was not precisely a flogging ship. There was nothing in the log that could be described as excessive, but there was a steady, almost daily drip of punishments for minor offences. Half a dozen lashes had been administered to some unfortunate seaman nearly every other day, and stoppage of grog or wine was commonplace. Carlisle was proud of the fact that the cat had only been out of the bag on one occasion in *Medina* – and that for theft by one of the quota men who had yet to understand the moral values of his new community. Punishment on this almost-moderate scale was no indication of dysfunctional leadership, and yet ….

It was more difficult to come to any conclusions about the state of the officers. Very little was ever committed to writing, and none of the commission or warrant officers could legally be punished without a court martial, requiring a gathering of captains, and that was quite impossible on a deployed ship. But Carlisle made a habit in his own frigate of glancing at the log slate every time he passed by the binnacle. This was a transient record of the orders that the captain or the master gave to the officer-of-the-watch. In a ship with free communication between the officers, the slate log would merely record navigational data to be transcribed into the fair log at the end of the watch, with a few orders that required emphasis – he occasionally used it for the purpose himself. But Carlisle had noticed that the open right-hand side of the slate was well-used in *Wessex*, filled with a barrage of orders to the officer-of-the-watch as if to compensate for lack of verbal communication.

Carlisle walked softly onto the quarterdeck and took up the slate from its hook on the side of the binnacle. Sure enough, it was teeming with orders from Godwin, not just to the officer-of-the-watch, but also to the sailing master. He had written small, but even so, the script was crammed in, running up against the wooden frame of the slate and filling every space.

Carlisle walked thoughtfully back to the dining cabin and resumed his seat bedside Jermy. There was no change. The surgeon was still in the cabin, fussing ineffectually around the cot, tweaking pillows and feeling the commodore's pulse. At a questioning look from Carlisle, he shrugged his shoulders and shook his head, desperately unwilling to admit verbally that his ministrations were to no purpose.

Sitting in the chair beside the fading commodore, Carlisle thought over what he had learned. He was now convinced that there was something wrong in the command structure of *Wessex*. Not only was the bond between the wardroom and the lower deck fractured – that essential understanding that kept three hundred and fifty men at sea, away from their homes and families, with a unified purpose – but it appeared that the bond between the captain and the officers was also severed. It was the first lietenant's role to be a bridge between the great cabin and the wardroom, but Godwin had chosen to establish himself solely on the captain's side of that divide. How much of that was a response to Jermy's failing health, Carlisle couldn't say, but he was now sure that there was no active communication between Godwin and the remainder of the wardroom officers. The ship was outwardly efficient; he had seen for himself how well the guns had been served, and how purposefully the two-decker had been sailed in the second attack on Port Louis. But without the stress and immediacy of action, a problem was brewing. He could see it in the sloppy way that work was carried out, in the sullen looks of the people.

Carlisle remained in the cabin. The squadron tacked at one bell in the first dog watch, a little later than he had planned, to compensate for the time lost in boat transfers when they had made no way to the north. Barbados lay right ahead, and if the northeast trade wind remained true, they would make it without any further tacking. The light faded, and the night watches were set. There was nothing else that required his immediate attention, and he felt that he could better address himself to whatever ailed *Wessex* once Jermy had passed away. That would provide a definite point from which he, as the new commander of the squadron, could start to make some changes.

The ship was unnaturally quiet. Sure, there were the usual noises of the wind in the rigging, the slapping of the waves against the hull and the working of the timbers as *Wessex* bullied her way to the southeast. But there was no sound of human activity – none. Like him or loathe him, the death of the captain of a man-of-war was a grave moment for all on board, from the oldest warrant officer to the youngest boy. It was like losing the head of the family, and it affected everyone. Even the bells had been silenced, substituted by a low murmur as the news of the turn of the half-hour glass was passed across the deck. Every few minutes the surgeon left his place at the far side of the cabin to confirm that the commodore still lived but he had not attempted any kind of medical intervention for many hours. Carlisle lost track of time. It was at some point towards the end of the middle watch – the *graveyard watch* as sailors called it, and not without cause – that Green looked up from one of his regular inspections and with a shocked face slowly shook his head. Carlisle felt for a breath, but there was nothing. There was no change in the commodore's features at all. He had looked like death since the afternoon, but now Carlisle could detect the loss of body heat. Jermy had passed away, cut his moorings and sailed to that undiscovered country.

'Mister Green, please call for the first lieutenant and the commodore's clerk and ask the master for our latitude and longitude.' The surgeon left the cabin gratefully, apparently happy to turn over responsibility now that the fateful moment had passed.

The Leeward Islands Squadron

CHAPTER FOURTEEN

Carlisle Bay

Sunday, twenty-sixth of December 1756
Wessex, at Anchor, Carlisle Bay

On the Friday evening after Jermy died the wind veered two points, forcing the squadron to follow it around until they could no longer fetch Carlisle Bay on the larboard tack. They spent Christmas day tacking to the north, all hands called at the turn of each watch to bring the ship about and maintain their line for Barbados. Then, when they had made their northing, to their great frustration the wind backed a full four points, and they had a fair sail into the anchorage, two points free, presenting a truly noble sight to the watchers on the shore. But Frankland was not there, just a small cutter commanded by a lieutenant who brought the news that the ships-of-the-line of the Leeward Islands Squadron were in English Harbour only three days earlier, and by his understanding were not planning on any operations against the French until they were reinforced. There was no homeward bound convoy scheduled until June, and although there was a constant threat to the island traffic from the French at Martinique, there was no need to be wearing out the small battlefleet until either it could achieve something against the enemy or there was a convoy to be protected. It was only nine months ago that *Warwick*, a sixty-gun ship, was taken by French seventy-four and two frigates off Martinique. Unable to open her lower gun ports in the heavy seas, with a hundred of her crew sick and without any other of Frankland's ships on hand, she had been forced to strike to the overwhelming force.

Carlisle had heard before he sailed that Rear Admiral

Coates was being sent out to relieve Townshend at Jamaica and that Frankland would benefit from some modest additions to his force. Indeed, *Wessex* was part of that intended reinforcement, as was *Medina*. It was part of the reasoning that contributed to Carlisle's decision to attack Port Louis a second time; he didn't relish the idea of delivering Frankland's new two-decker in a partly-destroyed state with no damage to the enemy as compensation. The privateer that dutifully followed them into the anchorage would be a visible confirmation that the French maritime effort had been meaningfully reduced. For Carlisle thoroughly understood the situation. The French battle fleet may threaten, and their frigates may cause sleepless nights for Townshend, but it was the commercially-funded men-of-war, the privateers, that caused the most considerable economic damage to Britain.

Carlisle was anxious to be on his way north, but Jermy must be decently buried first. The body certainly could not be held on board for the additional three days that it would take to reach Antigua – a minimum of three days and only if the trade wind didn't back northerly. A burial at sea briefly crossed his mind, but that could be justified only in the heat of a desperate action or when a friendly port was many days away. He would rightly be treated as a pariah in English Harbour if he handled the body of his commodore in that fashion.

To sailors of the navy, there are few more sombre sights than a ship in mourning for its captain. *Wessex* lay a bare half mile off Bridgetown in full view of Forts James and Willoughby to the north and Charles Fort to the southeast, her yards all acockbill and her ensign at half-mast. To see a King's ship in that state was terrible, and even the soldiers of the garrison were moved. From the promenade on the foreshore, she was stared at by the idle occupants of the town, and this being the day after Christmas day and a Sunday, there was no shortage of citizens with nothing better to do.

Jermy was rowed solemnly ashore to Charles Fort by his own boat's crew, bare-headed even in this tropical heat and keeping a slow time to the beat from a drummer in the following boat. All the boats of the squadron followed, filled with the officers of *Wessex* and *Medina* and as many sailors from *Wessex* as could be carried. The army had risen to the occasion. Jermy's coffin was lifted onto a gun carriage and trundled the few yards to the small cemetery behind the chapel, followed by all the officers of the garrison. A gun salute was fired from the fort, answered by the squadron in the bay, and to a final fusillade of small arms, Robert Jermy was laid to rest in the sandy soil of Needhams Point.

CHAPTER FIFTEEN

Passage to Antigua

Tuesday, twenty-eighth of December 1756
Medina, at Sea, Dominica west 20 leagues

It was good to be back at sea. Carlisle had felt compelled to stay an additional day at Barbados to satisfy the proprieties around the burial of a commodore. He had to call on the governor, drink sherry with his wife, relay the latest news from home to the garrison officers and be seen by the townspeople, for reassurance in these nervous times. Although well garrisoned, Barbados had every reason to feel nervous. The principal French West Indies base was an easy day's sail away, and the nearest British naval help was more than twice that distance. Any assistance from the Leeward Islands Squadron had a built-in week's delay, and by that time a determined French landing force could have overcome the forts and taken Bridgetown. Then, secure against anything other than a regular army, which didn't exist this side of the Atlantic, they could thumb their noses at Frankland's squadron. Anson certainly understood the necessity of a regular flow of wealth from the Colonies to pay for this war. However, in this first year of the conflict, he was at a loss to find the resources to adequately defend them while at the same time maintaining a sufficiently strong Western Squadron in the Channel to prevent the invasion of England.

Money was the key to victory over France, and Carlisle like most of his contemporaries understood the truth of the common saying, that the City of London was at the front line of the conflict. It had been said that the French could never run out of men and the British could never run out of money. The first part of that was correct, but the second part depended upon the navy's uninterrupted command of the sea. There was an essential symbiosis between the navy and the wealth of the nation; the navy was vastly expensive, and it needed a constant supply of money to pay for ships and men. The traders who generated the wealth of the nation that paid for those ships and men needed the navy to secure their lines of supply. The two were inseparable, and neither could stand without the other.

This short interlude ashore had strangely unsettled Carlisle. Barbados was a well-established colony; a jewel in the crown for a hundred and thirty years and a steady exporter of wealth to enrich the City of London, the investors and the landowners. That wealth had percolated down through British society; it was the reason that Britain, that small island on the edge of the European continent, could afford the build and man a navy that could challenge any other two of the great powers in combination. Barbados had become wealthy in its own right and with its rows of neat houses and its harbour, it resembled in style a fashionable English seaside town in the height of summer. Carlisle was struck by the ordinariness of it all, the carriages and the street vendors, the almost-fashionable dresses and the broadcloth suits of the men. How he envied the militia officers and their ladies strolling on the promenade. He had forgotten about the way that society in these islands strove so hard to mimic the home country, how so much effort was expended to make the islands attractive enough that the planters' families should wish to join them there, despite the harsh sun and the risk of disease. It simply hadn't occurred to him that, with his ship ordered to the Leeward Islands Squadron, possibly for years to come, he could have a normal family life in Antigua. In a moment of self-indulgence, he allowed himself to imagine life with Chiara at English Harbour. The small house and garden with a few servants – he could certainly afford that much by drawing an advance from his prize agent. Deployments from English Harbour were generally short, most cruises lasting days or weeks rather than months. In many ways it was an ideal place to bring a wife. But even as he dreamed, he knew that it could not be. He and Chiara were not married, not even engaged to be married, and surely the Viscountess Angelini would never allow her niece to travel to the West Indies without a wedding. 'It's only a daydream,' he thought, 'but I can allow myself to dream once in a while.' He quickly turned his mind back to his ship and his squadron, but he was unprepared for the almost physical shock of leaving that dream. It had seemed so possible for those brief few minutes, and he left it behind with regret and a sharp intake of breath – almost a sob.

Barbados was behind them now and Carlisle was walking the quarterdeck of his own ship. 'To hell with *Wessex*!' he thought, 'and to hell with Godwin.' He had moved back into *Medina* with real relief. *Wessex* was a broken ship for now. He doubted whether, under the morose and glowering first lieutenant, they were an effective fighting force at all. But he knew the limits of what he could achieve and with English Harbour only three days away he was inclined to hand the problem over to the admiral. The difficulty lay in the structure of naval command at sea. *He* had been appointed to command His Britannic Majesty's frigate *Medina*, nothing more. Godwin had been appointed first lieutenant and therefore second-in-command of His Majesty's ship-of-the-line *Wessex*. With the death of Jermy, there was no question about who succeeded him until the ship should again come under the command of an admiral, therefor Godwin commanded. The question of succession to command of the squadron was equally clear-cut. In principle, the squadron was small enough that it didn't need a commodore, and the navy had a very direct way of dealing with these *ad hoc* command situations: *where two or more of His Majesty's ships are gathered together, the senior captain shall command.* Carlisle as the senior of the two commanding officers, even though he commanded the smaller ship, was clearly the commander of the squadron. But that didn't make him a commodore, nor did it give him any authority over the inner workings of *Wessex*. His interference so far had only been possible because Godwin had been placed at a moral disadvantage after having withdrawn the squadron from Port Louis without authority. A grave offence and capable of being taken to court martial if Admiral Frankland felt ill-disposed. So, *Wessex's* command problems must wait, and Carlisle must hope that he didn't have to take the squadron into action in the next three days before the responsibility would be taken from him. His concern now was how much of his suspicions and fears he should reveal to the admiral. He had to weigh the obvious need for *Wessex* to be returned to a useful fighting unit against the possible damage to the officer corps, with one relatively junior captain making complaints, that could become formalised, against a senior lieutenant. Well, Carlisle would see how he was received by the admiral and what his plans were for the command of *Wessex*. At least the admiral wouldn't promote Godwin into the post; there were sure to be some favoured frigate captains under his command just waiting for such an opportunity.

Carlisle looked over his temporary squadron. He had placed *Medina* in the lead, more to establish his right to command than for any sound tactical or navigational reasons. *Wessex* brought up the rear with the prize nestled between them, protected from any predators. He was keeping well to windward of the island chain, but even so, he was very close to the area where *Warwick* was taken in March. He didn't want to take any chances with a dysfunctional fifty-gun ship, a frigate and an undermanned prize against a potential French squadron headed by one of their excellent seventy-fours.

The privateer had no name painted on her, and it was only in Barbados that Lieutenant Curtis revealed that he had found her name, *Duc de Choiseul,* in the logs. Carlisle had heard of him, or more accurately he had heard of the whole Choiseul clan, who were fast becoming the leaders of French foreign affairs. Whoever commissioned this private man-of-war had an eye to heavyweight patronage. If the admiral bought her into the service, would he give her a new name? It was amusing to guess what British sailors would make of her; they had a talent for nicknames for their ships, notably when the official name was French. *Cheesy Duck*, perhaps? He had given the command to Lieutenant Curtis in recognition of the part he had played in running the smoking schooner under the ramparts of Fort Royal. That was a courageous act that deserved credit and, in any case, the ship was too large for a midshipman to command on an ocean passage. Smith had been disappointed but buoyed up by the kind words that his captain had for him. The young man had tasted action, had acquitted himself well and could bask for a while in the glow of success.

The squadron would be in English Harbour on Friday, perhaps on Thursday evening if the wind held; if *Wessex* could squeeze an extra half knot of speed and if the land breeze didn't set in too early. English Harbour was on the south coast of Antigua and very convenient for a ship approaching from the southeast, but there was no getting in once the land breeze had started. It was a long and frustrating night at sea for any ship that arrived too late, keeping to windward for an easy approach in the early morning.

The sun was near its zenith, high overhead in these equatorial latitudes. The planks were warm underfoot, and the quarterdeck four-pounders were only just cooled sufficiently by the breeze to comfortably rest a hand upon. The ship heeled to the steady trade wind and buried her bow in each advancing wave, to spread a scintillating spray across the fo'c'sle and waist. Looking over the side, Carlisle was just in time to see a shoal of flying fish leave their natural environment and take to the air. Their elongated pectoral fins were extended, and their tails left that characteristically repetitive oscillating line in the surface of the sea. Carlisle had wondered about that snake-like wake, and now, when he was least expecting it and not really analysing it at all, its purpose came to him. Of course! That was the last effort of the fish's tail working furiously side-to-side to achieve sufficient speed for it to break the surface and start its glide. This new knowledge was only a little thing perhaps, but it made Carlisle inexpressibly happy.

Holbrooke was sat in his cabin, checking the watch and station bill. The allocation of men to their watches and stations should be easy. It was determined at the beginning of a commission and in principle was only changed when death or transfer to another ship created a hole to be filled. But in practice, it was a dynamic document that needed to constantly change as the qualities of individuals became better known and as seamen requested to change their messes or as their messes requested to change their membership. Was number seven gun a little slow at Port Louis? Would it benefit from a new second gun captain, perhaps taking one of the brightest from number eleven gun? Number eleven's gun crew was working together brilliantly; would replacing one of them make the whole smooth machinery fall apart?

A knock at his door disturbed Holbrooke's concentration. 'Oh well,' he thought, 'it's getting late anyway, I'll think about this tomorrow. Perhaps I'll ask Jackson to give me his opinion; he knows these men better than anyone.'

But Holbrooke was surprised to see that it was Jackson himself who had knocked at his door. His surprise was not only because he had just been thinking about the captain's coxswain, but also because it was not at all usual for anyone below the rank of warrant officer to seek out the first lieutenant in his cabin. It was only the trusted position that Jackson held as the captain's coxswain that allowed him to penetrate this far into the after part of the ship without being challenged. But it was a pleasant surprise, nevertheless. Holbrooke trusted Jackson, he felt that they worked well together, and he owed the coxswain a debt of gratitude for the way that he had followed Holbrooke onto the deck of *Vulcain* back in the Straits of Bonifacio, in the far distant Mediterranean.

'Jackson, good afternoon to you. Please come in.' The first lieutenant's quarters in a frigate were not large, and Holbrooke could hardly offer Jackson a seat, even if that were possible in the relationship between an officer and a rating. Jackson was more comfortable standing, in any case.

Jackson nodded towards the watch and station bill, 'I see you are working on that still sir, it's a never-ending task, isn't it?'

'Yes, I was just considering number seven gun, I feel that they may need a new second. What do you think?'

Jackson looked over at the sheet of paper on Holbrooke's tiny desk. 'They are certainly the weakest. Have you considered taking Fleming from number five, sir?

'I hadn't. Is Fleming ready for it?'

'I reckon so, sir. He's bright, and the other men follow him. He knows his gun drills too.'

'Very well, I'll consider that, thank you, Jackson.' He made some pencil notes in the margins.

'Now, I can't believe you have the second sight, Jackson. I have to believe it was sheer coincidence that brought you here when I needed you. But what can I do for you?'

'Well, sir. I was thinking about my future ...'

Tentatively at first and then with growing confidence,

the two men talked frankly to each other for the rest of Jackson's watch below deck. Holbrooke had not yet seen himself as having followers, but he knew that if he achieved promotion to commander, then he would have to consider how he built up a following to support his career. He knew that sea officer's careers were built on the exploitation of patronage and interest, and he knew that it worked downwards as well as upwards. If Holbrooke wanted to have competent men around him whom he trusted, he needed to nurture that trust. Yes, if he should be whisked away from *Medina* to command a sloop, he would want a nucleus of his own people. What Jackson was doing now, was to offer that loyalty when the time came.

And yet it was a tricky conversation. Loyalty to Holbrooke could be construed as disloyalty to Carlisle. A captain's coxswain was a member of the captain's inner circle of allegiance and patronage, and there was no knowing how Carlisle would respond if he knew about this conversation.

They parted with an understanding. Holbrooke considered but then rejected the idea of mentioning this to Carlisle. It wasn't a lack of loyalty that stopped him, it was a desire to avoid burdening his captain with what-ifs and maybes.

Jackson returned to the lower deck just in time for his watch to be called. He was satisfied with the meeting with the first lieutenant. If Holbrooke should be promoted, then he had a good chance of following the young lieutenant and picking up a bosun's warrant. If he should not be, then he would just have to wait for dead men's boots to achieve it. Either way, he was content.

CHAPTER SIXTEEN

English Harbour

Thursday, thirtieth of December 1756
Medina, at Anchor, English Harbour

They did indeed reach English Harbour before the land breeze, passing the familiar yet still curious rock formation around the point to the east of Halfmoon battery, looking for all the world like the after-lunch efforts of a drunken ecclesiastical mason. Pounded by the wind and sea, they had been carved into fantastic overweight parodies of great gothic pillars.

'Did you know that your father used to bow whenever we passed those rocks?' Carlisle asked Holbrooke, who looked mystified and shook his head. 'Apparently, they reminded him of Winchester Cathedral. He always told me that there is a famous fisherman buried there – he was paying his respects at long range.' Holbrooke's grin lit up his worried face; all first lieutenants are anxious coming into a new anchorage for the first time and with a ship about to come under the gaze of a commander-in-chief. 'Oh, of course, Izaak Walton. He is buried at Winchester, or at least there is a memorial to him in the cathedral. How like my father. Fly-fishing is his passion.' He spared a moment to look at the peculiar rock formations, looked around to check that nobody was watching, bowed briefly, then turned back to his duties.

They ghosted past Fort Berkeley and anchored just to the south of King's Yard in five fathoms of water on the dying gasps of the northeast trade wind. Sir Thomas Frankland's flag was flying in *Winchester*, lying a little further out in Freeman's Bay. *Medina's* thirteen-gun salute echoed back from the scrub-covered hills in the almost still air, answered with eleven from the flagship. Another finely balanced decision for Carlisle. Strictly speaking, with the death of the commodore they were no longer a squadron, and each of the two ships should have saluted the flag independently. But Carlisle had told Godwin not to fire a salute, in fact, he had put that order in writing before they left Barbados. His decision was made partly to assert his authority and partly to save His Majesty the cost of thirteen charges of powder. It was a decision that Frankland could easily take exception to if he should choose to put this young frigate captain in his place. Now, of course, there was no question of the continued existence of their small squadron. With the last of the thirteen guns, both ships had formally become part of the Leeward Islands Squadron, the greater part of which – the flagship, two sixties and a fifty – lay at anchor before them. On each of Carlisle's three ships, the red ensign – the default colours for ships sailing on Admiralty orders – was lowered and replaced by the white ensign, in recognition of their change of command.

English Harbour had developed considerably since Carlisle's last visit. The facilities on the western side of the bay had been improved, and the focus of naval activity had moved across the harbour from the careening wharf to King's Yard. As well as the careening berths and the same old hulk being used as a jetty, there was a small victualling yard and an ordnance yard. A naval hospital was being contemplated, but Carlisle had heard of no definite plans. The harbour was well protected by Fort Berkeley and the Halfmoon Battery facing each other across a bare cable of navigable water. It would take a bold enemy to force that passage. Carlisle idly wondered whether a pair of fire ships loaded with damp hay would have the same effect on these English gunners as they had at Fort Louis. It all depended upon the wind, he decided, but if the circumstances were right, it would be worth trying.

The harbour was very well sheltered from the weather

and impervious to the great swells that could so quickly build up, but compared with Port Royal at Jamaica, or with any other British naval base, English Harbour was a modest affair. The inner anchorages were too shallow for the new, larger seventy-fours, there was no accommodation for the crews while their ships were stripped out for careening and, worst of all, there was no dry dock. It would do for a frigate or a fourth-rate, but it was not a comfortable base for a third rate, which would be largely confined to anchoring in Freeman's Bay.

Captain Carlisle was rowed across to *Winchester* in his pinnace, his boats crew as smartly turned out as they could be, clean-shaven and freshly outfitted from the slop chest. The process of a newly arrived captain calling on the commander-in-chief, particularly on a station as observant of naval protocol as the Leeward Islands, was like a formal dance, a tribal ritual that was carried out with all the gravity that a man-of-war's crew could assemble. The incoming captain lost no time in making his call. Unless he was protected by significantly more patronage than Carlisle could muster, he would leave the detail of securing the ship in her anchor berth to his first lieutenant and make all haste towards the flagship. Ideally his boat would leave the ship even before she had settled back on her anchor cable. His boat would be rowed swiftly, but rowed *dry* – no spray was to touch the captain in his best uniform – a significant challenge in a naval boat where the captain always sat in the stern sheets, the natural destination for any spray from a carelessly handled oar. As the boat approached the starboard side of the flagship, a hail would come from the quarterdeck, 'boat ahoy!' to be answered by the coxswain of the boat with the name of his ship, '*Medina*,' thus informing the flagship that the captain of *Medina* was in the boat. Side boys would run down the side of the ship laying out baize-covered man-ropes to assist the great personage in his way into the entry-port. He would be piped aboard to the ritual tune of low, high and low notes on the bosun's call, derived from the whistled orders to haul away at the ropes to swing him onboard in a bosun's chair, in the days when that was the normal way of entering a ship. The flag captain would be on hand to greet him, with a representative selection of the flagship's officers lined up behind him. Hats would be removed, and introductions made, before the captain was conveyed to the great cabin to meet the admiral.

The ceremony was proceeding well until it became apparent to Carlisle that the flagship was not expecting him. There was a flurry of activity, officers scrambling for their hats and swords, man-ropes being rigged at the rush and side-boys cuffed and bullied into their stations. Carlisle was prepared to be offended. The flagship must have realised that Jermy was not commanding, his broad pennant was not flying in *Wessex* and the boat had come from *Medina*, a frigate, not the ship-of-the-line as they may have expected. 'Could this be a deliberate snub?' he thought. He climbed the few steps up the ship's side and in through the entry port, stiff-necked and ready to take offence. The pipes twittered, hats were removed from heads, and a harassed-looking lieutenant stepped forward to introduce himself. Carlisle was considering whether he should turn on his heel and return to his boat. This was an unpardonable breach of etiquette. 'Could it be aimed at me personally?' he thought. He stood, grim-faced as the lieutenant stumbled through an apology. He explained to the stony-faced captain that the admiral and his flag captain conducted their business from an office ashore, for convenience, but the flag remained in the flagship. He was aware that this could cause confusion in a newly arrived captain, perhaps Commodore Jermy had been informed before he left England? But here his explanation tailed off as he realised that he was on the point of quizzing a post-captain about the whereabouts of a commodore, under the nervous gaze of the ship's officers, the bosun's mates and the terrified side boys.

Carlisle started to relax, he could see the amusing side of this misunderstanding. Undoubtedly Jermy had been warned about this unusual arrangement, probably he had told Godwin, and it would be in character for that unpleasant and vindictive officer to withhold this critical information. More bows, the pipes twittered again, and he was back in his boat heading now for King's Yard. The rowers looked neither to the left or the right, they just rowed, their faces expressionless. The coxswain didn't even need the formal growl of *'eyes in the boat,'* to keep them to their business. They knew that something had gone wrong with the protocol of a call on the commander-in-chief, and no good could come from acknowledging that, by a word or a look.

The flag captain met him at the steps of the small house, set back a few paces from King's Yard on the scrubby hillside. It was hardly the suitable residence of an admiral, a member of parliament and commander-in-chief all combined in a single person, but it was in tune with the general feel of English Harbour, a naval backwater and a work in progress. Frankland's flag captain was the captain of *Winchester*, a few years older than Carlisle, but only a few months senior as a post-captain. Sir Edward Le Cras had spent a long time as a commander, right through the peace, and was only posted when the navy started expanding two years before. He and Carlisle had both benefited from the same opportunities for promotion that opened on rumours of war. He was a little junior for command of a fifty-gun ship, but then it was a flagship, and so he was nominally always under the eye of the admiral. Nevertheless, Le Cras' present position meant that he was not a man whom Carlisle should treat lightly. In any case, he had quite recovered from his anger at his reception in *Winchester* and was inclined to be friendly.

Captain Le Cras understood the situation immediately.

He politely asked about the commodore, expressed his shock and distress, but still managed to move Carlisle swiftly through to the presence of the Admiral. 'You are to be shown in directly,' he said as he opened the door to a large but ill-lit room. The admiral was sitting on a chaise longue positioned under the window at the back of the room, not at his desk. He had evidently been reading some papers by the last light of the setting sun, which soon would dip below the hills that enclosed the naval yard to the west.

Rear Admiral of the White Thomas Frankland was an unremarkable person. He was the second son of an East India Company director who had been governor of Fort William in Bengal at the time of Thomas' birth. He was also the second-born nephew of a childless baronet who had been a commissioner of the Admiralty Board when Thomas entered the navy. This relationship made Thomas the *Spare Dick*, as naval humour would mercilessly describe him, one brotherly heart-beat away from the baronetcy. His uncle had still been in post at the Admiralty when Thomas passed for lieutenant, which explains how he had been commissioned at the very early age of nineteen, even though Britain was at that time enjoying an unusually long period of peace. He was the MP for the family borough of Thirsk, which he held in the government interest, so he wielded significant patronage. Frankland had been at sea since he was thirteen, through peace and war, and had already gathered a certain amount of both fame and infamy.

In 1742, when in command of the small frigate *Rose* in the Bahamas, Frankland had taken a Spanish privateer, the *San Juan Bautista*. The vessel was commanded by none other than Juan de León Fandiño, the man who had cut off the ear of Captain Jenkins in 1731. That action, eight years later, had given Britain the *casus belli* for renewed war with Spain. In 1744, *Rose* was again in the news, having taken the Spanish treasure ship *Concepcion* of twenty-four guns, bound from Cartagena to Havana. The prize had a staggeringly rich cargo – gold, silver and jewels – the dream of every sea officer. However, Frankland had not chosen to condemn his prize by legal process, and the full value was in dispute and likely to rumble through the courts for years to come. It was said that Frankland had distributed the booty by the simple expedient of dividing the gold and silver by weight. Then after the original division of the spoils, he had found two chests of specie hidden in the hold. So vast was the first haul of precious metals and gems that this additional find of 20,000 and 30,000 pistoles was regarded as trivial in comparison.

Frankland had started his tenure as commander-in-chief of the Leeward Island Station by demanding that his predecessor, Thomas Pye, who was junior to Frankland, haul down his broad pennant as soon as he was superseded. This was strictly correct, but most men would have allowed the outgoing commander-in-chief to retain the symbols of his dignity as he left the station. Pye argued the point and was now awaiting court martial in Britain, a sorry affair that reflected poorly upon the brotherhood of sea officers.

This, then, was the man that Carlisle was about to meet. The man to whom he would owe allegiance for as long as *Medina* remained on the Leeward Islands Station.

'Captain Carlisle of *Medina*,' said Le Cras by way of introduction. 'Commodore Jermy died on the passage,' he added, rather brutally. Frankland looked up and raised an eyebrow. He stood and formally shook Carlisle's hand.

'Well, I'm pleased to see you, captain. We noticed the lack of a pennant but weren't sure whether that merely meant that Jermy had been superseded and the squadron had sailed without a commodore, although the packet has been and gone since you sailed from Sheerness, with no word of such a change. Those are your reports?' he asked, gesturing towards the thick, sealed envelope that Carlisle carried. 'Put them on the desk, my clerk will deal with them later,' he motioned to a seat beside his desk, 'but I will take a verbal report now if you please. Captain Le Cras, please stay unless you have urgent business elsewhere. I suspect this will be worth listening to.'

The admiral rang a small bell at his desk, and an African servant entered. Carlisle was disorientated for a moment – the scene was so reminiscent of his home in Virginia – until he remembered that African slaves were employed at the naval yard and Sir Thomas himself was a noted slave-owner. In fact, some sea officers wondered what took most of his time, his duties as commander-in-chief or his commercial interests. 'A glass of punch, Captain Carlisle?'

'With pleasure sir. If I may start with the commodore's death?'

'Certainly, then I would like to hear what you achieved at Port Louis; I can see that you have taken a prize.' The *Duc de Choiseul* was clearly visible, caught in the last rays of the setting sun. She was riding at anchor just off the careening wharf, her ensign staff proudly flying the white ensign over the French colours. Frankland could take pleasure in the sight, but he wasn't fooled by the white ensign, he personally gained nothing in the division of prize money. *Medina* and *Wessex* had been sailing under Admiralty orders when she was taken, and the commander-in-chief of the station was not entitled to a penny.

Carlisle chose his words carefully. He had been rehearsing for this moment since they left Barbados. He had little fear of being disbelieved, but it was essential to set the chronology straight so that his own decision regarding the command of the squadron should be unimpeachable.

'First, I should state that the cause of Commodore Jermy's death is uncertain.' Frankland frowned and fidgeted with a paperweight on his desk. The unexplained death of a commodore didn't sound pleasant and would be sure to cause a great deal of correspondence with the Admiralty and with his family.

'He collapsed during the first attack on Port Louis…'

'Wait!' said Frankland, holding up his hand, palm outward. 'There was more than one attack?' he asked, frowning.

'Yes, sir. The first attack on the nineteenth of December achieved little, so we attacked again on the twenty-first, with better success.'

'I see, and Commodore Jermy ordered both the first and second attacks?' Frankland had seized on the critical point immediately, he was no fool, Carlisle would have to be careful. This was not going the way that he intended. His carefully crafted narrative had been disrupted before it had really started.

'No sir, the commodore ordered the first attack but was incapacitated towards the end of that engagement. I ordered the second attack; the commodore knew nothing of it. He was unconscious in his cabin.'

It was vital not to dwell on the uncomfortable fact that Jermy had ordered a withdrawal before he was disabled. That would come out in the story, but Carlisle needed to frame it as a temporary withdrawal, not an abandonment of the attempt on Port Louis. Otherwise, it would appear that he had reversed a decision of his superior as soon as he was incapacitated. In all honesty, neither Carlisle nor anyone else could know what Jermy had intended. He had fallen before he could make clear to his first lieutenant or his sailing master whether the squadron's withdrawal was merely a re-grouping for a second attack or a permanent cessation of the attempt against Port Louis. Privately, Carlisle believed it was the latter. Jermy may have been the most active and courageous of officers before he became ill, but such constant and obvious pain clouds a man's judgement. Everything that Carlisle knew about Jermy in the last two months before his death suggested that his order to withdraw was the final act in his attempt on the French in Grenada.

Carlisle continued before Frankland had time to phrase another question. 'The commodore collapsed on his quarterdeck immediately following his order for the squadron to retire in the face of persistent and accurate fire from the fort – twenty-four-pound heated shot and nine-pounders. He had given no orders for a withdrawal to Barbados, and I was confident that a man of Mister Jermy's character wouldn't have contemplated abandoning the task before it was completed.' He looked squarely at the admiral, challenging him to disagree. 'The commodore didn't regain consciousness, and I considered it my duty to continue the task that he'd started and make another attack as soon as the damage to *Wessex* had been repaired.'

Frankland rose from the desk and picked up Carlisle's report, still sealed and unread. He appeared to be weighing it. 'I'll need to read your report before I make any further comment, Captain Carlisle. Meanwhile, there are three points I would like you to address,' he counted them off on his fingers for emphasis. 'First, when and how did Commodore Jermy die and where is his body now? Second, what damage did you inflict upon the French at Port Louis? And third, what's the damage to *Wessex* and *Medina*? I must decide whether another expedition against Grenada is required.'

Carlisle outlined the last days of commodore Jermy, his unchanging state, his lack of response and his eventual peaceful death and burial at Needhams Point. There was nothing that anyone in *Wessex* – and he was thinking principally about Godwin – could do to alter the facts. Carlisle had seen the surgeon's report. It had been reviewed and endorsed by his own surgeon, and the circumstances of the burial were uncontroversial. He knew that it had been the right decision to have Jermy buried at Barbados. In the cold light of an interview with the commander-in-chief, Carlisle could see how a burial at sea would have looked. It would have smacked of irreverence at best, subterfuge at worst.

The damage to the French required more careful explanation. It was not clear in the Admiralty orders what level of damage would be considered a success. The orders, which he had only read for himself after the first attack, spoke merely of *'destroying the privateers lying at Port Louis.'* There had been only three vessels that were clearly and unquestionably privateers, and he had sunk two of them and taken one. All the others in the port were merchantmen, although it was impossible to know whether any of them carried a letter of marque. They could, of course, be part-time merchantmen and part-time privateers as was the standard practice for both nations when away from home waters, ready to take a weaker British ship when the opportunity arose. In any case, he had burned and sunk a good number of those, and at least half of them would never sail again. Most of that had been achieved in the second attack. All that could be said for the first attack was that they had taken the schooner laden with hay – a poor exchange for the damage to *Wessex*.

Frankland heard his report without further comment. He left his flag captain to probe Carlisle about specific timings and the details of the vessels that were taken, burned and destroyed. Carlisle came with relief to an end of his narrative, with the squadron sailing from Carlisle Bay for English Harbour. It had gone better than he had expected after the first few interruptions. In fairness to the admiral, this unknown post-captain's actions had the potential to cause embarrassment. Jermy had friends in Britain, friends with political interest, no doubt. The fact of a man, even a commodore, dying in the West Indies within a few days of arriving was hardly a great surprise. Both the Leeward Islands Station and the Jamaica Station were notorious for a range of deadly diseases which were most dangerous to those newly arrived in the area. But any question of premature withdrawal, with accusations of cowardice lurking not far below the surface, could cause a political storm, and Frankland wanted none of it. Carlisle knew that his factual account of the two attacks and his assertion that Jermy had intended a second attack, would make much better reading than the alternative story, a senior sea officer incapacitated by disease, withdrawing after a pitiful attempt to obey his orders. That was not the narrative that their Lordships wished to hear.

Carlisle knew that his report, as written, would not be questioned. The attack on Port Louis and the destruction of the privateers would be hailed as a success – a modest, but significant feat of arms in the finest traditions of the service. None of the men in that room had any illusions. The three French privateers would be rapidly replaced by others; the privately funded war on British commerce was just too lucrative to be abandoned because of this irksome defeat. Grenada's privateers had suffered a temporary setback, nothing more. Nevertheless, Jermy's expedition would be remembered as a victory while Carlisle's name would appear as a footnote, at best. It was a little galling to realise that Jermy would take the posthumous credit for Carlisle's initiative and tactical genius, but that was the way of the service, and it would do no good complaining or feeling cheated. In the eyes of the British public and the political leadership, the damage to *Wessex* would even enhance the victory; it would be proof that the triumph had been hard-won. In any case, *Wessex's* poop deck and the great cabin could be repaired by the shipwrights at English Harbour in a few weeks, while *Medina* could proceed to sea with only a few days' labour to bring her back to full fighting trim.

Frankland seemed satisfied, relieved even. He may have guessed at the likely true nature of Jermy's decision to withdraw, but he could be sure that it wouldn't come out in Carlisle's report. The admiral had one more question for Carlisle. All the previous questions had been inevitable –

they were the general daily business of a commander-in-chief who would have been doing less than his duty if he had not asked them. Carlisle had hoped to avoid this last question, but he should have known, after Frankland's first interruption, that the admiral's intuition was keenly tuned. He missed nothing and saw through any evasions.

'Then tell me, captain, what is your impression of the leadership in *Wessex*? I will have to appoint a new captain of course, but how have her officers managed in the absence of Jermy?'

Carlisle hadn't wanted to answer this question, but he had spent more time in formulating a reply to this than he had over all the rest of his report. Long and hard he had pondered, but until that moment he hadn't decided how he would respond. It was not in the usual traditions of the service, as Carlisle understood them, to act as an informer against his brother officers. The efficiency of the fleet depended upon mutual trust among the commission and warrant officers. And of course, he could be wrong about his suspicions. But right or wrong, his testimony could destroy the careers of officers who were merely caught off balance by the slow progress from sickness to death of their captain. If that were the case, then he should tell the admiral that all was well in *Wessex*.

Alternatively, he could tell the truth about what he had observed at first hand. The lack of communication among the lieutenants and warrant officers, the atmosphere of fear, jealousy and mutual suspicion, the probability that the crew would not follow their leadership. And his suspicion, nay certainty, that the first lieutenant was at the centre of the problem. He didn't believe the other officers were at fault; he positively liked the sailing master, while the other lieutenants appeared an average assortment of their kind. But Godwin! At that moment he had a mental picture of the first lieutenant of *Wessex* smirking at him as Carlisle realised that Jermy had shared the secret of their destination with his first lieutenant but not with himself, the second in command of the squadron! God help him, but there was a sweetness in revenge, particularly when – and he knew this the instant he had made up his mind – it coincided the good of the service.

Carlisle tried to look like a man who was disinterestedly giving his opinion. No acrimony, no partiality – that was a hard part to act. He drew back his shoulders and looked Frankland full in the face. He had the curious feeling of the rest of the room fading away, of nothing left but the admiral's face. Like the view through a telescope when the subject fills the lens and all else beyond the indistinct circular boundary is invisible. 'Jermy has a decent set of officers,' he paused, 'but I fear that his first lieutenant took advantage of his illness on the passage from Sheerness to create an, ah, unfortunate atmosphere in the ship.'

Frankland's face was a mask. 'Go on,' he said, but moved not a muscle, regarding this new addition to his command as one would a cask of suspect beef. The thought flashed through Carlisle's mind, 'have I misjudged the temper of this man? Am I about to destroy my reputation on this station before I have hardly arrived?'

'There is no trust between the officers and they all appear to fear the first lieutenant. Of course, it's good that the first lieutenant has authority, but Lieutenant Godwin has taken it too far. The men do their duty, but their hearts are not in it. I moved onboard *Wessex* for the second attack and observed for myself the lack of willingness in the men. Commodore Jermy was sick before we left Sheerness and his ship has gone downhill without his guidance. They need a new captain and my recommendation would be to remove the first lieutenant to another position.'

A commander-in-chief on a foreign station had the power to move officers from one ship to another, safe in the knowledge that their Lordships, or more accurately the secretary to the board, would confirm and formalise that move. Carlisle also knew that they didn't like doing it.

Each action that required their Lordships' endorsement was one more small expenditure of the stock of authority that they had, the authority derived from their Lordships that could be eaten away too quickly if used frivolously.

'Do you believe that any more formal action should be taken against this first lieutenant, Captain?' asked Frankland.

Carlisle didn't pause. Giving the admiral the facts was right and proper but asking for a court martial – and that was what Frankland meant by *more formal action* – smacked of vindictiveness. 'No sir, I believe a move to another ship will be sufficient.'

'Very well Carlisle,' replied Frankland, 'thank you for your observations.' The admiral's use of his name in this collegiate manner without the formal 'Captain,' gave Carlisle hope that his assessment was not being disregarded. The lens of the telescope expanded, and the rest of the room came into view. Frankland looked over to his flag captain. 'Le Cras, would you look into this tomorrow? Go over to *Wessex* and assess the situation for me. I want to be able to give her a new captain before the end of the day, so I will expect your verbal report by noon.'

The Leeward Islands Squadron

CHAPTER SEVENTEEN

A Cruise

Monday, thirty-first of January 1757
Medina, at Sea, English Harbour west-northwest 10 leagues

Medina was battling against the trade wind, the fresh breeze on her bow filling her sails and her hull parting the blue swell and sending it surging aft in foaming white ruin. She had sailed that morning and was enjoying her break from the stifling authority of the commander-in-chief. English Harbour was a delightful spot; there were taverns ashore for the men, and the island was small enough that shore leave could be given without a severe risk of desertion. Of course, there was plenty of straggling – the casual lateness in returning from shore leave – bet it was not viewed with any particular severity. Unless the ship was under sailing orders, it wasn't a flogging offence, and the men knew it. But for a first lieutenant, English Harbour was a waking nightmare. The ship could be seen in great detail from the admiral's house behind King's Yard and in even greater detail from his flagship. In consequence, every detail of her upper decks and rigging was on display for critical inspection from dawn to dusk. The yards had to be precisely crossed at all times; a yard acockbill was regarded with a quasi-religious horror, an abomination to be exorcised with a full public censure for the instigator. Washing was only to be dried on one day of the week, sails were to be in immaculate harbour stow. Provisions, water, wood; all were to be struck below almost before they had been swung aboard. And the boats! The Leeward Islands Squadron gave birth to the expression *'a ship is known by her boats.'* Woe betide any midshipman who allowed any lack of concentration in his oarsmen that caused a missed stroke. There were always eyes ashore or on the flagship ready to spot such affronts to naval manners.

Holbrooke was therefore glad to be at sea. The liquor from the night before had dissipated, and he felt like a whole man again. He had not lost any of the crew unless you counted the two who had been landed to billets in Falmouth with various ailments. He had not even had to deal with the aftermath of fights with the soldiers from Monkshill Fort because after the first few nights there had been an uneasy truce, the sailors and soldiers agreeing to disagree on almost everything. Like himself, the crew had largely forgotten the excesses of the night before, and they had sailed at first light before there were too many watchers ashore and before the beginning of the sea breeze made it necessary to tow out of the harbour.

Medina had orders for what was in effect an independent cruise. They were to look into Basse Terre and Fort Louis at Guadeloupe, then on to the commercial port of St. Pierre and thence to Fort Royal at Martinique, the principal French naval base in the Caribbean. From there they were to head south to Grenada to check on the progress of repairs at the privateering base. So far, this was the everyday life of a cruiser of the Leeward Islands Squadron, but the second part of the orders was more interesting. They were to take the windward route north, staying to the east of the islands, picking up any prizes that they could along the way. They were then ordered to cruise to the north and east of Antigua, looking out for any trade heading towards the French territories in Lower Louisiana via the Old Straits of Bahama.

This looked almost like a peacetime yachting trip compared with being the junior ship in a squadron commanded by a sick commodore on an unrealistically tough mission. Except for those French seventy-fours at Port Royal. They were such swift and manoeuvrable ships that in most conditions they could out-sail – and undoubtedly out-fight – the relatively clumsy British frigates. That would be an ignominious end to their cruise. Holbrooke looked up at the maintop, 'keep a good look out there,' he bellowed, 'we are close to the French navy base.' A superfluous order but it made him feel better and confirmed that he could now shout without feeling that his head might explode.

The distances in this island chain still surprised Holbrooke. They were a mere thirty miles from English Harbour, but already French Guadeloupe was only twenty miles ahead, the lookout had reported the high land on his starboard bow thirty minutes ago, and Fort Royal was less than two hundred miles to the south. The navigation was also quite unlike anywhere else he had sailed. In the Channel, you could rely on using the tide to help you to your destination if the wind persisted foul. In the Mediterranean, the wind changed direction frequently. But here, the northwest trade winds dominated and there was no significant shifting tidal current to help, so the art of navigation was to jealously hoard your windward position, only giving it up grudgingly and when necessary. *Medina* was, therefore, close hauled to the trade wind, her bowlines and sheets bar-taught as the helmsmen fought to win every foot to windward in defiance of the wind. They were planning to pass in the night around the eastern side of Guadeloupe and its outlying island of La Desirade, then run downwind to Fort Louis to be off the port at first light. There was no knowing how the sea breeze would behave in that great southern bight, between Grand Terre and Basse Terre, but it was broad enough to tack out of if necessary.

A significant inclination of the mate-of-the-watch's head towards the ladder at the break of the quarterdeck warned Holbrooke that the captain was on his way up. Clutching his telescope, he part-walked, part-tottered down to the leeward side, taking a grip on the binnacle to avoid arriving in an undignified heap. The deck was angled like the pitch of a roof as the trade wind heeled the frigate to starboard.

Carlisle staggered as he reached the quarterdeck and the full force of the wind caught him. The helmsmen glanced at each other, not daring to risk a smile, and looked away quickly, painfully aware that their blank faces could not long withstand an exchange of knowing looks. It was an acknowledged fact among the crew that their captain took a few days to regain his sea-legs after a spell at anchor. Nobody had ever caught him being sea-sick, but it was widely suspected that he occasionally succumbed. And by the curious ethics of the lower deck, they loved him for this weakness. He stood for a few moments looking to windward, a sure sign of *mal-de-mer* according to sailors, who believed that gulping in mouthfuls of fresh air helped. They were right about the fresh air, but on this occasion, they were wrong about their captain's weakness. Carlisle was feeling perfectly well and was innocently bathing in this sense of freedom after a month in English Harbour. He *was* sometimes seasick, but he had long ago persuaded himself that it was only when the tide set against the wind, so the Mediterranean and the Caribbean were safe, as were all ocean passages, but the channel was a waking nightmare. Even the term used by sailors to describe the southwest approaches; *The Chops of the Channel*, made him turn green and long for firm ground. Having this cause and effect firmly fixed in his mind, he had felt no discomfort since *Medina* had cleared Ushant.

'Well Mister Holbrooke, how are we progressing?' He walked cautiously down to the binnacle and studied the traverse board as he spoke. He could see the half-hour pegs all in a straight line with no breaks in the pattern, no alterations of course.

'Six knots and a half on the log sir and we are holding our course southeast-by-east. We'll weather La Desirade if the wind doesn't veer.'

Carlisle looked at the dog-vane and felt the tension in

the weather shrouds. Eli, the quartermaster, watched him warily. He had been caught out once, responding slowly to a shift in the wind, but he wasn't going to be faulted this time. The helmsmen exchanged another wordless glance. They had both been on duty that day and could read old Eli's mind like a book.

'Good to be at sea again sir?' Holbrooke could see that Carlisle was in a relaxed frame of mind and felt he could push the usual boundaries between the captain and the first lieutenant.

'It is,' he replied, 'and particularly pleasing to be away from the station politics. I had no idea that such a small command could generate so many jealousies, so much jockeying for position and so much unseemly competition. Let's move to the taffrail for a moment.'

At the taffrail, the very stern of the quarterdeck, they were out of ear-shot of the mate-of-the watch, the midshipman, the quartermaster, the helmsmen, the marine and the messenger. The afterguard was mustered at the waist, yarning about their run ashore, so nobody need approach them except to heave the log each half hour and that was another twenty minutes away. Carlisle was evidently inclined to talk.

'You can't believe the manoeuvring that went on before Frankland appointed a new captain for *Wessex*. It's natural, of course; she is a plum job for anyone who has been on the station very long. Now that her cabin and poop are whole again she is in much better condition than either *Winchester* or *Bristol,* and even Robert Man had an eye to exchange out of *Anson*. Voluntarily exchanging from a sixty to a fifty! That shows the measure of the desirability of a newly-refitted ship. I even heard, and I believe it to be true, that Lachlan Leslie offered to pay Andrews to drop his claim. And Leslie has already had a seventy and an eighty, although always under the eye of a flag. But I can see why Le Cras wanted her so much, being a flag captain anywhere is a sore trial, but in the Leeward Islands

Squadron …!'

'You didn't consider throwing your own hat in the ring sir? You must have had a good chance after Port Louis.'

Carlisle looked at him sharply. 'I think you know why I didn't want that ship.' He paused and stared abstractedly out to windward. 'Apart from wanting to be in a frigate a little while longer – I haven't yet made my fortune in prize money, and there is little chance of that in a lumbering fourth rate – I didn't relish the thought of dealing with that crowd in *Wessex*.'

Holbrooke knew what he meant. The last he had heard, it appeared that while Frankland had agreed with Carlisle's assessment of the leadership situation in *Wessex*, he had not felt that it was acute enough for him to act. To Holbrooke's best knowledge, Godwin was still the first lieutenant. Probably the admiral was husbanding the opportunities that he had to make and break appointments; Frankland didn't want the Admiralty to reverse his decision on the new captain, and he had a basket full of other promotions and moves that were awaiting formal approval. The commander-in-chief of a foreign station had to be able to shuffle people around as sickness, the violence of the enemy and the real merit of people became evident. He also needed to exercise his patronage to fulfil promises to his followers. But there was a real danger that the Admiralty would take exception when too much freedom of action was on display, and reverse some of his appointments.

'And if I may say so, Holbrooke, I don't want to break up our partnership, and I don't want to break in a new first lieutenant. You are too junior yet to be the first of a fourth-rate; good heavens, you're too junior for even this frigate! No, I am best served by *Medina* for a year or two,' he patted the taffrail, 'and best served by you.'

'So, Godwin stays in *Wessex*?' asked Holbrooke quickly, he was faintly embarrassed by this praise from his admired captain, 'and he suffers nothing for that affair after the first attack?'

'Hadn't you heard?' He looked closely at Holbrooke. 'The appointment came out just before we sailed. He takes command of the schooner *Scorpion* today. Hardly a promotion, more like another twist in the endless station politics.'

Le Cras had some leverage in parliament, and he had shifted the awkward first lieutenant out as quickly as he could. Frankland had either to send Godwin for court martial or re-employ him. The former would reflect poorly upon the deceased commodore, and in any case, the charges may not stick. Re-appointed he must be, but no captain wanted a lieutenant of such seniority and poor reputation. A cutter command was the least of all the evils. If disaster struck and he put *Scorpion* ashore, then she was so small and insignificant that the Admiralty would hardly take notice. If he took a few coastal prizes, then Frankland would be a few pounds richer. Either way, a lieutenant of his seniority and experience could hardly make too much of a mess of this miniature command.

'It still leaves his poisonous legacy in *Wessex*,' said Carlisle, 'but Le Cras is just the man to bring about a change of style in that ship. I hope so because I for one wouldn't want to take her up against a French fifty in that state of unrest.'

CHAPTER EIGHTEEN

Fort Louis

Tuesday, first of February 1757
Medina, at Sea, Marie Galante Channel

Holbrooke stared eastward to where the sky was taking a blueish hue, and the lower stars were becoming indistinct. 'What time is sunrise Master?' he asked. Clouds were gathering; it looked like Guadeloupe could be in for a downpour.

'Six-thirty, or thereabouts Mister Holbrooke. But in these parts nautical twilight is fifty minutes earlier so we will be able to see and be seen in about thirty minutes.' Holbrooke shivered. He wouldn't have believed he could ever be cold in the tropics, but at this hour, just after two bells in the morning watch, he felt a slight chill. He must be thoroughly acclimatised to the weather to be cool only sixteen degrees north of the equator.

Carlisle was taking the ship in close to the land. At this hour in the morning, even this near to the shore, the trade wind reigned supreme, and *Medina* was on her favourite point of sailing; a broad reach with the wind just off her stern on the starboard quarter. They were under all plain sail; courses, topsails, t'gallants and the staysails. To any watchers, they were so obviously a man-of-war, and coming from this direction so unmistakably British, that there was no point in trying to hide their identity.

Holbrooke walked forward and dropped down from the quarterdeck into the waist. He had sent the hands to quarters half an hour ago; British men-of-war always did so before sunrise when there was any possibility of meeting the enemy. When the dawn arrived – and it was a fast transition in the tropics – an enemy could suddenly be revealed too close for comfort, and the ship could be in an engagement with minimal warning. It was such a sensible precaution and so commonly practised that it passed without comment, even among the men who had been on deck for the middle watch and had therefore only had half-an-hour in their hammocks.

The gun crews were all in places, clustered around the starboard guns, that being the side closest to the land. Like almost all men-of-war, their establishment only allowed enough crew to man one battery and a spare gun-captain for the opposite battery, so they naturally gathered on one side or the other. In action they would concentrate their available manpower on the engaged battery, leaving the additional captain to keep the opposite gun ready for immediate action. If they were asked to engage with both sides at once, it could be done, but the rate of fire would diminish. Holbrooke cast a critical eye along the deck. The men had been trained well, and after having been blooded in battle, they knew their business. The accoutrements of the great guns were all in place, even down to the battle lanterns in case they had to fight at night.

'What's the name of this place we are heading for sir?' That was Whittle, one of Carlisle's followers from Virginia. None of the Britons would have addressed his first lieutenant in that direct manner, but Whittle doggedly refused to adapt his manners and constantly sailed close to the wind in his relations with the ship's officers. Holbrooke didn't mind in the least, but he knew that the master and the other warrant officers thought it disrespectful.

'Fort Louis, one of the main commercial ports of Guadeloupe. We will be looking into Basse Terre later.'

'Funny that, isn't it sir. We hammered *Port* Louis only a few weeks ago, and now we are heading for *Fort* Louis. Do they name all their places after their kings?'

That raised a laugh among his gun's crew.

'We do the same, Whittle. How many Fort Georges are there around the world? And Fort Williams?'

'Aye, I guess you are right sir.'

'But now you mention it, Whittle, it was Fort Royal that gave us so much trouble in Grenada, wasn't it?

'Aye sir, it was. A right tough nut until we blinded them with the smoke.'

'Well, we will be visiting another Fort Royal, the capital city of Martinique, probably tomorrow. So, there are two Fort Royals,' Holbrooke held up his two fingers for emphasis, 'a Port Louis and a Fort Louis. I expect we will be on first-name terms with the French King before we are much older. All we have to do is to keep track of the *forts*, *ports*, *royals* and *Louis*, and not confuse them.'

Holbrooke moved on. He heard a soft thud behind him, like a rope's end hitting muscle. That was precisely what it was, the sound of the gun captain gently reminded Whittle that if anyone was going to talk to the first lieutenant, it would be him. The burst of laughter that followed it told Holbrooke that the men were in good spirits and looking forward to a sight of the enemy's territory.

Moving up the fo'c'sle, Holbrooke checked the preparations there. No great guns were provided on the fo'c'sle of these nine-pounder frigates, but there were four swivels on the deck under the care of a midshipman. They weren't the most agile of men that worked these guns. They weren't topmen, but they were, for the most part, experienced fo'c'sle hands, adept at handling the halyards, the sheets and bowlines and they didn't have to deal with the complexity of the great guns. The task here was much more straightforward. These were breech-loading weapons, the powder and shot were pre-packaged by the gunner and his mates into a cast iron container with a handle on one side. It looked like a big mug – a pint-and-a-half mug, so with the direct logic of the sea, that is what it was called. Whatever its inventor had named it, and whatever the ordnance depots called it, to generations of seamen it was merely a *mug*. Each gun had six of these ready to fire; two loaded with a ten-ounce ball and the remainder with cannister shot. They provided rapid fire and were lethal at close range, but ineffective at longer ranges because the joint between the mug and the barrel leaked explosive gasses horribly and restricted the muzzle velocity. It all looked in order. The most essential implement up here was the hammer that was provided for each swivel gun so that the wedge that kept the mug as close to the breech as possible could be thrust home hard. Holbrooke had seen the results of a swivel that had been fired before the wedge had been hammered; the blackened faces and clothing of the crew would have been amusing if it were not for the sight of a ball dropping harmlessly into the sea a bare twenty yards from the ship. Midshipman Smith knew all about the wedge and the other details of the management of swivels. He also knew that he had to keep his crews safely under cover until they were close enough – pistol shot or half-pistol shot range would be about right.

Satisfied that the ship was ready for whatever the dawn would bring, Holbrooke walked back to the quarterdeck along the leeward gangway. Twilight had started, and the stars were all but gone, just a few of the brighter ones were left haunting the western horizon. The eastern horizon was visible for at least seventy degrees either side of the point where the sun would rise. But all between was obscured by cloud; rain-bearing cloud as Holbrooke could easily see. As he watched, the threatened downpour started. It was an isolated shower, and only those that had to be exposed were soaked, the gun crews moving to the sides of the ship to take advantage of the cover that the gangways offered. But the shower at least wetted the decks which was always a good idea before action and saved four men a few minutes labour on the elm-tree pumps.

'Deck ho!' called the maintop lookout, undeterred by the rain. 'Sails on the starboard bow, just coming clear around that headland. You should be able to see them from the deck.' Three telescopes rose to three eyes. The captain, master and first lieutenant were all keen to know who those sails belonged to; man-of-war or merchant vessel, privateer or coaster.

'Not men-of-war, I think sir,' said the master, speaking slowly as he concentrated on keeping the sails in his cone of vision. 'A schooner and two snows, island traffic for a guinea,' he said.

'I won't be taking your bet master. Now, the question is, can we cut them off before they make Fort Royal?'

'It's not just Fort Royal you want to worry about sir. All of these little coves on the south side have good holding ground, and batteries are guarding most of them.'

'Nevertheless, we will try Mister Hosking, At the very least we will make them think about the defence of this coast, perhaps at the expense of something more vital. Come to starboard and let's stir them up.'

He watched the three vessels intently through his glass.

'Mister Holbrooke, open fire with the bow guns as soon as they are in range.'

The French vessels were well out into the bight before they realised their danger. They tacked immediately, one of the snows missing stays in its haste to escape from this apparent predator. *Medina* was heading directly towards Fort Louis with the wind on her starboard beam. The three vessels would be hard pressed to make it to safety on this tack. Presumably, they knew their own coast better than Carlisle but, in their position, he would have reached further into the deep bay. There were smaller ports in there, no doubt some of them protected by secondary batteries.

'There's good water right up to Hog's Island sir, but I've never been beyond there, and our charts don't help much.' He looked wistfully at the three vessels that had now seen sense and had abandoned the thought of getting into Fort Louis. They had all turned tail and were moving fast up the channel between Hog's Island and Basse Terre. 'I wouldn't be happy following them unless we take the way off her and heave the lead, sir.'

'Aye, you are right Master. Let's get as close as we can to Fort Louis, minding those twenty-four pounders, and then we can get out of this damned bay.' He cupped his hands around his mouth. 'Mister Holbrooke, can you try a ranging shot yet?'

Holbrooke waved in reply. He ducked below the fo'c'sle like a rabbit down a hole and almost immediately the number two gun fired, the most forward on the larboard side and, thanks to the curvature of the bows, the only weapon that would bear.

'Short, but right in line,' said the master, as a waterspout appeared only a few yards astern of the nearest snow, the one that had missed stays and had fallen behind its consorts. 'The next shot will reach her, but we won't catch her now unless we can dismast her.'

'Mister Holbrooke!' called Carlisle. 'When I yaw, give her the whole starboard battery then reload with bar-shot.' Carlisle had considered ordering the round-shot to be drawn, but that operation would take too much time. The gun crews would have enough to think about running from side-to-side so that both batteries could be fired in turn. 'What's the range to Fort Louis now, Master?'

'Just a mile and a half I would say sir. They will be trying their range in a moment.' As he spoke, a group of waterspouts appeared a cable short of *Medina*, followed by the dull boom of artillery brought down by the wind.

'Bring her off the wind, Master.'

Holbrooke sent his crews to starboard, the guns were already loaded and run out, and the spare gun captains were peering through the ports to see their targets. The crews immediately started training their pieces forward in anticipation of the yaw.

'Fire as you bear,' ordered Holbrooke, and the order was passed along the deck from gun to gun, the midshipmen in charge of sections repeating the orders to see that every captain knew what to do. The loaders were already reaching for the bar-shot in anticipation of the next broadside.

Number one gun was first to fire, followed by three, five and seven; all down the side each weapon spoke in fire and thunder as they saw the target. The fragile snow couldn't take much punishment, not even from nine-pounders and evidently, there had been at least one hit, the eruption of the broken woodwork from her taffrail clearly visible.

'Back onto the wind Mister Hosking.' But the master was already giving the helm orders, and the captains of the hands on the fo'c'sle and quarterdeck were ready with the sheets and braces.

Holbrooke watched with interest from the waist. He could safely leave the reloading of the guns with bar-shot to his midshipmen. He saw the damage to the snow; could see its desperate efforts to stay out of range, and he could imagine the passionate debate on board. Strike or run? If they knew anything about naval warfare, they would see that it would be foolhardy for the frigate to chase them much further and the vessel and its cargo was too valuable to give up lightly. That would be the logic of the situation as seen by the master and perhaps the mates; a logic undoubtedly approved by the owners and anyone who shared in the profits of the voyage. But the foremast hands sailed for wages and would not be impressed that their lives were being put in danger to preserve the fortunes of others. If she struck her colours now, it might just be possible to take possession of her before the fire from Fort Louis became too dangerous. It wasn't Holbrooke's choice; he was in the privileged position of watching his captain as he made the decisions.

All along the row of guns the captains were holding up their hands and looking expectantly at Holbrooke. He saw the last hand raised – number seven gun needed better leadership, they were slow – and waved his hat at Carlisle. Up went the helm and he saw Carlisle gesturing at him.

'As you bear men. Aim high and let's see if we can bring down a mast.'

Bar shot left the barrel in just the same way as round shot, but there were differences to the vessel under attack. First, the practical range was a little less because of the shot's poor aerodynamics. Second, it rarely had enough punch to burst through a ship's sides. Third, the sound. Sailors hated the howling noise of bar or chain shot passing overhead; it had the effect of terrorising a crew out of all proportion to its physical effects. And last, it did a much better job of cutting up rigging and bringing down yards and upper masts than round shot could achieve. Twelve rounds of bar-shot is a significant number to be fired at a small snow, and even at that extreme range, they were almost guaranteed to cause damage. Holbrooke watched as the main-topmast fell to larboard, it's shrouds and stays shot away. The gun crews were frantically reloading while mentally checking their stations for sail handling and manning the boats, they knew that if they were to take possession, the frigate would have to bring to, and a boat would have to be sent away.

At that moment the guns of Fort Louis spoke again, and two waterspouts emerged on either side of *Medina's* bows. The master looked anxiously at Carlisle, who nodded and with a wry smile ordered the frigate to be veered and taken out of the bight. It would have been irresponsible to risk the frigate for such a paltry prize, and in any case, they had made their point. Carlisle just hoped, illogically, that there had been no injuries in the snow.

CHAPTER NINETEEN

Prizes

Thursday, third of February 1757
Medina, at Sea, off Martinique

Medina looked into Basse Terre Roads on the leeward side of Guadeloupe in the afternoon of the same day that they had stirred up Fort Louis. They kept a respectful distance from the formidable batteries that protected that critical commercial port, but they had seen no men-of-war other than what looked like a small corvette anchored under the guns. There was no local traffic to be surprised this time; the warning had flashed across the island, that a British frigate was looking for trouble. In harbours and roadsteads the length and breadth of Guadeloupe, seaborne traffic had ceased. Satisfied that nothing more could be achieved and having completed their mission of reconnaissance, *Medina* turned her head southward. In the evening she passed the small group of islands called The Saintes (where, twenty-five years later and in a different war, Admiral Rodney was to break the French line and inflict a crippling defeat on their navy) and made an easy overnight passage to be off Dominica at dawn the next day.

Dominica had never been used by the French navy. It was a poor, underdeveloped island which only a generation ago had been, by mutual consent, a neutral territory, left to the native Caribs. But over the past thirty years, it had been steadily settled and developed by the French into a viable sugar-producing island. It was ripe for the taking and would be an excellent addition to the British Colonies in the Caribbean. However, a lone frigate could achieve nothing, and all that *Medina* could do was to coast along the leeward shore, observe the almost complete lack of seaborne traffic, and continue her passage south to Martinique.

The morning watch had been on deck for two hours, and the sun would soon show itself over the northern hills of Martinique. *Medina* was under reduced canvas, topsails alone, waiting for sufficient light to see what was going on in St. Pierre, the principal commercial port of the island.

Holbrooke was leaving the management of the watch to Midshipman Wishart, who was striding up and down the quarterdeck, trying not to look too self-important. In truth there was little to do; there were no sails in sight, they had a crew that hardly needed supervision, and the wind was comfortably abaft the larboard beam.

'Well, what do you think of our prospects today, George?' asked the chaplain. He and Holbrooke were close enough friends to use first names when speaking in private, and this leeward side of the deck, with a quartering breeze, was as private a place as could generally be found in a man-of-war.

'I'm feeling lucky today, David,' said Holbrooke with a cheerful grin while making the motions of shaking dice in his cupped hands. 'Martinique is a much more important island than Dominica, more like Guadeloupe, and I believe we may surprise some of the island trade, or perhaps even a French West Indiaman. Of course,' and here he paused, gazing up at the elaborate lacework of the mizzen rigging, 'we may also meet a French frigate or even one of their seventy-fours. A frigate we can handle, but a seventy-four?'

'This, I gather, is the main French base in these waters, is that so?'

'Yes, Fort Royal is their base, it's further south on this side of the island. We should be there this afternoon if we are not detained at St. Pierre. But you know, they don't keep a regular squadron here, they manage things differently and send squadrons or individual ships from France for clearly-defined missions, to return when they have finished. For us, that means that we don't know what men-of-war are likely to be here. *Courageux* and *Prudent* were hereabouts a few months ago. Both are very fine seventy-fours, better than anything of that rate that we can build. It was *Prudent* and two of their frigates that took *Warwick* last year, in these very waters.'

Chalmers looked steadily over to where Martinique would soon become visible. He would never truly understand these sailors. Here they were, a ship of less than half the force of the unfortunate *Warwick*, positively loitering in the area where she had been overwhelmed less than a year ago. 'Isn't this dangerous?' he thought. 'Shouldn't we be passing this spot as rapidly as possible?' True, the ship would soon be called to quarters, the guns would be made ready and, he recalled, he would have to at least show his face in the cockpit, where it was his duty to assist the surgeon with the wounded. 'But surely, surely the gravity of the situation requires more concern than is being shown?'

'Let me tell you about some conversations I had with the men in the dogs yesterday.' Chalmers had at least ten minutes to spare before the hands would be called and he would have to descend to the lower regions. 'They were discussing the action off Fort Louis on Tuesday.' Holbrooke's ears pricked up. He had wondered himself how the crew viewed that unsatisfactory affair. Nobody had been injured, and His Majesty had merely expended a few pounds of powder and shot. But they were on a cruise; they expected prizes and prize money, not a long-distance cannonade and a genteel withdrawal.

'I've observed how the lure of monetary reward motivates the whole ship, how everyone works harder when they have the prospect of prize money to show for their labours. So, I expected there to be a general grumbling after we let that vessel – a snow I believe – get away.' He looked down into the waist, where some of the crew were already moving around the guns, checking the equipment and adjusting the coils of the tackles. 'But nothing of the sort! They seem to have enjoyed it as a sort of recreation, a piece of fun with no injury and no great waste of effort.'

'Weren't they at all disappointed?'

'Not that I could detect. However, they very much expect to take some prizes on this cruise. They look to Martinique to fill their pockets for the next run ashore.'

'Ha! They'll be disappointed then. They must know that a prize must be condemned by a court first and then the prize sold, and the agents paid off. Eventually, months or years later, some money may filter through to their pockets.' Holbrooke knew only too well how long it took for prize money to make its way to the captors. Even in the straightforward case of Vulcain, which had been bought into the navy, there was no immediate sign of the prize money.

'But my dear George. Don't you know that on this station it's often the custom for captains to take matters into their own hands? I understand Mister Frankland himself is quite famous for side-stepping the process and making an immediate distribution.'

'Very true David. But I wonder whether Captain Carlisle will take a similar view.' Holbrooke knew his captain's mind quite well and was very familiar with the emotional burden that he carried from the Colonies. It was hard to imagine Carlisle exposing himself by taking such a cavalier attitude to the regulations. A sea officer with more influential friends – and Frankland was undoubtedly that, and a member of parliament – could do so, but Carlisle probably could not.

The two men were lost in their own thoughts. The shrill sound of the bosun's call brought them back to the present as a couple of hundred pairs of feet started rushing in all directions, at first apparently at random, but soon settling to a well-known pattern. It took less than ten minutes to clear for action and for all hands to be reported at their stations.

The outline of the hills of Martinique became more distinct, rimmed in silver turning to orange as the sun rose with the rapidity that was always a surprise to those used to higher latitudes. But long before the rays of the sun fell directly on this patch of the sea, it became evident that *Medina* was not alone. Only two miles to leeward a group of four merchant ships were heading north. They must have left one of the more southerly ports in Martinique the previous evening and had shortened sail overnight. Whatever the reason, there they were, and *Medina* was ideally positioned to take them as prizes. At the first gun, the sole schooner that flew colours struck them, and they all started their sheets and awaited the prize crews. They could neither flee from this fleet frigate in the open sea nor fight its overwhelming strength. Better by far to surrender, let the insurance companies bear the loss and resign themselves to a spell in the prison hulks that lined the upper reaches of Portsmouth Harbour and the Medway. Perhaps luck would be with them, and they would be exchanged without too long a spell of incarceration, they reasoned.

Medina lay comfortably to the moderate swell with the four prizes under her lee. It took until noon to examine each vessel and for Carlisle to determine that they were all lawful prizes. Their papers spoke of French ownership and their bills of lading detailed the cargoes of sugar, indigo, cotton and coffee that were being taken to Guadeloupe for onward trans-shipment to France. The hatches to the holds were sealed, and their crews were taken from the schooners and snows and confined to the mess decks under the fo'c'sle of the largest vessel, a ship-rigged old tub. The French masters and mates were brought aboard *Medina* to deprive the imprisoned crews of their leadership and thus to reduce the risk of an organised uprising. Common humanity would have persuaded Carlisle to give them a boat and send them all into St. Pierre; the prison hulks were not pleasant, and they stood a small but significant chance of never seeing their homes again. But one of the essential strategies of this war was to reduce the ability of the French to create a fleet capable of challenging the British navy, and Carlisle well knew that the most critical deficiency that the French Ministry of Marine faced was the shortage of skilled seamen. Their Lordships were firm – all French seamen taken prisoner were to be held. No local exchanges, no ransoms.

Medina lost a master's mate, three midshipmen, twenty hands and six marines to the prize crews; a substantial reduction in the manpower of a frigate, and they couldn't be reunited with their ship unless *Medina* returned to English Harbour on her way north. Nevertheless, it was an excellent transaction. There was at least a year's pay for each man on board, even after Admiral Frankland had taken his eighth, and all for a single gun and no casualties. If the prizes gave Dominica and Guadeloupe a wide berth, they would be in English Harbour and safe behind Fort Berkeley by Saturday afternoon.

Medina's activities had undoubtedly been observed from the shore of Martinique. Mount Pelée rose high above the remainder of the island, green to its very peak and yet looking volcanic and inhospitable. It was an excellent place for a lookout but perhaps somewhat uncomfortable and isolated. If the French commander had not utilised that lofty position, there were settlements, plantations, anchorages and batteries all around the coast, offering vantage points from where a lookout could have seen *Medina* making her captures. From there, it was a short horse-ride by a respectable coast road to St. Pierre and then on to Fort Royal. It was unlikely that any shipping would stir from Martinique for the next few days, but there was still a hope of northbound traffic from St. Lucia, St. Vincent or Grenada.

It was a cheerful ship's company that bade farewell to the four prizes, and a smiling set of prize crews that waved back. Although they had a two-day voyage with under-strength crews and unfamiliar rigs, at least only one of the prizes had to deal with the captives, and they had half a dozen marines for that task.

'What do you think of that morning's work David?' asked Holbrooke as he was taking his dinner in the gunroom.

'Neat, very neat,' the chaplain replied. 'I'm supposed to be above the base desire for money, but as I am informed that I share in the prize distribution, I can only say *God Speed the Prizes*!' He raised his glass to a sentiment that was echoed by all the other members of the mess, so loudly that the quartermaster two decks above nodded his old head in agreement.

'But tell me, why was the captain so pleased that all the prizes had been taken at the same time? What was the significance of that?'

'Well, do you see, every prize needs a prize crew to work the vessel to English Harbour. That's not so bad, but if there is a large crew of captives to look after then the crew may need to be doubled to act as guards,' said the Holbrooke.

'And then, if there is a significant passage to make, every prize needs at least a master's mate to ensure that she gets home safe and sound,' the master chipped in.

'But if all the prisoners can be put in one of the vessels, then only one set of guards is needed,' Holbrooke continued.

'And if they can all sail in company, then a master's mate can do the navigation for all four, and we need only send a youngster or a quartermaster as prize captain in the others.'

'So, you see, there is saving in men – skilled men and officers – so that we can continue the cruise and if fortune favours us we can continue to send in prizes.'

Chalmers was pleased with the explanation, and delighted with the thought of more prizes, particularly if they could be obtained in this bloodless way. Everything he owned was in the tiny berth that he shared with the surgeon. The chaplain had no family to fall back upon, no patronage in the church, no living in the country, no tithes. He was as destitute as a man of the cloth could reasonably be, and any addition to his paltry naval pay was very welcome indeed.

Holbrooke looked at his watch significantly, and all the others took the hint. The hands would be called to quarters in a few minutes, and the ship would be rigged for action. They were heading for the next episode of their cruise, a look into the anchorage at St. Pierre.

They approached on the larboard tack, pointing as close to the wind as ever they could. St. Pierre greeted them with a furious discharge of powder and shot from the fort and from a small battery on the south side of the anchorage. If there had been any doubt whether their presence had been reported, there was none now. The anchorage was crowded with vessels, many of them the larger French West Indiamen, loading for a voyage back to France. Crowded was the correct word, because when they had heard of the captures off the northern coast – which they did within an hour of sunrise – they had all moved closer under the guns of Fort St. Pierre. They had sailed, warped and towed, using whatever means they could to be safe from this marauder. With the greatest of incentives, it would be impossible to attempt anything against the ships in the bay, so after exchanging a few broadsides with the southerly battery, *Medina* put the wind on her quarter and stretched away southwards for Fort Royal.

CHAPTER TWENTY

Ambuscade

Thursday, third of February 1757
Medina, at Sea, off Martinique

The frigate was cleared for action again. The same crews at their guns, the same groups of seamen on the fo'c'sle, the same officers on the quarterdeck. But this time there was a different feeling on deck. It was fifteen miles from St. Pierre to Fort Royal, the principal French naval base in the West Indies. Fifteen miles on a twisting stone road that followed every spur of the mountains, every inlet of the sea but there was no doubt that a mounted messenger could make that journey in under three hours. Fort Royal would certainly have known of *Medina's* presence since the middle of the forenoon watch and would even know that she had taken prizes within sight of the shores of French Martinique.

Medina had orders to look into Fort Royal and report back to English Harbour with a count of the number and rates of men-of-war. That meant coming within a few miles of the anchorage, five miles at most. He wasn't concerned with the batteries, he could keep clear of those, but he was anxious about the French men-of-war. By the time he reached the Cul de Sac Royal – the deep bay that provided the sheltered harbour for Fort Royal which was positioned on its northern shore, the French could have sailed and been ready to meet him. They would have the weather-gage, and he would be hard-pressed to out-run one of the superb French seventy-fours, or even the more sedate sixty and fifty-gun fourth rates.

Carlisle looked at his watch. 'The French commander will have had four hours' notice of our arrival on this coast,' he said to Holbrook and Hosking, who had squeezed into this small space that the master used for his charts and instruments. 'He has had time to send a corvette down the coast, out of sight, and a third-rate could be weighing her anchor as we speak.'

'Could already have weighed,' responded the master, the voice of caution as always.

'Only if he slipped his cable I fancy, Mister Hosking.' He looked slightly irritated at being contradicted. Holbrooke had learned that it wasn't really the case that Carlisle was annoyed with the person who had corrected him but rather that he was disappointed in himself. The dissatisfied look came when Carlisle was trying to analyse his own failings – why had he not thought of that? Why had he not acted sooner? And all the other what-ifs that plagued the conscientious captain.

'But you are correct, of course. We must not underestimate our enemy.'

Hosking merely nodded. He had been at sea before this young post-captain was born and was not inclined to be patronised.

'If we take the worst case, and a ship of greater force than us slipped or weighed three hours ago, where could they be now?'

Hosking stepped off the distances on the chart. The results were encouraging. In this pure air and with a simple calculation of speed, time and distance, it was evident that *Medina* would be able to see the enemy from the masthead – they would not have had time to disappear below the horizon. There would be no line-of-battle ship ready to spring the trap when *Medina* was committed to the six-mile-wide entrance to the bay, between Negro Point and Black Cove.

'Could one of them have slipped around Diamond Rock, rather than sailed to the west?' Holbrooke voiced the concern that they all had.

'A ship-of-the-line could not have made it in that time,' said Hosking. 'But a frigate or corvette may have.'

They both looked at Carlisle. It was his decision. In an ideal world, they would have run southwest to give Fort Royal a wide berth until they could come back at a time when they weren't expected. However, there was a time constraint. Carlisle had only been granted two weeks for his cruise, and he had to visit their old friends at Grenada yet. There would hardly be time to come back inside the islands for another look at Fort Royal. Carlisle knew this was risky, but he was in high spirits after the captures of the morning and wanted to get this over and done. He wanted to be free to cruise upon the enemy's commerce.

Holbrooke spoke, moving his fingers across the chart to illustrate his point. 'Perhaps there is another way. We could cruise a few leagues off the bay until an hour or two before sunset. That will allow the sea breeze to die away, we will have the sun behind us, and perhaps, if there is an ambush, the French will spring it too soon, before we are trapped against the land.' He looked at his captain and the master; they were watching him with interest, rapidly thinking over this new plan. 'We would only lose three or four hours and still have a good count of the Frenchmen.'

Hosking nodded thoughtfully. Carlisle considered for a moment. 'Then let us make it so. Mister Hosking, we will cruise between these two points,' he indicated a line parallel to the mouth of the bay but six miles out to sea. 'Mister Holbrooke, the hands can secure from quarters, but the ship is to remain cleared for action. Set the sea watch and double the lookouts.'

'Aye-aye sir.' The two men turned away to their tasks.

'One more thing,' he said as they were squeezing out of the door. 'I want an extra lookout at the main masthead. His only task is to watch the water around Diamond Rock, nothing else. Any sign of a sail in that direction and I am to be told immediately.'

The afternoon wore on. There was a haze over the land, and little could be seen of Fort Royal at this range.

Some thought they could see at least three French two-deckers, some more, some less. Without a doubt, there would be keen eyes in the citadel watching this insolent frigate, but there was no movement from the anchorage. Perhaps the commander over there was reluctant to order his ships to sail when it was quite clear that *Medina* would flee at the first sight of canvas being shaken out on anything more substantial than a frigate. It would be a humiliating waste of effort.

But Carlisle had not yet discounted the possibility of an ambush. If a messenger had made that ride an hour faster than they guessed, if the French navy was at a higher state of readiness than he assumed, and if they had slipped their cable as soon as the British frigate was reported, then *Medina* could be trapped even now and not know it.

'Twilight at 6.48,' Hosking reminded Carlisle, who knew it very well, having been reminded hourly since giving the order to cruise off the bay.

'Turn the glass and strike the bell,' he heard the quartermaster say. Four double-strokes told him that it was the end of the afternoon watch, 4.00pm.

'Very well Mister Hosking. As soon as the watch is on deck, you may head in towards Fort Royal.' He looked over to the east. The master had done well, they could just fetch the entrance to the Cul de Sac Royal in one tack. In an hour they would be able to see what was in the anchorage. Carlisle felt strangely nervous.

'Give the starboard watch thirty minutes below deck, then at one bell you can beat to quarters, Mister Holbrooke.'

The marine drummer dutifully beat his drum, but it was only a formality. The starboard watch knew what was up and the more diligent of them were already at their stations. *Medina* was hard on the wind, on the larboard tack with the quartermaster and steersmen watching for every flaw in the north-easterly breeze that could be used to keep her pointed as high as possible. The French naval base and citadel were on the northern shore of the Cul de Sac Royal, three miles east of Negro Point, which marked the seaward limit of the north coast of the bay. The citadel itself was on a peninsula, and sheltered behind the peninsula, on its eastern side, were the wharves and storehouses of the dockyard. That was where any ships in ordinary would be berthed and where any careening would take place; like Antigua, there was no dry dock. The naval anchorages were all within a mile of the citadel in good holding ground of around fifteen fathoms. Further east, deeper into the bay, the water shallowed into a maze of sandbanks and reefs. It was easy to see why the French treasured this location; it was sheltered from the prevailing north-easterly trade wind, it had a wide mouth to allow the largest ships-of-the-line to come and go in most wind directions, and there was swinging space for a large fleet. Carlisle thought that he could get a good view of the anchorage if he went right up to the line from Negro Point to Black Cove. From there he could get an accurate count and a good idea of the rates of the ships at anchor. He was reluctant to go further into the Cul de Sac, but if he wanted to know what lay behind the citadel, in the dockyard, he would need to penetrate the very heart of the French naval domain, as high as Ramier's Island on the south coast of the broad bay.

'I'll decide upon that when I get a clearer view of the anchorage,' thought Carlisle. He still found it hard to believe that the French commander at Fort Royal had not prepared some sort of surprise for him.

'Lookout!' called Carlisle, tilting his face up to the main masthead. 'Are there any sails to leeward? Look carefully at the sea around that headland.'

'Nothing sir,' came the voice from on high. 'There are two small fishing boats on the south side of the bay, close to the shore, but nothing else.'

'Is it possible that the French have been asleep since we

took those prizes this morning?' he asked Holbrooke. 'If I were the French commander in that citadel or the senior officer afloat, I would be doing something, if only for the honour of the flag. Are they really content to allow us to sail right into the heart of their naval base.'

Holbrooke nodded. He had his telescope pressed to his eye trying to make some sense of the tangle of masts that he could see off the citadel, six miles away now. He was itching to go aloft, but it was hardly in keeping with the dignity of a first lieutenant, and he didn't want to disappoint Carlisle. It was his skill in counting and recording French ships at anchor in Toulon from the masthead – a year ago now – that had redeemed him in the eyes of his captain. That seemingly lowly duty, carried out with skill and zeal, had led to his first command of a tender to take the news to Port Mahon. That mission, successfully completed, had led to the second command of a prize barca-longa. His use of that small ship to turn the tide in a desperate battle with a French frigate had impressed the examining officer at his lieutenant's passing board and resulted in his commission as a lieutenant and his present employment. He restrained himself from making for the ratlines and was just about to start a wholly unnecessary inspection of the guns when Carlisle spoke again.

'Mister Holbrooke, I wouldn't normally ask you to do this, but would you oblige me by running up to the masthead to get a better count? I seem to remember that you are rather good at it.'

Holbrooke needed no second request. He turned sharply on his heels and with a broad grin slung his telescope over his shoulder and ran hand-over-hand up the larboard ratlines. He was out of practice, so his speed was nothing like an experienced topman's, but nevertheless, to a landsman, his progress looked extraordinary. Up and up he went, passing the maintop by way of the futtock shrouds, the fastest but most athletic route, over the startled lookout on the topmast crosstrees and even higher to a precarious perch on the t'gallant yard, his legs either side of the head of the mast. With both arms around the mast, holding the telescope to his eye, he had a broad view of the world from this ultimate high point of the frigate. Only a slender pole mast reached above him, the ship's pennant streaming away to leeward from its head.

He first satisfied himself that there was no man-of-war waiting for them to the south. As the lookout had reported, there was nothing in sight except a few innocent fishermen who were wisely giving this unknown man-of-war a wide berth. He could see Diamond Point in the clear air twelve miles to the south, but Diamond Rock was invisible around the corner. There was no sign of a sail at all. Then he settled to the systematic study of the citadel and the anchorage.

He could see four two-deckers at anchor. Two of them were noticeably more massive than the others, two Seventy-fours and a pair of sixties or fifties he decided. He could not yet see past the citadel into the dockyard and was not at all sure that the captain intended to go that far into the bay. He looked further left and could clearly see the citadel on its promontory. A sizeable defensive work, more significant than Fort Royal in Grenada. It seemed lower, nearer to the water, but that was just an illusion created by its greater size. They wouldn't be able to play any hay-smoke tricks on this fortification. And then to the left of the citadel lay the town of Fort Royal, a few hundred low colonial buildings with here and there the towers and spires of churches.

Returning his telescope to the anchorage, he could already see the two-deckers in greater detail as *Medina* had moved that much closer. Each ship's head was into the northeast wind, so Holbrooke could only see their sterns. But that was enough. No French sixty had the massive galleried quarters that he could see on the southerly pair, and no French sixty carried three bold lanterns on its taffrail. They were undoubtedly the newer kind of third-rate, the famous seventy-fours. Probably *Courageux* and *Prudent*, although the French policy of sending out single-purpose squadrons for specified durations meant that he couldn't be sure. Of the others, it looked like one sixty and a fifty. He looked closer. 'Yes,' he said to himself, 'that's the old *Warwick* at anchor nearest the citadel.' Like every sailor of the time, he yearned for the fame that would come with retrieving a British ship from its French captors.

Medina sailed on into the mouth of the bay. The sea breeze had diminished, and now it was the real trade wind, steady from the northeast at around fifteen knots. They were sailing as close hauled as could reasonably be expected in a square-rigged ship; the master, quartermaster and steersmen all watching the luffs of the courses and topsails for any sign that they were lifting – the giveaway indication that they were sailing too high and reducing the efficiency of the sails. The green slopes of the Basse Terre sped past their larboard quarter, and Negro Point was almost abeam.

'What do you see, Mister Holbrooke,' he heard the captain call through his speaking trumpet from far below. He was becoming impatient. The frigate was approaching the invisible line between Negro Point and Black Cove, the entrance to the bay. If there were a trap, then it would be infinitely more difficult to escape from it once *Medina* had passed that line.

'Two seventy-fours and a fifty at anchor, and a sixty that looks like the old *Warwick* sir,' he called back. 'But I can't see past the citadel, and there are certainly topmasts beyond there.'

Topmasts almost certainly belonged to ships in commission. If they were in ordinary – laid up without crews – their topmasts would have been struck. In truth, Carlisle was only waiting for a legitimate reason to sail right into the bay. He was in a devil-may-care frame of mind, and this report from Holbrooke was the spur that he needed.

'Mister Holbrooke,' he called, 'we will stand on. Let me know the instant that you have seen all there is to see.'

Holbrooke eased himself in his precarious perch. He had only expected to be there a few minutes, but now that it looked like a much more extended stay, he realised that his leg and arm muscles would soon be protesting. He turned and took a last look at Diamond Point before it became obscured by the headland leading down to Black Cove. There was still no sign of a man-of-war ready to ambush this lone British frigate.

The anchorage was even closer now. There would be no chance of reading the names of the two seventy-fours and the fifty – Carlisle certainly wouldn't get that close, and in any case, they would soon be visible from the deck, so he concentrated on the careenage behind the citadel. On *Medina's* present course, the frigate would stay to the southern side of the bay, out of range of the great guns of the ships in the anchorage and well beyond the reach of the guns on the citadel. That was well and good, but it meant that the closest they would approach the unknown ships that had their topmasts rigged would be around three miles. Close enough perhaps to determine their rates, but little else.

Ah, now he could see. The careenage had just opened to his view. One small two-decker, a heavy frigate and a light frigate or sloop – a *corvette* as the French called them. There was nothing else, no ships hauled down for scraping or breaming, just those three.

Carlisle paced the weather side of the quarterdeck. He was trying hard not to look concerned, but the rigid set of his shoulders and the fierce grip of his hands behind his back gave him away. He could see the French squadron at anchor, not more than two miles on their larboard side and he could just make out the ships in the careenage although he couldn't tell what they were. 'Am I foolhardy?' he thought, 'to linger this long in sight of the main French base?' He tried to analyse the situation; the wind looked steady, and *Medina* could not be caught on a lee shore, but on the other hand, the lack of frigates disturbed him. They could all have been sent away on cruises, but equally, there could be a powerful frigate – or two – even now moving to cut off his retreat from the bay. He looked nervously over his shoulder to the south, but his view down to Diamond Point was cut off, they were too deep into the bay. He looked again at the French two-deckers, they were all at anchor, their yards were crossed, and their sails were neatly stowed. If they were planning to get underway, he would expect to see them shortening their cables and preparing to shake out their topsails.

The urge to call to Holbrooke at the masthead was almost overwhelming, it was only the desire to appear unconcerned that prevented him from doing so. He could see Hosking looking at him in that way that he had; clearly, Hosking thought they should be on their way. 'I'll give it one more minute,' thought Carlisle. 'No, two more lengths of the quarterdeck. When I reach this ringbolt again, I will call Holbrooke.'

But Carlisle was relieved of the need, before he had made another dozen paces, to his relief he heard the call, sharp and clear from on high. 'Captain sir, three vessels in the careenage, all in ordinary. There's nothing more to see.'

'Mister Hosking, do you have room to veer?' he asked the sailing master, who was ready for the question, having been expecting it for the past five minutes.

'Aye, sir. We have five cables to Ramier's Island and its deep water all the way.'

'Very good. Veer the ship and take us out of the bay to the southwest.' He looked up to the main masthead. 'Mister Holbrooke, you may come on deck now.'

The bosun called his orders, the hands braced around the ponderous masts, the tacks and sheets were shifted, and the helm put to windward. *Medina* spun around almost in her own length and in a few minutes was settled on her new course.

'A fifty or sixty, a heavy frigate and a light frigate or sloop in the careenage sir. They're all in ordinary with their topmasts on deck,' reported Holbrooke when he had regained the quarterdeck.

'It's the absence of any frigates or sloops in the anchorage that concerns me,' said Carlisle. 'I'll be happier when that headland is abaft the beam, and I can see Diamond Point,' he said pointing at the green hills on their larboard bow.

'Deck ho! The nearest two-decker is loosening her sails. She has rigged a buoy to her cable,' called the lookout at the main topmast head. 'The sixty looks like she is doing the same.'

'Too late, I fancy,' said the master.

Carlisle snapped, the tension of bringing his precious ship so close to an overwhelming enemy force had shortened his temper, and he was in no mood for unwanted statements of the obvious.

'I'll thank you to mind the sailing of the frigate, Mister Hosking, and leave the enemy to me.' He turned away and looked hard to the south, trying to pierce the bold headland by the intensity of his gaze. What would they see when Diamond Point came clear? That was a mistake, to publicly rebuke the sailing master. He was just too important a person to alienate, but he would have to leave the remedy for another time.

'Send a lookout to the fore-top, Mister Holbrooke. He may give us a few additional seconds warning. Make sure he knows what he is looking for.'

The situation was clear to Holbrooke. The two French ships were preparing to slip their cables, may have done so already, and would cut off *Medina* from the north. It seemed very likely that Carlisle's suspicions were correct and that another French ship, a frigate or sloop, had been sent to the south to hide behind Diamond Point or even behind Diamond Rock itself, to prevent the British frigate escaping to the south. That would leave *Medina* with only one course of action – a run to the east with the whole Caribbean Sea to leeward. Not only would that mean the abandonment of her mission – she would never regain that ground to windward in time to visit Grenada – but the French seventy-four was almost certainly faster before the wind and would be close enough to remain in contact through the night. By cursed bad fortunate the full moon would rise in the east-northeast at about the time the sun would set. Unless there were a thick coverage of cloud, *Medina* would be as visible as if she were in sunlight. Probably the French commodore – Carlisle could see his distinguishing pennant flying gaily from the masthead – would wait unto daylight to attack.

'The first ship is underway sir. She's coming off the wind, her topsails are set, and she is shaking out her courses. The second is following,' reported Hosking. Evidently, he had shrugged off his captain's earlier rebuke.

Carlisle could see the French manoeuvres for himself. That was superb seamanship, to get underway so quickly. But of course, they had been preparing for this for some hours; *Medina* was witnessing the execution of a carefully crafted plan.

Ramier's Island was well astern now, and Black Cove was a little abaft the beam. Diamond Point would come clear soon.

'Deck ho! Sail on the larboard beam, just coming clear around the headland.'

This was the culmination of Carlisle's fears. He had learned a lot about himself in this war, he knew that he was sometimes too impetuous, he too readily dismissed the dangers and focussed on the tactical gains, and this was the result!

The ship was strangely quiet with the wind right on the stern and the waves subdued in the lee of Martinique.

Carlisle could hear the scrape of the master's shoes on the deck as he sought a firm stance to examine this newcomer through his telescope. He need not be concerned at Hosking sulking after his public rebuke, the sailing master had spent his life at sea, he had been checked by far more celebrated personages than this peculiar colonial.

'It's a frigate sir. It looks like a twenty-eight.' Any further comment was unnecessary. She was an even match for *Medina* and probably armed with nine-pounders like the British frigate. Any thoughts of a quick fight to brush her aside evaporated. This was no corvette but a powerful cruiser.

There was no immediate danger. It would take either the seventy-four or the frigate at least six hours to catch *Medina*. There was time to think. The sun was setting on their starboard bow in all its tropical splendour, burning the eye in its intensity as it slid swiftly towards the horizon. Eight bells sounded, 6.00pm, the end of the first dog watch. The hands were still at quarters, so there was no movement of men, no relieving of the watch. Carlisle looked astern, the full moon would soon be visible over the taffrail, but at present, it was still obscured by the bulk of the great sugar-producing island. There was hardly a cloud in the sky, and the northeast trade wind was steady at fifteen knots. The only variable that Carlisle could envisage was the onset of the land breeze, which would probably start early with this bright and cloudless sky. But they were rapidly drawing away from the land and away from the effects of the land breeze. So, there it was. *Medina* was like a sheep for the slaughter, being shepherded to the west, away from Carlisle's mission and only awaiting tomorrow's dawn for the butcher's knife to the throat.

He watched as a hoist of flags ascended the rigging of the commodore's ship. The second two-decker, presumably in obedience to the signal, hauled her wind and started beating back to the anchorage. Such confidence, such arrogance! That commodore was so sure

The Leeward Islands Squadron

of success that he was prepared to reduce his force by thirty percent.

'How to regain the initiative?' thought Carlisle. The normal sea officers' lament was, 'give me sea-room!' King Richard III didn't offer his kingdom for a horse at Bosworth field more passionately. However, in this case, the wide expanses of the Caribbean played into the Frenchman's hands; Carlisle needed the complications of the shore to even to balance. But the land was to windward, and they were moving away as rapidly as they could.

'Shall I set the stuns'ls sir,' asked Hosking. A reasonable request to stretch out the time until the two enemy ships came within range. Carlisle was tempted. In a court martial it would look good, he would appear to have done all he could to avoid capture. And capture was inevitable if they let the French shepherd them to the west until daylight. There would be no escape once they were within range of the two decks of thirty-two pounders that the seventy-four had available. Capture and imprisonment, perhaps until the end of this war.

No! Something must be done and done soon. Carlisle instinctively knew that he must not let himself be pushed away from the land. The complexities of navigation, the variability of the wind, the very presence of the rock-bound shore would go some way to even the odds, to give him his only chance. He made a snap decision.

'No, Mister Hosking, no stuns'ls. Bring her to starboard, four points off the wind. That should put our head just off northwest.'

That caught the master unaware. The new course would converge with the seventy-four's track. They would be heading straight for disaster. But Carlisle was watching the setting sun, and he knew that there was half an hour, no, an hour, between twilight and moon rise. Undoubtedly, the French commodore could engage them in that time, but Carlisle was almost sure that he would not do so. He was gambling that the Frenchman would copy his movements and stay to windward, waiting either for the moon or more likely for the dawn of the next day. All naval engagements had an element of chance about them, but a night engagement doubled or quadrupled that element. If he were the French commodore, he would not see the need to risk a night engagement.

He looked around him. Most of the faces looked grave, concerned. Only Holbrooke seemed at ease. There was more to that man than met the eye, as Carlisle well knew, and it wasn't blind faith in his captain that gave him this courage in the face of adversity.

'Mister Holbrooke, I am trying to avoid being pushed to leeward, I don't believe that we will be engaged by the enemy but make sure your guns are ready.'

'Aye-aye sir,' he replied and turned to the batteries.

'Mister Holbrooke, Mister Hosking, a word with you, if you please.'

They stood together on the starboard side of the quarterdeck. The three men could see that the seventy-four, now on *Medina's* starboard bow, had copied their movements and was also heading northwest. It looked absurdly as though the frigate was chasing the enormous third rate, trying to hem *her* in against the land, the hunted becoming the hunter. She was about two miles away and could at any time put up her helm and cross *Medina's* bow – a killing move. The French frigate was dead astern, about five miles distant. It was clear that the French were confident of taking the British frigate in the morning and sensibly keen to avoid any undue damage to their valuable prize.

Hosking was not usually a pessimistic man; cautious but not cynical, but he had walked over to the windward side of the quarterdeck with a long face and shuffling feet. Carlisle could sympathise, it looked hopeless, but he was determined to make a play for freedom.

'Gentlemen, here is what I intend ...' Carlisle outlined

his plan. Hosking looked doubtful, pulling at his long chin until his face looked like an old, mournful mule. Holbrooke's expression was supportive yet thoughtful. Indeed, Carlisle's plan was not without its risks, and it relied upon French over-confidence and their desire to await the dawn before taking their prize.

CHAPTER TWENTY-ONE

Escape

Thursday, third of February 1757
Medina, at Sea, off Martinique

Twilight had plunged the sea into a sort of transparent blackness. There was still a faint orange blush on the western horizon, the last vestiges of the spectacular sunset, while in the east a dull silver glow heralded the rising moon – the *full* moon – that had started to make its cold presence felt over the hills of Martinique. The stars, caught between these two competing illuminations, had not yet reached their full brilliance, but Venus was shining clear and bright a hands-breadth above the horizon as the sun lost its power to obscure that most beautiful of planets. In this magical twilight, both pursuing ships were entirely visible to the watchers on the deck of *Medina*. They were visible, but they had lost all their colour, they were mere grey cut-outs in the surrounding darkness, the inverse of the *silhouette* portraits that were becoming popular in England.

'Are you ready Mister Hosking? Then bring her about sharply, keep her five cables off the land.'

Medina came briskly through the wind, and now everything was reversed; the seventy-four was astern and the heavy frigate six points on the starboard bow. To the French, it must look like the desperate inchoate thrashings of a trapped animal, and they would probably expect more of this as the night wore on. Carlisle silently prayed that his action would not tempt either opposing captain to decide to bring the affair to its conclusion before dawn. His plan relied upon their certainty that he was trapped, even more so after his decision to stay close to the island rather than run into the Caribbean Sea.

Under normal circumstances, at anything less than two miles to leeward of a high shore such as that between Black Cove and Diamond Point, he would expect to be in a wind shadow. His move, therefore, looked suicidal, but that was reckoning without the land breeze. By its nature, the land breeze hugged the surface. Starting on the rapidly cooling highland, the cold, dense air would be forced down the slope, following the gentle hills and spreading out on contact with the sea, but always in a seaward direction. Carlisle gambled that the wind within five cables of the land would be considerably stronger than two miles to sea. Stronger, but less reliable with vicious gusts, particularly where the shore was heavily indented with coves between the rocky, tree-covered headlands.

Medina was now entering that zone. The seventy-four was covering any attempt to escape to the north, and the French frigate had just gone about as if to pen *Medina* in and prevent her escape to the east. She had lost ground in doing so and was now barely ahead of *Medina's* beam.

'Mister Hosking, take a bearing of the frigate and let me know how she draws.'

'Aye-aye sir,' he replied, looking a little less mournful. 'Let's hope she takes the bait.'

'Indeed, Mister Hosking,' said Carlisle, cutting off the conversation. He was in no mood to debate his decisions and turned away to look down at the guns in the waist.

'Starboard battery Mister Holbrooke, but I hope they won't be needed. In any case, they can relax for a while unless our friend out there loses patience.'

'Bearing's steady sir,' said Hosking. 'Their sails aren't drawing well at all,' he said pointing to the French frigate. The sailing master looked up and felt the steady wind on his cheek; they were not yet under the shadow of the shore. 'Stuns'ls sir?'

'I think not Mister Hosking. I don't want to give the game away too soon. In any case, we are likely to get some nasty gusts in a few minutes. Are all the hands at the sheets? You can take men from guns crews if you need them.'

As the two ships were on parallel courses, a steady bearing meant that they were sailing at the same speed. That was good. It would lull the French captain into a false sense of his own superior position.

Medina slowed perceptibly as she moved from the steady air stream of the Cul-de-Sac Royal into the wind shadow of the heights above Black Cove. Then the blessed land breeze asserted itself, and the frigate accelerated. The wind was fluky but strong, square on the larboard beam, filling the coarses, topsails and t'gallants. It was curiously silent in this smooth water with a stiff breeze whipping over its surface, like sailing in a duck pond.

'How's that bearing now Mister Hosking?'

'Just starting to draw right sir. We are starting to leave her behind.'

'How long before they notice?' thought Carlisle. If that captain knew his business, he would be taking bearings the same as Hosking was and it would rapidly become evident what was happening. Soon the French frigate's position of superiority would be reversed. *Medina* would be far enough ahead so that the Frenchman would have to decide – he could either bear up and move into the fast air-flow under the cliffs, which would put him astern of *Medina*, or he could stay to seaward and gradually lose position. In either case, he would soon be far enough to leeward or astern that he would be committed to a long chase. It was still very dangerous for *Medina*. The French frigate was probably faster than the British frigate, but its most significant advantage was off the wind; its captain would not fare so well in a luffing match, and that was precisely what Carlisle intended to impose upon him.

The seventy-four at least had seen the danger and was now firing guns to emphasise the gravity of the situation. The French frigate took the hint and her bow-chasers, the two most forward guns on her larboard side, opened with a roar. The dark night was split by the twin spouts of red flame. 'Much good may it do them,' thought Carlisle, but it confirmed that he was facing an equal; those were nine-pounders, not the twelve or even eighteen-pounders that he had feared. And not only were they enjoying a stronger breeze here under the cliffs, but the moon that now illuminated the Frenchman was not shining on *Medina*. In fact, the darkness was accentuated under the cliff by its contrast with the silvery illumination that was starting to spill over the peaks and out into the open sea, and the light was strengthening all the time as the full moon rose.

'Probably better to save our powder, sir,' said Holbrooke. 'There is scant chance of a hit, and we will only offer a better aiming mark.'

The frustration and rage of the French commodore could almost be felt in the British frigate. Only half an hour ago he was in the strongest of positions and assured of a valuable prize as soon as the day dawned, with no need for any damage or injury. He must still feel reasonably confident, but it had turned from a ninety-five percent certainty to a seventy-thirty chance. Carlisle was happy to work with those odds.

Another gun from the commodore heightened the tension. 'She's turning,' said Holbrooke, pointing to the ship on their starboard quarter.

She was indeed. The frigate, just over a mile on their quarter, was coming off the wind to bring her battery of fourteen guns to bear, an attempt to damage *Medina* and force her to action.

'A desperate move,' said Hosking. 'She will lose ground and she he has little chance of hitting us in this light.'

But Hosking nevertheless looked apprehensive. His words were meant to stiffen the steersmen rather than a statement of the real hazard. The light may have been weak, but the range was right, something between five cables and a mile. The men on the quarterdeck held their breath as the frigate spun quickly to starboard. Her captain was clearly competent, he manoeuvred that big ship with the ease of a sloop. Skilled, but overconfident, was the snap assessment that Carlisle made of his opponent's character. For it was now a contest between the two frigates; the seventy-four was, at least for the time being, out of the game.

When her whole battery was visible there was a pause, the French captain was ensuring that all the guns were pointed correctly. He must know that he had only one chance at this range – and the distance between the two ships was increasing rapidly; then it would be back to his numbers two and four guns.

The darkness was again split by spouts of red flame, but now there were fourteen, followed by a tremendous roar that reverberated from the cliffs, and then the crunch of round-shot impacting on solid oak with the curious whirling sound of oak and pine splinters flying across the decks. *Medina* staggered as she was hit, but they were lucky; the Frenchman had not had time to draw the round shot from his guns and reload with chain or bar shot. Although the guns had been well-pointed, the order to fire must have been given on the down-roll, so nearly all the hits were to the hull, just one having scored a furrow across the gangways but mercifully causing no casualties. At that range, none of the balls had penetrated the frigate's planking although the combined momentum had jolted *Medina*, throwing many of her people to the deck. The French captain should have waited another minute to let his ship settle after the turn.

Holbrooke was one of the few on the quarterdeck still on his feet, he and the steersmen who had naturally kept a tight hold on the wheel. By chance, the first lieutenant had been holding onto the quarterdeck rail, looking down at his guns when they had been hit. The captain, the master, and the quartermaster had all been caught without a hand-hold by the impact of at least half a dozen shot. Hosking had taken a head wound from a flying splinter and was clearly dazed, fighting to regain his feet; Carlisle was already upright, calling for damage reports and demanding that the master be taken below to the cockpit. But *Medina* was still sailing, her speed undiminished and her rudder answering to the tentative swings of her wheel.

The French frigate had immediately turned back onto the wind and was now pointing almost directly at *Medina*, trying to follow her into the faster air-flow close to the shore. At least *Medina* would be safe from her fire for a while. Like most square-rigged ships, she had no guns that could point right forward, and *Medina* had no weapons that could be trained astern. The days when frigates of all nations were routinely fitted with bow and stern-chasers had not yet come.

The three ships sped southward into the night; *Medina* in the lead, followed by the French frigate and, trailing some way behind, the seventy-four. The moon was shining through a cloudless sky over all the five miles of sea between Black Cove and Diamond Point; the main constellations were visible, and the minor stars were starting to show. There was no escape into the darkness for *Medina,* and it was evident that the French ships had abandoned any idea of waiting for dawn to make their capture – this British ship was just too slippery and must be pounded into submission as soon as possible. They were all hugging the shore and making their best possible speed in the treacherous wind. For it was dangerous; each headland and cove had its own pattern of land breeze, probably well known to the fishermen and local traders, but utterly unfamiliar to these great ships that did their business in deep waters.

'She's setting her starboard stuns'ls sir,' said Holbrooke. Now that the master was out of action, he had taken his place on the quarterdeck; the guns could look after themselves, and the bosun was quite capable of tending to the rigging. Carlisle nodded. He had considered making more sail and rejected it. The fact that the Frenchman had done so had not altered his opinion; any small gain in speed would be negated by the fluky wind as the passed from headland to cove and on to the next headland. The sails would not draw well, and there was always the danger of losing a spar as these hard gusts hit them.

Medina had taken some damage, and the surgeon had four patients now. The master who was merely concussed and had lost a patch of his scalp and three men of number twenty-five gun. One man had a crushed foot after his gun had been overturned by an unlucky shot that had entered straight through the gun-port, the other two had unpleasant but not dangerous splinter wounds. There were no deaths, thank God, but if the foot had to be removed, a critical few days was awaiting the young man as his body entered the race between natural healing and the onset of gangrene.

Diamond Point was coming up quickly, a black promontory outlined against the moon-silvered sea. Beyond Diamond Point was the angular shape of Diamond Rock, looking for all the world like an immense black gem, its pointed peak rising nearly six-hundred feet above the silvery surface. In 1757, to the British navy, Diamond Rock was just another tall basalt eruption that punctuated the island's coast. The men on *Medina's* quarterdeck could not imagine that forty-six years and two wars later it would become pivotal to British attempts to control access to Martinique and that bare island would briefly achieve glory by being commissioned as Her Majesty's Sloop-of-War *Diamond Rock*.

Carlisle knew nothing of this future history, and today it was just an island – a very convenient island. Carlisle knew that there were nearly two miles of navigable water between Diamond Rock and the nearest point of land, and those two miles were the key to his escape plan, for this reaching away to the south-southeast was all very well, but the game would soon be up. The land beyond Diamond

Point turned sharply northeast, right into the eye of the wind where the land breeze would be fighting a losing battle against the trade wind. If *Medina* merely continued her path, she would lose her present advantage of the land breeze and be quickly overtaken and overwhelmed before she could stretch across the wide bay to Salt Pit Point, the south-eastern extremity of Martinique.

Carlisle carefully considered his plan. His enemy now knew that he was not to be taken without a struggle. They would be looking for a quick conclusion and would have given up the hope of gaining an undamaged prize. They would want to bring the guns of the seventy-four to bear, and once under the threat of that broadside, Carlisle would have no option but to strike his colours. So, the frigate would pin him, preventing his escape and allowing the commodore to come up and finish the affair. The key was to keep the two enemy ships separated and to hit the frigate hard and fast so that *Medina* could escape.

'Mister Holbrooke, a word if you please,' the two men withdrew to the taffrail. Carlisle's plans were only half-formed; he had a vague idea that he would use Diamond Rock, but the details would have to develop when he saw how the French ships reacted. He was reluctant to share his immature ideas, even with this his closest friend, but he needed his intelligent assistance to make this work. 'I expect to engage the frigate in a running fight. Brute force won't help us. We must disable him, so draw the round shot from both batteries and load with chain shot. Do you have enough?'

'We can fire two full broadsides of chain sir, and then we will have to use bar. The swivels can help though, and I'll have them filled with langrage; I know the gunner has some already bagged,' said Holbrooke. 'And it would be quicker if we fire off the round shot sir, rather than draw it.'

'No. Our friend over there will guess what we are doing. You must draw the shot and reload.'

Holbrooke nodded. It was a slow and painful process to draw round shot. The guns had to be run in, then a worm, a sort of oversized corkscrew on a long ash shaft, had to be inserted and carefully twisted to catch the top wad and remove it. Then the muzzles had to be depressed to their limit with the quoins hammered home. At that point, with luck, the ball would roll out. If not, it would have to be coaxed out with the worm and rammer. As a last resort, the ponderous twenty-three hundredweight gun would be lifted and dropped using the great oak handspikes and two or three strong men. He called down to the upper deck to get the process underway.

'Remember, our objective is to disable the frigate. I really don't care about doing any physical damage; I just want to be able to sail faster than her.'

'I expect the French captain will have the same idea, sir. He will be slowing us down to allow his commodore to join him.'

'I wonder,' thought Carlisle, keeping this to himself. 'He has been humiliated already. Perhaps he can be persuaded to believe that he can take us himself, in which case he will try to pummel us into striking before that great ship-of-the-line can share the glory.' But aloud to Holbrooke, he said, 'I'm sure that's right. Let me know when you are ready.'

'Quartermaster, two points to larboard, steer directly for Diamond Rock, right ahead of you.'

'Aye-aye sir.' The quartermaster had heard many peculiar and questionable orders in his long years at sea and took the view that it was his part to obey the orders, he left others to do the thinking. It was a moot point whether, in the absence of a new order, he would take this fine frigate to its ruin on the hard cliffs ahead, with the certain loss of hundreds of men, or whether at the last moment he would take the initiative to turn one way or the other. A moot point certainly, but the answer was not to be seen in his face, which continued to gaze intently but imperturbably at the rock ahead, at his sails and at the two men on the wheel. 'Mind your course, Davison,' he growled, by way of showing his Olympian lack of concern.

Medina was clear of Diamond Point, and the wind had backed a little, now north-northeast or even north-by-east as the land breeze slewed around in its daily battle to balance itself against the trade wind. Diamond Rock was only a mile ahead.

'Keep them guessing,' thought Carlisle. He didn't want any of the hands to start preparing for a turn and give away his plan to the enemy. Carlisle knew his next move, but not the one after that; it all depended upon what the ships behind him chose to make of his manoeuvres. He was sure now that the frigate wanted to engage him, that the French captain would not be content with being a mere blocker of ratholes. Carlisle was also confident that the seventy-four would not want to get involved in complicated backing and filling close to the rock and with the wind still so uncertain. He intended to use that to his own advantage.

Five cables to go with the wind firmly on their larboard beam. The French Frigate was only a few cables astern and gaining slowly. The rock looked huge, towering above them like some sort of prehistoric monolith. Three cables, and anxious faces were turned furtively towards him. Only the quartermaster showed no emotion; he watched his luffs and watched his steersmen. There was no longer any need to look for the rock, it filled the view forward. In a deep recess of his consciousness, and even while planning his next manoeuvre, Carlisle imagined the question the court martial would ask after *Medina* had destroyed herself on Diamond Rock;

'*And as you approached the rock, Eli, was its bearing moving left, or was it moving right?*'

And the response from the imperturbable old quartermaster;

'Neither sir. It was moving up.'

Carlisle wanted this to be close. He knew there was deep water right up to the rock, that knowledge was essential to his plan.

'Three points to larboard quartermaster,' he ordered. Old Eli nodded and without any show of haste gave the helm order. The relief on the quarterdeck was palpable. The hands had been waiting for the order and now rushed to the sheets and tacks to adjust the trim for this new course. 'Hard on the wind,' Carlisle added. He looked astern. The Frenchman had guessed wrong. Barely able to believe that this British captain would willingly put himself to windward of the rock, he had already started to bear away in anticipation of staying to seaward of the fugitive. Too late he attempted to follow *Medina*, but the rock was just too close. He tried to tack but missed stays and hung in irons. For one glorious moment, it looked as though her momentum would take her gently up to the rock, to destroy her bowsprit with the certain loss of her fore-mast, but she managed to pay off at the last moment. To starboard! Now Carlisle knew what he must do. From the French perspective, the frigate should have followed *Medina* into the gap between Diamond Rock and the south-western shore of Martinique. That would leave the seventy-four to block the eastern side, *Medina's* escape route to the bay and beyond. *Medina's* only way out would have been back the way she came, and it would have been unusual if a frigate of equal force could not have held her in that two-mile gap long enough for the great guns of the seventy-four to join the battle. But now the French commodore's ship was committed to the two-mile gap while his unlucky consort was moving fast to the southeast, trying to sort out the confusion left after her failed manoeuvres.

'Hold your course quartermaster,' said Carlisle. He knew that he had to get the seventy-four to follow him into the gap. She was less than a mile astern, so it should be easy. Looking to windward Carlisle could see the other factor in his plan, his stroke of luck, at last. The dark patch in the sky that he had noticed twenty minutes ago had rolled nearer. It was an enormous cloud bank, not at all unusual at this time of year. In ten minutes it would obscure the moon, and in twenty it would be right overhead plunging the ships into darkness.

The seventy-four had taken the bait, how could he do otherwise? Carlisle thought that in the same situation he would have held off to seaward; it would have delayed the final encounter but on the other hand, would have made that encounter and its outcome more certain. Perhaps the commodore's trust in his subordinate had been broken, and he was determined to finish this himself. Or maybe his patience was at an end.

'Mister Holbrooke, are the stuns'ls ready?'

'Yes, sir. They can be set in less than five minutes,'

Carlisle looked astern again. The great bowsprit of the seventy-four, clearly visible in this silver light, was thrusting into the gap. There was no room to tack or to veer.

'Quartermaster, bear away, right before the wind. Shave that rock as close as ever you dare.' He felt the wind on his cheek. 'Mister Holbrooke, as soon as the wind is abaft the beam, set the stuns'ls.'

It was going to work. *Medina* spun around under the rapid turns of the wheel. Even old Eli had lost his poker face and was issuing helm orders as fast as they came from Carlisle. And now that strange silence, as a ship turns from fighting the wind to doing its bidding, the only sound the creak and scrape as the stuns'ls' booms were slid out through their irons. Astern, the darkness came upon them with frightening speed. The wind hadn't changed because the clouds were still some way off, but they had blocked out the moon, and the surf on the base of the rock showed its phosphorescent gleam in the gathering darkness.

At that moment the night was ripped apart by a stab of orange flame to larboard and the boom of a single gun. A hole appeared in the mizzen topsail, but Carlisle could tell by the sound that it was round-shot, not the disabling chain or bar shot. The French frigate had been duped, but Carlisle realised to his shame that he had momentarily forgotten about this smaller and nimbler adversary. The seventy-four was the lesser threat, and the commodore was now trying to extricate himself from the tight waters around the rock. If *Medina* could get away from the frigate, it would be at least an hour before the bigger ship could find and destroy them and, in that time, with this cloud bank rolling in, they would be lost in the wastes of the open sea.

'Open fire, Mister Holbrooke.' Before the words were fairly out of his mouth, *Medina* was shaken by the whole larboard broadside firing as one. The French frigate was still bows-on and only four cables away – she didn't stand a chance. What Diamond Rock had failed to do, *Medina's* chain shot completed. Her bowsprit and the maze of rigging that held it down and stopped the foremast from toppling backwards took the full force of fourteen chain shot at short range. Each chain shot carved a three-foot path through stays, halyards, sheets, tacks and the lighter spars. The bowsprit just ceased to exist. The foremast stood for a few seconds, but the frigate had been hard on the wind, and the loss of the forestays was fatal. The foretopmast hardly swayed at all, it just fell backwards, chopped off short at the foretop leaving a jagged stump as it tore through the system of stays that supported the mainmast and its staysails. Without the leverage forward the frigate shot up into the wind exposing her larboard battery, Carlisle gulped, was this the ruin of all his plans? But never a shot pursued the fleeing *Medina* as she ran free into the darkling Caribbean, leaving a broken frigate to be towed back to harbour by a furious commodore. As the bank of cloud reached the three ships, it brought a freshening breeze and a sharp downpour which only *Medina* was ready to exploit. Her stuns'ls filled with the fresh wind, and she simply vanished into the night.

CHAPTER TWENTY-TWO

Passage North

Sunday, sixth of February 1757
Medina, at Sea, off St. Lucia

Holbrooke was enjoying the sunset over St. Lucia. At ten miles to leeward, the island filled the western horizon, it's jagged peaks shrouded in cloud and the Pitons clearly visible at its southwest end. The sun was almost touching the clouds, turning them from fluffy white to deep pink, rimmed with silver and gold. *Medina* was sailing close hauled, pointing as high as she could to pass Martinique beyond sight of the watchers on the shore. They had no desire to stir up that hornet's nest again, and there was no doubt that the French commodore would be delighted to seize an opportunity to pounce upon this British frigate that had so humiliated him a few days before. It was an interesting navigational question that Carlisle and Holbrooke had to solve without the help of the sailing master, who was confined to his cabin until the effects of concussion had worn off. The trade wind had handily veered a point in the last twenty-four hours, giving them hope that they could make the beat past Martinique in a single tack.

Grenada had been almost uneventful. The French had been busy clearing away the evidence of the recent attack, and there was no sign of the two wrecks in the anchorage. The schooner that they had used as a smoke-ship had been removed and there was evidence of fresh masonry where *Wessex's* twenty-four pounders had left their mark. There were no ships in the anchorage; in that at least the raid had been successful. All the merchant traffic was crowded into the inner harbour, reducing the space available and slowing the operations of loading and unloading. It would be many months before they felt confident enough to use the outer anchorage again.

Medina was certainly recognised. Although they had approached from the northwest, where the land lines of communication were not so good as in the east, the garrison was ready for them. There must have been well-mounted messengers stationed at the north end of the island for just this occasion. The frigate was met with an impressive barrage that started before they were reasonably within range and continued as they skirted the maximum extent of the enormous waterspouts. Fort Royal was making its own smoke-screen this time, and the thick cloud of powder smoke that rolled down to meet *Medina* was still substantial enough to enter the eyes and nostrils after two miles born upon a brisk northeaster. Holbrooke had looked questioningly at Carlisle, standing beside his beloved guns. 'I think not,' the captain had said. 'We have nothing to prove to these gunners so let's stay clear.'

They put the wind right astern and rounded Point Salines five cables clear, confident that there were no fixed guns on the point and that the French could not have moved a field battery that fast, even in the unlikely event that they had one on the island. And here they were, a day later enjoying the sunset over St. Lucia.

'What next sir,' asked Lynton, the mate of the watch. 'Is it a straight passage back to English Harbour, or are we to have any more fun with the French?'

Charles Lynton and Holbrooke had been messmates before the older man had passed his lieutenant's qualifying board and before they had both been appointed to *Medina*. Lynton felt that he had a right to a certain familiarity with his first lieutenant when they were alone on the quarterdeck in the dog watches. *Alone* was, of course, a relative term on a crowded frigate when the hands were almost all on deck enjoying the beautiful weather and the break from the grinding daily routine of keeping a man-of-war at sea. In this case, Lynton meant that neither the captain nor the master – the other two pillars of authority beside the first lieutenant – was present on the quarterdeck.

'Don't come the green hand with me Mister Lynton,' replied Holbrooke, glaring at him with as much ferocity as he could muster. 'You know very well from your delving into things that don't concern you, that we have another eight clear days before the admiral expects to see our jibboom round Fort Berkeley. And even your limited navigation skills will tell you that we can make English Harbour in two days from here, so we have at least six days spare.'

Lynton, of course, did know this very well. He also knew that they had fulfilled the specific orders that Admiral Frankland had imposed upon them for this southerly part of the island chain. Grenada was the last, and they were now free to go a-hunting. But what he didn't know, the knowledge that he craved above all other knowledge, was which hunting ground his captain had decided upon. It was clear to all hands that the next few weeks was intended as a mere commercial venture, an opportunity to line all their pockets with prize money without concerning themselves with the broader conduct of the war. The four prizes that they had taken to the north of Martinique were only a taster as far as they were concerned; it gave them hope that their captain was thinking along the right lines. But you could never be too sure where colonials were involved, they had different ideas on many subjects; but so far, his views on prizes and prize money appeared sound.

Holbrooke found it hard to maintain a stern face in front of his old shipmate. This was why their Lordships generally appointed a newly-commissioned lieutenant to another ship, to make that break from midshipman or master's mate to the distinguished rank of lieutenant, without all the baggage of previous friendships and loyalties. In Holbrooke's case they had done just that, but in appointing him to the same new ship as his former captain – to their mutual satisfaction – he had inevitably shifted his berth together with many the captain's followers. It was a fine line that had to be trodden, to respect old acquaintances while imposing the authority that was needed to manage one of His Majesty's frigates. He moved to the very stern of the ship, to the taffrail with the white ensign snapping in the breeze over their heads, perhaps the best place in the vessel for a private conversation. Until the turn of the half hourglass when the log would be streamed, there was no reason for anyone to interrupt them, and if anyone did venture aft, he could be sent away quite legitimately, without causing comment.

'The captain feels that we have stirred up the French so much in these waters that they will have halted all sailings. We could, of course, hope for some traffic from France for Guadeloupe or Martinique, but it's a long shot, and they are unlikely to be valuable prizes in any case. The real value is in cargoes heading back to France. That is how we can hurt the French most and give ourselves a few guineas into the bargain.'

Lynton nodded in understanding. He had independently concluded that these waters were probably unhealthy for the next few weeks, but he hadn't reckoned in the relative value of cargoes between the eastbound and westbound traffic. As a mere master's mate, his share of prize money was significantly less than Holbrooke's, but it was still substantial and eagerly anticipated.

'And in any case, that French commodore is probably itching to find us. He must know that we will head back north again at some point, but probably guesses that we will pass to leeward of the island chain. I wouldn't be surprised if he has a couple of those two-deckers looking for us now. He'll be disappointed, but in any case, our best bet is to clear this area as fast as possible.'

'But where will we go sir?' Lynton couldn't believe his luck in getting all this free information, and he was pressing his advantage as hard as he dared. But Holbrooke was having none of it.

'Just you wait and see Mister Lynton. There are French islands all over this station, and trade routes that run to and from their homeland and between the islands. The captain just has to choose the best one.'

Holbrooke looked forward. Every man whose duties kept him on the quarterdeck – the steersmen, the marine, the boy and the quartermaster – were staring unashamedly in the direction of the two officers. They had no doubt of the subject of their conversation and passionately wanted the genuine news.

'Perhaps, Mister Lynton, rather than speculating on the captain's decisions, you could ensure that your watch is tending to its business. That main topsail luff is lifting quite disgracefully, and those sheets need to be started a few feet.'

Lynton jumped as though he had been kicked and went roaring forward to berate every man of the watch. It was a pleasure to see the deck a hive of activity for the next few minutes as Lynton vented his frustration on the more-or-less innocent seamen.

When the sun had set, Carlisle and Holbrooke sat together in the great cabin with all Hosking's charts spread before them.

'I shall rest easier when we are clear of these waters,' said Carlisle. 'If we meet that French seventy-four in the open sea we will have little chance. He won't underestimate us again; we can fight for honour, but we won't fight long. I guess that she can match our speed on any point and in any weather.'

'Then we need to be north of Guadeloupe sir,' said Holbrooke, 'as fast as possible.' He measured the distances by eye. 'Your orders are to cruise to the northeast of Antigua, I understand.'

'Yes, that's correct Holbrooke. Curious orders that take

The Leeward Islands Squadron

us far to the south then back past English Harbour. But that shows us how stretched the admiral is for cruisers. Still, at least we can leave this area as fast as possible without looking at all shy. The question that I am wrestling with is whether I should stop at English Harbour. On the one hand, we can retrieve Mister Wishart and his merry men, which will be a great relief to the watchkeepers, and we can take on wood and water. But then we stand the risk of our orders being changed by the admiral.' He stared abstractedly at the blackness beyond the windows of the cabin and then, as though he had just made up his mind, he turned to his first lieutenant.

'On the whole, Holbrooke, I believe we should call in, but only after we have had a look at our cruising ground – perhaps twenty-four hours or so. Mister Frankland is probably expecting us to do so having seen how many men we had to send in with the prizes. If I were him, I would be anticipating our arrival.'

'I think we can be certain of his good wishes at least sir. His eighth of the prize money will be very welcome, I'm sure.'

'Yes, the privateer, of course, brought him nothing as we were under Admiralty orders. If he resents that, and I'm not saying that he does,' said Carlisle, with a knowing look, 'if he resents that, then the four loaded merchantmen should have mellowed him a little.'

He turned to the charts again, pointing to the stretch of sea to the northeast of Antigua. 'What do you know about the area, Holbrooke?'

Holbrooke looked carefully at the chart. 'The direct route for French trade to Lower Louisiana takes them right past Antigua, past Hispaniola and through the Old Straits of Bahama. Of course, that's why Frankland tries to keep a cruiser to windward through the season. The French navy doesn't like that route, and the insurers have taken too many navigation losses north of Cuba, so they try to persuade the merchantmen to cut through The

Saintes.' He indicated the passage between Guadeloupe and the small group of islands off its southern point and then traced his finger westward right through the Caribbean Sea and into the Gulf of Mexico. 'Then they continue to Lower Louisiana. But they must pass Jamaica that way. Even when the French have a squadron at Cape François, it's a dangerous path, with Admiral Townshend and his nine ships sitting astride the route.'

'Aye, a good summary Holbrooke,' said Carlisle. 'The French have quite an advantage at Cape François, being to windward of Jamaica. But to gain from that, the merchantmen must beat up through the windward passage and then they still must pass through the Old Straits of Bahama. It's quite a puzzle for Townshend, stationing his ships for best advantage and keeping them supplied from his base so far to leeward. Did you know that he is being relieved by Coates? He may even be there by now. Coates is flying his flag in *Marlborough* and brings two sixties, a fifty and half a dozen frigates to reinforce the squadron.' Carlisle looked thoughtful. 'Sixty-eight guns. Can she stand against the French seventy-fours?'

'Something must be afoot for their Lordships to release that force from the Channel,' said Holbrooke. 'In any case, this is a difficult area for the French, between Guadeloupe and Cape François by the outside passage; a full thousand miles without a French naval base and with English Harbour across their path.'

He pointed to the islands to the west and north of Antigua. 'Montserrat, that's ours. St. Kitts is also ours, although I heard that there are French plantations on the island still.'

'I've been warned off St. Kitts and Nevis, Holbrooke. There is a sort of unofficial truce covering both while our government decides what to do. It seems that their ownership isn't clear-cut. I fear that a French ship trading with either of those islands would probably not be condemned by a prize court. We can look around the islands, but I won't risk taking anything that is trading with them.'

'Barbuda, Anguilla – both British. St. Bartholomew, now that is French through-and-through although a rather poor island. It may be worth looking into.'

'There's a good harbour here,' said Holbrooke. 'It doesn't appear to have a name, it's just called the *Careenage*, but there is a small town built up around it and some batteries to protect it.'

'Then here's the plan, providing we don't meet a French seventy-four in the next day or so.' Holbrooke was well aware that Carlisle had a personal superstition and always crossed his fingers when speaking of an undesirable event. He avoided staring when his captain's hand disappeared briefly behind his back. 'Does he know that he is so transparent?' thought Holbrooke, stifling a smile.

'We will stay hard on the wind tonight and tomorrow, aiming to be well to windward of Antigua at dawn on Tuesday. If there is nothing in sight, we will return to English Harbour. All being well, we can stand off and send a boat. We'll be in and out before sunset.'

Holbrooke looked at the distances to be run and thought about the men that had to be picked up, men who, entirely naturally, would spend their anticipated prize money before even the prizes were condemned. 'And if Wishart has let his men spread themselves across the island, he'll be at the masthead before his feet hit the deck,' said Carlisle.

CHAPTER TWENTY-THREE

A Commercial Venture

Wednesday, ninth of February 1757
Medina, at Sea, northwest of Antigua

The hail from the lookout was like a voice from heaven, the masthead being still invisible from the deck in this last few minutes before the sun pierced the eastern horizon. 'Nothing in sight sir,' he called in answer to the mate of the watch's shouted query. 'I can see the horizon clear to windward, but it's still dark to leeward.'

Medina was hard on the wind, beating up to the north with Antigua some fifty leagues under her lee. Lynton had obeyed his overnight orders to the letter, and now they were straddling the most direct route that any French merchant ship would take if bound for Lower Louisiana. Like all else at sea, the French were ruled by the winds and the currents. The general circulation of winds in the north Atlantic forced them south almost to the latitude of Madeira, then south and west right across the trackless void until they met the equatorial current that would sweep them past the Antilles, past Hispaniola and into the Old Bahamas Channel. It *was* possible to cross the Atlantic more directly – some of the early explorers had done so, and it was quite natural for John Cabot to take that shorter route from England only five years after Christopher Columbus's first voyage, two and a half centuries ago. Cabot had been fortunate to make the crossing to Newfoundland in only fifty days – it generally took longer and with ice-mountains and frequent gales it was a much more hazardous undertaking than the southern route. By the mid-eighteenth century, almost all the trade for the whole coast of Central and North America took the

The Leeward Islands Squadron

longer, but faster, passage through the tropical seas.

When the sun had risen and dispelled the gloom to the west, Carlisle came on deck. He stepped carefully around the men holy-stoning the quarterdeck and took a position beside the wheel. From there he could see all that he needed to see. *Medina* was heeling to larboard under the steady thrust of the northeast trade wind. The sails were set correctly, he noticed; only the lateen mizzen appeared to be spilling some wind. 'How is she steering, Palmer?' he asked the quartermaster. Palmer responded by shouldering the steersman aside and taking the wheel himself. He tentatively moved it a little to windward while watching the luffs of the topsails as they just started to lift. Then he moved it to leeward, and they filled again with a dull thump.

'As good as can be sir,' he said. 'She was griping a little, so we eased the sheets on that old mizzen two glasses ago, and now she is holding the wind as sweet as you could wish.'

'Very good,' Carlisle responded and picked up the traverse board. He could see an unvarying pattern of pegs; north-by-west all through the night and speeds alternating between six and seven knots, with half an hour of five knots just after midnight.

Out of the corner of his eye, he saw the marine walking forward to the bell at the break of the fo'c'sle. Two double strokes and a single stroke told him that it was six-thirty in the morning watch. The midshipman and the boy slid down to the leeward quarterdeck rail to cast the log. He heard the litany of orders with the part of his mind that wasn't taken up with planning his next move. 'Turn!' called the midshipman and the boy let the log-line run while the midshipman started the half-minute glass. 'Stop!' he called as the glass ran out and the boy nipped the line, dislodging the pin. 'Six knots and a half,' he heard the boy say to the midshipman. Carlisle always felt a sense of the ridiculous at these moments. He had distinctly heard the report that the ship was doing six and a half knots, but he had to wait until the midshipman had reported to the mate of the watch. Then for the mate of the watch – Lynton in this case, self-important in his acting role as the officer-of-the-watch – to march up to him, remove his hat and formally report what Carlisle already knew. The final absurdity came in the traditional form of the report, 'five bells sir, course north-by-west, six and a half knots on the log, *if you please.*' Carlisle often wondered what would happen if he was *not* pleased. Would Lynton conjure up a more acceptable speed? But he played his part as always, with a straight face.

'Very well Mister Lynton,' and he continued his musing on the best means to annoy the French and take some prizes. He knew that there was a high level of expectation among the people. Now, how to satisfy that anticipation?

The leeward side of the quarterdeck started to fill with officers, some keen to drink in the delights of this warm tropical morning, some merely fulfilling their duties to walk their rounds and to make reports.

'Good morning sir,' said Chalmers. The status of the chaplain in men-of-war was anomalous, to say the least. They were paid as able seamen and were only members of the gunroom mess by courtesy and then only if the first lieutenant chose to invite them to join. But Carlisle and Chalmers were old friends, and the chaplain didn't feel bound by all the traditional etiquette of the quarterdeck. He was completely uninhibited about talking to the captain without being invited to do so. 'What a glorious sunrise we had; Mister Lynton very kindly called me to witness it. For a quarter of an hour, the sun was trapped between the horizon and that bank of cloud that is fast overtaking us. The contrast between the silver of the sea and the salmon-pink of the underside of the clouds, all enveloped in the darkness on either side! If you saw a painting of it back in England, you would dismiss it as a wild fantasy. But we see it daily – and we are paid to do so!'

The look of sheer happiness in the chaplain's expression forced a smile from Carlisle. A smile that obliterated his official quarterdeck face, the face that he used to order men aloft, to chide the tardy and to send the offenders to the grating, on occasion, to have the flesh flogged from their bones. Carlisle was self-consciously aware of that face. It was necessary, but he knew that he must avoid it becoming his habitual appearance.

'And a good morning to you, Chalmers.' He beamed at the chaplain. 'So, you have been about since dawn, that is more than I can say. Have you thought about how we find some prizes in this wide ocean?' Carlisle asked, sweeping his arm around the weather horizon. The quartermaster looked solemn, regarding the chaplain with an unfavourable glance. He was accustomed to captains who would have confined the chaplain to his cabin for such a gross breach of protocol – approaching the captain on his own quarterdeck!

'Well, now you mention it, I was wondering what your purpose could be in taking us to such a desolate part of the ocean. No islands, no ships and I understand that on this course our next landfall will be Louisburg some two thousand miles to the north, held by the French if I'm not mistaken. If that's your objective, then I shall be sorry to exchange this tropical splendour for the fog and ice of the far north and a French prison hulk.'

'Ha! Never fear Chalmers. I won't take you to your death in the snow just yet. But look around you. Don't you see that you are on one of the ocean's great highways?'

Chalmers looked, but the sea appeared little different to any of the other seas that he had sailed over in the past year. Warmer than most, the waves perhaps rather more regular than he had experienced in the Mediterranean, but entirely devoid of ships.

'Well, I'll take your word for it, sir. I imagine that some happy confluence of geography, wind and currents causes you to say so. But I see nothing to confirm that, in fact …'

'Sail ho! Sail one point abaft the starboard beam.' The chaplain was interrupted by the masthead lookout. 'I can see the topsails of a ship sir. It looks like she is on the starboard tack and will pass astern of us.'

'Mister Lynton,' shouted Carlisle, his conversation with the chaplain forgotten, 'call both watches and then put us about to intercept that ship. And pass the word for the first lieutenant.'

The bosun's mate raised his call, and the shrill notes brought a rush of feet to the sheets and bowlines. Carlisle left the ship handling to Lynton. He knew that the young man could carry out this simple manoeuvre without supervision, but today there was a chase in sight. The hands would be excited and so would Lynton; this was an excellent opportunity to see how steady he could be.

Holbrooke threaded his way through the bustle in the waist. He had been inspecting the sail locker with the bosun and the yeoman of the sheets. In this climate, it was as well to turn over the sails every few days to discourage rot.

'A chase sir?' he asked as he approached, doffing his hat.

'Perhaps Mister Holbrooke, perhaps. Mister Chalmers here caused her to materialise out of thin air just as we were discussing the lack of trade.' Chalmers bowed in acknowledgement.

Medina's head came through the eye of the wind with a rattle of blocks and a flogging of the canvas. Lynton was doing well, but he was hampered by the waisters, who were determined to haul the sheets aft too soon, imagining that it would speed them towards their prey. For prey, they had all determined that she was. Able Seaman Whittle was at the masthead, and he wouldn't be deceived by a man-of-war, nor yet by a British West Indiaman, however small and fleeting the glimpse of a topsail as the two ships lifted together on the Atlantic swell.

'Now let's see whether young Lynton has grasped the situation,' said Carlisle. This was his preferred means of educating his quarterdeck officers; he needed them to think beyond the minute-by-minute set of the sails and course to steer. 'Mister Lynton. What will she do when she sees us?'

Lynton was used to this inquisition, but it didn't get any easier. 'She'll stand on until she is sure of us then …'

'Really Mister Lynton? Put yourself on the deck that innocent French Merchantman, for that is what I believe her to be. You have sighted a vessel, a large ship to windward of English Harbour, heading north where everyone else is steering either east or west. On seeing you, she alters course to intercept. Just how long will you wait for positive identification? Will you need to see her commissioning pennant? No sir, she will veer any moment. Wherever she was heading, she knows that she cannot get there with *Medina* in her path. She'll bear away for Guadeloupe or Martinique and hope that we lose interest.'

'Deck there! Chase has veered, she's heading south.'

'What course now Mister Lynton? Think quickly, that's your prize money slipping away.'

The quartermaster and the steersmen regarded Lynton with suspicion. That was their prize money slipping away also.

'I'll put her three points on my larboard bow sir, and we'll need the stuns'ls.'

Carlisle had already observed the bosun quietly sending the hands to their stations for spreading the additional canvas. His share of another prize would be remitted to his wife by the good offices of the purser. Nobody who had suffered under the bosun's tyranny would ever suspect him of delicate feelings, but he loved his wife with all his heart, and every penny that he made went straight back to be added to the family finances. Another few prizes and the house in Gosport would be theirs, mortgage-free and rent-free. The quarterdeck officers could play whatever games they liked, but he would be ready to supply the extra speed even before they knew they needed it.

'Very well Mister Lynton, make it so.'

In a way, it was unfair to ask these sorts of questions when Lynton was so deep into handling the ship – after all, he was not yet formally qualified for this role. But a frigate needed to be able to react fast to changing situations, and it was important that his officers could rapidly evaluate a situation and think tactically at the same time as they executed the necessary manoeuvres. He hadn't performed poorly after all.

Medina came swiftly to starboard, with some of the seamen on the tacks and sheets, others hurrying aloft to slide the stuns'ls' booms out through their irons. In five minutes *Medina* was transformed. From a ship fighting its way to windward, heeling to the sharp breeze, she had become a thing of tranquil beauty, slipping effortlessly across the swell with the wind on her quarter, her best point of sailing. Carlisle could see that Lynton had set a good course and the topsails of the chase were now visible from the deck. She was a typical ship of the French West Indies Company, short-masted and built for carrying capacity, not speed. She looked deeply-laden, probably with manufactured goods for the colonists along the Mississippi River. Short of an act of God, *Medina* would be taking possession of her by noon. But her master was right to play the game to the end. At sea, anything can happen in the time between breakfast and dinner. A squall could carry away the frigate's topmasts, a better prize could be sighted or – and not at all unlikely – a French third rate could heave over the horizon and turn the hunter into the hunted. Yes, if he were the master of that ship, he would run and keep running until *Medina* lobbed a nine-pounder under her forefoot.

Boom! *Medina's* number two gun snapped against its

breeching tackle, and a nine-pound ball raised a waterspout close under the Frenchman's bowsprit. Without further fuss the chase put down her helm, struck her colours and lay-to, quietly rising and falling on the long Atlantic swell. Her master was an expert seaman, and when Holbrooke was rowed across to take possession, he found the ship in good order and the crew still under control, although deeply displeased at the prospect of spending the rest of the war in a prison hulk in the upper reaches of Portsmouth harbour. Like all captured seamen, they had stuffed their sea-bags with their possessions. Anything left behind would be considered part of the prize, and it would be a miracle if they saw any of it again. In fact, they were lucky to have been taken by a regular King's ship; most privateers and the men-of-war of almost any other nations would have stripped them of their personal possessions, leaving them with only the clothes that they stood up in.

The reason for the master's spirit of co-operation soon became evident; he was shipping a modest quantity of his own money to invest in a speculative venture in Nouvelle-Orléans at the head of the Mississippi Delta. By the custom of the sea and the laws governing the taking of prizes, personal possessions were safe from seizure. But the rules were often ignored, and the master was very keen to befriend his captors and secure his property.

With English harbour now a mere eighty miles to leeward, Carlisle was confident that they could safely deliver their prize at dawn the next day. Lynton was given the command with a dozen men and a steady petty officer. The French captain and his crew were transferred to *Medina*, all except the bosun and carpenter who were held in the prize to assist in reaching the harbour. It carried a valuable mixed cargo of all the necessities and luxury items that a young colony could need. Bags of seed, clothes, blankets, tools, kitchen wares, uniforms for the militia, muskets and pistols, ball and powder, two harpsichords and even one of the new pianofortes. The cargo manifest was sent over to *Medina*, the hatches were sealed, and both ships filled their sails and bore away to the west for Antigua.

The Leeward Islands Squadron

CHAPTER TWENTY-FOUR

Consequences

Thursday, tenth of February 1757
Medina, at Anchor, English Harbour

Carlisle sat opposite Admiral Frankland. The atmosphere was positively cordial, the admiral was delighted with the success of *Medina's* cruise, and why shouldn't he be? He had received valuable intelligence about the French forces in Fort Royal, the enemy had been stirred up throughout the length of the Windward Islands, and he would personally be measurably wealthier from his eighth share of the prize money from the five vessels that *Medina* had brought in. And most conveniently, Frankland was in the peculiar position of sitting on the Vice-Admiralty Court – in fact by his force of personality he dominated it – so condemnation of the prizes would be swift and sure.

Carlisle should therefore also have been content, but he was not. His concern stemmed from being here, on dry land, at all. He had intended to stay in the offing, send in his prize, retrieve his men with the cutter and be on his way before noon. But a peremptory message from the Admiral had resulted in *Medina* being anchored now in her old berth just off the careenage wharf. He didn't know what this meeting was about, but if he was to continue his cruise he wanted to be underway in the dog watches to take advantage of the land breeze to waft him out past Fort Berkeley. If he were detained until the morning, he would have to tow out against the sea breeze which was hard work for the boats' crews and would mean half a day of his cruise lost.

'I've read your report, Carlisle,' said the admiral, tapping the folded papers on the desk in front of him.

'You did well to get so far into the Cul-de-Sac Royal and look into the careenage. All my other cruisers have been chased away before they have even passed Negro Point. What was your impression of the commodore's ship? Well handled? By the way, I believe her to be *Courageux*. We heard that *Prudent* sailed for Cape François last week. It was perhaps fortunate that you didn't face two seventy-fours.'

Carlisle chose his words carefully. It did no good to heap praise upon the enemy, but he had an important point to make.

'She is a fast ship and well-handled sir, but perhaps a little lacking in enterprise. A British seventy-four would have snapped us up in the offing before we could make things difficult in the lee of the land. Her sail handling was fast, but I had the impression that she may be short-handed and taking things rather one step at a time.'

'That would agree with everything we know. They have had a bad time with sickness and no reinforcements from France.' He rang a small silver bell. 'Coffee? I have an excellent blend that you may enjoy.'

Carlisle doubted it. He found that coffee as it was known in Britain and even more so on the continent didn't correspond to his Virginian notions of the brew. He liked his coffee in generous measures and much weaker.

'Thank you, sir, with pleasure.'

'Now, I expect you are itching to get back to sea to resume your cruise, perhaps even wondering why I am detaining you, eh?'

Carlisle merely inclined his head; he was unwilling to risk in any way questioning his superior's orders. Many post-captains, he knew, would have been demanding explanations by now, but Carlisle still lacked self-confidence when dealing with naval authority. He knew it was foolish and all part of the legacy of his colonial heritage, but he was unable to shake it off.

'It's partly a problem of your own making, Captain

The Leeward Islands Squadron

Carlisle,' said Frankland, looking vaguely dissatisfied and yet enjoying the discomfort he was causing.

Carlisle looked puzzled, wondering where this was leading.

'If you had been more forceful in your criticism of Lieutenant Godwin, I would have had him court martialled. We have enough captains here to form a board, and we could have put him on the next packet home.'

Carlisle stiffened. What had the wretched man done now?

'Le Cras wouldn't have him in *Wessex,* and nobody else would touch him. So, as you know, I had to put him in *Scorpion*, and now we have lost him and his schooner.' Frankland rapped his knuckles sharply on the desk, a habitual action that Carlisle had been told revealed his agitation.

Still, Carlisle remained silent. This was his cue to ask how *Scorpion* had been lost, but Carlisle wanted to distance himself from this issue. He didn't want to be involved, and he certainly didn't want to be tasked with solving the problem. A lost cause, he judged. But like his prize of yesterday, he would play the game out to its conclusion, hoping for some sort of reprieve.

'Dammit man, say something,' said Frankland. 'Aren't you even interested to know the facts?'

He wanted to respond, 'not in the slightest, sir,' but that could be construed as insubordination. He merely replied, 'of course sir. I presume he sailed in *Scorpion* and has not been heard from.'

'Just so,' replied Frankland, visibly controlling his temper. 'I sent him out the day after you left. His mission was simple; to take some messages to Barbuda and then to look into St. Bartholomew and report back. He should have been here two days ago. I wasn't immediately concerned. I assumed that he had been delayed in beating back, but yesterday I heard from Barbuda that he had not arrived there. That means that whatever happened, it was a week ago.'

Carlisle thought fast. Any number of disasters could have befallen that slender schooner. One thing was sure. Frankland had determined, by some obscure logic, that this was at least partly Carlisle's fault and consequently Carlisle and *Medina* would be involved in fixing the problem. There was little point, now, in trying to avoid it. 'Have you had any bad weather sir?' he asked.

'None, the weather has been perfect since you left.' Frankland stared aggressively at Carlisle, the very image of a man trying to shoulder off an unwanted burden.

'And *Scorpion* was well-found, with a good crew?'

Did he detect a slight shiftiness in the Admiral? A reluctance to answer the question? Was he being defensive even?

Frankland shifted his gaze, then looked squarely back at Carlisle. 'She was careened last month and inspected by the master shipwright. She's as well built a schooner as I have seen.' Frankland didn't answer the second part of the question but just stared belligerently at Carlisle, daring him to push for a response.

'Ah, so that's it,' thought Carlisle. 'The other captains had been dumping all their unwanted men in *Scorpion*.' It wasn't so unusual. Few foremast hands wanted a schooner; they were typically short-handed and offered poor accommodation. A draft to a schooner meant hard work and harder lying. Man-by-man she must have been denuded of her properly balanced company to be replaced by the lost souls and hard cases of the squadron.

Carlisle pushed recklessly forward. If he was to be involved and almost certainly held responsible for the outcome, he needed to know the facts.

'Her crew sir? The usual mixture of good and bad?'

'Forty in total. No master, but the bosun is a good man. No marines, of course. Some of the men would need watching, but Godwin knew that. Perhaps not the best crew in the squadron …'

And that was probably the most that he would get from Frankland. It was better not to push too far. If he had the chance he would talk to the flag captain, he would be more open – at least Carlisle hoped so.

'Very well sir. What are my orders?'

'Sail as soon as you have taken on wood and water. You must tow out if necessary. Find *Scorpion* and if possible bring her back. Godwin as well,' he said as an afterthought, his distaste showing clearly. 'My clerk has your written orders already, but I want to hear from you in no more than a week, one way or another.' He pushed a thin, sealed envelope across the desk, minimising his contact with it as if that would reduce his culpability.

'If that is all sir, then I'll hasten our supplies, and should be underway in two hours.'

'Thank you, Carlisle. Proceed to sea without further permission. Remember, I must know within a week, even if you have found nothing. And by the way, there is mail for *Medina*. My clerk has already sent it out to you.

CHAPTER TWENTY-FIVE

News From Nice

Thursday, tenth of February 1757
Medina, at Anchor, English Harbour

The flag captain was not much more inclined to be candid than the admiral. He had confirmed the physical state of the schooner – fit for sea in all respects – and had been only a little less guarded about the quality of the crew. By piecing together what the admiral had said, what additional information he had received from the flag captain, and by hearing the rumours from his own warrant officers, Carlisle gathered that *Scorpion* was a powder keg waiting to explode. The warrant officers were mostly good men, but none of them was a strong leader. The foremast hands were worse than he had guessed, the hard bargains from the larger ships of the squadron, ruthlessly dumped into the schooner. It was little wonder that the admiral and flag captain felt a measure of guilt. They had all been complicit in some way. Carlisle remembered that he too had discharged a couple of his own men when they first came to English Harbour – they had been *encouraged* to request a move – and he had no idea where they had gone. So probably even he was not blameless.

Back in *Medina*, Carlisle had no time to spare. He gave his orders to Holbrooke on the waist almost before the bosun's calls had ceased. The first lieutenant, sensing the urgency and his captain's irritation, turned without a word to expedite the embarkation of the wood for cooking and the last few barrels of water and to order the ship to prepare to weigh anchor.

'Pass the word for my clerk,' Carlisle called to the sentry as he walked into his cabin. There was a delay of a

The Leeward Islands Squadron

minute or so before Simmonds arrived, breathless and with the reason for his tardiness apparent in the weighty bags that he carried.

'Mail sir. I've sorted it, I was just finishing as you called. This one's the official mail,' he said laying a weighty sack on the table, 'and here is a bundle of personal mail for you. May I take the remainder to the wardroom sir?'

'Ah, thank you, Simmonds, this is just why I called you. The admiral told me that there was mail.' He reluctantly laid the personal mail to one side; half a dozen letters, and he immediately recognised Chiara's hand on three of them. 'Yes, you may take the mail to the wardroom, and give the mail for the crew to the purser. Tell him from me that the mail is to be distributed immediately; there is sufficient time before the last of the water is on board.'

There was a common shoreside myth that few seamen could read. But in *Medina* at least, only a very few had signed the muster list with an 'X,' that mark of educational shame. He knew that many of the people eagerly awaited the arrival of the mail, and only a few needed the help of messmates to read their letters.

The clerk turned to go, clutching the bag of mail for the wardroom and another for the foremast hands.

'Simmonds, before you go,' called Carlisle over his shoulder as he started looking at the official mail. 'The two men that we discharged when we were last in, where did they go?'

The clerk knew the answer immediately, it was a standing joke in the squadron, it seemed. '*Scorpion* sir, and a good day's work we did in losing them, if I may say. However, they're in good company now; there's not a sound man on the deck of that schooner.'

'Thank you, Simmonds. Now keep your damned opinions to yourself,' he snapped in irritation. He didn't care for the consequences of his actions to be flung in his face, even unwittingly.

'Sins, like chickens, come home to roost,' he thought

ruefully as he ignored his chastened clerk and turned back to the mail.

It was one of Carlisle's firm principles that official mail must come before personal correspondence. The admiral's orders needed to be read, even though he had already had heard them from the man himself. It was essential to confirm that there was no deviation between the written and the verbal versions; if there were it would need to be clarified before *Medina* sailed on this strange mission. Then there were the dozens of letters from the various offices of the Navy Board; queries on victualling accounts, discrepancies in muster logs, new orders for the condemnation of worn cordage. There was nothing that required Carlisle's personal intervention, but he needed to read each one and be sure that any action that was needed would be taken and that his officers received the information relevant to their parts of the ship.

Finally, he was able to dismiss Simmonds to deal with all the details and to draft half a dozen replies; that would keep him busy and out of Carlisle's way for a few hours. His clerk could commiserate with the other members of the gunroom mess. It was unlikely that any of them would yet be able to tell him why he had been checked by his captain for what seemed an everyday remark.

There were four letters from Chiara, each dated and sequentially numbered in her own efficient way. Really, she had more idea of how to ensure the arrival of messages to His Majesty's ships than did the Admiralty Board. She wrote an original and two duplicates of each letter, numbered them sequentially by the date of the original and gave each of the copies a numbered suffix. She then dispatched the original and each of the copies by different means, so that if the first was delayed or lost, the second or third had a good chance of arriving. Carlisle was therefore in the happy position of immediately knowing when a letter was missing so that in reading the latest arrival, he could make allowances if it had been received out of sequence. He settled down to read the letters from Chiara. He had learned that it was best to read the last letter first and then to go back and read the earlier letters. Otherwise he was continually itching to jump ahead and hear the latest part of a story, be it anything so mundane as the progress of the flowering of the winter jasmine. It was thus that he read the first duplicate of letter number seventeen, dated the twenty-second of November 1756.

'... *General Paterson has therefore agreed to arrange a passage for me. He says – and the viscountess agrees – that a neutral ship would be safest at least as far as Gibraltar, but he must take advice as to whether it is best for me to go to England to find a ship for Antigua or whether a ship may be found at Gibraltar. How I miss my Edward! You would know immediately how to make the fastest passage from Nice to Antigua. I expect you have already read the conditions that the viscountess has laid upon me for this journey, and I hope and trust that you will feel able to bind yourself by them ...*'

Carlisle was astonished; Chiara was taking ship for Antigua! He searched feverishly through the previous letters. There was only one actual duplicate, so there were two earlier originals that may hold a clue to these *conditions*. Here was letter number fourteen, dated the first of November, and letter number fifteen dated the eighth of November. But number sixteen was missing. It and all its duplicates must be rolling along on the northeast trade winds making their leisurely passage to Antigua. He should feel lucky, he knew, that a letter dated only eleven weeks ago in Nice was in his hands in Antigua. He quickly read the previous two letters, but there was no hint of Chiara taking passage for the West Indies, merely the oft-repeated wish that they could be together. Whatever had happened to precipitate this change must have been after the eighth of November. In any case, it was a well-formed plan, approved by Chiara's guardian and discussed with the regional governor by the twenty-second of November. Carlisle smiled. It was just like that family. There would have been an hour or two of discussion and then a firm, impulsive decision with action being taken to turn the wish into reality before the clock had struck twice. He could just imagine Chiara leaving her interview with the viscountess and sitting down at her desk to write the letters to engage the help of General Patterson and anyone else that she thought could be of assistance. The viscountess had never had any children, but Chiara was so like her in temperament that they could be mother and daughter, or sisters.

Then it hit him. If Chiara had fair winds to Gibraltar and there she found a ship bound for the West Indies, then allowing for all the mishaps that a world at war and the Atlantic weather could throw in the way, she could be in Antigua any day now. He would get no notice – he knew that – Chiara would not wait for the *second* packet that could carry her across the Atlantic, allowing the *first* to bring news of her imminent arrival. No, she would be on the fastest available ship, the one with the earliest departure time. He involuntarily walked over to the stern windows in case a ship had slipped quietly into the harbour while he had been reading, but of course, the packet's anchorage was empty.

'*There is some additional news,*' Chiara continued, '*my cousin will be sailing with me.*'

Carlisle remembered the young man in his soldier's uniform who was so envious of Chiara's experience when she had been rescued from the supposed Barbary corsair. He had listened so eagerly to details of *Fury's* clashes with the *Vulcain*, and the eventual capture of the French frigate. The viscountess – it was typical of the Angelini family that the matriarch was always referred to by her title – hoped that Edward would be able to find some employment for the young man in his ship. Carlisle even remembered his name – Enrico, perhaps an Italian form of Henry; he must ask Chalmers, he was likely to know.

'Now that's an interesting idea,' thought Carlisle, 'a subject of King Charles Emanuel on the quarterdeck of a frigate of King George's navy.' Certainly, there was plenty of precedent for that kind of arrangement, but with the delicate political situation in Sardinia and the King's unknown allegiance in this war, he would need to tread carefully.

'But I'll worry about that when it happens. After all, I may appoint whomsoever I wish as a midshipman.' For midshipman it must be; the navy made no exceptions in the matter of the training of its lieutenants and in any case, Enrico was presumably a Catholic and unless he was prepared to perjure himself, could not take the oath required before a commission could be granted. Of course, the formidable Viscountess Angelini would know all that already, she would have sweated the information out of Paterson before she would ever have agreed to her nephew joining her niece on this adventure.

There was no other useful information in the letter. Carlisle was tempted to call Simmonds back and ask him to search for the missing letter number sixteen, in the highly unlikely event that it had been mislaid on its way to the cabin. But he knew that if he gave such an order, it would only betray his anxiety, and the rumours would spread throughout the ship in minutes. The personal affairs of the captain were always of the highest interest to his officers and crew. No, he would have to accept that he would hear no more until he returned to the harbour. By then he may have some idea of when Chiara was expected and perhaps some notion of these damned *conditions*.

CHAPTER TWENTY-SIX

Barbuda

Friday, eleventh of February 1757
Medina, at Sea, off Barbuda

It took little thought to decide how to proceed with the search. Clearly, Carlisle must head first for Barbuda. If *Scorpion* had come to grief before she had contacted the inhabitants, then he may find some sign of her on the way, or he may discover wreckage around the island. But in his heart, he had no enthusiasm for this mission. Godwin had probably decided to head for St. Bartholomew first and was even now trying to beat back towards Barbuda against the wind and current. An almost unimaginable error for a sea officer, disregarding all that was known of the conditions in the eastern Caribbean, and Carlisle knew that Godwin was a competent seaman. But there was hardly any other explanation that made sense; if the schooner had been taken by the French, the Admiral would have heard by now, wouldn't he?

As the sun rose the next day, they sighted Spanish Point at the southern tip of Barbuda. It was a low-lying island, its highest point no more than a hundred feet above the sea, and was, therefore, easy to miss in the vast tracts of the ocean. An error of a dozen miles in navigation – no great distance on a sea passage – could easily result in a missed landfall. How good a navigator was Godwin? He had no sailing master to support him. Could he have simply missed the island?

'I think we will look at the windward side first, Mister Hosking,' said Carlisle. The sailing master had declined to be put ashore in English Harbour, and this was his first day out of his cabin. He looked pale and shaky and moved about the deck from one hand-hold to another, but otherwise, he appeared fit for duty. 'You have visited Barbuda before, I understand.'

'Five years ago, sir. I'm no pilot for these islands, but I can take you to a safe anchorage and keep you clear of the reefs.'

'Let's look at the chart in my day cabin master, are we safe on this course for a while?'

'Aye, if we come up another point we'll weather Spanish Point and have a clear reach along the windward side.'

In the cabin, they looked at the master's only chart of the island. It was an unfortunate example of draughtsmanship which didn't give Carlisle much faith in its accuracy.

'It's quite deep water on the eastern side as you can see. There is a lot of coral, but only out to a couple of cables from the shore and we will be able to see anything as large as a boat without having to go very close. What high land the island has is all in the south; you can see there is a bit of a bluff running down to the southeast coast. There are no anchorages or harbours on that side at all.'

Carlisle could see what he meant. No vessel would approach the island from the eastern side, but perhaps Godwin had tried to coast around to get to the north. It was illogical and unlikely, but this task must be addressed methodically, exhausting all possibilities, or they ran the risk of being sent back to try again.

'When we have passed up the eastern side, we will need to give the north coast a very wide berth,' Hosking continued. 'It's all coral there. Some seventy-five years ago the old *Woolwich,* a four-gun sloop, was wrecked there and a merchant brig with her. You could still see their bones when last I came this way, but the Islanders come out and take the timber whenever they get a calm spell; there's precious little good wood on Barbuda so there may be nothing left to see by now.' On the chart, he indicated the far north of the island, heavily encumbered by a wide fringe of coral. 'However, the only entrance to the lagoon is on the north side; there's a small channel through the reef, it's big enough for a boat but nothing larger. If you don't know about that reef, you could easily come too close looking for an anchorage or seeking a short way around to the west.'

"The anchorages are all here, I presume, Mister Hosking,' said Carlisle pointing to the two bays on the western side of the island.

'Yes, the most convenient is this one,' he replied, pointing to the northern of the two bays. 'It's a safe landing on a narrow strand. There's a small battery there, probably only one or two men from the militia. They hoist a flag, and the town will send a boat to row us across the lagoon. Don't try swimming though, the lagoon is full of sand sharks. The locals believe it's a nursery for the monsters.'

Carlisle shuddered. Sand sharks had an evil reputation, fuelled by tales of the old buccaneering days. They lay unseen on a sandy bottom until a meal passed above them when they would rise fast and strike savagely. Many of the old tales were unreliable, he knew, the result of a rum-fuelled imagination, but he didn't care to discover for himself whether they genuinely deserved their fearsome reputation.

'This passage in the north; you say a boat can get through there, is that not the best way to the town?'

'Well, it's a long pull from the anchorage. Whether we anchor or stand off, it will be about a six-mile stretch for the boat, from the anchorage or from the north beyond the shallow coral. For a quick visit, the beach is best.'

'There's a battery on the beach; you said it was small, what sort of guns does it have?' asked Carlisle.

'Just a single six-pounder in a timber and sand emplacement, when I was last here. The militia may have added to it when the war started, but it's only a token gesture. The island is quite indefensible without a regular regiment. I expect the battery will be manned though.'

'How much water in the anchorage?'

'Three fathoms about five cables off the strand and the bottom is sand and shells. We will need a good hand on the lead, and we probably won't be able to anchor less than a mile off, but it's good holding ground and perfectly sheltered from the northeaster.'

'Then let's go around to the east, giving this northern headland a wide berth – it looks like it's called Goat Island Point on the chart – and come to the anchorage from the north. How long should that take?'

Hosking stepped off the distances with his dividers. 'It's all fair winds except for a tight beat to the anchorage at the end. We should be there by eight bells in the afternoon sir, perhaps sooner.'

'Then make it so master. Are you fully fit now?'

'Fit enough sir,' he replied. 'I can take you around this island at least.'

They found nothing on the south or east coasts. If *Scorpion* had been wrecked, it would be here, under the eastern bluffs where the swell from the constant trade winds beat against the coral-fringed shore. There was no sound reason why Godwin should have chosen this route to get to the only settlement on the island, for Codrington was on the west side, the leeward shore, sheltered in the coral lagoon. If Godwin had landed, he would undoubtedly have anchored close to the beach that Hosking had pointed out and sent his boat in, but that evidently had not happened.

Still, Carlisle wanted to exclude Barbuda definitively, so they rounded Goat Island Point, Billy's Point and Cook's Bay Point giving them all at least three miles clearance for the coral reefs. They anchored in five fathoms with an excellent clean bottom of sand and shells, just as the master had said. The tiny battery with its solitary flagpole was visible a mile to the east, a lonely outpost of humanity in the otherwise empty vista.

Carlisle and Chalmers sat side-by-side in the stern sheets of the longboat. It grounded a few yards from the point where the golden sands were lapped by the waves. Carlisle had a good boat crew, and they knew how to treat their captain and the chaplain. All but Jackson, the coxswain, jumped out of the boat as soon as it had grounded, to reduce the draught, and then by brute force pulled it up the beach as far as it would go. A pair of eight-foot deal planks were run out over the bow and Carlisle and Chalmers made their way to the shore dry-shod. There was no need for a signal from the battery; *Medina* had been seen in the early morning from Spanish Point. The Islanders kept a vigilant lookout as they were unprotected apart from the small and questionable militia. Until *Medina* was identified as a friend, she had been watched with the greatest care and eyes had followed her passage around the island.

He called himself the governor, but in fact, he was the manager of the Codrington estates on the island, the family having been granted a lease by King Charles – or King James, nobody could quite remember which. David Jones was a very tall, thin man. He walked with a limp, a legacy of the last slave uprising, and he went nowhere alone; he was perpetually protected by two well-armed English indentured servants.

'No sir,' he said shaking his head definitively. 'We have seen nothing of a King's schooner, not for a month or so now when *Scorpion* last came this way. I was only aware of the problem two days ago when our own schooner came back from St. John's and told us that *Scorpion* had not returned to English Harbour. I rode clear round the island looking for signs of a wreck, but there was nothing. Where she is, I don't know, but she didn't come to Barbuda.'

'Could she have landed her dispatches without you knowing, at first light perhaps?' asked Carlisle.

'No, captain,' he replied emphatically. 'We keep good

lookouts around the coast. We saw you to the south before dawn; nothing could land here without my knowing.' There was just a hint of defensiveness in Jones, perhaps merely a dislike at being thus questioned by a King's officer. Carlisle knew that they were in danger of alienating this self-styled governor.

'At night, possibly?' asked Chalmers.

Jones gave him a look he reserved for simpletons and chaplains. 'Not with our reefs. To the east they would have grounded and broken up before they reached the land, to the north and south they would have struck coral, and to the west, we keep watch all night. There has been no schooner here.'

Scorpion had apparently not been near Barbuda, and she had not been wrecked on the island. That at least cleared away any question that she had been here. There was still a possibility that she had foundered on passage from English Harbour, but that seemed unlikely, given her sound material state and the fair weather, which the governor had confirmed.

They made their farewells and left Jones scowling at their backs.

Carlisle and Chalmers were thoughtful as they were rowed the long mile back across the lagoon by the local boatmen. But Chalmers was always eager to talk to anyone new, and the old man, the trusted black slave at the tiller, seemed ready to chat. He was shy and reserved at first, but his age gave him a certain freedom of speech, even in this august company. Carlisle was in the bows, looking intently to the north at the distant passage into the lagoon and occasionally back to the west, to the town of Codrington, trying to imprint it on his memory in case he should ever need to come here again. Chalmers idly engaged the man in conversation; he was interested in the conditions that the enslaved Africans lived under, but when they had exhausted that topic the old man looked at him with a wholly different expression, secretive and cautious.

'You're looking for a schooner, your honour?' he asked quietly.

'Yes,' replied Chalmers, thinking this was only the old man's way of making conversation. 'A King's schooner, it should have visited here a week ago, but it hasn't arrived.'

'I seen a schooner sir,' he said, and looked thoughtful, his lips moving as he counted back the days. 'Maybe a week or so ago.'

Chalmers wasn't really taking the man seriously, and Carlisle couldn't hear.

'You saw a schooner? Where was that?' he asked casually.

'I sleep some nights at the gun over yonder,' he said, pointing ahead at the narrow strip of beach with the small battery. 'The men there like to take a little rum, and they give me some if I keep watch for them.' He moved the tiller a little to starboard. His crew of four were not inclined to exert themselves, and the starboard oars were noticeably less efficient than the larboard; the boat was making its sedate way crabwise across the lagoon.

'One night I saw a sail over there,' he pointed to the southwest, 'just before the sun went down. It was heading that way,' he pointed away to the northwest. 'I told the soldiers, but it had gone by the time they came to look, and they didn't believe me. I think it was that schooner which comes here from the big island.'

Chalmers considered what he had heard. It was probably nothing, but he called to Carlisle anyway. The old man was less forthcoming in front of the captain. He could recognise authority and had learned to say no more than was necessary to those who had the power to hurt him, but with encouragement from the chaplain, he repeated his story.

'Were they the same soldiers?' Carlisle asked, pointing to the two men at the battery. Are those the men who were on watch that night?'

The old man was looking worried now, afraid that he was getting himself into trouble. This naval captain would be gone in an hour, but he would be left to face the soldiers.

'No sir, it was a different two. They are different every night.'

Carlisle looked hard at him. Was he telling the truth? Or was he afraid of implicating the soldiers in this affair? It was impossible to say, but no good would come of pressing the point. What did he have to gain by fabricating this story, but a few moments of fame? Both Carlisle and Chalmers understood that the opportunity for this man to be important, even for ten minutes, was an adequate reason for making up stories. But he didn't look like he had just invented this tale, and it fitted too closely the timeline for *Scorpion*; a timeline that the old man was unlikely to have known.

When they grounded on the beach, Carlisle strode over to the battery. No, the two militiamen had not been on watch on that night. No, they had not seen the schooner. They confirmed that their watchkeeping rota had them out here only one night in four. No, in the time left before it became dark it was not possible to find the men who were on watch that night.

By the time they had finished questioning the soldiers, the boat from the town was halfway back across the lagoon. The old man had wasted no time in leaving the scene, apparently concerned that he had said too much. However, both Carlisle and Chalmers knew that his story had an authentic ring to it. But why would *Scorpion* have shown her topsail – the old man was sure that it was the square topsail that he saw, it had a cloth of a much darker colour on the starboard leach, it was quite distinctive – and then turned away again? What game was Godwin playing? The trip to Barbuda had not been in vain after all. They knew that *Scorpion* had not touched there, but they were reasonably confident that in the evening after leaving

English Harbour, or perhaps the next evening, she had approached from the southwest to within about eight miles and then slipped back over the horizon. But where had she gone?

CHAPTER TWENTY-SEVEN

Theories

Friday, eleventh of February 1757
Medina, at Anchor, off Barbuda

The two men sat in silence in the stern sheets of the longboat. Each was thinking through the puzzle that they had been presented with, each falling back on his own experience, his own expertise. Inevitably it was Carlisle who spoke first. Chalmers was a much better listener than a talker and was perfectly happy with the dead silence that most men found oppressive.

'It makes perfect sense that *Scorpion* should approach from the southwest,' mused Carlisle, half to himself, 'that's the direct route from the western side of Antigua, and it would have avoided a hard beat into the wind to get around to the east of the island. A schooner can lie closer to the wind than we can; from the west side of Antigua, she would have had a straight beat on the starboard tack to make the anchorage at Barbuda.'

'Is that significant,' asked Chalmers. 'I ask in all ignorance of navigation. Were his actions quite normal up to that point?'

'Well, we know that *Scorpion* left English Harbour at seven bells in the morning watch. She had something like fifty miles to sail to the point where the old man said she was sighted. A schooner of her kind should have averaged at least six knots the whole way, so he was there maybe an hour or two later than he would have expected. It was growing dark, too late to approach an unfamiliar anchorage without a pilot.' Carlisle looked thoughtful. 'Perhaps Godwin realised that he would be anchoring in the dark and decided to stand off until daylight.'

'What would he have done overnight?' asked Chalmers.

'He wouldn't have wanted to get set to leeward of Barbuda, so I would have expected him to tack and stand out to the east. Then in the morning watch, when it was light enough, he could run back around Spaniard Point and come to the anchorage.'

'But the old man said that the schooner disappeared soon after she was sighted. That suggests that she reversed his course.'

'And that makes no sense at all. Godwin would have been set to leeward overnight with the devil's own job to beat back to the island in the morning.' Carlisle thumped his fist on the gunwale of the boat. 'Unless he decided to carry out the second part of his mission first; unless he stretched away to St. Bartholomew overnight.'

It was hard to believe that Godwin would so far disobey his written orders to visit St. Bartholomew before Barbuda. But that was what the logic was telling him.

The longboat bumped alongside *Medina* as the daylight was fading.

'Weigh anchor, Mister Hosking. Set all sail and lay a course for St. Bartholomew. I wish to be off the Careenage at first light.'

'May I speak to you in your cabin, captain?' asked Chalmers in a low, confidential voice. He apparently didn't want to be overheard. 'I may have a different perspective on this problem.'

'Very well. Are you happy for Holbrooke to join us? The master and the bosun are quite capable of taking us to sea without our supervision,' he replied, matching his tone to the chaplain's.

'Mister Hosking. Pass the word for the first lieutenant, I would be pleased if he could join me in my cabin.'

The three men were seated around the table in the day cabin. The charts of the islands were still laid out, held down by various navigational instruments. Briefly, Carlisle told Holbrooke what they had learned.

'Now it's your turn, Chalmers. What's this idea of yours?'

The captain and the first lieutenant looked expectantly at the chaplain. He had something of the reputation of an oracle, and neither man would readily dismiss his ideas. There was something disproportionately valuable in having the views of an intelligent man whose experience of life was so different to the two sea officers.

'Well, I believe I have followed the navigational logic, and it seems to me that Godwin was at the right place and only a few hours later than he expected. You will know better than I, but those few hours could easily be explained by the normal uncertainty of a sea passage, even one as short as that from Antigua to Barbuda.'

Carlisle and Holbrooke exchanged sly glances. Only the chaplain could refer so casually to the *normal* uncertainty of a sea passage. But they knew what he meant.

'The range of possibilities appear to come under four headings.'

Chalmers extended the index finger of his right hand onto the edge of the table. It was a peculiar way of gaining attention and emphasising his points – almost intimate when used in such a small cloistered gathering.

'First, the old man's story is incorrect. Either he was mistaken, or he fabricated it, or what he saw was another vessel altogether. In that last case it raises the intriguing possibility that there was a second vessel out there; if that were so, then *Scorpion* could have fallen victim to an enemy cruiser.'

The possibility that *Scorpion* had been taken had occurred to Carlisle and Holbrooke, but they hadn't connected it to the sighting off Barbuda.

'But that possibility leads us nowhere. If the schooner really was taken a week ago, it could be anywhere by now, safe in any of a dozen French harbours,' replied Holbrooke.

Chalmers ignored him and laid a second finger on the

table; the gesture was mesmerising.

'Then, the story could be true – and I believe he was accurate as far as he could be. *Scorpion* really did approach Barbuda at nightfall and then retire. However, if Godwin did what you suggest he should have done overnight and stood out to the east after he was below the horizon, then again it leads us nowhere. He could have foundered or been taken, and there is nothing we can usefully do a week after the event.'

Carlisle and Holbrooke were starting to see where the chaplain was going. Chalmers laid a third finger on the table.

'That leaves the last possibility. That the old man's story is accurate in all respects, including the direction that *Scorpion* took to leave the vicinity of Barbuda. In that case, *Scorpion* really did approach Barbuda at sunset and then for reasons that we don't understand, departed to the northwest.'

'Then it's almost certain that he has taken it upon himself to make for St. Bartholomew,' said Carlisle. 'Perhaps he thought to save time on his mission by choosing not to waste a night standing off Barbuda. If so, then he is a worse navigator than I had imagined, and he has taken no account of the prevailing winds.' Carlisle looked thoughtful, 'but he didn't strike me as professionally incompetent, for all his other failings.'

'Then why else would he have headed away to the west?' asked Holbrooke. 'A chase perhaps?'

'There is another possibility if we accept that the old man was both accurate and honest,' said Chalmers, portentous laying a fourth finger on the table. 'I hardly like to mention it, and it's why I asked that we speak where we can't be overheard.' All three men leaned closer to the table; like conspirators around their victim. 'From all that I have heard of Lieutenant Godwin, and with the bad character of the crew that he was given – I only repeat what is common knowledge in English Harbour – could there have been an overthrow of authority, a mutiny?'

The power of a single word was never so clearly revealed. Rembrandt would have done justice to the scene. The three men around the lamplit table, the rest of the small cabin in semi-darkness, the shadows creating a portentous atmosphere. But no painting could have recreated the sharp intake of breath from the captain and first lieutenant. All three faces were suddenly solemn. *Mutiny* was not a word to be casually bandied around in the eighteenth-century navy.

They sat a few minutes, quietly pondering this new line of enquiry. It was Carlisle who broke the silence, Chalmers having reverted to his listening mode while Holbrooke was struck dumb, overawed by the very thought of discussing mutiny.

'It fits the facts,' said Carlisle cautiously, 'but then so does the idea that *Scorpion* was taken by an enemy cruiser. At present they are the only hypotheses that make any sense at all.' He sat back in his chair and said with more confidence, 'in any case, both theories lead us towards St. Bartholomew as being the next French island to leeward, suitable for both a fugitive's hideout and a safe harbour for a prize. In this wide ocean that is the next point of reference for the hunt.'

He looked earnestly at his two companions. 'God willing, there is a more palatable explanation than either of those. We are already heading for St. Bartholomew,' he could feel the changed motion of the frigate as the long swell took her abaft her starboard beam and could hear the orders and bustle of setting the stuns'ls, 'so let's consider what we should do in the morning. Meanwhile, not a word of this to anyone. Even the rumour of this could blight Godwin's career and that of the warrant officers in *Scorpion*. Until we know the facts, this supposition must stay a secret between us three.'

Medina spread her sails to the quartering breeze and stretched away, west by north for the tiny French island that was now the centre of the quest for the errant schooner.

CHAPTER TWENTY-EIGHT

St. Bartholomew

Saturday, twelfth of February 1757
Medina, at Sea, off St. Bartholomew

The rugged green-clad peak showed clearly ahead as the sun rose astern of the frigate. St. Bartholomew was no Barbuda. Although it was smaller, it was also considerably more broken and much higher, formed by some volcanic activity in the far distant past. The nearest summit on the eastern side of the island towered nearly a thousand feet above the blue sea and trailed a permanent white cloud to leeward. The whole island was dominated by this and smaller hills, becoming less lofty as they trailed away to the west.

It was to the west of the island that *Medina's* business took them. Like all these islands in the Antilles, the constant pounding of the north-easterly trade wind made the eastern side of each island unsuitable for a harbour or for an anchorage. Thus all maritime affairs were conducted on the western side.

The little groups of fishing vessels that had left their harbours before the sun rose quickly hauled their nets and raced inshore when they saw the frigate approaching. It was not usual for men-of-war to interfere with the fishing industry, but it was better not to take chances. The frigate passed Les Roques and Coco Island to seaward, their telescopes scanning every cove and inlet for a sign of the schooner. Nothing, no wreck on the shore, no tall masts reaching above the fishing vessels. They struck the stuns'ls and hardened onto the wind around Negro Point on the southwest corner of the island. There was no chance of surprising the French inhabitants; *Medina* was clearly visible from the island and had been since dawn. There was no sign of *Scorpion* and no sign of a French cruiser, but they had not yet looked into the main harbour of the island.

'Mister Hosking, bring us between the Sugar Loaf Island and that group of islets off the Careenage. I'd like to have a good look at the harbour.'

'Aye-aye sir,' replied the sailing master. 'Its deep water right up to the Sugar Loaf, but I'm not sure about those other islands, I've never been that close.'

There was a Sugar Loaf island or hill on most of the French Caribbean islands, *Le Pain de Sucre* in their own language. A fitting way of acknowledging both the foundations of the prosperity of the islands and the remarkable resemblance between an eroded volcanic peak and a conventional sugarloaf, the typical form into which sugar for European homes was moulded before being shipped across the Atlantic. This Sugar Loaf Island was the least like its namesake that Carlisle had seen. A sugarloaf should be a rounded cone, but this island was more like a penny bun.

The Careenage was full of masts, none of them very tall. Holbrooke had climbed up to the maintop for a better look, and he was seated comfortably against the mast, his feet stretched out to the hammock cranes. His first thought was for the batteries on the peninsula that protected the careenage; he counted three, none of them very large and none posing a significant threat to *Medina*, although they would make a cutting-out expedition perilous. They were fast coming to the point where his view of the Careenage would be cut off by the first group of islands close to the shore – The Saintes – again a common name for a clutch of tall isles. He just had time for a quick sweep with the telescope. He could see a lot of small coasters, a few of them were schooners and about the same size as *Scorpion*; any of them could be the missing man-of-war. But then just before his view was obscured, he saw something – or thought he did – that made him rub his eyes. He had just seen the flash of two white flags at the masthead of a vessel, then it was gone, hidden by The Saintes. The French used the Bourbon standard as their national ensign, it was white with gold fleur-de-lis, but from a distance, it appeared predominantly white, and so was the ensign for the Leeward Island Squadron, as long as it was commanded by a Rear Admiral of the White. Could it have been a white ensign under a French Ensign? He probably saw what wasn't there, his mind conditioned by last evening's conversation. He would have to wait until they moved further north, past the islands.

'Deck ho!' came the call from the masthead. That was Whittle on lookout duty, the best eyes in the ship. 'Captain sir. I just caught a glimpse of a white ensign under another white or grey flag. It's flying on a schooner in the bay, but its obscured by the island now.'

'I believe I saw the same thing,' shouted Holbrooke. 'Possibly a white ensign under a Bourbon flag. I'll get a better look once we are past the islands.'

'Mister Hosking, take us further north. I need a clear view into the bay,' ordered Carlisle. Then *Scorpion* was a prize. Had she been captured in a fight or had a mutinous crew handed her over to the enemy? In either case, the French would undoubtedly display her as a prize, and the act of hoisting the two ensigns, the victor's above the vanquished, was the conventional way of emphasising the fact.

At that moment there was the faint sound of a gun, two guns; a puff of smoke appeared in the position of the southern battery. There was no sound of a passing shot and no water spout. Either the guns were so small that *Medina* was well out of range, or they were firing to warn the frigate off, choosing not to waste ball at that range.

The seconds ticked by agonisingly, The Saintes slipped aft, and the mouth of the Careenage opened. Holbrooke knew that he would have only a minute or so before his view was again obscured, this time by the next group of islands, called with a stark lack of imagination *Les Islettes*. He could see the first few vessels alongside the wharves, and then, suddenly, the schooner came clear, and there was no longer any doubt. He let Whittle give the bad news to the quarterdeck, while he hurried down the ratlines to report.

'It's *Scorpion* sir, for sure, and she is flying the French ensign over the white. She is the fourth vessel in from the seaward point of that natural mole. And there's a battery right on the point, no more than three or four hundred yards from her.'

They were interrupted by the sound of a shot howling overhead.

'It looks like that battery on the point has heavier metal than the last one,' said Carlisle with his telescope to his eye, 'but they are no better at pointing their guns. However, that's a nine-pounder, and it has our range; we have seen all we need to see.' He lowered the telescope.

'Mister Hosking, take us out to the north of the Sugar Loaf.'

With the wind on her starboard quarter, *Medina* drew quickly out of range of the battery's guns. The blank looks on the quarterdeck said it all; there was nothing to be done. A cutting out expedition in the face of an alert enemy with fixed batteries was not to be undertaken by a frigate's crew. Carlisle's duty was clear, to return to English Harbour and pass the problem on to the admiral. He didn't expect to get such a warm reception as when he came in with a prize at his tail.

'Take her around the island and then set a course for English Harbour, Mister Hosking. We should be there tomorrow in the morning watch, I would guess.'

Carlisle and Holbrooke looked wistfully astern. It went against the grain to leave the schooner there, under French colours. Both men knew, however, that they would not be thanked for throwing away lives on an attempt such as

The Leeward Islands Squadron

this. If Frankland felt it important enough, he could mount a regular expedition against St. Bartholomew. He could batter the guns into silence, and he could land a strong party to secure the peninsula and cut out *Scorpion* and the other French ships by main force. But *Medina* had neither the guns nor the marines to attempt such an operation. No words were needed; they must reach back to English Harbour as fast as they could.

They were still watching the receding shoreline of the Careenage through the gaps in its guardian islands as The Sugar Loaf came onto their larboard beam. The battery had stopped firing, the range was too great, and *Medina* must present a problematic target between the islands.

'Hands to veer ship,' called the master.

'He's still not quite right,' thought Carlisle. A week ago, the master's roar could have split a topsail; he clearly wasn't fully recovered from the blow on his head. He spotted a small lugger out of the corner of his eye, close to the island, but it was no threat, and they would leave it at least two cables to leeward. It looked ready to sink, it was so low in the water. 'Perhaps they had a good catch,' thought Carlisle idly, considering the miracle of Jesus in the Sea of Galilee. Where that memory had sprung from, he was unable to say, but the image of a great catch of fish – too many for the boat – always occurred to him whenever he saw a small fishing vessel with a good haul.

Medina came around quickly and put the wind on her larboard side. The wind was fair for the western side of Antigua; they could take advantage of the sea breeze in the morning to coast around the southern shore and take them up to English Harbour. They should be anchoring and reporting by the middle of the forenoon watch. Carlisle was not looking forward to that.

'Captain sir. That lugger is signalling us,' said Holbrooke. 'He looks quite frantic.'

It was an unremarkable craft, one of the many that could be found in any of the French islands. A descendant of that hardy breed of boats that fished and smuggled around the Breton coast.

'They're running down towards us sir.'

'Mister Hook,' he said to the marine lieutenant, 'a file of your men in the waist if you please. They may level their muskets at that boat until we are sure of its intentions.'

He heard the heavy clump of booted feet as he stared at the boat through his telescope. They certainly were signalling, and they were intent upon intercepting *Medina*. He could see a man in the bows, a second at the sheets and there was a third at the tiller, although the sails were masking him. Reason told Carlisle to ignore the boat, it was probably just a French fisherman looking for a quick sale. But in full view of the shore, less than two miles away? That was a risky business that could lead to a charge of trading with the enemy.

'Lay to Mister Hosking.' He had made a snap decision, based on his gut instinct rather than reason. He was out of range of the guns at the Careenage, and there were no enemy ships in sight. He could afford an hour for a conversation with a French fisherman; who knew what useful information he could glean? And in any case, it would be an excellent opportunity to practice his French.

Medina lay with her larboard bow to the wind. The man in the bows of the lugger had stopped signalling, and it looked like they would make a neat approach to the larboard waist. Holbrooke cupped his hands to hail, to warn the boat to stand off until their intentions were known. But at that moment she veered, and the figure at the tiller became visible. Blue and white, a sea officer's uniform! Holbrooke was quick to take in the situation and changed his French hail to the conventional naval challenge.

'Boat Ahoy!'

Only fifty yards away now, and the figure in the bows, equally quick-witted, responded. The man's reply was brought down by the wind, loud and clear, 'aye, aye,' the correct response indicating the presence of a commission officer in the boat.

Carlisle and Holbrooke exchanged glances – there was only one British sea officer who could be in a boat in these waters, and that was evident to all on the quarterdeck. Carlisle saw Lieutenant Hook signalling for his Marines to lower their muskets. 'Belay that,' he said quietly, 'keep the muskets pointing at the boat, Mister Hook, I'm not yet sure what we are dealing with.'

Holbrooke signalled for the boat to come alongside, the universal downward sweep of the arm.

'Mister Holbrooke, get those men on board and take the lugger in tow. I want Godwin in my great cabin, and you are to guard the other two in my day cabin. They are not to speak to anyone other than you or I.' Whatever story there was to be told, Carlisle wanted to manage it rather than to let a few fragments of information cause all sorts of rumours. If *Scorpion* had been taken by an enemy in a fight, then there was no need to hide the facts. But if she had suffered a mutiny – and that looked more and more likely – then it was vital that the men be isolated from his crew. Carlisle was confident in the loyalty of his people, but mutiny was insidious, it caught hold of men's imagination and wouldn't let go.

Godwin came on board looking dour and surly. Neither Carlisle nor Holbrooke knew the other two, but none of them said a word. Clearly, Godwin had insisted on silence. 'Good,' thought Carlisle, 'at least he has retained some common sense.'

'That's *Scorpion's* master's mate and bosun sir,' whispered Hosking. 'Philip Stevens is the mate, a good man, but I don't remember the bosun's name.'

'Thank you, Mister Hosking. As soon as the lugger is secured, take us back to our course for Antigua.' He looked at the inquisitive faces on the quarterdeck, 'and please do your best to damp down the speculation until I have discovered the facts.'

CHAPTER TWENTY-NINE

Mutiny

Saturday, twelfth of February 1757
Medina, at Sea, off St. Bartholomew

Miles Godwin looked as though he had spent a night in an open boat, but he seemed well otherwise. The stubble on his jaw suggested that he had shaved less than forty-eight hours ago which gave Carlisle some point of reference. His uniform was not clean, but not yet disreputable. He was no longer the bullish self-confident man that Carlisle had first met in the great cabin of *Wessex* three months ago. Much of the arrogance had been swept away by the events at Grenada and the disappointments of English Harbour. Godwin knew as well as any sea officer that command of a small schooner was not a promotion from first-lieutenant of a two-decked fourth rate. He was subdued, but there was still the ghost of the man visible; defeated but not conquered and he met Carlisle's inquisitive gaze with a steely, defiant scowl. The two men were not on good terms, and they both knew it. In this situation, Carlisle would generally have offered refreshment and let the lieutenant tell his story in his own time, but he didn't feel inclined to be the one to extend the olive branch.

'Well, Mister Godwin, I see *Scorpion* is in the Careenage, and yet you are here.'

Godwin had backbone, he had to admit. There was no sign of defeat on his face. He stared straight back at Carlisle and let a dozen seconds pass before he replied. Enough time to deliver the unspoken message, 'damn you, Edward Carlisle.'

Godwin opened his mouth to speak, shifted his position in the chair and made a second attempt. He blurted out the single word; '*mutiny.*'

The fateful syllables hung in the air, the most dangerous word in the service. Carlisle kept his face impassive, privately blessing his decision to keep the master's mate and the bosun incommunicado.

'The crew rose against me the evening after we left English Harbour. The master's mate, the bosun and a few of the seamen were all that remained loyal. I had no midshipmen, no volunteers, no gentlemen at all to second me.'

Carlisle didn't respond. There was apparently a long story to be told here, but he would let Godwin tell it in his own time. Meanwhile, *Medina* was moving fast away from St. Bartholomew, towards Antigua. Was that the right thing to do? Nothing substantial had changed; it was still an impossible task to cut out the schooner. In fact, the need to report to Admiral Frankland had only become more urgent.

Carlisle listened to the story with a stony, severe face. In truth, Godwin could hardly be blamed; the seeds of the uprising had been sown when all the squadron's refuse had been dumped into the schooner. Nevertheless, Godwin was heading for trial for the loss of his ship, and a court martial convened on the Leeward Island Station and made up of captains who had been complicit in discarding their worst men into *Scorpion* would hardly be inclined to fairness. Set aside Carlisle's established antipathy towards Godwin, the man was far too dangerous to befriend, or even to be offered the ordinary civilities.

Scorpion had sailed from English Harbour at first light on Wednesday a week ago. It was the first time that Godwin had taken her to sea, but she had swept out of the harbour quickly enough, the men pulling at the great oars with little murmuring until the sea breeze came to their aid and allowed the sails to be set for a course around the coast to the east. The schooner had then picked up the trade wind and set her course close-hauled for Barbuda. Godwin was aware of the nature of his crew, but he also knew the nature of this appointment – a chance to rebuild his career from the ashes of the Grenada expedition – and he knew that he was in no position to argue with the admiral.

The trouble had started as soon as they had stowed the sweeps and set the sails. Once out of sight of authority, the hands effectively refused to turn to. It was only dumb insolence and clumsy disobedience to start with, but by mid-afternoon, they were refusing to touch sheet or halyard. Only the master's mate and bosun could be relied upon; the few hands who didn't actively support the trouble-makers were cowed, and they kept themselves below decks. Godwin found that he could not go forward of the wheel without being jostled and threatened. The ringleader was an able seaman named Dawson, a big, articulate man with the carriage of a prize-fighter and the gift of oratory of a barrister. It appeared that he had been the leader of the men for some time although he kept a low profile while they were at anchor in English Harbour.

Seeing how things stood, Godwin had considered turning back for English Harbour, even though he knew that it would reflect poorly upon him in this his first command. That he didn't was almost solely because he was concerned that such an action would precipitate the mutiny; he knew that it had got that far out of his control. He planned to go ashore at Barbuda and demand help from the militia.

Carlisle heard all this either directly or by innuendo. Godwin was careful not to talk about his professional aspirations, but his thinking was quite clear and along the same lines as any other sea officer caught up in this situation. Carlisle almost felt sorry for him.

'We had made a slow passage, being unable to set sufficient sail due to the hands' refusal to work. I sighted Barbuda just before sunset. Not being familiar with the island or the anchorage, I ordered the ship about so that we could stand off to the east until the morning.'

Carlisle nodded cautiously. 'Just as I supposed,' he thought.

'But the hands refused, saying that if they had to sail through the night, it would be in a direction that they chose. It became clear that they'd planned this before we left English Harbour, but they had not intended to take any action until they were off St. Bartholomew.'

Godwin now started to show the first signs of strain.

'I had laid out a pair of pistols in my cabin before we sailed. I left the deck to collect them, intending to use them to enforce my will on the crew. But as I stepped out of my cabin with the pistols in hand, they were waiting for me. They pinioned me, tied my hands behind my back,' he lifted his arms to show the raw wounds from the rough hemp cordage that they had used, 'and threw me into my cabin with two of them to guard me. I heard a short scuffle on deck, and then the master's mate and the bosun were pushed in to join me, both with their hands tied. Then I felt the schooner alter course and from the direction of the setting sun I knew that we were heading northwest, for St. Bartholomew or beyond.'

'Just as the old man said,' thought Carlisle. 'He saw them sail away to the northwest, but nobody would believe him.'

Godwin continued; the tension was showing, the stress of having to confess these failings to the man who had been most responsible for putting him into this position when he should now still be, the first lieutenant of *Wessex*.

'We were boarded by a boat from shore soon after dawn, and a pilot took us into the Careenage, that would be Thursday. I know now that we were expected, the bastards must have been planning this for weeks.' Godwin's agitation was showing clear; the man was close to tears. 'I could hear them cheering on deck. Then some soldiers came and took the three of us away, and we were kept in the town lockup.'

He told this part of the story with his eyes firmly fixed on the deck below him. 'At least he feels some shame,' thought Carlisle. He tried to imagine facing other sea officers after having his ship taken from him without a drop of blood being spilt in its defence.

'Could I have a glass of water, sir?' asked Godwin. 'I have had no drink since yesterday.'

Carlisle's orders for everyone to keep clear of his cabin had been obeyed, and his servant was nowhere to be seen. He called through the closed door for the sentry to pass the word. It took only a few minutes for the water to be produced and some biscuits and fruit. Carlisle used those few moments to evaluate his own handling of the interview. He was harsh, he knew, and that was not in his nature. He justified it by the need to keep his distance from this man. After all, it was highly likely that he would have to sit in judgement on him soon, and their relationship already had an unfortunate history. 'However, I have made my point,' thought Carlisle. 'I can afford to show a more human face.'

Somewhat refreshed, Godwin continued.

'We lay in that stinking gaol for three nights until the Governor came to visit. He is a reasonable man, and he immediately ordered us to be held under guard in a room in the barracks. We saw nothing of the mutineers in this time, but the soldiers were very free in their conversation in the next room to the one where we were held – we could hear almost every word that they said. We discovered that the mutineers were still living on board the schooner and that the governor was waiting for a chance to send her to the French navy at Fort Royal.'

Carlisle started. 'They would sail the schooner to Martinique?' he asked.

'Yes, sir. And then we heard two days ago that a frigate was being sent to escort her. It's expected today, to sail back to Martinique as soon as *Scorpion* clears the harbour.'

Carlisle held up his hand for a pause. They hadn't sighted a frigate yet, but most likely a Frenchman would sail inside the island chain, to the leeward of Dominica, Guadeloupe, Montserrat and St. Kitts, to keep clear of Frankland's squadron. On *Medina's* present course, they probably wouldn't sight each other at all. The prospect of meeting the frigate was very attractive, particularly if – as seemed likely – she was the same ship that they had dismasted off Diamond Rock a week ago. 'Was that enough time for a repair?' thought Carlisle, 'certainly, if the dockyard at Fort Royal was as competent as it looked.'

'Could the French have known that they were overheard?' asked Carlisle. Two things came to mind; first, this could be a trap, the information being fed to Godwin and he then being allowed to escape. *Medina* could be faced with that great brute of a seventy-four where he expected only a frigate. Second, if it wasn't a trap, would the French change their plans when Godwin escaped, guessing that he may have overheard their conversations?

'No sir,' replied Godwin, positively. 'I am sure that they had no idea that we could hear them. There was a solid wall between the two rooms except at a point where a hatch had been filled in with wood panelling. That was where we could hear them, by putting our ears to the panelling. They had no reason to believe that they could be heard.'

'Very well, how did you escape?' This was the test. If the escape had been too easy, then the danger that they were being lured into a trap was too high.

'We had been watching the guards' routines and saw that we had about ten minutes when the lawn outside our window was unguarded. In the middle watch, we removed the putty from around the window, jumped out and ran down to the shore between the two batteries, only a few hundred yards. We were looking for a larger boat, but they were all in the Careenage, and that was far too risky. However, we found that little lugger and sailed out to the

Sugar Loaf without anyone spotting us. I expect we weren't missed until breakfast time. We weighed her down with stones and sank her in a small cleft in the rocks and hid through the day. We planned to raise her last night, but there were too many boats around, still looking for us I believe. When we saw *Medina*, we bailed her as fast as we could. You perhaps saw that she is still almost swamped; we only managed to get the water a few inches below the gunwales. However, it was just enough. If it had taken us five more minutes, we would have missed you.'

Carlisle stood and walked to the chart; it gave him time to think. Was it possible that the three men had not only escaped from their prison but found a boat and spent two nights and a day unobserved on a rock little more than a mile away from their gaolers? On the other hand, was it feasible that the French could have designed such a complex operation of deceit?

'Pass the word for the master,' he called.

Hosking knocked and walked in. The contrast between the tension in the cabin and the master's imperturbable demeanour was ludicrous. As Godwin's tale had unfolded, Carlisle had become first depressed and then, as this last information was revealed – the possibility of a fight with a French frigate – he became more and more energised; he was literally on the edge of his seat. The master, however, knew none of this. He may have guessed at the events that led to this lieutenant having come aboard, but they were only guesses.

'Mister Hosking, as soon as we have sunk St. Bartholomew, bring the ship onto an easterly heading. I don't want our change of course to be observed from the shore or by any French vessel. I'll be on deck in the next half an hour.' Hosking turned to go. 'And Mister Hosking, keep a sharp lookout for a French frigate.'

CHAPTER THIRTY

The Hunt

Sunday, thirteenth of February 1757
Medina, at Sea, off Montserrat

The eastern horizon was aglow. Twilight was only minutes away, and already the faces of the men on the quarterdeck were becoming more distinct. *Medina* had cleared for action an hour ago, and the hands were at their quarters, excused from the usual morning watch routines of scrubbing the decks and polishing the brightwork. They knew their captain well enough to be sure that it was no mere merchant ship that they were waiting for, tucked in here to the south of Montserrat with the tremendous barren cone of the Soufriere volcano towering three thousand feet above them. They also knew about the mutiny by now; it was hard to suppress that kind of news.

Carlisle had wrestled with his conscience. Should he have returned to English Harbour to alert the admiral to this possibility of intercepting a French frigate only sixty miles to leeward of the British naval base? Certainly, if two or three ships of the squadron could have sailed before dark to be in position at dawn, the capture would be a mere matter of a few guns and the running down of an ensign. But that was the rub; could he have made English Harbour in time, and would any of the squadron be ready to sail at that short notice? As with most operations at sea, it came down to a careful judgement of speed against time and distance, all against the background of the weather. If the French frigate and the schooner left the Careenage in the afternoon watch, they would be off Montserrat at dawn. That was cutting it too fine for Carlisle. He had been confident that he could have *Medina* in position to meet the Frenchman, even allowing for a detour to the east to mask their intentions.

So here they were, in a position and at a time derived from fine calculations against a host of variables and plain unknowns. Had the frigate arrived and departed on time? Had she taken the leeward route back to Fort Royal? Was she alone? Had *Medina* been sighted, lying in wait? Had the escape of the prisoners caused a change in plan? Carlisle had a hunch, and he was determined to act upon it. Godwin's story about his flight sounded plausible, and it was unlikely that it had been engineered by the French. Even if the three Englishmen had been seen being rescued by *Medina* – and that was possible – the governor must have assumed that the escapees knew nothing about the frigate and would be relatively unconcerned. *Medina* had been seen departing east, presumably to report back to English Harbour from whence the governor might expect that a cutting-out expedition would be launched. That alone would convince the governor that he should be rid of this schooner as soon as possible. As much as anything can be certain at sea, Carlisle was confident that the frigate and schooner would pass to the leeward of Montserrat sometime in the morning or forenoon watches so that they could make Fort Royal in Martinique at dawn the following day.

'Mister Holbrooke, who do we have at the masthead?'

Holbrooke was certain that Carlisle already knew that Whittle had been sent up there fifteen minutes ago, but Whittle at the masthead had become something of a good luck charm. Carlisle believed in luck, although he was reluctant to admit it, and for this particular spell to work, he needed to be *told* that Whittle was at the masthead.

Keeping a straight face, Holbrooke replied, 'It's Whittle sir. He would have been up there all night if he had been allowed, but I thought it best to reserve him for the dawn.'

'Quite right,' said Carlisle, 'and all else is in order?'

They had talked through how this engagement may fall

out. There was little chance of using the land once they were to leeward of the island, but it was a convenient place to lurk until their prey should appear. *Medina* was the equal of most of the French frigates, only the heavy fifth rates could out-gun her, and he was prepared to have a go at even those. If it were their old friend from last week, then they would be well-matched on paper. Carlisle had outwitted that ship once already and believed that he could also out-fight her. It would be a slugging match, where the better gunnery would win – the faster and more accurate gunnery – and in that Carlisle felt he had the advantage over any frigate that floated. His men were well drilled – obsessively so to an outside observer – and they had been blooded in three successful actions; the privateer luggers off Ushant, the raid on Fort Royal and Port Louis in Grenada and the engagement with this same frigate off Diamond Rock. They had also taken prizes; they were all of them wealthier by the division of the value of five fine French merchantmen. Then, there was also the small matter of Carlisle's reputation. Enough of the crew had served with him in *Fury* to know that he had the bloody-mindedness to carry through a tough sea-fight, and those who had not served with him had been forced to listen to his exploits being re-told around the mess tables long into the night.

His crew was in top form, standing on tip-toe ready and eager for the start. If he couldn't take any French frigate that swam with this crew, then it was a sad case for the British navy.

Carlisle had one real concern, and that was the schooner. Her light build and tiny armament meant that she could hardly influence the course of the battle. But what would she do? If there were a substantial number of the mutineers still on board, they would be desperate to avoid a fight that could only end badly for them. Either they would help the French to win against their countrymen and therefore be hunted down by the navy with even more persistence than usual, or they would be taken by *Medina* and hauled before a court martial, where they could expect little mercy. No, if the mutineers were still on board, they would want to sail as fast as they could for Martinique and leave the frigate to deal with *Medina* alone. Carlisle didn't want to take the frigate and lose the schooner, and he was prepared to take risks to prevent her escape.

'You have a double load of chain shot in the starboard battery, Mister Holbrooke?'

'Yes, sir. Chain shot to starboard, round shot to larboard.'

The sun's upper rim was just piercing the horizon. The volcano to starboard was caught in a noose of light, turning the ash-grey slopes to pinks and oranges, each lava gully showing up in stark relief against the long morning shadows. A shoal of flying fish broke the surface on the larboard quarter, the very best of omens for Carlisle. He watched as the last one lost height and, with its fins folded against its flanks, slipped back into its watery realm. Carlisle dearly loved to see flying fish.

'Sail ho! Sail on the starboard bow, five miles or so sir. It looks like a frigate.'

Every man on deck stood stock-still, fearing that by moving they would miss the exchange between their captain and that most lucky of able seamen.

'Is there any sign of the schooner, Whittle?' replied Carlisle.

'Nothing sir, no schooner.'

That was disappointing. The first hitch in the plan. If the schooner was not with the frigate, then where was she? But the frigate was true to her time. She would be taking the most direct route to Martinique, and that led five miles off Montserrat.

'Deck ho! I see the schooner now sir. She is close under the lee of the frigate. You can just see her foremast

The Leeward Islands Squadron

over the frigate's bowsprit. It looks like *Scorpion*.'

Carlisle breathed a sigh of relief. It was not essential to re-take *Scorpion* – sailing into English Harbour with a French frigate behind her would be quite enough glory for *Medina* and her captain. But the absence of the schooner meant that the Frenchman would have less constraint on his tactics in the coming fight. He would not have to worry about his defenceless charge and could concentrate wholly on fighting *Medina*.

'Mister Hosking, two points to starboard if you please. Then a course to take me close under that frigate's bow.'

'Aye-aye sir.' Hosking rubbed his hands in pleasure at the coming fight.

The Frenchman would undoubtedly see what Carlisle intended, but he had the disadvantage of being to leeward – Carlisle had the weather-gage, and at least in this opening phase, he could decide when and how the combat should be opened. The Frenchman had to react to Carlisle's opening move, and it was Carlisle's clear task to deceive him for as long as he could.

Medina was running free with the north-westerly trade wind right on her stern, the wind and waves making almost no sound on this point of sailing. She was stripped down to fighting rig; topsails and staysails, the lower yards chained and puddened and the splinter nets rigged. In the general silence, the sanded decks crunched under the feet of the officers while the men at the swivel guns nervously swung their weapons on their mounts. Hook's marines provided bright patches of red where they were distributed in the tops and along the hammock nets.

'She's hauling her wind sir.' said Hosking.

'Very well. Let's give her something to think about. Come half a point to starboard as though I am determined to pass her larboard to larboard.'

'Mister Holbrooke, we have a chance to hit her hard with the starboard battery. She won't want to come off the wind and let us get around her stern, so I believe she will try to force us further to the north. She has about two more points that she can turn to larboard.'

'Mister Hosking, you see the situation? Let her believe she is forcing us to starboard.'

'Aye-aye sir.' He turned to the quartermaster, 'give her half a point to starboard, Eli then hold her there.'

'Half a point to starboard it is sir.'

The French frigate moved a little more to larboard of the bowsprit, and she could be seen turning closer to the wind.

'Not wishing to tempt fate, Mister Holbrooke, Mister Hosking,' said Carlisle privately crossing his fingers behind his back, 'but if he continues to follow us around until he is hard on the wind, I will wait until our bowsprits are almost touching and turn to larboard. We must pass very close to take advantage of our double-shotted guns. But make no mistake gentlemen, she will be ready to fire also. I only hope that most of her gun crews are attending to the larboard battery.'

The two frigates, equal in size and armament, rushed together at a combined closing speed of fourteen knots. What had been a distant prospect from the deck of *Medina* rapidly became a solid reality, just twenty minutes from first sighting to the now-inevitable engagement. Holbrooke looked around the deck, nodded to the bosun and then made a closer study of the men at his guns. Everything was ready, and there was no need to disturb them with unnecessary orders. He was forcibly reminded of Henry IV's speech before the walls of Harfleur; *I see you stand like greyhounds in the slips*. That phrase had real meaning today as he looked at the gun crews. They were eager for battle, just waiting for the word to unleash their fire and destruction on the enemy. 'Now, if we can just preserve that spirit to the end of the business, even when guns are dismounted, half of the men are down, and the deck is slippery with blood. If they can still be so eager to fight then, nothing can stand against us,' he thought. He remembered previous occasions when he had gone into battle with Captain Carlisle. The three times they had fought *Vulcain*, a much bigger ship than their old *Fury*. How his soul had been stirred as he saw *Fury* hurtling into that last engagement, how his heart had nearly stopped when the battle turned against Carlisle, and his snap decision to throw his pitifully small crew of the tender *Chiara* into the fray. Only he knew how close he had come to turning away and beating back to Gibraltar, although his crew may have guessed, and that was a guilty thought that he would take to his grave.

'What did I learn that day?' He had thought about it so often in the past year that the conclusions seemed to merge. Training, preparation, tactical thought, morale; all these were important, but the key point was burned into his consciousness. It was the key to winning a sea fight and the key to naval preferment if you were not fortunate enough to have strong patronage or interest. 'Boldness, that is the key to winning,' he remembered. 'When you have prepared yourself, your men and your ship for combat, at the end you must be prepared to roll the dice. To charge when others urge caution, to turn at bay when all about you cry retreat, to throw in your own life as you would the last chip in a game of hazard.' The very recollection of his new life's principle stiffened him, and another look at the gun crews reassured him. They were ready.

Holbrooke looked up and saw that the frigate was a mere mile away now. Yes, it was the same ship that they crippled a week ago. She had a new bowsprit; the lighter colour of the wood flashed in the slanting dawn sunlight. But it was noticeably too short for the rest of the rig, and it would give their opponent a tendency to gripe, for the bows to continually seek the wind. Apart from the strain on the steersmen, it meant that she would be slow in stays and may prefer veering to tacking. What was the port admiral thinking when he sent this half-repaired ship out? Perhaps he believed this was a simple escort task, with little chance of meeting the enemy. Well, he was about to be proved wrong. Holbrooke turned to point this out to his captain but saw that he had already seen it and was discussing the implications with Hosking, pointing to starboard.

'Mister Holbrooke,' shouted Carlisle urgently. 'Stand by the larboard battery, I'm going to force her to tack or to show us her stern. Either way, we have a chance to rake her. The chain shot will do at that range.'

The nearest gun crews had already heard the captain, but discipline held them in place until Holbrooke bellowed, 'larboard battery, men. Out quoins, aim high but wait for the word.'

There was a rush of feet as the crews ran to the other side of the deck. This is where discipline and preparation told. Each pair of guns, larboard and starboard, had only a single crew, but each crew had two captains. It was the duty of the second captain to have the disengaged gun ready for immediate use so that when the gun crew stepped across the deck from the opposite side, everything was in order; the gun loaded, the sponges and rammers in their places, the linstock with its slow match waiting in its tub. The second captains didn't disappoint him; they were knocking out the quoins, increasing the elevation of the guns, even as the crews slotted easily into their allotted places.

'If he holds his course, the captain will cross his bow and force him to tack or veer,' he called down to his men. 'Either we will destroy the captain's cabin, or we'll make a mess of his new bowsprit.'

That raised a cheer. It was an interesting question; how much do you tell the men? It could have a harmful effect on morale if they knew the plan and it doesn't work. '*No plan survives contact with the enemy*,' was another important principle that Holbrooke held close. But in this case, it was hard to see what else the Frenchman could do. If he bore away now, at this pace, he was just asking for *Medina* to cross his stern. And in any case, he was probably not capable of bearing away quickly with that short bowsprit.

Closer now, and Holbrooke could see every detail of the Frenchman's bows. The bowsprit was new, but the jib-boom was utterly absent. Holbrooke could imagine what had happened in the yard. The shipwrights had fitted the bowsprit and were waiting for the new cap and saddle iron to be forged before they replaced the jib-boom, but the frigate was sent to sea before those essential pieces of ironwork were ready. Holbrooke thought that he would have lashed the jib-boom in place if he had been sent to sea in that state. It was a tricky job and only a short-term fix, but it was well within the capabilities of a competent bosun.

Holbrooke felt rather than saw *Medina* turn to starboard. The Frenchman hesitated and then put down his helm to tack. That would have been a useful manoeuvre if they had the leverage of a jib to haul the bows right through the eye of the wind and onto the starboard tack. As it was, the French frigate flew into the wind very quickly but was reluctant to pay off on the new course. A party of a dozen fo'c'sle hands were hauling the clew of the fore topmast staysail out to starboard, but the ship responded very slowly. They weren't exactly caught in irons, but they were helpless against the manoeuvrable, well-handled frigate that was *Medina*. Holbrooke looked back at the quarterdeck and could see Carlisle's intention. He was going to cross the Frenchman's bows at very short range, taking advantage of his inability to come off the wind to bring his battery to bear.

'Fire as you bear,' shouted Holbrooke as *Medina* rushed across her adversary's bows.

Number two gun roared, followed by all the remainder of the battery in rapid succession as they saw their target. The range was less than half a cable, and they couldn't miss, even with the target moving rapidly left. With the quoins removed and *Medina* heeling to larboard, the guns were pointing about ten degrees above the horizontal. The chain shot hurled itself against the beakhead and the spars, the rigging and the sails, tearing great rents wherever it passed. The new bowsprit miraculously survived, but the forestay and fore topmast stay parted, and the beakhead was shattered. Until they rigged new stays forward, the ship would be unmanageable. All they could do was strip the main and mizzen masts of their sails and run to leeward under the foresail and fore-topsail. Anything else would surely bring their fore topmast down. By sheer good fortune, *Medina's* larboard battery had been loaded with chain shot. It had been intended to disable the schooner leaving *Medina* free to deal with the frigate, but the order had been reversed, and now it was the frigate that was disabled while the schooner awaited their attention.

A great cheer came from *Medina*. The Frenchman had not managed to fire a single shot in retaliation, and now her gun crews would be busy repairing the destruction to her bows. *Medina* ran on to the northwest; Carlisle was intent on preventing the schooner from escaping. The frigate could wait, in any case, she could hardly evade *Medina* on this crystal clear day with only the broad Caribbean under her lee and twelve hours to sunset.

CHAPTER THIRTY-ONE

Scorpion

Sunday, thirteenth of February 1757
Medina, at Sea, off Montserrat

Carlisle shouted across the quarterdeck. 'Veer ship, Mister Hosking, lay me a cable to windward of *Scorpion*.'

'Aye-aye sir,' replied the sailing master.

Carlisle studied the schooner. He would dearly love to know how many mutineers had been left aboard and how many French sailors had been drafted in. The Frenchmen could fire a gun for the honour of their King before striking their colours, but the leaders of the mutineers would be fighting for their very lives. A court martial may find ways to pardon the majority, but any that were found to have instigated the mutiny, or taken an active leadership role, would inevitably swing from a yardarm in English Harbour.

Scorpion was a mile away and running fast to the southeast. She had come up a little, and it looked like she was heading for the nearest French territory, probably Guadeloupe. Montserrat was closer, but she would have to get past *Medina* to reach the dubious safety of that small island. If she could make it to Guadeloupe, she could take shelter under any of the French batteries that were scattered all along the western side, even if she couldn't reach the protected road of Basse Terre at the southern end of the island. But it was forty miles to Guadeloupe; she would be lucky to make it by noon, and with the wind abaft the beam, *Medina* would overhaul her in an hour.

'Mister Holbrooke, we must take *Scorpion* as rapidly as possible. Otherwise that gentleman astern will elude us.' They both looked at the frigate. She was game enough and was running down to protect the schooner. But Carlisle and Holbrooke knew that it was a mere gesture, a point of honour with no tactical substance behind it. Now that the frigate was disabled, and even though her guns were unharmed, *Medina* was perfectly capable of dealing with both the French vessels, either individually or separately. In her present state, the frigate was, of the two, the least able to make her escape; Carlisle would deal with her once the schooner was re-taken.

'Captain Carlisle sir.' It was Godwin; he had found his way onto the quarterdeck. Well, it could do no harm now; the whole ship knew about the mutiny. 'May I have a prize crew to re-take my ship?'

Now that was something that Carlisle hadn't anticipated. Of course, Godwin was entirely correct. It was his ship, and until ordered otherwise by the commander-in-chief, he was still the captain. Carlisle knew that but had pushed it to the back of his mind. There was something wrong about it, allowing this man to sail his command back into English Harbour – this man who had so publicly failed in his first duty as a captain of one of His Majesty's ships. Carlisle paused for a moment and looked at Godwin. Any hint of remorse or apology from Godwin would have won him over, but the wretched man just glowered back at Carlisle, belligerence in every muscle of his tense face. Bringing his ship back into English Harbour would make a difference to the court martial board and could lighten the punishment or even swing the verdict. He had it in his power to aid this man in the difficult days to follow. Any hint of an unbending, the slightest nod towards fellowship would have swayed Carlisle. All this passed through his mind as he stood there, all this and the remembrance of the weakness he had shown in not demanding a court martial for Godwin after the Grenada raid. His decision was made, and in this instance the good of the service and his own inclination perfectly aligned.

'No sir, you will not return to *Scorpion*. Leave the deck

immediately and return to my day cabin.'

Godwin winced. He opened his mouth to argue, but nothing came out. He stood rooted to the spot. His hesitation was his downfall and led to the final humiliation.

'Mister Hook,' he called to the marine lieutenant, without taking his eyes off Godwin's face. 'Be so good as to escort Lieutenant Godwin to my day cabin and set a sentry on the door. He is not to leave without my permission.'

He turned back to Godwin. 'To avoid any further misunderstanding regarding your status, you may consider yourself under arrest.'

It was difficult for Carlisle to dismiss from his mind that distasteful encounter with Godwin but banish it he must. Although he had crippled the French frigate, he had not drawn her teeth, and she was still trying to impose herself between *Medina* and *Scorpion*. The battle required the captain's full attention.

'Mister Holbrooke, are your guns reloaded?'

'Yes sir, all loaded with round shot.'

'Then be so good as to join me on the quarterdeck.'

Holbrooke ran up the quarterdeck ladder and remove his hat as he met his captain.

'You see the situation, Holbrooke. The frigate is still trying to get between *Scorpion* and us, but *Scorpion* appears to have no faith in the frigate's power to protect them and is stretching away for Guadeloupe.'

Holbrooke nodded. The positions of the three ships were entirely clear in this crystal morning. It was quite a shock to see that the sun had not yet risen more than three or four times its diameter above the horizon. As if to confirm that so little time had passed, the ship's bell tolled three double strokes. It was only seven o'clock, and already they had achieved so much.

'What I don't know is whether *Scorpion* is under the command of mutineers or the French navy. I must give my attention to the frigate, but please study *Scorpion* and let me know what you see.'

Holbrooke retrieved his telescope from the binnacle. *Scorpion* was dead ahead at a mile; there was no need to climb into the top, but it was difficult to observe the schooner from the quarterdeck, so he walked forward to the fo'c'sle. From this vantage point, he could see that she appeared to be under regular control. There was a uniformed officer on the quarterdeck and a man at the wheel. He was about to return and report to Carlisle when he saw four men run aft. It looked like an argument; there was a scuffle, he distinctly heard the *pop, pop* of pistols being fired, and the uniformed man was knocked down. The schooner immediately put down her helm and headed east, close hauled on the larboard tack, closer than *Medina* could hope to follow her.

Holbrooke ran aft. 'It looks like there has been another mutiny in *Scorpion* sir,' he said. 'I saw the captain knocked down and now she has hauled her wind. It looks like she is trying to separate from the frigate.'

Carlisle nodded. It was what he had feared. The British mutineers had no intention of being taken and were presenting *Medina* with a choice of either the frigate or the schooner.

'That frigate will take hours to make enough repair to lay a course with the wind even a point forward of the beam. Let's see if we can stop that schooner. Commence firing as soon as you can hit her, Mister Holbrooke.'

'Chase that schooner, Mister Hosking, you may use all the sail that you need.'

The schooner was fine on the larboard bow. Only numbers two and four guns would bear, and they started firing immediately. Although *Scorpion* was sailing closer to the wind than *Medina*, she was sailing a little slower, meeting more resistance from the swell put up by the trade wind than the more massive ship. It was long range for accurate firing, but they could see spouts very close to their target. The gunner had come on deck to personally point the guns.

'A hit, I believe sir,' he said with satisfaction as a shot from number two gun failed to raise a spout. In his glee, he rubbed his hands on the leather apron that he wore in the powder magazine and had not yet removed. 'He cannot stand many more of those.'

'Keep at it Master Gunner. We can't get any closer, so this is the best range we can give you.'

'It'll be sufficient sir. Another hit, it looks like.'

As they watched, the schooner flew into the wind, and its fore-and-aft sails flapped wildly in the stiff breeze.

'Mister Holbrooke,' Carlisle called from the quarterdeck. 'I will put her close under my lee. Take Sergeant Wilson with you and a dozen marines and secure the schooner as quickly as you can, then lay a course for English Harbour. Wave to me when you have control; I want to be after the frigate as soon as possible.'

They came over the low sides of the schooner with a rush, but there was no resistance. Four men lay dead on the quarterdeck and two more lay moaning in the scuppers. A group of Frenchmen were gathered around the foremast looking bewildered, while another group of British sailors – mutineers presumably – were trying to ingratiate themselves with their new captors. It was a pathetic scene. The men were trying to come forward to plead their cases, disconnected snatches of their appeals reaching Holbrooke's ears.

'Sergeant Wilson, get all those men, British and French, down below and batten the hatches,' ordered Holbrooke. He would not have any of them on deck until he was safe in English Harbour.

'Jackson, put a man on the wheel. Your course is close-hauled on the larboard tack. We need to make some easting.'

Wilson was an efficient man with ten years' service, and he wasn't going to take any nonsense. The marines herded the men below at bayonet point, ignoring all their pleas of innocence and regardless of nationality. There was many a drop of blood on the deck where a man hesitated and was encouraged by a prick of the bayonet. It was hard luck on the French who could have expected better treatment having not resisted the boarding, but this was no time for niceties. Holbrooke guessed the identity of the bodies – they were most likely the ringleaders, shot by the French captain who had also met his end – but he was taking no risks.

Holbrooke noted with approval that Wilson, at his own initiative, had put two men on the starboard swivel gun and pointed it inboard at the grating covering the hatch. The Frenchmen and mutineers could see the brutal antipersonnel weapon and recognised the grim, determined expressions on the marines manning it. They knew that any attempt to force the hatch would be suicidal.

Holbrooke waved his hat to Carlisle, who waved back and turned to give an order. *Medina* came slowly off the wind and veered as her head passed through the southwest and settled on a course to chase the frigate, which was now four miles downwind and seemingly heading into the vastness of the Caribbean Sea. There was little else the Frenchman could do until she contrived some way of setting a headsail.

CHAPTER THIRTY-TWO

L'Arques

Sunday, thirteenth of February 1757
Medina, at Sea, Montserrat northeast-by-east 6 nautical miles

The jib provides little extra motive power when sailing before the wind, its primary purpose in those circumstances is to keep the ship's head off the wind and relieve the pressure on the rudder. Consequently, the French frigate was barely sailing any slower than *Medina*. The two ships hurtled away into the Caribbean Sea, southwest-by-south with the trade wind at their backs. The Frenchman's tactic was obvious; with her lack of manoeuvrability she could not expect to win a fight against *Medina*, so she must run as fast as she could and hope to still be out of cannon shot by nightfall. By then she may also have made some sort of repair that allowed her to set a headsail and there would then be a better than even chance that she could lose the British frigate overnight.

Likewise, Carlisle knew that he needed to catch the Frenchman before she disappeared in the dark. His only concern for the next few hours was to make *Medina* sail as she had never sailed before. Her t'gallants and spritsail had been set as soon as Holbrooke had indicated that the schooner was safe, but there were still improvements that they could consider; rarely-used sails that could be dragged out of the locker and bent onto forgotten halyards.

'Mister Hosking, what do you think of the spritsail topsail?'

The master squinted forward, moved his head from side to side and looked at the long swell pushing up their stern as each wave reached them.

'I wouldn't do it, sir. It has a nasty tendency to push the bows down, and this swell is already doing enough of that.'

Privately, Carlisle agreed. The spritsail topsail was a legacy of the days when men-of-war had no jib boom, and the bowsprit was set at a higher angle.

'The royals then?' Carlisle knew the master's dislike of the royal sails. Main and fore royals were a recent innovation in frigates, though there was no mizzen royal. In fact, they had only been set in *Medina* as a drill, and there had been no occasion to use them otherwise.

'Well, we can at least try them, sir. If they are ever to be of any use, then these are the right conditions. I'll tell the bosun to take it step-by-step; it won't do to endanger the t'gallants.'

The master gave the orders. The topmen knew how to set the royals, but it would still take at least twenty minutes.

'Now sir. I would like to brail the mizzen. I feel we will use less rudder without that great leverage aft.'

'Very well, mister Hosking.' Carlisle paced the weather side of the quarterdeck as the bosun supervised the changes to the sail plan and the master gauged the effect on the ship of each shift. When it was complete, and the log had been cast, he walked over to Carlisle with a look of deep satisfaction and touched his hat.

'I must say that I may have misjudged those royals. We have an extra half knot, sir.'

'And that may make all the difference,' replied Carlisle. 'It's ten hours to sunset, she is four miles ahead, and we have not been gaining at all. That half knot will put her in the bag unless she can find any extra speed.'

Out to the west, the sun was hurrying towards the horizon, and there was only half an hour of light left. It had been a close-run thing; Carlisle would not have believed that the French captain would squeeze so much speed out of his crippled ship. *Medina* had closed to two cables before opening fire, enduring the stinging harassment of the nine-pound stern-chasers for the last two hours. It had been a miracle that they had not had any casualties, and what *Medina* had suffered in canvas and cordage was rapidly repaired by the bosun. Half a dozen shots from the forward guns had not induced the Frenchman to strike his colours, but when Carlisle in exasperation yawed and gave her a full broadside, the Bourbon ensign had come fluttering down from its staff at the taffrail.

Charles Lynton and Chalmers had been rowed across to take the surrender, Lynton to be the visible presence of authority now that Carlisle had no lieutenant to offer. Chalmers went for his command of the French language.

The frigate was *L'Arques*, named after the beautiful little river that drains the country behind Dieppe. As the longboat came back with the French captain alongside Chalmers in the stern sheets, Carlisle left the quarterdeck to the sailing master to await the defeated captain in his cabin. The Frenchman's casualties were light; no dead and no amputations. *Medina* had suffered no casualties at all, and each was deemed to have acted with honour, according to the code of the sea. Carlisle therefore confidently expected a cordial meeting and had planned to invite his captive to a substantial supper.

He was almost proved right. The French captain was outwardly courteous and grateful for the consideration that was being shown him, though he was a beaten man in more than one way. Yes, he had lost his ship, and that was the fortune of war; a court martial would probably be lenient when it knew about him being sent out before his repairs were complete. But as Carlisle had already guessed, this mission was something of a last chance to redeem himself, thrown to him by his exasperated commodore. The French captain had little hope of being employed at sea again; the supper was, therefore, a dull affair. Carlisle's cheerfulness was unable to conquer the Frenchman's gloom and even Chalmers, that master of the passive inquisition, found himself unable to draw the man into conversation. They gave up in the end and offered the Frenchman the use of Carlisle's sleeping cabin, where he could be under the watchful eye of the sentry.

The boats shuttled back and forward between the ships until long after dark. All the French officers were transferred to *Medina,* and a good nucleus of seamen and marines was transferred from *Medina* to *L'Arques* – enough to work the ship back to English Harbour a hundred and twenty miles dead to windward. With a long beat to the north of St. Kitts and a second leg direct for Antigua, it should take less than three days, and Carlisle hoped to be at anchor with his prize by Wednesday evening. Meanwhile, the task of keeping two hundred Frenchmen under guard with a crew stripped to the bone through men being sent away to man the prizes – a frigate and a schooner, no less – meant that there was little prospect of a relaxing cruise.

Long after sunset Carlisle and Chalmers were sat together in the great cabin, picking at the remains of the cheese from the failed supper party and savouring a glass of the precious Madeira.

'There's something odd about that ship, you know,' said Chalmers, studying the colour of the wine against the cabin lantern, 'something wrong with the feeling on board.'

'Oh, and what is it that looked odd?' replied Carlisle. He was only half paying attention – the chaplain's rudimentary grasp of naval matters hardly qualified him to make a useful comment – and he was still working through everything that could go wrong with so many captives on board.

'There was none of that feeling of professional competence that I get in most British ships. Certainly, in *Fury* and here in *Medina*, I have always felt that I was in the hands of experienced seamen. I have the same feeling when I go on board the other ships of the squadron, but it was different in *L'Arques*.' He took a fragment of cheese from the plate. 'Tell me Carlisle, are the French short of seamen?'

'Well, it's almost a tradition that the French have more difficulty in manning their fleet than we do. They have no impress service, you know, they gave it up a century ago. But they do have what they call the *class system*, where they keep a register of seamen and draft them into the navy by age classes when required. It's very unpopular with the seamen although from the outside it looks more humane than the press gang.'

Carlisle looked at Chalmers to check that he was still following. He was aware that a sea officer holding forth about systems of manning the fleet can become very tedious.

'The problem is that the *classes* simply do not provide enough seamen. Of course, we know that, and to make matters worse for the French, we do everything we can to take their seamen prisoner, and then we avoid exchanging the good ones until the war has ended. Our commissioners for the exchange of prisoners are very experienced at weeding out the landsmen and sending them back to France while keeping the true seamen penned up in the prison hulks. Admiral Hawke was cruising in the channel, taking French merchantmen and their crews even before this war was declared. So as the war goes on, you can expect to see the quality of the French man-of-war's men decline, but it shouldn't have happened yet.'

'Nevertheless, that is what I saw,' said Chalmers. 'There was a core of good petty officers attending to all the skilled work, while great herds of bewildered men were being pushed from place to place. I have seen nothing like that before, although I understand that it happens when there is a large intake of pressed men. The officers appeared to know their business but were reluctant to interfere. The overall impression was that the ship was held together by a handful of experienced petty officers.'

Carlisle pondered on Chalmers' remarks. He was an astute observer, and his lack of background knowledge of the navy often allowed him to see problems more clearly. If the French were already having difficulty manning their ships when their navy was still little more than half the size of the British fleet, they would find it even more difficult as the war progressed. With the French so dependent upon the *guerre de course*, how would they manage the allocation of seamen between the navy, the merchants and the privateers? They took the decision in the last century to centrally manage that conundrum, while Britain took a more chaotic approach in using the impress service, even though it was so hated by the seamen and reviled by the broadsheets. Perhaps this war would offer some evidence as to which system best-provided men for the fleet. In any case, he would put a note into his report and let Frankland know that the French manning problems were already starting to bite.

The Leeward Islands Squadron

CHAPTER THIRTY-THREE

Reunion

Wednesday, sixteenth of February 1757
Medina, at Anchor, English Harbour

Holbrooke had quite a story to tell when he reached English Harbour in the forenoon watch on Monday. Admiral Frankland's last definite knowledge of the schooner was when it weighed anchor for Barbuda two weeks before. The story of mutiny, imprisonment of the officers by the French, their escape, their rescue by *Medina* and then the re-taking of *Scorpion* was a dramatic tale. The admiral raised his eyebrows when he heard that Carlisle had kept Godwin in *Medina* rather than restore him to the schooner – his lawful command – but made no comment. He would have to deal with that problematic officer when *Medina* returned.

The balance of power in the Leeward Island Station was Frankland's principal interest. It was what kept him awake at night, thinking about the consequences if one of his ships – any one of them – should meet a French seventy-four at sea. He was concerned now for *Medina* and her prize, for a prize the Frenchman almost certainly was. When the frigate and *Scorpion* failed to arrive at Fort Royal, it was reasonable to assume that the French commodore would send a strong search party northward. *Courageux* or *Prudent* could be at sea even now – probably were at sea – sweeping up the island chain looking for the missing frigate and schooner.

Hastily stored, wooded and watered, *Winchester* and *Wessex* sailed from English Harbour that evening, leaving a score of men each in the fleshpots of Falmouth and St. John's. The gravity of the situation was highlighted by Admiral Frankland taking personal command, flying his flag in *Winchester*. The squadron reached northwest with the trade wind on their starboard beam, reasoning correctly that Carlisle would take a long tack north to keep clear of Martinique and the French navy. They found *Medina* and *L'Arques* on Tuesday at the end of the forenoon watch as the two frigates rounded St. Kitts for the last leg back to Antigua. It was therefore with a with a strong escort that Carlisle returned in triumph to English Harbour, taking the first of the sea breeze to anchor in Freeman's Bay. The garrison was expecting them, and the army had provided a band, a splash of scarlet and gold on the ramparts of Fort Berkeley, the instruments twinkling in the morning sun. An unusually gifted trumpeter absurdly gave a rendition of Handel's *See the Conquering Hero Comes*.

'A little rich for the capture of a mere frigate,' thought Carlisle, but he appreciated the sentiment.

'Let go!' shouted Carlisle, and the great bower anchor dragged its cable down into the clear, warm waters of the bay. English Harbour appeared much the same as he had left it; the same blinding sunshine, the same scrub-covered hills and the same mix of naval ships and boats. The only addition was a packet boat swinging at her anchor in Freeman's Bay. Carlisle was exhausted, mentally and physically. He knew that the packet was significant in some way, but he just didn't have the spare mental capacity to address the puzzle.

For the past four days, Carlisle had hardly slept, with two hundred French prisoners to be guarded day and night by his depleted crew and the terrifying prospect of meeting a strong French force at sea. He had sent prize crews into *Scorpion* and *L'Arques*, many of his best men and a significant number of his marines. And he had not yet made his report to Frankland. Apart from a shouted conversation over fifty yards of heaving sea – the admiral naturally wanted the squadron back in English Harbour without delay – the admiral knew only what Holbrooke had told him. Carlisle could foresee a problematic interview when he had to explain why he had arrested Godwin and confined him to a cabin on board *Medina* rather than restore him to his own *Scorpion*. The written report had taken every moment that could be spared from the needs of the two ships. His clerk had written the first draft, a sound, workmanlike attempt that nevertheless failed to set his actions in confining Godwin in a positive light, and Carlisle was acutely aware that he was open to criticism and very keen to shut off that possibility with a written justification.

As the anchor cable snaked out of the hawse hole, the longboat was hauled alongside and manned. By the time the cable was made fast to the bitts, Carlisle was being piped over the side, and the boat shot away towards the flagship. He had departed *Medina* to the accompaniment of only a single bosun's call and two side boys, all that could be spared from the tasks of working the ship and guarding the prisoners. By contrast, he was greeted at the entry port of the flagship by the full ceremonial required for a post-captain – a chorus of calls, six side boys and all the flagship's commission officers. If Frankland planned any kind of reprimand, he was at least providing the outward signs of a very cordial greeting.

Carlisle looked over his shoulder before he allowed himself to be ushered to the great cabin. The visible evidence of his success was laid out before him in the intense tropical sunshine, framed by the flagship's entry port. All his ships were safely at anchor behind the guns of Fort Berkeley and The Half Moon Battery. His beloved *Medina*, *L'Arques*, *Scorpion,* the ship that he captured to the northeast and the four merchantmen that he took off Martinique only twelve days ago – it seemed like a lifetime. Carlisle realised in an instant that he had nothing to fear from this interview with the admiral. Here was substantial evidence that the Leeward Islands Squadron was contributing to the war effort, evidence that would make good reading on the streets of London and be welcomed by an embattled Admiralty still reeling from the disaster at Minorca. The pressures on the Devonshire Pitt government would be eased at least for a day or two, Frankland would be enriched by his eighth share of the value of the prizes, even *Scorpion* would be likely to yield an *ex gratia* payment as she had been more than twenty-four hours in French hands. If Frankland privately disagreed with Carlisle's actions regarding Lieutenant Godwin, he would take it as a *fait accompli*. Godwin's career was wrecked – he would be lucky not to be broken by the inevitable court martial – and Carlisle found it hard to feel any pity for a man who had spurned so many opportunities to unbend.

It was an hour later that Carlisle was shown back to the entry port. The same ceremony but now in reverse, the only difference being the unexplained absence of *Winchester's* officers and the addition of the admiral who had come to personally see Carlisle over the side. There was a strange hush over the ship as he took his seat in the stern sheets of his boat beside Jackson, who had magically appeared in his rightful place.

'Now how has Jackson managed to get back to my boat so soon?' thought Carlisle, who had last seen him boarding *Scorpion* with Holbrooke. 'And was Jackson fighting back a grin? Damn him, the man had probably been drinking.' With a shove from the bows, the boat turned and headed towards *Medina*.

'Captain Carlisle,' called the admiral from the entry port. 'You should remove your hat, sir.'

'How strange, what on earth was Frankland talking about?' thought Carlisle. But at that moment he was startled by a single gun from the bows of the flagship, and then the anchorage erupted as a great cheer arose from every ship. The yards of all the squadron were festooned with sailors, and they were cheering – cheering him,

The Leeward Islands Squadron

Captain Carlisle, the post-captain from the Colonies. That explained the absence of the officers from the entry port.

'Your hat sir,' whispered Jackson, now smiling broadly. He wouldn't have missed this for anything, he would have swum past shoals of sand sharks – if that is what it took – to be at the tiller of his captain's boat at this moment. Carlisle was rowed back to his frigate past every ship of the squadron, bare-headed in recognition of the extraordinary honour. The cheers continued, echoing back from the hills until the longboat hooked onto *Medina's* chains.

Carlisle hauled himself through the break in the gunwale and onto the waist. He was dazed and disorientated by having been cheered by the squadron – an honour that few sea officers were granted, and none ever forgot.

'Mister Hosking, be so kind as to ask Mister Holbrooke to come to my cabin.'

'Mister Holbrooke is not yet on board, sir. Shall I send a boat ashore for him?'

'No thank you Mister Hosking, I'm sure he has some business ashore, and we will see him soon,' replied Carlisle, hiding his irritation. 'But that is odd and slightly disappointing,' he thought. 'The first lieutenant's clear duty is to report on board as soon as his ship has anchored.' Carlisle had expected to be met on the waist by Holbrooke, and in any case, he had a host of tasks to unload on him. 'Let me know when he returns; I will be in my cabin.'

Carlisle had not even reached his cabin when he heard the call from the quarterdeck, 'boat approaching sir. It's Mister Holbrooke.' There was some whispering that Carlisle couldn't catch, but if it was important, he could rely upon the officer of the watch to let him know.

Carlisle threw himself into his chair. Exhaustion was threatening to overwhelm the euphoria of his reception by the admiral. He was on the point of loosening his stock when there was a knock at the door. It was Midshipman Lynton, with a look somewhat like the one he saw on Jackson in the longboat, a suppressed grin.

'If you please, sir, Mister Holbrooke will be on board in two minutes.'

'I know that very well, damn you,' said Carlisle letting his annoyance show. Was there no rest for the captain of one of His Majesty's frigates? What did Lynton expect him to do, greet his first lieutenant – who should have reported an hour ago – at the gangway?

'Sir,' said Lynton crestfallen. 'There is a lady in the boat with him, and I very much believe it's Lady Chiara … from Nice.' Lynton stood indecisively. Should he add that she looked unreasonably beautiful, should he comment at all? But the decision was taken out of his hands as Carlisle leapt to his feet and rushed through the cabin door, thrusting Lynton to the side in his haste. He reached the quarterdeck in half a dozen strides to see the boat only thirty yards away. There were six oarsmen, two less than usual to allow space for the passengers. He could see the young soldier Enrico, and in a flash of insight, he knew at least one of the viscountess' mysterious conditions. For there, sat bolt upright in the space normally occupied by the stroke oar, sat the mysterious and formidable chief-of-household of the Angelini family – *Black Rod* as he had been dubbed on account of his impressive bearing. There was a midshipman at the tiller and Holbrooke. But he had eyes for none of these, because – incredibly – his beloved Chiara was sat beside Holbrooke, smiling delightedly below her flowered hat. Old Eli, the quartermaster, turned discreetly away as he saw the tears on his captain's face.

EPILOGUE

Pitt's Strategy

What became known as the *First Newcastle Administration* collapsed in November 1756, shortly after *Wessex* and *Medina* sailed from the Downs. The Duke of Newcastle and his cabinet had been severely criticised for their handling of the war, Britain having lost Calcutta in India, leading to the tragic incident of *The Black Hole*, and Oswego on Lake Ontario. But it was the debacle at Minorca that sealed his fate, at least for the next six months. It could have been worse. Months later it was a commonplace, heard in the taverns and salons, that Byng was shot so that Newcastle wouldn't be hanged. Henry Fox, the Secretary of State for the Southern Department and Lord Anson, the First Lord of the Admiralty, followed Newcastle into the wilderness. But not before they had set in train the events that caused *Wessex* and *Medina* to be sent under sealed orders to the West Indies and initiated Carlisle and Holbrooke's adventures on the Leeward Islands Station.

The incoming administration was headed by the Duke of Devonshire, who promoted a new man into the Southern Department, William Pitt, known to history as *Pitt the Elder*. In this post, Pitt was responsible for Southern England, Wales, Ireland and the American Colonies, and for diplomatic relations with the Roman Catholic and Muslim states of Europe. With it came the responsibility for the naval and military strategies for operations in those areas, in effect the majority of Britain's naval and military effort in the Seven Years War.

Pitt had already served as Paymaster General of the Forces, but for some years he had wielded influence that belied his relatively junior ministerial role. By his straightforward approach and ostentatious honesty – some would call it self-serving political opportunism – he had become a favourite of the people, earning the popular name of *The Great Commoner*. Now, with Devonshire sitting in the Lords, he found himself in the much-coveted position of Leader of the House of Commons – the *de facto* Prime Minister. Earl Temple became the First Lord of the Admiralty, a relatively harmless six-month punctuation in Anson's brilliant career.

Pitt, almost alone in the cabinet, thoroughly understood the value to Britain of its burgeoning empire and particularly the Thirteen Colonies in North America, and this at a time when the sugar plantations in the West Indies were the jewel in the British economic crown, overshadowing all other trade. Consequently, his war aims at this point were focussed on securing Britain's American Colonies without sacrificing any of the valuable possessions in the West Indies, the East Indies, or those in Africa.

Pitt knew that the British North American Colonies could never be at peace while the French held Canada. This point that had been demonstrated by France's 1754-1756 push down the Ohio valley that had precipitated this war, an attempt to link up with their countrymen in Louisiana through the Mississippi basin. French dominion of the Ohio and Mississippi would have confined the Thirteen Colonies to a narrow strip of land between the sea and the Appalachian mountain range, while France would be left free to expand westward across the Great Plains and the Rocky Mountains to the blue Pacific Ocean. Pitt knew that if Britain didn't act, France would hold the north, the south, the west and the centre of that vast continent, denying the British Colonies the opportunity to increase and keeping them under constant threat of overland invasion. Under those conditions, it would only be a matter of time before they fell under French domination.

France's American strategy had one great and – as it was to prove, fatal – weakness. The very existence of Canada, known as *New France* to the French, was dependent upon its sea communications with its homeland, but ever since the end of the War of Austrian Succession in 1748, Britain had been the dominant European maritime power. Consequently, the British grand strategy was inherently maritime, to cut off the sea lines of communication between France and New France and when their garrisons and economy were sufficiently weakened, to invade. When that was achieved, Pitt planned to apply the same strategy to the lesser threat of the French settlements in Louisiana.

Britain's involvement in the continental war would be designed to support the maritime grand strategy and protect its colonies. Frederick of Prussia (he was not yet known as *Frederick the Great*), Britain's only Great Power ally, would be offered cash subsidies to keep him fighting and to tie down French manpower and finances on the continent, thus preventing them building a navy to rival Britain's. Otherwise, Pitt had little interest in continental affairs apart from the continuing need to ensure that no single power dominated Europe. In Pitt's mind, the only vital ground on the continent – and then only reluctantly acknowledged – was Hanover, George II's personal fiefdom and Electorate, the place where he had spent the first thirty years of his life and to which he was particularly attached. It was generally understood that if Hanover were lost, then something substantial would have to be exchanged for it in the eventual peace negotiations. If that something were Canada, then the war and all its miseries and all its expense would have been for nothing.

During the winter of 1756 Devonshire and Pitt shook off the defeat at Minorca and the disappointments in North America and India and planned their naval deployments to hold the line until they could muster the forces to take the offensive against France. In this, they benefitted from Anson's careful stewardship of the navy as more and more ships became available and – of the utmost importance – the men to operate them. In the mid-eighteenth century, the navy was still predominantly a volunteer service, with the impress service – the *Press Gang* of lurid fame – supplementing the numbers by forcibly recruiting those who used the sea as their profession.

Rear Admiral Thomas Cotes was sent to relieve Townshend in Jamaica, flying his flag in the sixty-eight-gun *Marlborough*, with two sixty-gun ships, a fifty-gun ship and six frigates to supplement the existing three ships of the line. This gave Cotes a respectable battle squadron of seven ships which, if concentrated, would be the equal of anything the French were likely to deploy to that theatre. Frankland had to make do with his three ships of the line and numerous frigates and smaller vessels.

With no significant French squadron in the Caribbean and, so far, no strategy of territorial conquest, Cotes and Frankland could concentrate on the commerce war – the protection of British commerce and the interdiction of French trade. The deployment of the ships to support this commerce war was a well-understood science. The ships of the line were stationed to keep a watch on the two main French naval bases in the region, Fort Royal at Martinique and Cape François at the western end of St. Dominique, leaving the frigates to cover the main trade routes and the sloops and smaller vessels to protect British trade from privateers.

While the opening months of 1757 hardly looked any less gloomy for Britain and its navy than the closing months of 1756, and British politics was in a hopeless mess of its own making, we can nevertheless see the first glimmerings of a winning strategy shining through the gloom of political confusion. To quote Winston Churchill, speaking in a much more hazardous situation nearly two centuries later:

> *'Now this is not the end. It is not even the beginning of the end. But it is, perhaps, the end of the beginning.'*

Carlisle and Holbrooke will return, in the third book of the series, to implement the British naval strategy in the second year of the war.

NAUTICAL TERMS

Throughout the centuries, sailors have created their own language to describe the highly technical equipment and processes that they use to live and work at sea. This holds true in the twenty-first century. When counting the number of nautical terms that I have used in this series of novels, it became evident that a printed book was not the best place for them. I have therefore created a glossary of nautical terms on my website:

https://chris-durbin.com/glossary/

My glossary of nautical terms is limited to those that I have used in this series of novels, as they were used in the middle of the eighteenth century. It is intended as a work of reference to accompany the Carlisle and Holbrooke series of naval adventure novels.

Some of the usages of these terms have changed over the years, so this glossary should be used with caution when referring to periods before 1740 or after 1780.

My online glossary is not exhaustive; a more comprehensive list can be found in Falconer's Universal Dictionary of the Marine, first published in 1769. I have not counted the number of terms that Falconer has defined, but he fills 328 pages with English language terms, followed by a further eighty-three pages of French translations. It is a monumental work.

An online version of the 1780 edition of The Universal Dictionary (which unfortunately does not include all the excellent diagrams that are in the print version) can be found on this website:

https://archive.org/details/universaldiction00falc

BIBLIOGRAPHY

The following is a selection of the many books that I consulted in researching *The Leeward Islands Squadron*.

Sir Julian Corbett wrote the original, definitive text on the seven years war. Most later writers use his work as a stepping stone to launch their own.

>   Corbett, LLM., Sir Julian Stafford. *England in the Seven Years War – Vol. I: A Study in Combined Strategy*: Normandy Press. Kindle Edition.

Three very accessible modern books cover the strategic context and naval operations of the seven years war. Daniel Baugh addresses the whole war on land and sea, while Martin Robson concentrates on maritime operations. Jonathan Dull has produced a very readable account from the French perspective.

>   Baugh, Daniel. *The Global Seven Years War 1754-1763*. Pearson Education 2011. Print.

>   Robson, Martin. *A History of the Royal Navy, The Seven Years War*. I.B. Taurus, 2016. Print.

>   Dull, Jonathan, R. *The French Navy and the Seven Years' War*, University of Nebraska Press, 2005. Print

For an interesting perspective on the life of sea officers of the mid-eighteenth century, I would read *Augustus Hervey's Journal*, with the cautionary note that Hervey was by no means typical of the breed, but he is very entertaining and devastatingly honest. For a more balanced view I would read *British Naval Captains of the Seven Years War*.

Erskine, David (editor). Augustus Hervey's Journal, The Adventures Afloat and Ashore of a Naval Casanova: Chatham Publishing, 2002. Print.

McLeod, A.B. British Naval Captains of the Seven Years War, A View for the Quarterdeck. The Boydell Press, 2012. Print.

I recommend *The Wooden World* for an overview of shipboard life and administration during the seven years war:

N.A.M Rodger. The Wooden World, An Anatomy of the Georgian Navy. Fontana Press, 1986. Print.

THE AUTHOR

Chris Durbin grew up in the seaside town of Porthcawl in South Wales. As a sea cadet, he had his first experience of sailing in the treacherous tideway of the Bristol Channel. He was a crew member on the Porthcawl lifeboat before joining the navy.

Chris spent twenty-four years as a warfare officer in the Royal Navy, serving in all classes of ship from aircraft carriers through destroyers and frigates to the smallest minesweepers. He took part in operational campaigns in the Falkland Islands, the Middle East and the Adriatic. As a personnel exchange officer, he spent two years teaching tactics at a US Navy training centre in San Diego.

On his retirement from the Royal Navy, Chris joined a large American company and spent eighteen years in the aerospace, defence and security industry, including two years on the design team for the Queen Elizabeth class aircraft carriers.

Chris is a graduate of the Britannia Royal Naval College at Dartmouth, the British Army Command and Staff College, the United States Navy War College (where he gained a postgraduate diploma in national security decision-making) and Cambridge University (where he was awarded an MPhil in International Relations).

With a lifelong interest in naval history and a long-standing ambition to write historical fiction, Chris has completed the first two novels in the Carlisle & Holbrooke series, in which a colonial Virginian commands a British navy frigate during the middle years of the eighteenth century.

The series will follow its principal characters through the Seven Years War and into the period of turbulent relations between Britain and her American Colonies in the 1760s. They will negotiate some thought-provoking loyalty issues when British policy and colonial restlessness lead inexorably to the American Revolution.

Chris now lives on the south coast of England, surrounded by hundreds of years of naval history. His three children are all busy growing their own families and careers while Chris and his wife (US Navy, retired) of thirty-six years enjoy sailing their classic dayboat.

FEEDBACK

If you have enjoyed The Leeward Islands Squadron, please consider leaving a review on Amazon.

This is the second of a series of books that will follow Carlisle and Holbrooke through the Seven Years War and into the 1760s when relations between Britain and her restless American Colonies are tested to breaking point.

Look out for the third in the Carlisle Holbrooke series, coming soon.

You can follow my Blog at:

www.chris-durbin.com

Printed in Great Britain
by Amazon